SOMEONE'S
GOTTA
GIVE

Praise for
Someone's Gotta Give

"Imagine Andy from *The Devil Wears Prada* as a thirty-something mom toiling in the cutthroat world of private philanthropy. A heartfelt look at the cost of 'having it all' on working mothers, and a clear-eyed send-up of the do-gooders (and do-badders). I cheered for Lucia the whole time."

—SALLY FRANSON, author of *Big in Sweden*

"A fast-paced, funny exploration of the juggling act of motherhood—with entertaining forays into the world of upper echelon Brits, including royalty and, of course, Colin Firth—told with an honesty that will be instantly relatable to fellow jugglers."

—SOPHIE BRICKMAN, author of *Plays Well with Others*

"In this delicious debut that is equal parts warm and biting, Miranda examines the pressure on women to 'do it all' with humor and whip-smart accuracy. A must-read for all of us who've felt like something (or someone) just had to give!"

—ASHA ELIAS, author of *Pink Glass Houses*

"Amidst a fabulous cast of characters, down-to-earth Lucia takes center stage as she navigates expat- and mom-life in between the odd event at Buckingham Palace. Full of heart and humor."

—JANE COSTELLO, author of *It's Getting Hot in Here*

"An absolute delight—a sharp, funny, and heartfelt exploration of identity, purpose, and the many hats we wear (sometimes all at once). This book will make you laugh, think, and cheer. A must-read for anyone searching for their place in the world."

—GLORIA CALDERÓN KELLETT, award-winning television writer
and producer of *One Day at a Time*

Praise for
My What If Year

"Miranda writes with humor, grace, and a joyful curiosity that's a delight to read."
—BIANCA BOSKER, author of *Cork Dork*

"With her winning combination of chutzpah, self-deprecating humor, and determination, Miranda turns midlife (or mid-career) malaise into a hilarious memoir that is both engrossing and inspiring."
—ANNABELLE GURWITCH, author of *I See You Made an Effort*

"Delivered with such refreshing audacity and wild charm. For anyone looking for a breath of inspiration."
—MARISA RENEE LEE, author of *Grief Is Love*

"Funny, heartwarming . . . Miranda teaches us that sometimes uprooting our lives is what leads us and our families forward."
—EVE RODSKY, author of *Fair Play*

"For every woman who imagined a different life and told herself, 'You just can't.' You can, Miranda shows us, and in the process of trying on the lives in your fantasies, you just might find the one you want for real."
—PAMELA REDMOND, author of *Younger*

"This hilarious, witty memoir had me saying 'YAY YAY' from the very beginning! An inspiring read that will make every reader want to supercharge their own careers."
—MEAGHAN B. MURPHY, editor in chief at *Woman's Day*,
author of *Your Fully Charged Life*

"Miranda gives us permission to get curious, hold tight to the wisp of a new idea, and honor the voice that whispers, 'What if there's more?'"
—ALICIA MENENDEZ, MSNBC anchor,
author of *The Likeability Trap*

SOMEONE'S GOTTA GIVE

A NOVEL

ALISHA FERNANDEZ MIRANDA

Zibby Publishing
New York

Someone's Gotta Give: A Novel

Copyright © 2025 by Alisha Fernandez Miranda

All rights reserved. No part of this book may be used, reproduced, distributed, or transmitted in any form or by any means without the prior written permission of the publisher, except as permitted by US copyright law. Published in the United States by Zibby Publishing, New York.

ZIBBY, Zibby Publishing, colophon, and associated logos are trademarks and/or registered trademarks of Zibby Media LLC.

This book is a work of fiction. Names, characters, places, historical events, and incidents are the product of the author's imagination or are used fictitiously. Any resemblance to actual persons, living or dead, events, or locales is entirely coincidental.

Library of Congress Control Number: 2024952422
Paperback ISBN: 979-8-9906304-0-6
eBook ISBN: 979-8-9906304-1-3

Book design by Westchester Publishing Services
Cover design by Nicolette Seeback Ruggiero
Cover art © amesto, Ints Vikmanis, Fontinia, Lisa Agustini93, and Foxy Fox all for Shutterstock.com

www.zibbymedia.com

Printed in the United States of America

10 9 8 7 6 5 4 3 2 1

For my parents, Alex and Mindy, who taught me right from wrong and how to pick my battles.

Surplus wealth is a sacred trust which its possessor is bound to administer in his lifetime for the good of the community.

—*Andrew Carnegie*

Did you hear my covert narcissism I disguise as altruism?

—*Taylor Swift*

Prologue

"*Mamita*, what are you still doing here?"

Lucia looked up from her phone, glowing unnaturally bright under the dark Texas sky. The heat of the day had receded; at 101 degrees, it was practically balmy for a summer night in Austin. Still, Lucia's hair was three times its normal voluminous size. Her dark curls were already escaping the messy bun she had thrown up after the last of her donors left the ArteAustin festival. She pushed the loose strands away from her face with both hands in a futile attempt to clear her field of vision.

Lucia's boss, Milagros, slowly came into focus. Only her face was visible under the strings of fairy lights that crisscrossed the lawn. Lucia clearly made out pursed lips and a creased forehead: the picture of concern.

"It's not that late, is it?" Lucia asked, looking around the lawn at the thinning crowds.

Milagros frowned. "It's after nine. You should go home. Don't think I don't know that you've been here after closing every night. Above and beyond, as usual. Have you even eaten anything today?" She started rooting around in her bag; Lucia loved this about Milagros and most of the moms she worked with—they never went anywhere without a 7-Eleven's worth of snacks.

"I ate, I ate, don't worry." Lucia laughed. "We had six food trucks here, and I've tried a different one every night." This evening's menu had been Texas BBQ—she had specifically saved the best for last. But when had she actually eaten? Judging by the very dry, baked-in sauce stain on her shirt, it had probably been hours ago.

Missing regular mealtimes because she was so wrapped up in her work was not unusual for Lucia. More than once, Milagros had pulled one of a seemingly endless supply of smooshed granola bars out of her bag, like a rabbit from a hat, handing it over just when Lucia's blood sugar was about to dip into the danger zone.

"Fine." Milagros raised her hands in submission. "But I know you. You'd sleep here if they let you. Go home, you deserve some rest."

It was the final night of Summer Under the Stars, ArteAustin's major fundraising event of the year. All week, the festival had been full of music, spoken word, art, and poetry, courtesy of the clients that ArteAustin served: asylum seekers, new immigrants, and refugees. They came to the nonprofit for legal help, advocacy, mental health support, and a place to express themselves creatively through art. It was Lucia's job to bring in the cash that made this all happen.

She grinned to herself. "You're right," she said, stowing her phone in her pocket and standing up. "I do deserve it."

"Amen. You kicked ass this week!"

Lucia crossed over to Milagros and gave her a hug.

"*Bueno*, I have to run. Frank just texted, and the kids are still wide awake." Milagros rolled her eyes. "Good thing I love that man so much. He probably didn't even remember to feed the cat."

"You go. I'll be right behind you, I promise," Lucia said.

But she didn't head to the exit. There was no one waiting at home to greet her with a one-armed hug while sheepishly hiding a bowl of forgotten cat food behind his back. It was just her, a few dead houseplants, and Colin Firth, and he would happily wait for her arrival to stream in on demand, all disheveled hair, sexy see-through shirt, and furrowed brow.

Milagros was right, though; she did deserve a little break. She made her way over to the last remaining stall—the bar, of course—and ordered herself an ice-cold beer in a glass bottle.

When Lucia joined ArteAustin, straight out of college over a decade ago, she had applied for a caseworker role. She wanted to help individuals and families, people like her grandparents who came from Venezuela in the 1970s and had to completely start over without knowing a word of English. Without a law degree, she could do very little as a caseworker, they told her, but how did she feel about fundraising? They had an opening for a fundraising assistant, and she could start right away.

Lucia was passionate about the mission and, as it turned out, was an incredible fundraiser. She had a way with people, especially rich ones. She easily slipped into the role she had played for her entire life—that of translator, someone who could feel as comfortable in a donor's glitzy McMansion as she did in her nonprofit's office, where funds were often so tight there was a limit to the number of paper clips each staff member could use in any given month. For her, it was the best of both worlds.

Her colleagues called her a workaholic, both to her face and behind her back, but she didn't mind. There just weren't enough hours in the day to get everything done that needed doing, and she found it easier to channel all her energy into following her professional passion, sometimes at the expense of everything else. What was the expression? Do what you love and you'll never work a day in your life?

She loved it. All of it. The early mornings and late nights, the unused gym membership, the friends who still included her on their WhatsApp groups as a courtesy but knew she'd never show up to drinks, the fact that she hadn't been on a date in three years, two months, and five days (not that she was counting). It was a small price to pay for a job she adored. For helping people who needed it. For waking up every morning feeling like she had a clear purpose in life and she was working to achieve it.

Lucia wandered away from the crowd, plopped down into a lawn chair, and kicked off her shoes, curling her toes in the crisp, dry grass. The cicadas were so loud that she struggled to make out the song being played by the all-female mariachi band, the closing act of the festival. She took a slug of icy beer and savored the taste.

Based on the amount of money ArteAustin had brought in over the week of the festival—that *she* had brought in from the high-net-worth donors in her portfolio—they'd be able to launch their childcare support service across the city in the fall. She sank back and reveled in the moment. She had her colleagues, her career, her calling. She had a cold beer on a hot night. It was enough.

She closed her eyes, feeling entirely content, when she heard a loud thud just in front of her, followed by an exclamation not often heard in Texas: "Oh bugger."

Lucia's eyes popped open. Sprawled face down on the ground in front of her was a man. He made an effort to stand up but teetered unsteadily. She stood and reached out to buttress him, wrapping her fingers around noticeably firm biceps.

He turned to face her. The biceps were attached to a very attractive face. "Goodness, I'm mortified," he said in a Hugh Grant–esque British accent. So he was hot *and* British.

"I believe I tripped over your shoes. It's my fault entirely. And now I've stained my trousers."

"In that case, I'm the one who should be mortified." She awkwardly retrieved her shoes from behind the stranger and slid them back on, quickly returning her grip to his biceps. In case he had a concussion, she told herself. "Your pants are the least of your problems," Lucia said. "Your nose is bleeding."

"Oh dear, is it?" He reached up to touch his face, his fingers coming back covered in blood. "How dreadful."

"Isn't it, though," Lucia said, playfully mocking his accent (she couldn't help herself). "Come on, let's go get some ice."

She guided him back to the bar, her beer forgotten, her feeling of contentment replaced by a stirring in the pit of her stomach, a place usually reserved for cravings for *queso fundido* or churros, doughnuts, or any fried pastry dusted with cinnamon. This was new, unfamiliar, and not unpleasant.

They were offered a red-and-white-striped dish towel filled with ice. He pressed it to his nose, wincing slightly. Lucia took another towel, moistened it in a glass of water, and gently dabbed his face where some of the blood was drying. It was an intimate act, given that he was a stranger, but she felt completely comfortable.

"Not my ideal first impression," he said.

"It could have been worse," she offered generously.

"How, exactly?"

"You could have gotten blood on me. Although, I'm already covered in BBQ sauce, so maybe I wouldn't have noticed."

He laughed, and she decided it was the best sound she had ever heard. And then that feeling was there again. One she hadn't felt for a long time, or possibly ever.

A feeling that perhaps it wasn't enough—that maybe she was missing something, after all.

Three Years Later

Chapter 1
A Casual Dinner

"Lucia? Lucia? Wake up, love."

Lucia felt a gentle nudge on her shoulder and heard a deep, soft voice that sounded very far away. For a heartbeat, she thought she had fallen asleep at her desk and bolted upright. But once her eyes focused, she realized it was just Ollie (her husband—sometimes she still couldn't believe she had a husband). She wasn't in an office, but in their living room, on the gray-green sofa that cost more than her first car.

Precariously balanced beside her was a cup of tea, which was cold. It was for show more than anything. She hated tea, but it felt appropriate. When in Rome, as the saying went. Or, in this case, London, where declaring you preferred coffee was an offense akin to insulting someone's mother, or much worse, the queen.

She heard a xylophone and a nursery rhyme about a bobbin plink-plonking in the background. What even was a bobbin? Probably some torture instrument from the Tudor times, Lucia surmised. It would be just like the Brits to make up a song for children about something like that.

She reached up to touch something on her chin: dried custard from the doughnut she had scarfed down at teatime. Even as a grown-ass, thirty-eight-year-old woman, she still could not manage to eat without leaving a trace. ("How can someone so smart be so messy?" her grandmother had once asked her. Lucia had shrugged, her mouth full of crumbs, and said, "I guess I can't be great at everything.")

"I must have dozed off," she said, rising from the sofa and offering Ollie a quick peck on the cheek. "Sleep when the baby sleeps, right?"

"Of course, love," he said, rifling through the mail. "No doubt you and Marley had a busy morning," Ollie said, without a hint of irony.

Busy. That was one of those words that seemed to have undergone a transmutation when she crossed the Atlantic and became a British resident. In her new environment, an elevator was called a lift, silverware was cutlery, and plain old garbage had been promoted to much-fancier-sounding rubbish; busy, too, meant something different.

From a certain perspective, their morning had been busy. First there was a drawn-out debate over whether one could wear a party dress over pajama pants (Marley won), followed by a rush down the leafy-green streets of Notting Hill to Singy Songy, which Lucia believed was the ninth circle of hell. Who in their right mind willingly gave a drum to a toddler?

Singy Songy was followed by baby ballet. (Admittedly adorable because: tutus. But not exactly riveting. Lucia couldn't very well distract herself with a naughty romance novel—her preferred form of entertainment—without being reported to child services.) All of that before noon.

Then, it was time for a refuel, in this case a quick doughnut pit stop for Lucia, followed by a bowl of pureed peas and apples for Marley, capped off by a spiral down a Google rabbit hole that started with the question "mess-free potty training in 24 hours or less?" and ended with "are my common bathroom cleaning supplies giving me cancer and killing my sex life?" By the time she put Marley down for her nap, she was just as exhausted as if she had, like Ollie, spent eight or nine hours in front of a desk.

"Well, it was a double-doughnut day," she said.

"That bad?" Ollie asked, looking like a dejected puppy.

She knew there wasn't any point in telling him about the exhausting or annoying or boring parts of her day. Or that on the afternoons when she wasn't napping, she counted down the hours until he got home from work, until she would have another adult around to share things with. As much as she loved how much her life had expanded since she'd met him—she was married with a baby in a brand-new country—it had contracted at the same time.

No, there was no point at all, she told herself. He wanted so badly for her to love London, love her new life—because he loved her, and anyway, they were still in the honeymoon period. Making him upset was the last thing she wanted.

"Of course not, not at all." She brushed the custard off and plastered a smile on her face. "They were just really good doughnuts."

A noise floated their way from Marley's room, and both of them turned to face the door, their bodies on high alert in the way only parents are when their baby stirs. "I'll grab her," Ollie said. "You wake up and get yourself ready. Mummy will be here soon, and we need to leave for Gaz and Pip's around half six."

The fake smile on her face morphed into a real one. She had been so excited about this grown-ups' night out for weeks. They were "going round" to the house of Ollie's "schoolmates"—Gavin (better known as Gaz) and Philippa ("just Pip, darling"), plus two other couples. Maybe she'd get to finish an entire sentence tonight. If she could still put one together that didn't rhyme.

Marley's delighted squeals wafted into the bedroom. She was such a happy baby, always giggling or laughing. Yes, there was the occasional tantrum—usually because Lucia had deigned to pick the wrong color bowl at breakfast—but one look at her dark curly hair (from Lucia) and big blue eyes (from Ollie and some recessive gene buried deep in Lucia's Venezuelan lineage) and all was forgiven. Having a baby, she had learned, was allowing your heart to walk outside your body. She was filled with both a love she didn't know she was capable of and a terror she didn't know existed. Motherhood was incredible that way.

It could also be incredibly lonely. She had made a grand total of zero friends since she'd moved; unless she counted the guy who sold the doughnuts at her neighborhood bakery, but she suspected he only liked her because she was a generous tipper. It wasn't for lack of trying or that people weren't nice; they were, at least at surface level. But her excellence at connecting with people as a professional didn't seem to translate to her mom life. She was about as good at making friends in London as she was at not dripping custard down the front of her shirt, which was to say, appallingly bad.

Last week at the library, she and about a half dozen yummy mummies were sitting together on the carpet in their yoga pants, trading tips about the best organic-yogurt brands. It was, by her current standards, a fairly successful conversation—she contributed something interesting about antioxidants she had read in an article (or possibly an Instagram caption) and managed to complete at least two full sentences without interruption.

When the library volunteer finished her reading of *Goodnight Moon*, and everyone began to swoop up their kids, Lucia swallowed her apprehension and asked one of the women (the blonde one whose name was either Hannah or Anna or Sara), "Do you want to get some lunch after this? There's a new sandwich shop down the street, and I hear they have an actual playroom in the restaurant. And a valet to park the strollers. Living the dream!" She smiled, her heart pounding like she was back in the middle school cafeteria.

"It's buggies here, not strollers," Hannah/Anna/Sara corrected her with a half frown, her expression a mix of kindness and pity. "The thing is we're all headed off to Emma's. Have you met Emma? She's our uni friend. She's sometimes here on a Tuesday? With little Louis?" They were sentences but phrased as questions, so Lucia nodded yes in response; she was sure she had met an Emma, or maybe a Gemma, at some point.

Lucia couldn't stand to be pitied, not ever and certainly not while wearing her dressiest leggings, so she plastered what she hoped was a genuine-looking grin on her face. "No worries," she said, a British expression that she used often, even when she did, in fact, have many worries. "Next week, maybe." She waved goodbye, hanging back while the clique left so it didn't look like she was following them like a creepy stalker.

Socializing on this side of the pond seemed to come so easily to everyone but her.

Tonight, she was absolutely convinced, would be perfect. It had to be. She had been introduced to Ollie's friends on multiple occasions, but their encounters had been brief, the conversations superficial, which she chalked up to being so entrenched in motherhood and her new life in London. Despite holding not one but two degrees, it had taken her almost a year to adjust to the fact that the door leading to the passenger seat was now on the other side of the car (the wrong side, if you asked her). Now that Marley was a toddler, she had a bit more breathing space in her day and thinking space in her brain, and she hoped she'd be able to forge a deeper relationship with these people who meant so much to her husband.

After all, in every excellent British romantic comedy—and Lucia had seen them all—there was always a scene in which the school chums would gather at a beautiful country pile or someone's impossibly cozy dining table that seated ten, and plied with wine and shepherd's pie, they would tell jokes and take the piss out of one another (in a loving way) and be generally droll and charming. This was exactly how she pictured the evening going, and she couldn't wait to be a part of it.

"What's the vibe tonight?" she yelled toward the living room. "Am I going for *Downton Abbey*—formal wear to dinner; or more like *The Holiday*—relaxed country-cottage chic?"

She popped her head out the bedroom door. Marley and Ollie seemed completely engrossed in an episode of *Peppa Pig*.

"Hmm?" he muttered without looking up. Lucia walked over to him and cupped his chin so his eyes met hers. It was a good, strong chin, with a cleft in it. A prerequisite for her to find anyone attractive.

His gaze broke from the screen, and his eyes met hers before scanning downward.

"Sexy," he purred.

Lucia followed his gaze. She was shirtless, wearing her most raggedy maternity bra, the one that had started out white but was now a color more akin to dried-breast-milk ivory, with a safety pin holding the front clasp together, the result of a particularly aggressive attempt by baby Marley to access lunch.

She smiled in spite of herself. "Hey. Eyes up here, mister," she said, playfully nudging his chin back up. "Focus! Tonight! What. Is. The. Vibe?"

"Anything is fine, darling, they'll love you in whatever you're wearing, like I do, *cariña*."

She dropped his chin and walked back to the bedroom. "This is a big deal," she said. "They're your friends. I want to feel like part of the gang. For once."

Ollie placed Marley in her Jumperoo and followed Lucia into their room. "And by the way, it's *cariño* with an O at the end," she said. "Even though I'm a woman. But A for effort." He caught up to her and wrapped his arms around her waist, nuzzling his nose into her neck. She ran her fingers through his sandy-brown hair, graying slightly at the temples in a way that made him look distinguished, not old. "Be serious, though; answer me, *por favor*."

"Casual, darling, very casual," he said, disentangling himself from her. "It's just Gaz and Pip's flat. Two other couples besides them and us—Belly, Colz, Caz, and Loony."

"Your friends have the weirdest names. Remind me again? Belly is Annabel, I know. Your ex," Lucia said with a raised eyebrow.

"While I do find your jealousy somewhat alluring," Ollie said with a glint in his eye, "Belly and I were over one hundred years ago."

Lucia wasn't jealous exactly, but it was not lost on her that Belly was, in fact, her polar opposite. It almost boggled the mind that one man could have been attracted to them both. She was blonde, thin with no boobs, no hips, and no belly to speak of, and almost certainly capable of finishing a bowl of soup without spilling a drop. She played polo "like a fiend" and had been a high-powered lawyer, leading her firm's pro bono practice until she quit upon having her first child (of a planned five) with Colin, a.k.a. Colz.

"But please, if this jealousy is fueling any sort of primal need to claim me as your mate, feel free."

Lucia rolled her eyes, even though her insides warmed at the thought, and went back to assessing her wardrobe, settling on a basic black shift dress. It was boring but inoffensive. After her trendiest cowboy boots got yeehawed all night long the first time she'd worn them to a pub, she had become more cautious about which elements of her background—and wardrobe— she chose to exhibit in public.

"Anyway, OK, so the other couple must be Charlotte— that's Caz—and Loony, who is really called . . ."

Ollie stopped buttoning his shirt.

"Good god, would you believe I don't even remember Loony's real name?"

He resumed his buttoning and pulled a black sweater off its hanger. As soon as the temperature went below sixty-five degrees Fahrenheit, Ollie always wore a black or brown cashmere sweater. This stability and reliability were part of Lucia's attraction to Ollie in the first place. After his chin.

She had no idea that, when Ollie fell into her life on that sultry summer night three years ago, it would set her on an entirely different path, like a pinball flicked off—or on—course. He had been traveling around the US having a "grown-up gap year," attempting to visit all fifty states, but after they met he didn't go any farther. He did eventually make it to Nevada, where they eloped in Vegas six months and a missed period after their meet-cute. Lucia quit her job and put all her possessions on a cargo ship headed across the Atlantic. Before she knew it, she'd woken up one morning a mother, a wife, and an expat.

She didn't regret it—not for a second—but sometimes it felt like she had sleepwalked into a brand-new existence.

Tonight was important. She wanted Ollie to see she could fit into his London life. Caz and Gaz and Jazz or whatever they were called would love her.

The doorbell rang. "That's probably Mummy," Ollie called from the bathroom. "Can you get it, love?"

Lucia shuddered involuntarily at the prospect of having to greet her mother-in-law and went to the door.

As a motherless daughter, Lucia had secretly harbored a dream that she'd get a second chance at a maternal connection when she got married. She had been raised by her grandparents, Venezuelan immigrants to the US, after her mother's death when she was only four years old. Lucia had never felt unloved a day in her life but had always wondered what a healthy, supportive mother-daughter relationship would feel like.

Unfortunately, it didn't seem like she was going to find out anytime soon.

It wasn't that Moira hated her—more like she had exhausted all her affection on Ollie and his sister, Isabel. And now, of course, on Marley. There wasn't much left for Lucia.

Or maybe Moira really did hate her, she thought.

Lucia smoothed the front of her dress to make sure it was neat and presentable, the way Moira expected her to be. Their relationship was polite and cordial; they kept their interactions to a minimum and never discussed anything that mattered. There were three safe topics: Ollie, Marley, and that old British standby, the weather.

Lucia opened the door. "Hello, Moira. Thank you so much for coming," she said graciously.

Moira stood there in her uniform: a pale cardigan over a matching top (she owned the same twinset in every color), sensible pumps, and a permanent grimace. Unlike Lucia's free-flowing locks, Moira's gray curls were pinned tightly to her head.

"No trouble at all," she said, walking past Lucia. "Anything for my Peanut." This, her nickname for Ollie, always made Lucia gag.

"He'll be right out," she said, following her into the living room where she watched Moira's eyes appraise the cleanliness of everything. If this was a test, Lucia was sure she had not passed. "So . . . Warm outside for this time of year, isn't it?"

"Quite," she said, perking up. "I was just saying the same to Imogene, that's my neighbor, you know, the loveliest woman, Oxford educated and an incredible baker at that."

It was possibly the longest Moira had ever spoken to her without Ollie in the room. It was cordial, even. But, in true Moira fashion, more was coming.

"Cooking is such an important skill for a wife and mother, don't you agree?" Moira said, sniffing at the air and inspecting the half-empty box of doughnuts on the counter.

"I've always been better at eating," Lucia replied—a joke, but Moira didn't laugh.

"So many lazy women, just pottering along with store-bought treats when everything you can find out there can be easily whipped up in here, with the right skill and constitution. But I suppose in America it's fast food all the time. Mackey Donald's is basically your national dish, isn't it?"

And there it was.

"What was that, Ollie?" Lucia pretended to hear a call from the bathroom. "I'll just go check on him, Moira. Marley's in front of the TV."

"Of course she is," Moira replied.

Lucia waited until she was out of sight before rolling her eyes so far back they almost got stuck and then went to finish getting ready.

"Harold." Ollie said as she entered the bathroom.

"What?"

"Loony's real name, it's Harold."

Lucia reached over and plucked a piece of her long, dark hair off Ollie's shirt. "You're the loony one," she said affectionately. In her world, she not only knew but often called people by their first, middle, and last names, and sometimes even their mother's maiden names. This was his world, though. Hopefully soon—maybe tonight—it would feel more like hers.

Chapter 2
Lost in Translation

Gaz and Pip's London pad was just a fifteen-minute walk through Notting Hill from Lucia and Ollie's flat. Neither of them needed a jacket as they strolled hand in hand down the street. All around them people's moods had clearly been buoyed by the weather. An older woman walking a dog actually smiled at them as she passed.

"I'm nervous," Lucia admitted.

"What on earth for?" Ollie replied, genuinely puzzled. "Nothing could be more relaxed about tonight, and you look ravishing." She smiled at him because he meant it, but he was no help. In his eyes, she was charming, witty, and whip-smart. Once upon a time, she'd seen herself that way—but that was back in Texas, back at work, before. She used to walk around with the certitude that she would be able to fig-ure out the solution to any problem posed in her professional life. That confidence didn't apply anymore; the required skills for wifedom and motherhood (particularly the British vari-ety) seemed to exist just outside her grasp.

They merged onto Portobello Road. The brightly colored facades looked bolder in the sunshine, and the pubs were full of revelers enjoying what could be the year's last warm day (any warm day in London could be the last, so it was important to behave accordingly). This part of Notting Hill was her favorite—where the posh residents who looked like they just stepped out of a Richard Curtis movie mingled with the market-shop owners who had manned stalls for decades, where you could get a Michelin-star meal or the best Jamaican patty you've ever eaten without having to go farther than across the street. This London, the international one where Lucia occasionally picked up a snippet of Spanish that made her heart both sing and sink with homesickness, this was the one she loved. She hoped that one day she'd feel at home here, too.

But today was not that day. They turned off the market road onto a crescent full of houses that looked like wedding cakes—tall, white, and ornate. She didn't dare engage in one of her favorite pastimes—checking the house price listings app to see how much the properties were worth—for fear of what she might find.

That was probably for the best because Gaz and Pip's pad was not a pad, per se, as it had been described. It was two houses, at least, fused together to create one gigantic mansion.

Lucia smoothed her dress as Ollie rang the bell. They were greeted by a waiter who asked what they would like to drink. "Dry martini," Ollie ordered, grinning widely as Gaz entered the foyer and slapped him on the back, calling him an unmentionable word that Lucia had recently come to know was a British term of endearment. "Not in front of the missus," he said, winking at Lucia and following Gaz into the house.

"And for you, Mrs. Barrow?" the waiter asked again.

Lucia made direct eye contact with him and smiled. He was young, attractive with an unspecified southern Mediterranean

21

accent. She made a point to always befriend the home staff of her clients and now, she guessed, her friends—in part because it was plain good manners and in part as a beacon to them, and to herself.

"Um, gosh, I'm not sure," Lucia stalled, distracted by Belly walking into the room wearing pink palazzo pants paired with a transparent silk top. Lucia did a double take at the sight of Belly's lacy black bra. "Can I have a beer? Ice-cold, if possible, please."

"Oh, Lulu," Belly screeched. Lucia winced at hearing the childish nickname, which made her feel like a Teletubby. "You are *hilarious*. Tsk, tsk, a lady doesn't have a lager at a dinner party. Not in polite company, of course. Get her a champers, like mine. Come, we're all in the sitting room gossiping about how awful Caz's new highlights look. We are so wicked." (Lucia made a note in her mental dictionary: casual dinner = formal catered affair.)

Belly led Lucia into a large open-plan living room decorated sparsely in white, gray, and birch. She thought with a pang about how she would have loved to tell her *abuela* about this fun fact: The superrich London set filled their living spaces with as few things as possible. The opposite was true where she grew up. Stuff equaled money, and the more you had, the more you showed it off. Every frame in her grandparents' home was gold and ornate; every porcelain statue of a carousel horse was displayed with pride by the front door, "for company." Back in Austin, her rich clients' homes were no different; their basic style ethos was the same as the middle-class Venezuelans, only with better brands and a lot more longhorns hanging on their walls. But for über-wealthy Brits, less was truly more.

"I love the crown molding," she said, using a term that, like lager, she had only recently learned.

"Do you really?" Pip asked. "Truthfully, I think it's ghastly. We tried to get rid of it, but it's an original feature and this is a listed building, so no luck."

"Right," she backtracked. "I guess some people might find it . . . um . . . gauche."

"Indeed," Pip replied. "I can see *you* wouldn't want to be gauche, would you? Quite the opposite." She eyed Lucia's boring black shift up and down. Lucia reddened. She was Miss Marple in a room full of Pussycat Dolls (if the Pussycat Dolls wore McQueen). Pip just laughed lightly. "Kidding, too, naturally. Of course, black is the new black." She linked her arm (sleeved in bright-blue chiffon) with Lucia's and pulled her down onto the sofa.

The women moved on from ribbing to discussing when they could all get away to Belly's new cottage in the country (which Lucia now very much doubted was a cottage at all). "We didn't need it, of course, but we had to get it for the dog," Belly said forcefully. "She loves the fresh air. Every dog deserves a home in the countryside, wouldn't you agree, Lucia?"

"Sure. I love dogs. Dogs are great." It was the only response she could come up with as she downed the last sip of champagne in her glass. They moved on swiftly to the topic of the best private schools and which waiting lists they had already put their future, as yet unborn, children on.

Great, Lucia thought. Not only could she not come up with a single intelligent or interesting comment, but on top of that, she had already ruined her eighteen-month-old's entire academic future by not putting her on even a single waiting list. She shifted her weight on the sofa. The irony was, Lucia was usually so good with rich people—it had been her entire job, cultivating high-net-worth donors and convincing them of all the reasons to love ArteAustin and, by extension, love her. She was highly skilled at the fake-it-till-you-make-it approach, especially if it meant a potential donor was more likely to open their checkbook.

But that was business. There was a protective layer in those conversations—it wasn't about Lucia herself, just the work, the mission, the cause.

Here, she had nothing to hide behind. Her boring dress, her new-world vocabulary, her unfashionably curly hair—everything was on full display. These people were social connections, her husband's very best friends in the world, and yet she had nothing personal in common with them. When it came to just being herself, she had no idea how to bridge the chasm that existed between her and these women who seemed to float through life on a cloud of Chanel.

She drank more quickly than she intended to, for liquid courage and because expensive champagne is delicious, and focused again on their conversation, which was still on the subject of children.

"Well," Caz launched, "we've just brought over an au pair from Sweden, and she seems marvelous. Don't worry, she's not attractive." They all laughed, so Lucia did, too. "She's live-in, which is great, but I do think it's vital to spend quality time with my angel darlings, don't you? I try to see the children for an hour a day if I can, most of the days in the week."

The boys entered the room and announced that dinner was served before Lucia could question how Caz filled the other twenty-three hours of her day. As they all got up to make their way to the dining room, Lucia watched with fury as Belly whispered something to Ollie, placing a possessive hand on the small of his back. She was filled with a visceral need to snap one of her tiny collarbones like a glow stick.

They traveled in a pack down a long hallway lined with portraits and tapestries. "Why is it that two people and one average-sized baby need so much space?" she wondered aloud and much less softly than she had intended.

"Well, how else were they supposed to fit an Olympic-sized pool in the basement, silly?" Belly admonished.

Lucia stopped just outside the dining room in front of a familiar image. "Oh wow, Philipp—I mean Pip! Is this a Graham Sutherland? I thought his portrait of Winston Churchill was destroyed? How did you come across it?"

An awkward silence followed before Ollie crossed over and whispered into her ear. "Lucia, that's Gaz's grandfather."

Belly, overhearing, swatted Ollie on the arm and then held on, a fraction too long for Lucia's liking. "Ollie, your wife is just too precious. It's as if she just arrived on English soil this morning." She turned to Lucia with a mock frown. "Come now, Lulu, we don't all look the same, you know."

Lucia tried to recover, but like spilled talcum powder, any attempt to make it better only made it worse. She felt their judgment of her compounding with each error she made.

At every turn, Lucia felt off-kilter. Like any group of life-long friends, their banter was full of inside jokes and offhanded references to cultural touchpoints from their childhoods. During the starters, Colz leaned in and pronounced the words *lovely jubbly* with a wink. With no context whatsoever, Lucia was sure it was a comment about the size of her ass until Ollie explained it was a line from the "classic" British TV show *Only Fools and Horses*. She certainly did feel like a fool (or a horse's lovely jubbly).

The main course arrived, a beautifully presented golden-roasted bird that resembled a tiny chicken. Quail? Partridge? She wasn't about to ask.

"Bon appétit," Gaz exclaimed as they all began daintily slicing off slivers of meat. Lucia took her fork and knife, bringing her elbows tight into her ribs like a T. rex while she performed delicate surgery on this ridiculously small main course. She felt like Tiny Tim cutting one bean into fifths for his whole family to share.

When she looked up, they were all watching her. "What do you think of the quail, Lucia?" Belly asked with her eyebrows raised expectantly, her mouth twitching in delight at Lucia's discomfort. "A bit small perhaps? Everything's bigger in Texas, isn't that right?" She laughed, and Lucia was overcome with a sudden urge to shove a baby potato up Belly's nose.

Lucia popped a morsel into her mouth, preparing to offer an eloquent comment about how much she enjoyed game, when her back molars crunched down on something so hard she nearly broke a crown.

"Oh yes, mind the shot," Gaz said.

Lucia attempted a gracious smile before spitting the small metal pellet into her napkin.

By the time they arrived back at home, Lucia felt like she might as well get a giant red L-plate, the kind put on a car to signify a learning driver, tattooed on her forehead. At least it would distract from her bright-pink cheeks, in a permanent blush of embarrassment, and probably her broken tooth. What would the appropriate thank-you gift be for a dinner like this? Her dental bill?

She flopped into bed and wished the duvet would swallow her whole. She had never felt more like an outsider in her life, so unable to blend in, which was really saying something. She couldn't keep up with their pop-culture references or dress the right way or enjoy eating their stupid tiny birds.

"It was, I'd say, an unmitigated disaster," she told Ollie as he got into bed with her.

He just laughed. "You are charmingly adorable," he said, lying next to her. "I love so much that you're trying to fit in with my friends." He moved into big-spoon position and wrapped his body around hers. His warmth made her feel so comfortable and safe, even if there was a good chance she'd choke in her sleep that night on a quail femur lodged in her esophagus. "Don't fret, they'll warm up. It just takes time."

"OK, but just tell me one thing. Didn't that portrait really look like Churchill?"

Ollie chuckled and kissed her again before rolling over. He was snoring softly in under two minutes flat, but Lucia couldn't sleep. She got up to check on Marley. Her daughter was curled up in a corner of her crib, just as still as could be. Lucia gently placed one hand on Marley's back to make sure she was still breathing. Reassured, she climbed back into her own bed and stared at the ceiling. She felt aimless—in the physical sense, in this strange country, but also in the bigger, soul-searching, purpose-driven way—and worse, she had no idea how to fix it.

Chapter 3
Playground Mom

This was perhaps a controversial opinion, but Lucia hated playgrounds. All playgrounds. She had been to many, and the Diana Princess of Wales Memorial Playground in Kensington Gardens had to be, objectively, one of the best. Even the journey there was beautiful—entering the Broad Walk of the park through the wrought-iron Black Lion Gate, then crossing into the gardens themselves through the wildflower meadow, which, on a late September day like this one, was filled with an explosion of dahlias and hydrangeas in full bloom. The playground itself was every child's dream: a giant pirate ship at the center, marooned on a sandy beach, slides and seesaws, a musical play area and a small village of toddler-sized wooden houses. The perfect place for a kid to have an adventure. There was even a coffee shop for the grown-ups.

Lucia hated sitting at the playground. Maybe it would have been more fun if she had a friend to pass the time with. It had been two weeks since the epic fail of a dinner with Ollie's crew, and she hadn't received a single invite to join Belly or Pip for lunch or a playdate or a quick midafternoon manicure. So, this afternoon, she was resigned to a monotonous hour or two of scrolling through social media—she didn't like spending too much time alone with her thoughts, afraid of what she might find there—and looking up every ten seconds to make sure Marley wasn't in mortal danger (as in dangling upside down from the crow's nest of the ship) or wandering under a visiting playgroup's rainbow parachute (a suffocation risk) or stealing another kid's rice cake (this had happened more than once). Playgrounds were giant death traps, she thought, full of big hazards for little hands. Little hands that, on multiple occasions after playing at the Diana playground, touched Lucia's face in the most precious, loving way possible, only to leave a residue of something that she never, ever wanted to know the source of. To Lucia, the whole experience was just *yuck*.

Unfortunately for her, Marley loved the playground, and Lucia loved Marley, and it was the most effective way to tire her out before nap time, so they had found themselves there—just the two of them—many an afternoon since Marley was old enough to toddle around independently.

Today at the playground something was different. Or, rather, someone. Amid the sea of Lululemon-clad mummies was the most strikingly beautiful woman. She had sleek, dark hair that matched her dark skin and eyes, and wore a designer coat over a faded yellow T-shirt with "Just Stop Oil" printed in black lettering across the chest. Her fingers—with their long, perfectly manicured nails—were wrapped around a book. The cover was scandalous, especially in their current surroundings. It featured a tall, muscly man dressed as a farmhand (he couldn't be getting much work done with his shirt unbuttoned down to his belly button), while a buxom woman popping out of a milkmaid outfit stared up at him suggestively. The title was, simply, *Stable Boy*. Lucia decided immediately that the woman reading it was amazing.

Ensuring Marley was happily occupied building a sand-castle and picking her nose, Lucia pushed her buggy over to where her new best friend was sitting. She took the empty spot at the end of the long bench, but the woman didn't look up. Lucia was going to have to start this conversation herself.

"Hot day for this time of year, isn't it?" she said. A dull, safe topic, but it was true, at least; they were having an unseasonably warm September.

The woman looked over. "Well, that's climate change for you, innit."

Lucia moved a bit closer to peek at the cover of the book. "Oh, is that by Tilly Willington? I've just finished the one about the sexy handyman and the orphaned heiress who inherits the hotel where he works," Lucia casually mentioned.

The woman's eyes danced in the sunlight. "*Room Service?* I haven't read it yet, but I love this one," she replied in a smooth accent that was 100 percent London, as she flashed the cover at Lucia. "How about *Slow and Steady* with the race car drivers? The whole thing with the head of the pit crew being her long-lost fiancé was a bit much, but my god, Tilly Willy can really write a sex scene."

"I haven't read it. But now I feel like I should." Lucia smiled and extended her hand. "Lucia. Or in this context, Marley's mom." She gestured at Marley, who had found an unsuspecting victim in a little boy whom she had dispatched to collect some twigs.

The woman took Lucia's hand and shook it. "Susanna. But everyone calls me Sooz. And that little builder's assistant over there"—she pointed at the boy doing Marley's bidding—"is my Atticus. Looks like they're friends already."

Lucia sent a silent prayer up to whichever god looked after desperately lonely mothers that this would be true for them, as well. With someone to chat with—and not just anyone, but someone smart and funny who loved reading and hated playgrounds almost as much as she did—the time passed quickly. Before she knew it, she and Sooz had been talking for over an hour. Sooz ran a "little sustainable beauty blog" (which Lucia discovered later had more than three million followers and only covered environmentally friendly, nontoxic, cruelty-free products) and, even better, was a passionate activist.

"I've only been arrested twice," she said. "But the second time I glued myself so well to the railing of Buckingham Palace that it took a crew of five to pry me off and throw me in jail."

"That is so badass," Lucia replied, awestruck. "I've always done my social justice work from behind a desk." She told Sooz about ArteAustin, her face brightening when she shared the story of the Garcia family the nonprofit had supported for years. Lucia had taken a special interest in their case, personally testifying during their citizenship hearings (not a typical role for a fundraiser, but she had a habit of getting attached). When they got permission to stay in the US, they all cried, Lucia included. The next day, Mrs. Garcia showed up with sixty of Lucia's favorite tacos—carnitas with extra hot sauce. "I shared a few, but they were so good," she told Sooz, "I ended up freezing half of them and eating one every day for a month."

"Sounds like you love what you do," Sooz said admiringly, and Lucia's heart sank, just a bit, at the memory. "So what are you up to now, work-wise?" she asked.

"You're looking at it," Lucia said, pointing at the playground. "It all happened so fast. I met Ollie, fell in love, we moved here, and then I gave birth, and Marley was so small and helpless, so of course it made sense to look after her full-time. Plus I didn't *need* to go back to work right away."

"Ahh, I see," said Sooz. "Rich husband."

No one in Ollie's circle ever mentioned money unless it was to complain about how expensive something they could easily afford was. But they were rich, to her at least, richer than anyone in her usual social circles. They attended elite schools, wore designer clothes, were the kind of people who would spend seventy-five pounds on a candle. She loved that Sooz was just open about it. "Yeah, I guess you could say that," she replied.

"A stay-at-home mum. Best job in the world," Sooz said.

Lucia frowned, a shiver rolling down her spine at the term *stay-at-home mom* (even if it was an apt description). "Well, I love Marley and our time together," she replied. "It's a privilege, and I don't take it for granted."

She peered across at Marley and Atticus, who were throwing leaves at each other, their laughter echoing across the park. "It's the cutest job in the world," Lucia continued. "But the best?"

As a fundraiser, Lucia had never given less than 100 percent and reaped the rewards of her effort with complete confidence in her ability to tackle whatever was thrown at her.

But you couldn't rely on smarts and a plucky can-do attitude alone to figure out how to get a screaming toddler back to sleep at 4:00 a.m. or to determine whether baby-led weaning was superior to spoon-feeding. And worse, everything she read on Mumsnet or BabyCenter made it seem as if the stakes could not be higher, one wrong move and your baby would be traumatized forever. If she didn't offer Marley at least forty-five minutes of full eye contact every day, was she already tanking her chances of getting into an Ivy League school? In this world, mom world, there were no right answers, only lots and lots of differing opinions.

On many days, Lucia could feel, like a phantom limb, the missing electric current of pride in her work—the sense she'd done not just a good but a great job and that she was living up to the promise she had made to her grandparents: to make the world a little bit better for those less fortunate than her. In her earliest memories she felt driven by this purpose. Without it, she worried she had lost a piece of herself.

"I'm not sure," Lucia admitted. "Does that make me a horrible mother?"

"Mate, not at all," Sooz said, looking at her pointedly. "I started up my blog when I was pregnant with my older daughter because I was bored out of my bloody mind. I had been speaking to people in verse. So I know what you mean. But also, you know, a beauty blog isn't saving the world. That's why I started with the environmental activism, showing up where it matters. We've got to do some good in the world before we leave it, that's what I think. Honestly, it's the best gift I can give my children. A future where they're not living in climate-controlled caves underground or in space or whatever." She looked down at her phone. "Shit! I have to go. Call with *Vogue* in ten."

She handed the phone to Lucia. "Babe, pop your number in and I'll text you. Atticus and I are going to a march next week." She scooped Atticus up with one hand, depositing him in the pushchair before he even knew what was happening. "I'll message you the details. Come with me to a protest. It'll feel good to get back to doing something that doesn't involve a Gruffalo."

Lucia waved as Sooz departed. "Or a sexy librarian!" she yelled after her.

"*Between the Covers!*" Sooz exclaimed over her shoulder. "I love that one." And with that she was gone.

Lucia looked at the time and realized she needed to be going, too. She retrieved Marley from the sandpit and, after wiping her down with antibacterial gel, placed her in the buggy and started walking home.

"Such a great day at the playground, *mamita*, don't you think?" she said to Marley, who was already half asleep. Sooz was so refreshing. Lucia hadn't met anyone like her since she'd left Austin. She was honest, funny, sharp-witted, and sharper tongued. And she seemed to love her job. When had Lucia ever met a working mother who seemed like she had this whole work–life balance thing figured out, running from the playground to a call with Anna Wintour (or one of her minions) without breaking a sweat?

Becoming a stay-at-home mom had been Lucia's choice. She didn't regret it, but sometimes it felt like she'd blinked and two years had passed by. It had, in fact, been that long since she last saw the inside of an office (or any side of a paycheck). She hadn't considered how long she might stay home with Marley. And she certainly had never discussed it with Ollie, who seemed so content with how their life as parents was structured. But here was Sooz, who seemed to do it all—work, mommy life, even activism.

Maybe there was another paradigm out there, another example for her to follow.

Perhaps the playground wasn't so terrible after all.

Lucia hummed to herself all the way home, making her way through the entire Destiny's Child back catalog as she put Marley down for her nap, made an obligatory cup of tea with no intention of drinking it, tidied the flat, did a plank for a solid fourteen seconds, signed a petition about fracking, folded the laundry, and then woke Marley up and started on dinner.

"Something smells heavenly," Ollie said as he opened the front door.

"A guaranteed benefit of a Latina wife: You have a seventy-five percent chance of coming home on any given day to frying onions and garlic." He came around to where she was stationed behind the stovetop and gave her neck a nuzzle.

"I knew there were other reasons besides your perfectly formed rear end that marriage was an excellent idea." She turned and kissed him—the teasing of her lips on his signifying a promise of more to come.

"Nice to see you in such an excellent mood. What's the occasion?" he said.

"Well, since you asked, I made a friend today. And let me tell you, she's such a badass. She works as a beauty—"

"Oh, actually, darling, that reminds me." He pulled out his phone, scrolling down with a furrowed brow. "Just before I forget. Belly and I were chatting today, and she mentioned that if you ever fancied a playdate, you should just message. Here, let me text you the number."

Lucia frowned. "I actually have Belly's number already." Lucia recalled exchanging numbers the first time they'd met, when Belly had said, "Call me anytime, I'm sure we're going to be the best of friends." The subsequent text chain was entirely blue: Lucia had messaged several times over the months to set something up, but Belly had never bothered to respond.

"No, not her number," Ollie said, still scrolling. "Ah. Here it is." He tapped a few times, and a moment later, Lucia's phone pinged. "Who's Fernanda?" she asked.

"Fernanda. Belly's nanny. She thought you might want to reach out to organize a playdate for the children."

That makes sense, Lucia thought. She didn't qualify as friend material for Belly—clearly not friendly enough to have casual midday chats like she and Ollie seemed to have—but it was fine for her to spend time with the help. If Belly was trying to send Lucia the message that she didn't rank, then she had succeeded.

"Slick move. Stone-cold, but slick," Lucia said under her breath.

"Hmm?" Ollie questioned, having already moved on to something else. "What did you say?"

"Nothing, darling," Lucia said, refocusing on the dinner in front of her. "Nothing at all."

"Let me say hi to my other best girl," he said, making his way over to Marley's bouncer. "Really quite kind of Belly, don't you think?"

Lucia thought it best not to answer him.

Chapter 4
Mummy's Little Activist

The following week, Lucia was full of nervous excitement as she hauled the buggy up the steps from the Tube station and stepped out into Trafalgar Square. It was overcast, and there was the tiniest chill in the air, a warning that fall was just around the corner. Even under a cloudy sky, the Landseer lions at the base of Nelson's Column looked as majestic as ever.

Lucia scanned the crowd for Sooz, who had indeed followed up with an invite to the demonstration to which Lucia had immediately replied: Yes, yes, a thousand times yes. When Sooz sent back a GIF of a drenched Mr. Darcy, Lucia knew they were destined to be soulmates. It was only that morning, when she was figuring out what one wears to a protest in London, that she realized she hadn't bothered to ask what they were protesting.

Truthfully, it didn't matter. She had a date with a friend to do something that was going to have a net-positive impact (on someone, somewhere). She'd chosen her outfit carefully, wanting to look neither too militant nor too much like a West London mummy who just got lost on the way to the butcher. She'd settled on a pair of stretchy jeans and an oversize sweater that had been designed by one of ArteAustin's artists in residence.

She had worn the sweater to Singy Songy once before, and a fellow mother had asked where she could get one of her own child's drawings printed on an item of clothing. She was so embarrassed that she mumbled something about Kinko's, quickly changed the subject, and hid the offending item in the back of a drawer where it had remained ever since.

If she was being honest with herself, though, she loved the sweater and was proud to be wearing it again today, to be bringing a little bit of her past life into her new one. She hoped Sooz, who seemed to like her just as she was, would agree.

Lucia stood with Marley by the fourth plinth to wait for Sooz, who appeared a minute later.

"Hi hi hi, love, sorry I'm a bit late," she said as she hugged Lucia. She smelled like jasmine and sandalwood and was wearing a lime-green T-shirt that read "Plus Ça Change." The *Plus Ça* was crossed out with an X and the *change* was bolded in capital letters. She'd paired the top with a black miniskirt, high boots, and matching lime-green nails. "I have a prezzie." She reached into her bag and pulled out a Marley-sized T-shirt that said, "Mummy's Little Activist."

"Atticus has a matching one," Sooz said. "Now we're all dressed to protest. Love your jumper, by the way. Can't slouch on the *lewks* just because we're taking a stand against a fashion brand, now can we?"

Lucia beamed and followed as Sooz led them over to the front of the National Gallery. A small stage had been set up with speakers, and the crowds were starting to gather. Just a few hundred people, but not bad for a weekday afternoon, Lucia thought.

"I just can't believe the Gallery would let Plus Ça sponsor their exhibition. They shouldn't be taking money from that pig

Charmless Chatto full stop, and certainly not money that comes from fast fashion."

So that was the purpose of the protest. Lord Charles Chatto was the CEO of Plus Ça, one of Europe's biggest fast-fashion chains. Their clothes were cheap and cute, and teenagers lined up outside their stores every time they had a new drop, leaving with bag loads of items. Most ended up in landfills, but Chatto was unrepentant about his environmental footprint and the nearly annual exposés on the shocking conditions in the factories that made Plus Ça's clothes. The newspapers had coined the moniker Charmless Chatto (and were no doubt still patting themselves on the back for their clever alliteration).

More people were surrounding them with placards that read: "Who Made Your Clothes?" and "Living Wage Now!" Lucia realized in horror that her own jeggings were Plus Ça. She almost never shopped there, but this pair was purchased in a moment of weakness, immediately post-Marley, when she didn't want to invest in any expensive pieces of clothing before she lost the baby weight. Which hadn't happened just yet. She pulled her sweater down farther on her hips, hoping no one would notice.

"They sound like prime evildoers, for sure. But do you really think they should have turned down the money?" Lucia questioned. "I mean, the National Gallery needs it, the owner of Plus Ça has it. Why shouldn't they take it and do something good? If they turned it down, what would this Chatto guy do? Buy another plane or horse or Rolex?"

Sooz pressed her lips into a line as she looked at Lucia thoughtfully before responding. "It's not even the money that's the problem. It's the halo effect, right? Plus Ça hasn't given an anonymous donation. They want their name splashed everywhere, so when people think of them, they think they're doing good. Wealthy people, big donors, companies doing awful things—they think they can whitewash their images by giving away money and hoping no one notices how they made it. It's rubbish and we shouldn't allow them to get away with it."

Lucia felt a part of her brain that had been dormant spark, fundraiser mode activated after a long nap. She was about to prod Sooz further when a woman with fiery-pink hair stood up on the dais and grabbed the mic.

It wasn't that she disagreed with Sooz—she did, in principle, think she was right. Her donors at ArteAustin had lots of different reasons for giving—to gain political or social capital among their peers, their faith maybe, or sometimes because they did truly love a cause. She rarely felt it useful to question their motives. What did it matter where the money came from as long as it was going to a good cause? Back in Texas, she had turned a blind eye more than once to how it had been made (mostly oil, of course) and gratefully took their checks. Fundraisers didn't often have the luxury of deciding whose dollars were clean and whose weren't. On balance, she believed it was worth the little trade-offs for the impact the money would have.

After three speeches and a few rousing rounds of rhyming chants, the crowds started to move inside the Gallery. Marley had enjoyed the event immensely, waking up from her nap about halfway through the speeches and using the cacophony as an opportunity to scream gibberish at the top of her lungs. Lucia moved to join them, but Sooz pulled her back.

"Let's go grab a snack, mate. I need a sugar rush after all of that."

"No protesting inside?" Lucia asked, but only half-heartedly.

"Naw. It could get rowdy in there, and I never bring the baby to ones where I might get arrested. He's too young to have a record. Aren't you, my boo-boo?" Atticus, clearly an experienced activist, was sound asleep.

Sooz led the way toward a bakery she knew in Covent Garden. "That was fun," Lucia said between mouthfuls of chocolate cake. "It had never occurred to me that social justice could be such a family-friendly activity. Marley loved chanting in time to the beat, and this was way better than Singy Songy, in that I didn't almost die of boredom. And we got to have cake. Win-win."

"The way I see it, parenting is all about balance, right?" Sooz agreed, grabbing another forkful. "We do one activity for them and one for us. That way it's fair."

Their conversation flowed seamlessly, dancing between deconstructing 1970s feminist paintings and how to sneak veggies into recipes for chocolate muffins. They had mom life and life life in common. Lucia felt like a more vibrant, interesting person in Sooz's presence; for the first time since she had arrived in London, she could be herself.

They parted ways with hugs and promises of a cinema date next week. Sooz got on the Tube, rushing home for an evening of calls with the West Coast, but Lucia decided to brave the ninety-minute walk. Unlike Sooz, she had nowhere to be. Marley was peaceful as they ambled down Piccadilly, passing men and women in suits rushing in and out of the private clubs and restaurants and offices that lined the street. You could feel the busyness emanating from their pores. Rushing here, rushing there. Lucia envied them. They had somewhere to be, someone waiting for them, something important to do. They had a sense of purpose, something that had eluded her since she'd left Austin, and ArteAustin, behind.

She cut through the Green Park, where the trees were dressed for fall, half green and half yellow, caught between the seasons. Not fall, she corrected herself. Autumn. No one here said fall, even though they all knew what it meant and it was, empirically, easier to spell.

Buckingham Palace gleamed in the distance. Maybe she should look into booking a tour, she thought. How cool would that be?

By the time they reached Hyde Park Corner, Marley had fallen asleep, and Lucia was so lost in her own thoughts that she was startled by the buzz of her phone in her pocket.

It was a text from a number she didn't recognize:

Hey, hon, it's Helen Macpherson from Austin. Long time no habla! I heard you were in London now. Are you working? I know a great job going at our bank.

Helen! She hadn't thought about Helen in forever—a big-haired, big-bosomed, brassy Texan who, after inheriting hundreds of millions, had been one of Lucia's major donors at ArteAustin. Helen had married a bespectacled Dutchman and moved to Monaco, which she said was for the sunshine but everyone knew was for tax reasons. Lucia hadn't seen her since, and that was at least five years ago. It was all very out of the blue.

Lucia reread the text and was convinced it was sent to the wrong person. Her? At a bank? She shot off a quick reply:

Hi! Are you sure you meant to message me? Lucia Gutierrez from ArteAustin? Yes, I am in London. But I don't have any finance experience. I think you might be mistaking me for someone else—but it's lovely to hear from you.

She reread the message, fixed three errors—Lucia could not bear to send any message with a typo—and hit Send.

Helen's response was immediate:

Yes, silly goose, I know it's you. The job isn't on the numbers side. It's a private bank, our private bank, working with wealthy clients on their philanthropy. Sat next to someone at a dinner party, and she said they were hiring. I thought of you. Maybe you'd like giving away money more than asking for it! Should I connect you?

Another person might have waited to respond or asked more questions, like, "Which bank?" or even, "What is the job?" Another person might have gone home to think about it, to discuss it with their partner and consider what they'd do about childcare, or maybe even do a little bit of research.

Maybe it was the afterglow of the protest, the delight of having a friend, or just the sheer desire deep within her to fill her days with more than doughnuts (albeit great doughnuts) and naps in front of afternoon reruns of *Midsomer Murders*. She'd never know.

Lucia immediately responded:

Yes. Why not?

Chapter 5
The Interview

Lucia looked up at the glass-fronted building and slowly approached the revolving doors.

She was going to a job interview. That no one knew was happening because she hadn't told them; not Sooz, who was babysitting; not Ollie, to whom she had flat-out lied. Maybe if she didn't tell anyone, she thought, it wasn't real. And if it wasn't real, it didn't matter if she bombed. Spectacularly.

After she'd responded to Helen's text, it had taken a few weeks to hear back. She had assumed the bank wasn't interested after all. She tried not to take it personally and focused instead on spending as much time as possible with Sooz and Atticus. They crisscrossed London, experiencing things that were outside of the day-to-day lives of Ollie and his friends—filling their bellies with Trinidadian curried mutton at Brixton Village, canvassing for an upcoming local by-election in Tooting, and even going to a performance art exhibition on a houseboat in Regent's Canal. She was finally enjoying herself and figured, with only a tinge of regret, that it wasn't so bad this bank didn't want her.

And then one night, as Lucia lay in bed with Ollie reading beside her, she was doing one final scroll of Instagram (though desperately trying to break the habit of bringing her phone into bed, she was, so far, failing) when an email came through. It was from an HR woman at Eastern Currents Bank with the instruction to send her résumé and book an interview slot.

"What are you looking at, *amor*?" Ollie asked, throwing an arm around her. She quickly brought her screen down on her chest.

"Just a notice about changing the class time for kid yoga," she replied quickly. "Babies, not goats."

"Either way, sounds nice," he said sleepily. He kissed her and rolled over to face the other side.

Lucia waited for his breathing to deepen and then picked up her phone again. She felt a flash of guilt about lying. She could have told him—should have told him—about the text from Helen and the interview. But she was afraid of the can of worms it might open.

She had no inkling of how he would feel about the whole idea. Ollie knew how much Lucia loved what she'd done in Austin and how sad she was to leave it, so he must have known that she would want to go back to work again. Didn't he?

The truth was, they had never explicitly spoken about what would happen when—or, she guessed, if—she went back to work. Ollie often made comments about how happy he was that his girls got to spend their days together, or how he could relax at work knowing Marley was so well taken care of. Moira, a stay-at-home mom herself, was, in his eyes, the shining paragon of womanhood. He never explicitly said that's what he wanted Lucia to do, but what if it was?

She didn't know. That was one of those hard topics or questions that they assiduously avoided, letting it bounce off the impenetrable bubble that their new love had created around them. The honeymoon period was still ongoing, even if a few tiny cracks had appeared. She and Ollie rarely bickered and had never had a real fight. The idea of it roiled the pit of her stomach. If she was being honest with herself, she was afraid that he could fall out of love with her as quickly as he'd fallen into it.

There was no point in trying to find out now, over an insignificant interview that would probably end up being for nothing. It wasn't as if she was going to get the job. She was completely out of the professional loop. It had been a year and a half since she had read anything that didn't feature either of the phrases *throbbing member* or *preventing colic*.

Still, a little voice had convinced her to go and give it a try. "You never know," it said. And anyway, she thought, it would be nice to put on her hell-yes dress, the only item of work clothing that still fit her postbaby body (even if she did have to wear two layers of Spanx). Electric blue with a peplum (the Spanx could only do so much) and a matching blazer. She waited until Ollie left for work in the morning before fishing it out from the back of her closet and putting it on. It still did the trick!

Lucia texted Sooz to ask if she could drop Marley off for a few hours, so she could have an informational coffee with the head of a nonprofit that worked on immigrants' rights—just a little white lie to avoid having to explain things in more detail. Sooz replied with a torrent of jubilant emoji, a naughty GIF of a dominatrix, and the words of course.

Sooz lived only a few blocks away in a sweet eggplant-colored terraced house on Portobello Road. Thanks to her home-price-stalking app, Lucia knew these homes cost seven figures. In Notting Hill, where a studio flat in a fifth-floor walk-up could go for the same amount, these full houses were considered crown jewels. They almost never went on the market. Leave it to Sooz to live in the cutest house on the most sought-after street in town.

She rang the bell, and Sooz answered, wearing a matching sports bra and leggings, and a healthy glow on her face. "Did I interrupt a workout?" Lucia asked, giving her a hug.

"Christ no," Sooz said. "Some days are just not made for underwire bras. Atticus and I were doing a bit of baby Zumba on the telly, so I guess that counts as my exercise today. Come in, come join us," she added, unbuckling Marley from her stroller. She ran to where Atticus was adorably shaking his hips in front of a wall-mounted TV, nearly knocking him over with affection.

"Hold on, hold on," Sooz said, turning back to Lucia and looking her up and down. "What a stunner."

"Why thank you," Lucia said, spinning around. "It is my best outfit, having earned that distinction by being the only outfit from my prebaby life that still fits."

"Well, *you* look fit. If this charity knows what's good for them, they'll offer you that volunteer role on the spot."

Lucia again felt a tiny stab of guilt, but it subsided quickly in the wave of excitement. All dressed up and divested of her usual accessories—stroller, diaper bag, dried baby food on her shirt—she felt like an actual adult woman.

Sooz led her into the open-plan living room, full of color and light. Marley was demonstrating salsa dancing for Atticus as the baby Zumba instructor on the screen took them through a merengue.

"*Wepa, dale mami,*" Lucia said, laughing at Marley's unco-ordinated but confident hip shimmies. "I taught her everything she knows."

"I have no doubt," Sooz agreed.

Lucia looked at the large, super-stylish melting clock on the wall. Though the numbers were blurred in Dalí fashion, she could tell she needed to leave now. She got up to go, but Sooz stopped her.

"Wait! You look amazing, but I just got in a whole batch of mica-free eye shadow samples that will make this blue dress pop. Two minutes for a mini makeover?"

"From the expert? How could I say no?"

It took more than two minutes, but it was worth it. Lucia barely recognized herself in the mirror. "I *do* look amazing," she said at her reflection, admiringly. "Sooz, you are a miracle worker."

"That's why they pay me the big bucks." She shrugged. "You already looked great when you came in, but this just elevates it. OK, don't be late." She shoved her out the door. "Knock 'em dead, babes."

"Bye, *mija*," she yelled to Marley who ignored her completely.

Lucia whistled as she walked to the Tube station, staring at herself in each window that she passed, her confidence increasing with each step. She bounded down the steps to the train and boarded the eastbound Central Line for the journey to Liverpool Street.

In her head, she reviewed everything she had learned while cramming last night and this morning. Eastern Currents was one of the country's oldest and most revered financial institutions, founded by private bankers for discerning masters of empire from London and Liverpool and Glasgow who had set out to make their fortunes in Hong Kong or Johannesburg or Lahore. This made their footprint truly international, operating around the world with headquarters in London and advising clients on how to grow their money, make more of it, and sometimes, how to give it away.

That was where the position of philanthropy advisor came in. Advisors worked with the bank's clients to help them do more good with their sizable personal wealth. Getting paid to give away other people's money, instead of constantly asking for it, seemed like the most desirable career in the world.

With a solid fifteen minutes to spare, Lucia found the Eastern Currents building and crossed herself for good luck (she wasn't religious but couldn't shake the superstitious elements of her Catholic upbringing). She let the revolving doors spin once, then twice. Then she took a deep breath and walked through to the reception desk.

Two women in black blazers with red scarves tied jauntily around their necks were typing at the speed of light, their perfectly unchipped red polish visible every time they clacked down on their keyboards.

"Good morning, I'm here to see Celeste Le Fevre," Lucia said. No turning back now.

"Name please?" said one of the receptionists without peeling her eyes away from her computer screen.

"Lucia Gutierrez-Barrow," she replied. "Sorry, I know it's a mouthful."

"Fine, yes, please look up at the camera," the receptionist said, gesturing behind her.

"Wait, which one? Ah, I see it. Cheese." She grinned wide. The receptionist did not bother to look at the image as she printed the badge and handed it to Lucia. "Just take a seat please. Someone will be down shortly."

When Lucia looked down at the temporary ID card, she was shocked to see that it was one of the best photos of her that had ever been taken in her adult life. Her dark eyes popped, and her face bore more than a passing resemblance to Salma Hayek. This was a rare stroke of luck; her passport, her driver's license, her gym ID card photos were all horrendous, so bad that Lucia was embarrassed every time someone looked at them and didn't say, "Are you sure this is you? This person is much, much less attractive than you are." But today, her grainy ID photo made her look like a supermodel, a testament to Sooz's extraordinary skills with an eye-shadow brush. She hoped it was a good omen.

Lucia said thank you and walked over to the waiting area. The walls were covered in art, both contemporary and traditional. At the center of the atrium, a gigantic wooden pillar covered in an ancient looping script reached almost to the ceiling. It was impressive, if extraordinarily phallic.

She started to sit down on the ikat-print sofa when a pencil-thin man with pale skin and a floppy shock of dark hair came toward her with darting eyes.

"Mrs. Gut . . . Gooty . . . Mrs. Barrow?" he asked, fixing his gaze on her.

She had long since resigned herself to the fact that no one in the UK would ever be able to pronounce her name correctly. "Hi, yes, that's me."

"Please, come with me. I'm Thomas, Celeste's assistant. I'll take you upstairs to meet Ms. Le Fevre."

Celeste Le Fevre was born in Paris but had been at the bank in London for almost two decades, steadily rising in the ranks until she reached her current role, head of philanthropy. She was a bit of a superstar, it seemed. Last year her team had set the record for the largest single donation by a client in the bank's hundred-plus-year history, to build a girls' school in Tamil Nadu, India. Lucia had found a photo online from the school's ribbon-cutting ceremony featuring Celeste front and center, a slim, attractive, pale woman, wearing a kurta and holding a Dior bag, posing with smiling students in gingham dresses and braided pigtails. She didn't seem to have a digital footprint from before her life at Eastern Currents, her bio stated vaguely that she had "worked in international development" prior to joining.

Thomas guided Lucia through the entry gates to a bank of elevators and pressed ten.

"So, early start this morning?" she asked, in the interest of small talk.

"Not too bad," he said.

"And . . . Do you enjoy working here?"

"Yes."

This guy was giving her nothing, she thought, as they got on the elevator.

The view on the way up was impressive, 360 degrees of glass, affording them a view of the building's wide atrium as they rose.

"This glass is so clean," Lucia said, grasping for something to cut the awkward silence. "I wish I could do this to my own windows."

Thomas looked at her oddly—as if he had no idea what cleaning a window might even entail or why, for that matter, she felt any need to speak to him—and then went back to staring at his shoes.

It was fine, she thought. As much as she wanted to, she didn't need to charm Celeste's assistant. She pulled out the ID and looked at it once more, for luck. "I swear, it's the best picture I've ever taken," she muttered under her breath.

The elevator announced, "Tenth floor," and she stepped forward, crashing face-first into the not-yet-open glass door with the full force of her body. She ricocheted backward, almost sending Thomas tumbling to the floor. The impact knocked the wind out of her, and a searing pain signaled that she might have broken her nose. At the very least, it was going to bruise.

"Oh my, are you alright?" His eyes were wide like saucers.

No, she was not alright, she thought. She glimpsed a smudge of Sooz's mica-free eyeshadow on the previously spotless glass and wondered if she had a concussion.

While trying not to wince, or cry, she arranged her features into what she hoped was a normal, uninjured expression. "Yep, I'm fine. Sorry about that. Heh."

He raised an eyebrow but gestured for her to leave the elevator, holding his arm out to block the door for fear that she would crash into it again. She exited, safely this time, then let him lead her through a long corridor of conference rooms. Each was named after a city where Eastern Currents had claimed market superiority: Kuala Lumpur, Jakarta, Nairobi. He walked her to the very end of the hall—Dubai—and opened the door.

Lucia noticed three things immediately.

The first was the view, overlooking the wide expanse of the older part of the city with the dome of St. Paul's Cathedral like a diamond at its center. Lucia loved old London, where buried deep under the concrete and steel were coins and shards of pottery from Roman times, ancient history literally underneath their feet.

The second was the painting on the wall. She recognized the distinctive style as that of Malini Shambala, an Indian artist from the 1960s. Lucia had minored in art history in college, almost on a whim—it was never a career path that seemed open to her, a working-class Venezuelan American whose childhood home featured seven hundred images of the Virgin Mary and nothing else that could be called art—but she had always found a quiet inner peace in museums that eluded her in the other spaces of her life.

After a class on political art of the Indian diaspora, Lucia became a huge fan of Shambala's work. She remembered the specific piece in front of her now. It was a large canvas that took up almost half the wall, in the style of Picasso's *Guernica*—but instead of shades of black and white, this was full of bright colors and patterns, women in saris of pink, green, and yellow that exploded off the canvas.

Lucia had seen a lot of art since then, but this Shambala painting was a personal favorite. She knew it was in a private collection and never imagined she'd get a chance to see it in person. At least the day wouldn't be a total waste.

The third and final thing she noticed was that the woman sitting in front of her was wearing an ivory suit. Even before having kids, wearing all white required hubris that Lucia didn't possess. How did anyone make it through an entire day without spilling a drop of coffee on their pants or stabbing themselves in the shoulder accidentally with a blue ballpoint pen? To date, Lucia's entire wardrobe had been selected for its ability to hide stains. Since Marley's arrival, she would have dressed in Teflon if she could have. A woman wearing white had a poise and manual dexterity that Lucia couldn't even fathom.

Celeste was even more attractive than in the photos online. She was thin and toned, with skin that looked unnaturally taut for a woman in her early sixties but not so stretched that she looked like the Joker. Her hair, sliced into a short bob with severe bangs, was a soft caramel hue. She wore subtle makeup and a simple but enormous emerald pendant, roughly the size of an eyeball, on a chain around her neck. She wasn't beautiful in a classic sense—her features were too angular, and her face looked like it never smiled—but she demanded your attention.

Celeste frowned as she typed a message on her phone at a furious speed. Lucia stood awkwardly, waiting to be acknowledged. Her head was pounding. Risking a *faux pas*, she decided to sit down. Another minute passed before Celeste finally looked up.

"So," she began, placing her phone in front of her. "You have a good CV. It is not great, but you come very highly recommended."

"Um, thank you . . . I guess?" was all she could say. No one had ever started an interview with an insult. Maybe this was a power move; she tried to regain composure. "I mean, thank you. Helen was one of my favorite donors," she said, which wasn't a lie. Helen was demanding—she needed a lot of hand-holding—but she was kind and generous to a fault.

Celeste's phone buzzed on the table, and she picked it up, scowled, and started typing away again. Lucia had no idea if she had even heard her answer.

Another minute passed in silence, until Celeste looked up again. "What is a favorite donor for you?"

"That's an easy question." Lucia smiled broadly, delighted to be asked something she could answer. "First of all, they give unrestricted gifts—no strings attached—which Helen didn't do at first, but eventually I got her there. Second—they respect my expertise." Lucia thought back to the many, many people she had met in her career who thought that being an expert on manufacturing semiconductors meant that they were automatically an expert on, say, education policy or how many staff a nonprofit should hire.

"Third—they care about impact. Fourth—of course, they fork over a lot of cash."

This caught Celeste's attention, and she dismissed reason five with a wave of her hand. "The money is important to you? I thought you 'charity people'"—at this she sneered—"only cared about doing good."

"If only," Lucia sighed. "Of course, I have the issues that get me out of bed in the morning. My family immigrated to the US, so protecting the rights of refugees and immigrants is personal for me. I suppose I'm an immigrant, too, here in the UK. And I guess you are, as well."

She watched as Celeste's nostrils flared. "I am here for work," she sneered. "Not an immigrant. No one would mistake me for British, I should hope." Lucia made another mental note: Never call a French person British, or vice versa.

"The money, though, that's key," Lucia continued, trying to cover her gaffe. "The money makes the impact happen. It can't be ignored. That's why no matter who my favorite donor really is, every donor is my favorite donor. The donor is always right."

"In that we agree," Celeste said, calmer now. "Here, the client is always right." She paused before continuing. "I don't like to hire people from nonprofit backgrounds. They are too soft. They care, of course they care, about people, children, climate . . . We all care. But they are not ready to make the sacrifices required to do the work. To convince the clients to give, and give more and more money away, we must keep them happy. Sometimes there is a cost, but it is worth it. And, of course, we are rewarded, as well. Do you see it?"

Lucia nodded in agreement. There were sacrifices to be made in any job. Lucia had sacrificed a social life, untold hours of sleep, nights out with friends, even regular Pap smears to achieve the mission at ArteAustin. But as long as they were leading with their values, the sacrifices were always worth it.

"I do," she said, nodding again. "I really do. I've never shied away from making sacrifices to ensure the impact is achieved."

"Hmm," Celeste said. "And you have children?"

Lucia was startled by this question. She was fairly sure it was not legal to ask if she had kids, but she answered, anyway. "A daughter. She's one."

"And will you have more children?"

Lucia was entirely sure it wasn't legal to ask *that* question but answered honestly. "Maybe one day, but not anytime soon."

"Children are a joy," Celeste said. "I have a daughter and a son, all grown now. But I had full-time nannies when they were babies. Children can get in the way of a career."

Although the sentence ended with a period, Celeste looked at Lucia expectantly as if she had asked a question.

"Not for me," Lucia said.

Celeste looked back down at Lucia's résumé, flipping the pages and skimming quickly over the words Lucia had carefully selected to describe her years of experience.

This woman was an enigma. Was she done asking questions? Was she bored? Lucia had no clue how badly this interview was going. But something about Celeste made Lucia want to try harder.

"Listen, I may not be your ideal candidate on paper," she said. "But I'm a quick learner, I'm smart, and I work hard. I care about making the world better, but I'm not naive enough to assume that happens without sacrifice. This job is kind of a dream for me. As a fundraiser, I have always wondered what life is like on the other side of the balance sheet. I can promise you I will give you one hundred percent dedication."

Celeste looked her straight in the eye. "Are you certain of that? Because I require one hundred percent. *Non*, more than that. I have a big agenda, an important one, this year especially. Many things are happening, and I need the right team surrounding me. I expect nothing less than complete loyalty, and it will not always be easy, it will not always be fun, but at the end of it you will be richly rewarded."

"Absolutely," Lucia said. "Making the kind of impact you have the potential to make here, with the assets at the bank's disposal, is the biggest reward I could ask for."

"*Bon*," Celeste said. "That, as well."

Celeste was quiet again, opening her mouth as if to say something then stopping herself. After another moment, she said, "I have enough. You are done now."

Lucia stood up and held out her hand in parting, but Celeste had already returned her attention back to the incoming messages on her phone. Awkwardly, Lucia dropped her hand and turned to leave. This had been the shortest interview of her life. "By the way," she said on her way out, unable to help herself. "That painting is extraordinary."

"Hmm?" Celeste said, still glued to her phone.

"The Shambala. It's glorious."

Celeste looked up. "You know Malini's work?"

"Know it? I love it. I've never seen this piece in person, though. It's been a real privilege."

And even though she had her back turned, she knew Celeste watched her as she walked out the door. She made her way downstairs, reaching out to tap the elevator door and ensure it was open before passing through, and exited the building into the cloudy day. Clearly she had tanked. But on the bright side, she wouldn't ever have to admit to Sooz or Ollie where she had been.

She thought about Marley waiting for her. If she hurried, she'd be in time to put her down for her nap. She'd feel her warmth as she pulled her close, inhaling the fresh scent of her baby soap. Her heart swelled with love for this little person she had made.

Sooz had sent her a photo of Marley and Atticus blowing bubbles in the garden. The accompanying message said:

Your daughter is a dream already, but if she turns out to be half the woman you are, the world will be lucky. Hope your coffee went well, love. xx

She smiled to herself. Who needed this job? She already had so much. She could make it enough. Even if that little voice inside her begged to differ.

Chapter 6
Patricos

Lucia missed the first call when it came in.

She was at the library, where she had been sitting for forty-five minutes in her formal sweatpants (the ones without holes), listening to puppets sing "Frère Jacques" and failing to come up with anything to add to the rather animated conversation among the other moms about how early was *too* early to put your child into violin lessons. (Consensus: It's never too early.)

It wasn't until after the puppet had been passed to Marley and she had shoved it into her mouth, causing an uproar from the librarian, that Lucia hurried out of the library and saw the call notification from an unknown number. But there was no voicemail. She promptly put it out of her mind, focusing instead on the most important part of her day: caffeinating with her daughter.

Coffee together was one of the few rituals from her childhood that Lucia was adamant about passing on to Marley. Every morning until she went away to college, Lucia would sit at the breakfast table with her *abuelo*. He would pour himself a *cortado* and Lucia her own *café con leche* (just milk and sugar until she was old enough for real coffee). They'd have their cups together, and she always felt very grown-up. After they finished, Abuelo would clear their mugs from the table and put his hand on her shoulder. "*Vamos, mija,*" he would say. "Let's go do something great."

Now she was the one with the *cortado*, and Marley had the warm milk, which, thankfully, had the opposite effect of coffee. As Lucia went to put her down for her nap, she leaned in to kiss her. "Have a good rest, *mija*," she said, already thinking about how she was going to spend the next ninety minutes.

"*Pio pio, mama,*" Marley begged, offering the pout that Lucia could never resist, no matter how boring it was to repeat the same song about chickens over and over again. Lucia couldn't carry a tune in a bucket, but she sang it twice, then kissed her daughter once more before softly closing the door behind her.

As she stepped into the kitchen, her phone buzzed on the counter. There were two new missed calls from an unknown number, one voicemail, and a text from Helen. Lucia immediately clicked on the text:

Hon, the bank just called me for a reference. I gave them such a rave they probably think you paid me!! I think you're in!!!! Go, girl, go!!!

Lucia's heart pounded and her hands shook as she checked her voicemail next. It was a formal-sounding message from someone named Linda in HR at Eastern Currents asking her to please phone back. She had good news.

Lucia paced back and forth in the living room, wanting to return the call but hesitant to do so. This was one of those moments in life when taking the next step would change everything. There was still a chance to stop the train—she could decline the offer, if it was in fact an offer, or defer until she could have a proper conversation about it with her husband. But even as she was aware of those possibilities, she was also entirely certain that wasn't how this would go. She knew in her heart of hearts that, with trembling fingers, she'd dial Linda in HR's number and say she would accept the job. They would tell her about the salary and benefits and suggest a start date, but none of that would matter. She'd just say yes. She knew she would.

And that was exactly what she did.

Linda congratulated her on being offered the position of philanthropy advisor, reporting directly to Celeste, and explained that her new boss was "adamant" that she start immediately—next week at the latest. Linda mentioned a salary that was triple what Lucia had been making at ArteAustin, and Lucia swallowed a squeal. Just because she didn't need the money didn't mean she wasn't delighted that it was she who was making it. Linda promised to email over the contract, NDA, and new-joiner pack by end of day.

As soon as they hung up, Lucia made two more calls: one to her mother-in-law, whom she loathed to ask for favors but knew would be delighted to babysit Marley that night. And the second to Patricos, her and Ollie's favorite local spot, to make a reservation.

London is a big city made up of small neighborhoods; even with so many glitzy attractions a short Tube ride away, she found that people tended to stay within a few blocks of their homes. She and Ollie were no different, which was how they found Patricos, their regular spot for a romantic meal or, if they were with Marley, a quick and delicious 5:00 p.m. dinner that ended with tomato sauce everywhere. The staff at Patricos didn't mind—they made everyone feel like a regular (even if you weren't), argued loudly with one another in Italian (which was similar enough to Spanish to feel comforting), and added garlic to every single dish (Lucia's idea of heaven).

Patricos offered homemade pastas, focaccia still moist with olive oil, and heaping salads—unfussy food in a warm environment, so unlike the places Ollie's friends had insisted they try, whose menus always seemed to include a quail egg in bacon reduction for thirty-eight pounds. Literally, fifty dollars for bacon and eggs. She was so hungry after those meals that she typically picked up a slice of pizza on the way home.

Lucia arrived at Patricos first, back in her hell-yes dress for the second time that week. Shortly after, Ollie, who had been messaged with a cryptic request to meet her for a surprise, breezed in straight from the office in his work clothes. He placed his briefcase down on the floor and leaned in for a kiss. She loved that he still carried a briefcase to work even though the entirety of the legal profession (and all other professions) had gone paperless. It was just like him to stick with something so traditional and proper.

Lucia felt a wave of guilt wash over her. Was she the kind of wife who took a job and hid it from her husband? Apparently so.

"You look enchanting as usual, *amor*," he said with a wide grin as he sat down. "Tell me then, what are we celebrating?"

Lucia fumbled. What had she been thinking? The idea that she, the woman who couldn't even make it through a casual dinner or morning playdate without embarrassing herself at least twelve times, could waltz into a bank full of British people and just fit right in? She didn't fit in anywhere here. She had one friend. Not to mention she had forgotten basically everything she ever knew about fundraising. She was addled from sleep deprivation and had no idea if the effects of baby brain would be permanent. And what did she know about philanthropy as a fundraiser, anyway? Oh my god, she thought. Had she made a horrible mistake?

Ollie looked at her, his brow furrowed with concern. Her breathing slowed. She just needed to tell him and everything would be fine.

Antonio, their waiter, had overheard Ollie. "Celebrating, *signora*? Prosecco then! A bottle!"

Lucia regained her composure. "Absolutely," she said. "Why not? *Grazie*, Antonio."

He scurried off into the kitchen, and Lucia took a deep breath. "Yes, sorry, love. I went into my own head for a minute. But something great did happen."

Immediately Ollie smiled in relief. "Marvelous. Did Marley do something wonderful today?"

"No. I mean yes, she does something wonderful every day, but that's not what this is about." Nerves of steel, just come right out with it, she told herself. "The victory today was mine."

"Splendid!" he said, his entire face lighting up. "Do tell, don't keep me in suspense any longer."

"The thing is . . . I got a job."

Ollie's pale cheeks flushed, just briefly, before he recovered. "That's extraordinary. A job. I'm surprised, I'll admit. I had no idea you were looking." She watched the ramifications of her admission sprout in his brain, showing on his face in real time. He didn't look mad—more confused. She waited for the next questions on the tip of his tongue: What's the job? Did you have an interview? Why did you keep this from me? But instead he said, "Didn't we agree you'd stay at home with Marley for a little while longer?"

"When?" she asked, her voice involuntarily notching up an octave. "When exactly did we agree to that?"

Antonio arrived with the prosecco, pouring out two glasses and waiting for the foam to die down before topping them up a little bit more. Sensing the tension, he backed away quietly, but the moment had been enough to give Ollie a chance to respond.

"I suppose you're right. We never agreed to it, or even discussed it for that matter. I just thought . . . I assumed, I suppose . . . that you'd follow the same path as Mummy." Lucia cringed. "As Belly, Caz, and Pip."

She felt heat rising in her veins, but before she could explain how little she cared about emulating the life choices of her sworn frenemies, he reached across the table and put his hand on top of hers. "But of course, that was foolish. You're nothing like them."

"Is that a bad thing?"

"Not at all, *cariña* . . . I mean, *cariño*," he corrected himself. "It's precisely why I love you. And ultimately, all I want is for you to be happy. To be able to make you happy."

His eyes glistened with feeling; how could she be angry? Sure, maybe they hadn't known each other long enough to have had discussions like this, but they had time. As long as they could talk to each other, openly and with honesty, they didn't need to be mind readers. They'd figure it out, eventually.

"I'm sorry. I didn't mean to get angry. I love our life here, of course I'm happy." This was stretching the truth, but seeing how it immediately put Ollie at ease, she continued. It wasn't a lie. Just a slight exaggeration to keep the peace. "I love being home with Marley, and I should have told you about the interview. I didn't think there was a snowball's chance in hell that I'd get the job. But I did, and it's too good to pass up." She focused on the good things—the size of the bank's coffers, the impact their clients had made so far—and played down the disastrous interview and the weird vibes Celeste gave off. By the time their food arrived, the whole story was out.

"Darling, it all sounds fascinating. And you know I fully support your ambitions. Your generous heart, your passion to help others—it's what attracted me to you in the first place. And now, you're offering me the chance to be the trophy husband to a powerful banker who makes the world a better place? You can keep me in the lifestyle to which I've become regrettably accustomed." He winked, threading his fingers through hers. She was unable to sustain any anger at him when he looked at her like that. "I just want to make sure you know what you are getting into. And that we're . . . that you're ready for it."

"I am ready! I'm so ready," she yelped. "I want to . . . No, I need to get back to work. Please, just support me on this?"

Ollie didn't realize the extent to which she needed this; how could he? She hadn't been totally honest with him about how lost she felt, and not just geographically, every day. That was on her, not him. But surely he could read between the lines, sense her stagnation? Even if he couldn't—she needed him to back her. She knew that one way or another, this job was a step toward helping her get back to herself. That was the person whom he had fallen in love with after all.

Ollie smiled, although there was a hint of sadness behind his eyes. "If it's what you want, then I am fully prepared to do whatever you need to make it happen."

Lucia sighed again, this time with relief. "Great. What I need right now is for my husband to toast my success." She picked up her prosecco glass with her right hand and reached for Ollie's hand across the table with her left. "That and a full-time nanny."

"To new beginnings. And to my hot banker wife. I look forward to my future career as a gentleman who lunches."

Lucia excused herself to go to the bathroom and e-signed the contract right then and there.

The next day, Lucia received a call from a personal shopper at Crease, the hottest work-wear boutique in Knightsbridge, inviting her to set up an appointment as a gift from her "loving and apologetic gentleman who lunches." When she texted Ollie in thanks, he only replied:

She knows the budget, so just say yes to whatever she suggests. Hot bankers need hot wardrobes.

She immediately texted Sooz, inviting her to come along. Even the window mannequins displayed in posh Knightsbridge boutiques made Lucia feel deeply unfashionable—she would never have deigned to go into any of the stores, at least not alone. She knew that Crease, with its hand-tailored suits and locally sourced wool, would, thankfully, meet Sooz's sustainable fashion requirements.

Thirty-six hours later, Lucia was standing in the center of a private dressing lounge with an ivory carpet so pristine that she considered taking her shoes off before stepping inside.

"Turn around, please, I need to see it from the back."

Sooz twirled her manicured finger at Lucia, who obliged by spinning around slowly in the charcoal-gray suit she was trying on.

"It's nice," Sooz admitted begrudgingly. "The exact suit a sellout would wear. Albeit one with an amazing arse."

Lucia took the insult and the compliment in stride. "Thank you. But I'm not selling out. This job is going to give me the chance to make some real change. Maybe even more than I ever made as a fundraiser. We're talking about serious money here to do good." She told Sooz what she had learned about the partnership between Eastern Currents and noted philanthropist Jagamir Patra. He had donated enough money to provide free school breakfasts for a year to every child in Tower Hamlets, a part of East London where it was greatly needed. "That's thousands of kids with hot meals in their bellies every morning. Who knows what they might go on to do?" Her voice gained confidence as she spoke.

"Oh babe," Sooz said. "That's lovely. But Patra, he's one of the richest men in Europe. While he's feeding those kids in East London, he's fattening his pockets by paying workers at his factories less than a pound a day. He gets richer off the backs of others, makes a splashy, headline-worthy donation that, honestly, is probably less than his annual mineral water budget, and then he gets called a hero."

Lucia stripped down and handed the suit back to her personal shopper, nodding to indicate she should add it to the yes pile, and took a black jumpsuit from her hands. "Maybe," Lucia said. "But isn't it better than if he gave nothing at all? He's going to do what he does, anyway. At least someone in need is benefiting. I'm going to be able to facilitate that. Come, help me zip this."

Sooz put down her glass and walked over to Lucia, frowning in displeasure. "I'm not sure that's how to make change."

"Tell that to a ten year old starting his day on an empty stomach." Sooz zipped her up, deftly for someone with three-inch nails, and Lucia spun around to meet Sooz's fierce gaze with one of her own. "Look, you're not wrong. I'm not naive enough to think early-morning pancakes or beans on toast or blood pudding or whatever kids here eat for breakfast is going to solve world hunger. But this is how change starts. I'm going to be making change, real change, from the inside. I'll help him see how he can use not just his money, but everything at his disposal to create a positive impact."

"Humph," Sooz said, stepping back. "This one's a keeper, too. Tilly Willy would write a wicked sex scene about unzipping a jumpsuit like that."

Lucia blushed. "Anyway, you and I both know it's not only about that kind of change. *I* need a change. I'm not cut out to be a yummy mummy. I'm a hot mess, my leggings aren't nearly expensive enough, and my hips are way too wide for high-waisted jeans." They laughed. "I have to find my purpose again."

Sooz rested her hand gently on Lucia's arm. "Oh, hon. You are a great mum, but I know what you're saying is true. I'm sorry I've been so negative. I am proud of you for getting the first job you even went for. I just want to make sure you are somewhere that will value you, that's worthy of your brilliance. I can see you're lost. Any idiot can see that." Lucia wondered, with a fleeting pang, why Ollie hadn't. "Take the job, you do you. But do me a favor and don't get even more lost while you're in there. That world, the world of private jets and superyachts and trying to use generosity to gloss over all manner of sins—it's easy to lose your way. Don't forget who you are and promise you won't forget why you're there."

"I promise," she said, reaching out her pinkie for Sooz to hook with her own.

"Another glass, please," Sooz yelled out of the fitting room. "We must toast to Lucia's new employers, the imperialist bastards! And bring in that yellow peacoat from the window."

"That's the spirit."

"You'll never make any change if you only wear gray and black. Boring. My mate is going to be a philanthropy advisor at Britain's oldest, poshest, snobbiest bank. You better add a bit of color to their world."

"They won't have any idea what's hit them!" Lucia said, spying a bright-pink silk scarf and whipping it off the mannequin with a flourish. She managed one complete twirl just before the whole display tipped over and crashed to the floor.

Chapter 7
First Day Jitters

On her first day of work, Lucia woke up early to make sure she and Marley could have their morning coffee together. Gretel, their newly hired nanny, arrived with German precision at the exact appointed time. Even though it had been just under a week since she'd accepted the job, Lucia had managed to interview eight nannies. They were all lovely—experienced, with great references—but Lucia had found something wrong with each one. Too young, too old, too pretty (she hated herself for thinking this, but Caz had been right). Gretel, however, was perfect (just not too perfect). She was capable, seemingly unflappable, and warm but firm. She had attended Germany's top nanny training school where graduates went on to serve CEOs, royalty, and world leaders. She was empirically attractive but thankfully not Ollie's type. And she spoke perfect Spanish, almost better than Lucia's, which had gotten rusty from disuse since she had moved to London. She was Fräulein Maria incarnate. Lucia offered her the job on the spot.

The hiring may have been easy, but the reality of leaving her baby with this highly qualified stranger turned out to be an entirely different ball game. From the moment she woke up, Marley could tell that something was amiss (probably because she wasn't used to her mother wearing makeup so early in the day). She wrapped herself around Lucia's leg like a sloth, her grip surprisingly strong. It took Ollie and Gretel together to pry her arms open. The baby ballet had been paying off.

By the time Lucia was ready to say goodbye, Marley refused to kiss her and instead knocked her entire bowl of cereal onto the floor. Lucia hovered, but Gretel shooed her out the door, deftly refilling Marley's bowl with one hand and sweeping up the mess with the other.

Lucia paused on the landing, filled with an uncomfortable mix of emotions. Maybe she should go back inside and give up on the entire prospect of leaving the house for work? She'd just stay home until Marley went away to college.

But in a matter of seconds, she heard her daughter's adorable laugh from the other side of the door and recalled that it was kazoo day at Singy Songy, a fate worse than death. She could do this.

To be a commuter on the Tube, crossing London from its residential neighborhoods in the west to its gleaming commercial skyscrapers in the east during rush hour, was nothing like she had ever experienced before.

The orderly queues she had gotten so accustomed to when traveling off-peak were nowhere to be found. Rush hour was a free-for-all of silent passive-aggressive stares, as people pushed, shoved, and elbowed to get down to the platform. Once the train arrived and opened its doors, a wall of people materialized, blocking her entrance on either side. Two trains filled and departed before she had had enough and pushed her way on just like everyone else.

Then, there was the ride itself. There were no seats. She focused on hanging on to the strap above her for dear life and breathing in and out through her mouth, as her nose was unpleasantly lodged in the armpit of the much taller man to her right. If this was a trial set out for her by the work gods, she was determined to pass it.

Finally, the doors opened at Liverpool Street, and she, along with everyone else in the western hemisphere, disembarked and moved as one monolith into the station and up the escalator. When she reached street level and the throng of suits disbursed to get on with their days, she almost fell to her knees with gratitude for the fresh air.

Setting aside the fact that she would have to repeat this journey in the evening and then again tomorrow, she pulled herself together and walked toward the Eastern Currents building, repeating her mantras to herself out loud: "I am smart. I am capable. I can do this."

She stepped into the grand lobby where dozens of men and women hurried around her, talking on phones or to one another about interest rates and currency hedging, giving her whiplash. But she felt something else, too: a rush of excitement. She was one of them now, a woman with somewhere to be.

Lucia paused before approaching the reception desk. Standing there in her new yellow coat, she felt certain this was all an elaborate practical joke. She was probably famous among the staff for being the woman who crashed into the elevator door during her interview. They were about to tell her that, of course, she didn't really get the job; they just wanted to see her again so they could laugh in her face.

Her phone buzzed twice: a text from Ollie (Good luck today, amor!) and one from Sooz (Get it, girl, and remember to give 'em hell, with three emoji of a smiling devil for emphasis). Lucia smiled and stepped up to the reception desk.

"Hi. I'm Lucia Gutierrez-Barrow. You might remember me. From the amazing ID photo?" she joked. The receptionist stared at her like she was speaking in tongues.

"Anyway, today's my first day."

A few clacks later, the receptionist handed her a permanent ID card. To her delight, it featured the same headshot from her interview.

"Can I get this in an eight by ten?" she joked.

"Pardon?" asked the receptionist without looking up.

"Never mind. Ignore me. Thank you," she replied cheerily and wandered over to the waiting area determined not to make a fool of herself today.

She watched the financial news ticker roll by on a screen in the lobby. She had spent the weekend cramming macroeconomic concepts, studying up on currency hedging and amortization and other things that she figured she should know now that she officially worked in the financial services industry. All the little green arrows were pointing up. That was good. The more money her clients made, the more they put into their bank accounts, which meant the more money the bank had at its disposal. They called it AUM—assets under management—and this number mattered to everyone. Bonuses depended on it, shares rose or fell because of it.

Lucia's job depended on it, too. Eastern Currents—bankers to the royal family (she had already decided what she'd cook the first time the heir to the throne and his wife dropped by her house for dinner)—had the most assets under their management, by a large margin. To open an account at Eastern Currents, one needed to have a minimum of thirty million dollars to their name (those were the small-fry clients).

Someone, at some point, had figured out that the bank's extremely wealthy clientele cared about philanthropy. They wanted advice and guidance on how much to give and whom to give to. If their private bank could help them make decisions about their charitable giving, the more money they would want to send their way.

The scale of wealth—and therefore the potential scale of impact through giving—was in the billions, with a big fat *B*. It was Lucia's job to make sure that as much of it as possible went to the right places. That could mean climate change or school breakfasts or (her heart swelled at this) helping refugees get on their feet in their new countries. The possibilities were endless.

"Lucia? Hi. I'm Melissa Cook. I'll be showing you around today."

Lucia had assumed every person at the bank would be like the ones she had met so far: impeccably dressed in business-formal attire with attitudes to match. This woman was the opposite. She had a warm smile and Coke-bottle glasses that covered shockingly green eyes. A mass of frizzy blonde hair framed her round face. She wore minimal makeup and a bright-red caftan over black cigarette pants. Lucia's eyes were immediately drawn to her statement necklace. It was made of silver bottle tops that jingled as she moved.

Lucia shook Melissa's hand, and they walked through the barriers toward the elevator, looking like ketchup and mustard amid the sea of black and gray power suits. Lucia hesitated for a moment before getting in, and Melissa laughed.

"A quick learner, excellent," Melissa observed. "We heard all about your little accident." She chuckled.

Lucia held her face in her hands. "Oh my god, I'm so embarrassed."

"Don't be silly, it happens more than you'd imagine." Melissa's accent was broad, from somewhere in the middle of the country, Lucia guessed, although placing accents was not her forte. She had stopped guessing when she'd asked her favorite barista what part of England he was from and he'd replied, "South Africa."

Melissa pushed a button on the digital panel, and they got into the elevator together. "Everyone tends to start early, to catch our colleagues in Asia before their business day finishes. I arrive by half eight—I'm one of the later ones, but I have school drop-off, and breakfast club doesn't start till half seven, so there you go."

Friendly *and* a working mom? Melissa was great. "How long have you been at the bank?" Lucia asked.

The elevator dinged as the doors opened on the eighth floor. "Far too long, I reckon. One of these days Celeste will finally have enough of me." She let out a noise halfway between a seal's bark and an overexcited hyena that Lucia could only assume was a laugh. It was awkward but strangely charming.

Lucia opened her mouth to ask what she meant, but as they turned the corner, her attention was drawn elsewhere. Like a magpie her eyes went straight to the shiniest object. Except here, *everything* was shiny.

Even though ArteAustin's budget had grown year over year, especially with Lucia running the fundraising operation, the bulk of their money always went to the people they were helping. How could you justify a new laptop when yours worked perfectly fine (if it was plugged in at exactly the right angle and the temperature didn't exceed eighty-seven degrees)? That money would be better spent on lawyer fees for an immigration hearing. The staff were accustomed to making do with what they had. The rustic feel of the office, once born from necessity, became a design choice.

If ArteAustin was like a grandma's charming attic, Eastern Currents was like a surgeon's operating room. In Switzerland. Neat rows of desks, all in the same tasteful shade of gray, were lined up like soldiers in formation. Along the back wall were individual, glass-enclosed offices for the bigwigs. At first, the offices appeared to have no walls separating them from the bullpen. But then Lucia caught a glimpse of a man, speaking into a headset and pacing angrily, as he pressed a button, and the glass fogged up, becoming opaque. Like a magic trick! She waited for someone to yell, "Ta-da!" but no one did.

Melissa walked her over to an empty desk where a gleaming black monitor and a sleek black chair—ergonomic and a marvel of design—awaited her.

"This is yours. I'm just across the way. Well until I'm out on the street." Melissa laughed nervously again, clearly some sort of defense mechanism.

"I'll let you settle in," she continued. "We've got a team meeting in about fifteen minutes, so you'll meet everyone then. Coffee bar is on floor five. Loos are just on the other side of the lifts. Pens, supplies, anything you need, just ask the secretaries and they'll order it for you."

Lucia placed her bag down and surveyed her desk. Next to the monitor, there was a brand-new MacBook, an iPhone—the latest model—and a landline with a Bluetooth headset. She took out two frames from her bag—a picture of her and Ollie, young and sweaty on a Galveston beach, and a black-and-white photo of Marley, eyes wide as saucers peering up at the camera. She also pulled out a small statue of the *Virgen de Guadalupe* that had belonged to her grandmother. It was a symbol of good luck, but the statue's bright colors seemed out of place amid the sea of chrome. She bent over so no one could see, kissed it once, and stuffed it into her drawer.

Her laptop had been set up in advance, and she opened her inbox to twelve emails from "Le Fevre, Celeste." She spun around in her chair to ask Melissa what she should watch out for when it came to Celeste and bumped right into a man who had evidently been looming over her. She hadn't even heard him creep up.

"Watch the shoes," he said. "Gucci."

"Oh, I'm so sorry." She rolled her chair backward and reached out her hand. "Hi! I'm Lucia. Nice to meet you," she said, meeting the gaze of a tall, handsome man with smooth dark skin. He looked quite young, in his late twenties. She took in his suit (a fantastic cut), the shoes in question (suede), and the small gap in his front teeth (quite appealing).

"Charmed," he said, shaking her hand warily, as if her enthusiasm might rub off. "Tristan, the more experienced philanthropy advisor."

"Oh great!" Lucia said, smiling. "So it's you, me, and Melissa: the Three Musketeers."

"Hmm," he said, looking her up and down. "I'm more like the Lone Ranger—that's a reference an American would understand, yes?" He pointed to himself. "And you two are Tweedledee and Tweedledum." He waved a finger between Melissa and her.

Lucia laughed. But Tristan remained stone-faced.

"I wanted to ensure you saw Celeste's email. We need a dossier on the Janssens by noon. You'll have to do it right after the team meeting."

Dossier? Janssens? She hadn't seen the email, but his crossed arms made it clear he wasn't open to questions. "Yep, absolutely," she said smoothly. "I'll take care of it." She was sure she could figure it out. "Frankly, I'm just delighted to be out of my house, in clothes that don't have an elastic waistband, surrounded by respectful professionals at the top of their game. My most recent boss was a little diva. She never let me go to the bathroom alone and freaked out if her milk was not at the perfect temperature. Also, she threw fruit at me regularly."

Lucia grinned broadly—she always found that cracking a joke disarmed people—but Tristan remained frozen, without so much as a twitch of the upper lip.

"You'll find yourself right at home here, then," he quipped.

Like a savior from the heavens, Melissa interrupted their conversation. "Oh brill, Lucia, you've met Tristan. He's like a boiled sweet. Hard on the outside and also hard on the inside." She let out another bark-like laugh at her own joke. Tristan made a face of disgust and walked away.

"Is he always that serious?" Lucia said.

"He's not so bad. He cares about the work, even if he has a different way of showing it. We don't always agree, but he's courteous. More than I can say for everyone here. Ha. Anyway. Let's go, it's time for the meeting."

Lucia followed Melissa into a large conference room with another amazing view, this time of the Thames in the distance. There was a full videoconference setup that included microphones and cameras at every seat around the large, polished black table.

"I feel like we're at the UN," she whispered to Melissa.

"The UN's systems are nowhere near this nice," she whispered back.

They took their seats. It was so quiet you could hear every squeak of the leather chairs. Tristan reclined, crossing his legs like he didn't have a care in the world. She could see the tiniest fraction of a practically invisible sock, which gave her an odd sense of relief, as if wearing socks he wanted to hide meant that he cared, just a little, about what people thought of him. Melissa was fumbling with a pen, shaking it and scribbling, with little success.

Lucia felt a draft as the door opened. Celeste entered, looking effortlessly chic in a slim-fit hunter-green suit and a white silk blouse, her skin dewy like she had come straight from a facial.

"Is it ready?" she asked, without so much as bothering to acknowledge her assistant, Thomas, to whom the question was addressed.

"Yes, Celeste, we're all ready to go. We have Asia on the line," Thomas replied. Two faces popped up on the screen.

"Let's begin," Celeste started. "Nancy, Xin Li, are you ready for the Asian Philanthropy Conference next week? What have you prepared?"

Melissa interrupted just as Nancy started speaking.

"We should introduce Lucia, don't you think?"

If looks were daggers, Melissa would be bleeding on the floor, but she met Celeste's steely gaze with a softer but equally firm look of her own.

"*Bon.* Lucia, Asia. Asia, this is Lucia."

Lucia stood up, but the camera didn't follow, leaving just her midsection on the screen. The double layer of Spanx she was wearing was not meant for a close-up on an HDTV. She grimaced, vowing to do a hundred sit-ups a night, or at least ten, and sat back down.

"Good morning, or evening, to my colleagues in Asia. My name is Lucia Gutierrez-Barrow. I most recently worked as a fundraiser—"

"Yes, yes, enough." Celeste cut her off like the Academy Awards orchestra.

"Anyway, I'mdelightedtobehere and lookforwardtoworkingwithyou." Lucia smashed her words together to finish as rapidly as she could, smiling at Celeste, who did not smile back.

"Now that we are done with interruptions, Nancy, please go."

Nancy and Xin Li took turns updating Celeste as to the various VVIPs who were attending the conference—top clients and government officials—and the reception the bank was hosting at one of Singapore's swankiest hotels.

"That's all from us, Celeste," Nancy said. "Lucia, you must come out and visit us here soon. I will take you for the best black pepper crab in the world. I hope you like spicy food?" Lucia's mouth began to salivate at the thought of the crab and the idea of an all-expenses-paid trip to Singapore. The farthest she traveled at ArteAustin had been to visit a donor in Oklahoma, and she didn't even get to stay overnight.

Nancy continued. "Oh, and quite a few of our prospects for the Asia conference plan to attend GIFGAL in the spring, so we'll let you know who they are in due course."

"Sorry, what's GIFGAL?" Lucia asked.

Celeste gave Melissa an annoyed glare. "Has she not been trained yet?"

"Considering she's been here for less than an hour, we hadn't gotten to that part of her induction," Melissa retorted, turning to Lucia. "GIFGAL stands for the Global Innovation Forum for Giving and Loving. It's the philanthropic event of the year, designed to raise as much money as possible. Plus, it's no great hardship that it's on a private island in the middle of the Caribbean."

"Yes, thank you, it is enough," Celeste said. "Don't forget," she said, addressing Thomas, who was scribbling furiously.

"We will need rooms for Nigel, Brendan, me, Tristan, and"—she sighed—"Melissa."

Melissa beamed as Celeste continued down the agenda.

"Tristan," Celeste said, turning her chair to him. "Prospective client update."

As Tristan began to talk about someone called St. James, the door opened. A protruding belly entered the room attached to a man with a large bristly mustache who seemed deeply invested in whatever was happening on his phone. "Carry on," he said, taking a seat at the head of the table.

"Good morning, Brendan," Celeste said, practically purring. She smiled like a cat, too. It was unnerving—everything was in the right place, but there was no warmth in it, only calculation.

"We just had the Asia update; everything is taken care of." Her whole vibe had changed since he'd walked into the room. So Celeste was capable of something resembling charm; she was smooth and deferential. Lucia was about to get a master class in subtle ass-kissing, she thought.

"Good, good," Brendan murmured. Lucia didn't think he had heard or cared, but it was enough for Celeste, who gestured to Tristan to continue.

Tristan went down a list, a who's who of the UK's wealthiest families, starting with prospects (clients of the bank who didn't give philanthropically yet) and then active clients (who did). Rothesay, Perry, Fitzherbert, Gordon-Lennox. Duke this, baroness that. Lucia frantically tried to write everything down, but her pen couldn't keep up with all the hyphenated names.

Now Tristan turned to her. "You'll be shadowing one of us first before you see any clients on your own," he said to the room and then, under his breath, "If you survive that long."

"We are done?" Celeste asked in a oh-so-French manner that indicated the question was rhetorical.

"Not quite," Melissa said. "Sunita Sanderson."

A collective groan went up.

"Look I know you don't like her, but we have to deal with this."

Lucia couldn't help herself. "Who is Sunita Sanderson?" she asked.

"The upstart wife of Lord Sanderson of Somerset. His third wife. Or is it fourth?" Tristan grinned at Melissa, who rolled her eyes.

"Third. And she's lovely," Melissa interjected. "But she has made some enemies. She has very progressive ideas about how to deploy their capital. Since she and Lord Sanderson got married, he's given away nearly three-quarters of his vast fortune to charities working on climate change."

"That's fantastic," Lucia said.

Celeste whipped her head around. "No, not so fantastic. This means his money has gone out of the bank. AUM is down. We are not happy."

"Right," Lucia said. "Sorry." She wrote "AUM" in huge letters and underlined it three times in her notebook.

"Neither is his eldest son, who was set to inherit it all," Tristan added.

Melissa continued. "Sunita wants us to set up a fund within the bank to support their climate efforts and raise money from other clients, too. That would be good for our AUM. But Fredrick, the son, has said he'll pull his own personal account if we, and I quote, 'help that harlot spend his inheritance.'"

She glanced over at Brendan. "The management team want our position before they decide. If my opinion is worth anything . . ." Celeste let out a *pfft*, but Melissa went on, "The answer should be obvious. Surely we want to be part of the climate change fund. Not only is it one of the most significant issues of our generation, but this sounds like it could be vital for getting more money into the nonprofits that need it."

Celeste rolled her eyes. "It is not such a clear-cut decision. Fredrick will still inherit a lot; he is one of the top clients and also a big philanthropist in his own right. Besides, climate change is very . . . political." She looked over to Brendan, sweetness and light in her eyes. "If you please, what is your esteemed position?"

"Hmm . . . All good points, indeed," he said, still entirely engrossed in his phone. Lucia could have sworn she saw him place a bet on a football match. "You decide, Celeste, it's your team. Just let me know when you do." With that Brendan stood up and left the room.

Celeste kept the smile frozen on her face until he turned the corner and then looked back at the team with a vicious expression. "We go with Fredrick. He will also do some good works with his money, and we don't want to anger anyone. For the long term, we are better with him. It's done, no one speaks of it again. I do not tolerate dissent here."

Lucia thought she must have misunderstood the context of Celeste's decision and raised her hand to ask a follow-up question, knocking over the microphone in front of her. The sound of feedback ricocheted around the room, and everyone covered their ears. When it ended, Celeste glared at Lucia. "Put your hand down. This is not primary school; if you have a question, just ask it."

"I'm just wondering if you can explain your comment about climate change being too political," Lucia asked. Celeste was silent, so she went on. "I just feel like I'm missing something. Climate change isn't politics. It's science."

Celeste held up a hand. "Stop," she said firmly, as if she was scolding a naughty toddler. "There is nothing to discuss. Our clients prefer causes that are clean and free from reproach. Easy for everyone to understand. Children, animals, etcetera."

Lucia wanted to probe further, but she noticed Melissa staring at her. In a smooth, almost imperceptible motion, Melissa brushed one finger over her closed lips.

"OK. Right," Lucia said. "Thank you, Celeste."

The meeting was over.

As Lucia left the room, she heard the jangle of bottle tops behind her, and Melissa appeared by her side.

"Come with me," she said.

They went into a private office, and Melissa pressed a button, fogging the windows and blocking them from view. "Sorry you had to deal with that on your first day."

"Yeah . . ." Lucia grasped for words. "Celeste definitely doesn't mince words, does she?"

"Too right," Melissa said. "I often wonder if she's done some deal, like every time she delivers a backhanded insult, a devil gets its horns." She grinned.

"I was only trying to understand why Celeste made that call. The bank publicly proclaims itself a climate warrior. Isn't it weird that she would find a climate fund too political?"

"We toe a fine line here. What happens in public isn't always the same as what goes on behind closed doors," Melissa said, resigned. "The Sanderson battle has been raging for a while. I agree it's the wrong decision, but she was right about one thing; Fredrick will do a lot with his funds. Even if it's for a less— how should I put this?—urgent cause."

"I get it, but does Celeste genuinely believe that climate change is too political?" Lucia's head started to spin with questions.

"Hey, don't fret. We all go through a bit of this soul-searching at the beginning. It'll pass." Melissa patted her on the back. "Sometimes we disagree on the best way to do good. But the important thing is we're here—you and I—and there will be others like us. The 'soft charity people' as she says. It's our role to keep holding them to account, even when the decisions they make are misguided."

Melissa was right. Lucia just needed to take a long-term view, that was all.

"Of course, I know. I'm just out of practice, I think." She stood up and brushed off an invisible speck of lint. "I need some time to get used to how things are done, to get back into the swing of things. Learn the lingo here. And figure out how to take the Tube during rush hour without sweating through my entire outfit. I know it's only day one, but is it too early to ask for a vacation?" Lucia joked.

"Speaking of, I can't bloody wait for GIFGAL," Melissa said, as they walked back to their desks. "This job comes with a lot of headaches, but it'll all be worth it when I'm sipping a piña colada with my toes in the sand. This is the closest I've gotten to a proper holiday in three years." She sighed. "Celeste has never let me go before, but they need an extra body this year, and mark my words, I'm going to take full advantage of every second."

"I'm sure there will be plenty of good work to do, too," Lucia replied, winking.

"Yeah." Melissa snorted. "On my tan."

They giggled together, like old school friends. Then, Lucia sat down at her desk and typed, "what does a British person mean by a dossier?" into Google. She felt better immediately.

Chapter 8
Curtsy Practice

As her cab sped down The Mall, Lucia still couldn't believe it had only been one week since she'd started at Eastern Currents and already she was going to an event at Buckingham Palace. She let out a tiny squeal.

Tristan muttered something under his breath that sounded like *rube*.

"Ignore him." Melissa said with a giant grin. "Quite a location for our annual Eastern Currents Philanthropy Day, eh? The day I stop being impressed by the majesty of Buckingham Palace, please have the guards lock me in the Tower."

"That can be arranged," Tristan retorted.

Lucia pinched the inside of her wrist to make sure she wasn't hallucinating. She wasn't jostling for space out front with the hundreds of tourists desperate to catch a glimpse of the Changing of the Guard or waiting around the side entrance to the Queen's Gallery, hoping to bag a ticket that would allow a peek at a few empty rooms, dusty vases, and armchairs for display only. She was being waved in by a police officer, straight through the main entrance. For a self-proclaimed Anglophile who, as a child, had pretended to be Diana on her wedding day, donning a pillowcase as a makeshift bridal veil and walking down an imaginary aisle to exchange vows with Prince Charles (her dog wearing a bow tie), this was the ultimate life goal unlocked.

Toto, she was definitely not in Texas anymore, she thought.

As soon as they were out of the cab, Tristan practically sprinted ahead to create some distance between himself and Lucia and Melissa, who did stick out just a little bit. Lucia was dressed conservatively in a black skirt and blazer, as per Celeste's instruction not to wear her "flashy American clothes," but her jaw trailing on the floor still gave her away as the commemorative-mug-buying superfan that she was. Melissa wasn't fawning over their surroundings, but in her bright-green tunic and signature bottle-top necklace, she didn't look like she fit in with the other suits entering the palace, either.

"This is insane," Lucia whispered as she retrieved her passport from the security guard checking IDs and she and Melissa were ushered into the entryway, a long hallway lined with antique swords. "Is it a special anniversary or something? Is that why the bank is able to host this event here?" she asked.

"Not particularly special, no. We host Philanthropy Day here every year. Eastern Currents has banked every member of the royal family since the late 1750s—the legitimate and the illegitimate ones!"

Lucia picked up an ashtray branded with the royal sigil and, before anyone could stop her, snapped a surreptitious selfie, shooting it over to Sooz with a message: Man, they'll let any old riffraff in here these days. She was able to sneak a quick peek at the response—Please convey to the royals my sincere feelings about the monarchy, followed by three skull and crossbones emoji— before handing her phone over to security, who would store all devices until the event was over. Lucia prayed they didn't see Sooz's message, which would likely be enough evidence to try her for treason.

"This is your job now, love. Better get used to it." Melissa smiled. "So listen, your aim today is to mingle. The audience is clients and prospective clients, plus a few key members of the royal family. Chat everyone up and get them excited about philanthropy. But don't be aggressive about our services. We're not allowed to do any actual pitching in the palace, house rules." She raised a finger to her mouth. "The key is to remind them of all the benefits of giving without being too pushy. *Tell* them what we do, but don't *sell* them what we do. Less is more. OK?"

"Um" was all Lucia could say. The sight of Elton John— sorry, *Sir* Elton John—entering in a silver-sequined dinner jacket had distracted her. The most famous person she had ever seen in the flesh prior to this was a state senator from Texas, and he looked more like her elementary school gym teacher than a VIP.

"You'll be fine, pet. Be yourself. But not too American. You'll get the hang of it."

They entered an elegantly decorated room that was alive with conversation. Melissa made a beeline for an older woman whom Lucia recognized as the ex-wife of one of the Beatles. She was wearing a fur coat and sunglasses even though it was seventy degrees and raining outside.

She scanned the room, clocking not one but two Spice Girls. Nearby, she spotted Celeste in a bright-orange pantsuit. (It seemed the no-flashy-colors rule was for Lucia only.) She was in conversation with a hot young actor rumored to be the next James Bond. Celeste caught her eye and made a swirling motion with her finger: the universal sign for go circulate. OK, Lucia thought, grabbing a glass of water from a passing waiter. I'm in Buckingham Palace. I remember how to do this. Be myself but not myself. Here goes nothing.

She weaved through groups of chatting celebrities of one sort or another, trying not to gawk. She guessed that even the people she didn't recognize were important. They smelled important. The whole room smelled important, or expensive at least, like they were pumping in a fragrance—fig and lemon—through the vents.

Lucia moved closer to a portrait of Queen Victoria, trying to see who the artist was, when she bumped into a woman.

"I'm so sorry," she said.

"Not at all," the woman replied. They locked eyes, and for a second, Lucia thought they knew each other; the recognition was one-sided. The woman in question was the host of *The Great British Bake Off* and one of the UK's most celebrated chefs. Lucia knew her, but she definitely did not know Lucia.

"I was actually just leaving." The chef smiled. "Nice to meet you, Mr. Cutler," she said to the man she had been chatting with. She turned to Lucia and softly muttered, "Good luck with this one, deary."

Introductions were quickly made, although Lucia already knew Brody Cutler by reputation—he was the definition of a tech wunderkind, enrolling at Stanford at fifteen, only to drop out two years later and sell his music-pirating app for a large fortune. He was dressed like he was trying to cosplay an elder statesman: tweed coat with leather elbow patches, Steve Jobsian black turtleneck, and a wisp of an oiled-up goatee that looked like it had taken significant effort to grow.

"I've never done 'philanthropy,' per se," he said, raising his fingers into air quotes, "but I'm very into social and environmental justice and all their related causes and forms."

"That's excellent," Lucia said, sipping her water while she considered how else to respond. It was Fundraising 101: The key to chatting with well-to-do types was to make the conversation about the most important person in the room (them). This strategy engendered warmth and allowed you to build a relationship. She thought back to an interview with him she had read in *Forbes* (a notorious one where he went on and on about the need to reduce carbon emissions, given aboard his private jet. The small one, not the big one).

"Congratulations, by the way," she said. "I hear you're getting married."

"Yes, indeed, thank you. I'm not a fan of the institution, per se, but it's important to my fiancée's family, so down the aisle we'll walk. I've just come from my bachelor party last week in Turks and Caicos."

"I bet that was wild," Lucia said.

"Actually, no," Brody deadpanned. "I'm passionately committed to ending the exploitation of women, so instead of the traditional entertainment, I hosted a panel discussion with exotic dancers discussing their career paths. It was highly disruptive."

Lucia, who had trained herself to paste a placid smile on her face when she heard her donors at ArteAustin spout all sorts of nonsense, nearly spit out her water.

"That does sound . . . disruptive," she said, taking another sip to stifle her laughter. "So, what brings you to Philanthropy Day? Since you're not into 'philanthropy,'" she said, mirroring his air quotes back at him.

"I'm here to find ideas. Disruptive ones. That's what the world needs." He went on without really making eye contact with her. "More tech people solving these problems." Personally, Lucia believed that was probably the last thing the world needed, but nothing more than a mutter of assent seemed to be required. "Most nonprofits are bloated and wasteful," he went on. "Their CEOs get paid huge salaries, and they use all their donations to pad their fat wallets."

Lucia pinched the inside of her wrist. She had heard this baseless misconception more than once in her career, and it always drove her batty. Brody's base salary for a day would have been enough to keep an organization like ArteAustin afloat for a year. Who did they think was going to run the programs if no one got paid?

"I want to fund something that has never been done before and is going to fix everything."

"Wow, that would be—" Before she could say more, they were interrupted by the entrance of a tuxedo-clad man.

"Ladies and gentlemen, the princess will be arriving shortly. Please make your way to your designated tables for the greeting."

Saved by the bell. Or the butler. Brody wasn't really looking for input, anyway—she knew his type. He meant well, and (according to him) he was brilliant; surely those two things combined would make him better equipped than anyone else to solve all the world's problems at once. What he wanted was affirmation, a pat on the back for his intended altruism and original genius. His attitude was a reminder that Lucia had always struggled to come to terms with this part of the philanthropy world.

"That's our cue. Really nice to meet you, Mr. Cutler, and do reach out if you want some help with all that . . . um . . . disruption. My team and I are always here if you need us."

"Cool, cool, my people will call your people. Namaste."

"Sure, namaste," she said to him, scanning the room for Melissa to help her parse her highly disruptive feelings about this conversation. Melissa had become her trusted guide in this strange new territory.

She couldn't find her friend, but the princess waited for no one, and certainly not for Lucia, so she quickly made her way over to a high table with the number eight on it. They were fundraising for the National Academy of Diagenetic Sciences (NADS, but she kept that humorous acronym to herself, unsure if the word held the same meaning on this side of the pond). As was customary at meet and greets hosted by a member of the royal family, everyone attending was divided into small groups and assigned to a table. The princess would visit each table in order, greet the attendees by name, and take a photo to be sent around as a souvenir afterward.

Lucia knew she was supposed to curtsy when she greeted any royal, so while she waited alone at their table, she thought she would get in a few practice rounds. She was surreptitiously bending and straightening, bending and straightening, when a woman with short spiky hair who looked to be in her seventies approached the table with a quizzical look on her face.

"My dear, are you perfectly alright?"

"Um, yes, sorry. Just . . . uh . . . stretching my calf muscles," she said, too mortified to admit what she was doing.

"You can't lie to me; you were practicing your curtsy, weren't you? Oh, don't bother," she said laughing. "Her royal pain in my arse doesn't care a fig if you curtsy for her or not. I do love her, though."

Did she mean . . . the princess? Lucia had never heard a British person speak about a royal with such naughty amusement. Who was this delightful creature who was happy to say out loud what others were only thinking? Lucia combed her memory of the dossiers she had read on everyone who would be in their small group today, until—

"You must be Lady Simmons," Lucia said. "It's a pleasure."

"Just Rona. And please, don't curtsy. Let me spare you the embarrassment." She let out a deep, throaty laugh.

Rona's profile had stood out amid a sea of lawyers, hedge fund owners, and property magnates. A former social worker, Rona had lived a regular life until her great-aunt died, leaving her a sizable fortune. Rona was now a frequent giver of large cash gifts to small nonprofits—both in the UK and around the world—that supported women and girls.

It seemed Rona had not gotten Celeste's wardrobe memo, either. She wore what appeared to be a tracksuit covered in a pattern of palm leaves and flamingos. She would not have looked out of place in a Miami Beach bingo hall, but here she attracted attention. People were doing double takes as they walked by to find their tables.

Lucia loved her already.

She gave Rona her best curtsy. "Awful," Rona declared, and Lucia blushed. They started to chat about the grant Rona had just made to open a girls' school in Pakistan—a country she and her husband, Francis, had visited many times and had fallen in love with.

"I like to be hands-off with my donations, you know, no fuss, no fanfare," she said. "But Seema, the executive director of the school, has become a friend, so she sends me photos and updates all the time. I would never ask for them to do that extra work, but I love them." Rona opened her phone to her photos. "This is Bisu, she's fifteen and wants to be a biochemist. And here's Ushma, she's a brilliant tennis player. She gave me a run for my money last time I was there, and I know I'm old, but I'm pretty good. My knees are better at bending than yours, anyway."

Rona's whole face lit up as she handed Lucia her phone to scroll through the images on her own. "Francis and I never had any children, which I don't regret, by the way, but I love these girls—and Seema—like my own. I know I'm supposed to say money can't buy you happiness, but the truth is it can come pretty bloody close. There is nothing more extraordinary than knowing you have the power to change someone's life for the better—and then doing it."

This was music to Lucia's ears. People like Rona were the reason she loved her line of work.

Lucia's thumb continued scrolling until she reached a boudoir photo, obviously of Rona, stark naked and tastefully posing on a four-poster bed. "Whoops," she said, grabbing the phone away from Lucia. "That's for Francis."

"What's so funny?" Melissa sauntered up to the table looking at Rona and Lucia, the former laughing like a hyena, the latter bright red in the face.

"Nothing, darling Melissa, just showing Lucia some pornography."

"That'll be Rona for you. How are you?"

"Simply magnificent. I must say, I just had the most wonderful session with a thermodynamic cupper. It was positively orgasmic." Rona's phone rang, and she looked down at it. "I'm so sorry, ladies, I must take this. We just bought some shares in something called Tock Tick, and no one could explain what it does, so I had to go straight to the source. Tell the princess I'll only be a moment."

Rona walked off yelling into her phone in Mandarin. Melissa shook her head. "She is a character, that one. But one of our best."

Lucia watched her go with admiration. "It's so refreshing to meet someone here who gets so much joy out of the giving part of philanthropy, you know?"

"I do." Melissa nodded emphatically. "You know Rona always gives unrestricted gifts and lets the charities use them however they want. Paying staff, keeping the lights on. She once funded the salaries of the entire management team of a North London domestic violence shelter *and* sent them all on a spa day. I've received dozens of thank-you letters for her, sharing beautiful stories of how meaningful her gifts were. She reads them but never takes credit for anything. I keep a few at my desk for the days when I have to deal with a particularly awful client."

"How do you do it, though? Deal with the challenging ones?" Lucia asked, recounting the highlights of her conversation with Brody.

"Peach schnapps."

"I'm serious." Lucia made a gagging motion.

"Ah, pet." Melissa exhaled, laying a hand on Lucia's shoulder. "Even Rona didn't start out as Rona. When I first started working with her, a million years ago, she was generous, yes, but cautious. 'How do I really know the charities are going to use my money wisely? How can I really measure the impact?' She wanted to control how her donations were spent. She was afraid. A lot of them are, really, that's where it comes from. Afraid to do the wrong thing or to put their money where it won't be enough to make a real difference or be wasted. People's attachment to their money is deeply psychological and intimate. Philanthropy is as much about addressing what's in their heads and hearts as it is about anything else."

"So what changed?"

"Time. Little by little, she began to trust more. And learn more. She gave her first gift, then her next one was bigger, and sure enough she's morphed into the flamingo-covered pillar of generosity you see before you." Melissa gestured at Rona, who was wrapping up her phone call in the hallway, while the princess patiently waited.

Brody Cutler still at the forefront of her mind, Lucia asked, "Do you really believe everyone has the potential to be like Rona?"

"It's a good question, but Celeste would say it's the wrong one," Melissa said. "Although Celeste would say it more rudely than that. She'd say it doesn't matter if everyone gives like Rona as long as they give something. Through us, of course, so it counts toward AUM." Melissa gestured back over at Brody. "Mr. Cutler over there has over one hundred million pounds banked with Eastern Currents, and we're one of his small accounts. If we allow Brody to think he's doing good, invite him to the palace, introduce him to the right people, he'll give more. The bigger impact, that will come with time."

Lucia knew that fundraisers had to be patient. Sometimes she would cultivate a potential donor for years before they would give anything at all. "That's Celeste's answer. What's yours?"

"Don't mind silly me. I often disagree with Celeste about the trade-offs required to move someone along the path to better giving. I like to think my standards are higher, even though we're all trying to get to the same place." Melissa waved Rona over again; they were holding up the greeting schedule. "But you can't deny that Celeste is the one with the corner office."

Lucia sighed. "I guess you're right. I can't expect miracles right away, but there is power in the journey."

"Exactly," Melissa said. "Now." She put down her drink and rearranged the folds of her tunic. "Here comes the princess. Have you practiced your curtsy?"

"Yes, but it didn't help."

"No matter. Just smile. And don't make a joke about NADS," Melissa said as the princess approached and she dipped herself into a graceful genuflection.

* * *

That night at home, when Lucia recounted the entire day for Ollie, beat by beat, she hammed up her impressions, stroking her chin thoughtfully like Brody, practically bending to the floor as she reenacted her curtsy for the princess. He laughed so hard tears were coming out of his eyes. Lucia was thrilled to have something more interesting to share with him than her research into a new brand of organic baby formula.

"She was right, *amor*, that is a terrible curtsy."

"*Que que*?" she said in mock anger. "Next time I see Belly I'll make sure to ask her for a long demo."

"I saw her today actually," Ollie said. "She sends her love."

Questions popped into Lucia's head: When did you see her, and why? What did she say about me? Did she touch the small of your back in the way that drives me insane?

But she let it slide, like a drop of water off Brody Cutler's greasy goatee. The last thing she wanted to do was spoil this moment of joy with Ollie. She fell next to him on the sofa and draped her legs over his. Then, taking his wineglass and placing it on the coffee table, she pulled his face close to hers.

"You know," she murmured softly in his ear. "Now that I'm like one degree of separation from royalty, I think you probably have to treat me like a queen."

"With pleasure, your majesty," he said, meeting her lips with his own.

Chapter 9
All Aboard

Lucia yelled at her beeping alarm to shut up, but it stubbornly refused to listen. "Five more minutes," she groaned. Ollie took it as a command and rolled over her body to turn it off himself.

"I can get up with her, darling," he murmured.

"No, it's fine. I want the time with Marley," she grumbled, hauling her weary bones out of bed. She splashed some cold water on her face and poked at the bags under her eyes. Maybe Sooz could recommend an under-eye mask, she thought, although she needed the kind of chemical megastrength remedy that likely didn't exist in a nontoxic, climate-neutral variety.

Lucia could try to get more than four or five hours of sleep a night. But at this stage that seemed unlikely.

The last few weeks at work had not involved the equivalent glamour of her visit to the royal palace, but that did not mean she wasn't enjoying herself. On the contrary, she delighted in solving the research challenges Tristan presented her with, uncovering an obscure fact about a client or identifying the perfect nonprofit to match a donor with. She felt invigorated. But it had been a challenge to adjust to the rhythm of working-mom life, and she was sleeping less than she had with a newborn (which was really saying something).

Finishing her workday in time to get home before Marley went to sleep was a dream that died a painful death in week two of her tenure, when Lucia had tried to leave at 5:30 and Celeste had loudly demanded in front of the entire office, "When I am here, I expect you to be here." Given that Celeste rarely arrived before 11:00 a.m., fresh from a salon or Pilates class or both, that usually meant the team was forced to stay well into the evening.

By the time Lucia crept home, Ollie was waiting and ready to play. In spite of knowing she was burning the candle at both ends, she couldn't resist those puppy dog eyes and that adorable cleft in his chin. She missed sleep, but she missed him more. So, she pushed herself, doubling down on the charm and energy she imagined was required to be a good wife. They ate dinner and drank wine together at a very European hour, then binge-watched nonsense on Netflix. Once Ollie fell asleep, content in the fact that he was loved, cared for, and attended to, Lucia would sneak out of bed and finish everything else she still had to do.

It turned out it was a lot harder to be a card-carrying workaholic at the office now that she had other people's needs to consider besides her own.

One more splash of cold water and then she padded over to Marley's room where her daughter was already babbling away and prepared to greet the day after a healthy eleven hours of sleep. Was it weird to be jealous of her baby's schedule, she wondered. Marley had insisted on wearing her elephant costume to bed every night since Halloween, so Lucia reattached the trunk (as per her daughter's daily request) and held her close as they lay on the floor staring up at the glow-in-the-dark stars on her ceiling. She sang songs in Spanish, the same ones her grandparents used to sing to her, for Marley's benefit mostly but also to keep herself from falling back asleep.

She soaked up her baby as much as possible during this extra hour before Ollie arose. After playtime, she carried Marley to the kitchen table, like she had done every morning over the past few weeks, and the two of them had their coffee just like Lucia and her *abuelo*—a *café con leche* for Lucia, as milky and sugary as ever, and a cup of milk foam for Marley. "*Vamos, mija*," she said just as Gretel arrived to take over so Lucia could get ready for work. "Let's go do something great."

"Moo," replied her daughter, still unclear about the difference between an elephant and a cow.

Lucia prayed the caffeine would kick in soon.

She got dressed, hugged her family goodbye, and headed out the door to the office, boarding the Tube with less trepidation each passing day. Arriving at her desk, she planted herself in front of her screen with a stack of dossiers to prepare; the mounting tower of empty coffee cups piled next to her was the only sign the hours had passed.

She was startled out of her flow state by a shadow hovering over her.

"*Allons-y*. Let's go."

Lucia looked up to see Celeste impatiently tapping the toes of her stilettos. She looked ominous—in yet another power pose? (Every move Celeste made was a power pose.)

Celeste treated Lucia with more or less open hostility. No matter what she tried—flattery, clear communication, setting and managing expectations, bribes of chocolate, even praying to the *Virgen de Guadalupe*, who remained wedged in the back of her desk drawer—she still seemed to disappoint her boss at every turn. She wished things could be different, that they could be allies or that Celeste would consider being her mentor. She also wished she cared less about Celeste's opinion of her, but until that happened, she had resigned herself to playing the long game of wearing her down.

This morning, though, she was not in the mood to kill Celeste with kindness—just to kill her. It was 10:00 a.m. and already a three-coffee morning.

"Let's go," Celeste repeated in a shrill, clipped tone. "Now or we will be late." Celeste never asked, only demanded.

Lucia quickly minimized her latest dossier and opened her calendar—it was, as it had been this morning when she'd last checked, empty for another two hours. She was relieved that at least she hadn't forgotten something. She put her game face on and gave a winning smile.

"Good morning, Celeste," she chirped. "Not a problem, but can you remind me where are we going?"

Celeste let out an impatient sigh. "To meet Tamsin. Of course. She is the top tier—the most important person, really—and we must bring her on as a client." Her Eye of Sauron swiveled across the room and landed on Tristan. "First Melissa was supposed to come, but of course she is off today, something about a dentist appointment for her child. I don't know why she couldn't have gone alone, but no matter . . ." Lucia remembered that Melissa's daughter was seven, so maybe not the appropriate age to go solo to get a cavity filled, but those little details about people's lives didn't matter to Celeste, who continued, "Tristan was meant to invite you to take her place. Did he invite you?"

Lucia followed Celeste's beam of anger toward Tristan's stricken face as she watched it dawn on him, in real time, that he had screwed up. She was quiet for a beat longer than she needed to be and made direct eye contact with Tristan before responding.

"Of course. Tamsin," Lucia replied smoothly. "Yes, I'm aware of the meeting. I just meant, which room is it in?"

Tristan exhaled, and Lucia sent a discreet nod in his direction. He would, at the very least, owe her one now.

Celeste rolled her eyes theatrically. "Room? No room. It is on the river. Come, we will be late. Why do you always ask such ridiculous questions?"

Lucia took a deep breath as she reached into her desk drawer to grab a pen and notebook. She felt *la Virgen* and tapped her once, then twice for luck. If she was going to spend a whole morning on her own with Celeste, she was going to need as much luck as she could get.

Since getting Celeste to like her seemed, at this point, a bridge too far, Lucia had been working on developing a thicker skin. She had been observing Celeste closely and was starting to suspect that she was rude on purpose. Yet another, more sinister kind of power pose. While Lucia seemed to be the target *du jour*, Celeste was generally mean to everyone who wasn't a boss or client. Lucia tried not to take it personally, to use each slight to fashion a new plate onto her armor, making her more resistant to the attacks. It was working—some of the time, at least. She had cried in the bathroom only twice that week.

Lucia dashed after Celeste into the elevator, then out through the lobby doors and into a waiting town car. As they started to drive south toward the Thames, Celeste put on her sunglasses and went right back to work, attending to her call list, often speaking loudly in French. To a French client? A French maid? Lucia didn't know, but she was grateful she didn't have to make small talk.

Six weeks and Lucia was still trying to prove herself. She hadn't been given her own roster of clients and had yet to take a meeting alone. She had shadowed quite a few. Meetings with Melissa were great—she always learned something helpful and was able to contribute—but Celeste and Tristan had thus far treated her like an actual shadow, expected to sit silently in the corner unless someone wanted a cup of coffee or tea. She didn't know how she was supposed to demonstrate that she could do this job, much less make any sort of impact, if she wasn't allowed to open her mouth.

She took out her own phone and opened an email from Tristan that said, "Thank you thank you thank you. I'll name my finest chinchilla after you." Attached was the dossier on Tamsin St. James.

Tamsin was the only child of Bernard St. James, born Bernie Crumb. He'd changed his name after making his first hundred million. Tamsin's mother was Bernie's fourth wife, but not his current wife. She had been a glamour model—her big break, posing topless on *The Sun*'s infamous Page 3. Tamsin had clearly gotten her looks from her. It wasn't from Bernard, that much was certain.

Bernard's father drove a black cab as his father had done before him, but Bernard had been determined to make something more of himself. He fought tooth and nail (with a face that looked it) and became one of the fiercest traders in the City of London. Bernard was one of the few to get out of the market before the financial crisis—people wondered if that stroke of genius had been intuition or a bit of insider trading, but it really didn't matter. He was already richer than Midas by that point, anyway. He subsequently expanded his empire and now owned the largest logistics and supply chain management company in the world.

Tamsin was his only child (that he knew of), and it was a widely known fact that as soon as he died, she would inherit hundreds of millions in liquid assets—cash—plus a property portfolio to rival the royal family's. Around the bank she was known as the Great White Whale—no one had yet landed her as a client. Bernard had been with Eastern Currents for years, but Tamsin was being courted by every bank on either side of the Atlantic.

As part of this strategy, Celeste was dispatched once a year to discuss philanthropy and showcase why the bank would be the perfect partner for Tamsin. Someone on the management team had followed a logical thought process: Young people like doing good for the world, so what better way for the bank to secure the next generation of wealth than to get them excited about the bank's commitment to philanthropy? This simplistic logic worked a lot of the time and was the reason Celeste and her team had their jobs to begin with.

It was clear that Celeste couldn't stand Tamsin, but Lucia had heard Celeste ooze disdain for clients behind their backs, only to instantly turn up the charm to the max as soon as one of them walked into the room. Lucia was in awe of how easily Celeste could impersonate a caring human being when it mattered. In spite of that, Tamsin had remained vague and noncommittal.

The journey was short; just fifteen minutes later, the car pulled over in front of the Tower of London. Tower Bridge with its cheery blue-and-white cables shined in the late-autumn sunlight. The bridge was packed with tourists, smiling for selfies on the exact site where the heads of traitors of the realm were once staked and displayed.

Celeste led the way down the cobbled road to a pier on the river. She was so fast, even in heels. Lucia struggled to keep up, sure she was going to break her ankle. Next to the public boarding platform, where the river cruises embarked, was a separate gangway leading to the biggest yacht Lucia had ever seen.

Celeste marched up the ramp with purpose, and Lucia, awestruck, followed. A staff member ushered them into what looked like the formal living room of a Barbie Dreamhouse. The hot-pink carpeting and zebra-print sofas were a lot, even for Lucia, who loved color. In the center of the room was a sunken hot tub, slightly steaming, that could easily fit twelve people. (Lucia briefly hallucinated that she'd just stepped into a Tilly Willy romance novel and glanced around for any scantily clad cabana boys.) The superyacht's large windows overlooked City Hall and Potters Fields on the opposite bank; Lucia waved to a passing sightseeing boat, its deck full of gawking tourists with their phones out.

She and Celeste sat silently in the room for a full minute. Lucia had counted sixty ticks on the wall clock shaped like a German shepherd before Celeste turned to speak.

"Ta-ma-sin is impossible," she said in a low voice, pronouncing her name with three syllables. "She is not interested in anyone but herself and her TikTok followers and her dogs." She grimaced at the word, making it clear that she was not a fan of furry creatures. "But she will have great assets at her disposal one day. I have a lot of plans for how we can deploy them, but I cannot get anything out of her, like drawing blood from a stone. Sit, listen, be quiet, and learn. Do nothing and leave it all to me."

Finally, a young woman, teetering on impossibly high heels, sauntered into the room. Lucia knew Tamsin was just twenty-three, but the makeup on her face made guessing her age a challenge. She was so thin and her eyelashes so long, she looked as if the weight of them might tip her right over.

She wore a tight, low-cut, dark-blue minidress with a blazer over it and had a kelly green Birkin bag hooked over her arm. Her extensions were bleached within an inch of their life and her smile—gleaming, white, Hollywood teeth—added to the idea that you weren't looking at a person so much as an Instagram filter.

"*Bonjour, ma cherie,*" Celeste said, standing up and air-kissing both of Tamsin's cheeks as if they were the best of friends. "It has been too long. Since when? Mustique?"

Lucia moved in closer and introduced herself. "It's lovely to make your acquaint—" Just as she was extending her hand, a tiny Yorkie mysteriously materialized from within the depths of Tamsin's handbag and nipped her.

She pulled her hand back quickly.

Tamsin laughed. "Sorry, sorry, that's just Lady Barksalot. She doesn't like meeting new people, but she'll come round, won't you princess? That's right! Who's a good doggy woggy?" Tamsin made kissy-faces at the dog in the bag, who continued yapping. "Lucy, did you say? Pleasure to meet you."

Tamsin took a seat, pulling the pup out of the six-figure handbag and placing her on the floor, which seemed to subdue the barking, at least temporarily. Lucia could not wait to tell Sooz about this entire setup. Although, maybe she had better not. Sooz would likely rage about the sizable carbon footprints of both large yachts and tiny terriers.

Celeste inquired about Tamsin's new business venture—designing custom jewel-encrusted, dog-shaped handbags—as another member of the staff entered carrying a tray with two glasses of water for Celeste and Lucia and a margarita for Tamsin. (It was only 11:00 a.m. in London, but it was five o'clock somewhere.) The waiter also set down a plate of Tunnock's Tea Cakes. Without even considering if Celeste would somehow berate her for a lack of decorum, Lucia reached for one. Tamsin had done the same, and their fingers bumped.

"I love these." Tamsin beamed. "I keep a stash in all the houses. And the yachts. Even the jet! My gran used to buy them for me when I was little, and they always remind me of her."

"You know, my *abuela*—my grandmother—used to buy these for me, too," Lucia said, remembering them fondly. "Although in the States, we call them Mallomars. I was so excited to find something similar over here. They are hands down one of my favorite things about this country."

Tamsin asked Lucia where she was from. Her eyes lit up at the mention of Lucia's Venezuelan heritage. "Like near Tulum? God, I love Tulum. The men there are so sexy," she said appreciatively. Lucia didn't have the heart to tell her that Tulum was in Mexico, fifteen hundred miles away from Caracas. With her mouth conveniently full of marshmallow, she nodded as if in total agreement.

Maybe it was the chocolate, but either way Lucia found herself warming to Tamsin. Under the layers of makeup and clothes, there was a sweetness and vulnerability. She seemed fragile, like a baby bird swathed in YSL; Lucia felt like she wanted to protect her. And feed her a million more tea cakes.

Finally, it seemed Celeste had had enough small talk. "*Bon*," she said. "What have you been thinking about your giving? Are you ready to try with a few donations this year? How can we help you?"

Tamsin frowned slightly and bit her bottom lip. "I haven't thought much about it, to be honest. It just doesn't . . ." She paused, deciding what to say next. "It doesn't get me very excited. I mean it's all so *boring*. It's not that I don't care about starving children. I do, of course. It's just that everyone is doing starving children now, and I don't know. I want something more . . . unique."

Lucia's training snapped into place. She knew the key to getting people on the journey to giving, as Melissa would call it, was tapping into a primal feeling that would motivate them. Within just a few minutes, she could tell that Tamsin craved attention, that she wanted to be viewed as a standout in a crowd. She wasn't going to do anything that wouldn't make a splash on social media. Lucia could get her to support a good cause, if only she knew which button to push.

But Celeste didn't seem at all concerned about doing anything more than checking off this perfunctory meeting from her to-do list for another year. "Ah well," she said, looking pointedly at the clock on the wall. "Whenever you are ready, we are here for you as you require."

"Actually, I have one quick question," Lucia said, avoiding Celeste's instant glare—although she could almost feel the icy daggers pricking her neck. "What do you care about? Like really and truly care about. What lights you up inside?"

Tamsin contemplated the question. "Lady Barksalot. Making Daddy happy. And shoes." She seemed satisfied with her answer.

"OK," said Lucia. Celeste was still staring her down, so she knew she should not say anything more or share any other ideas of her own, but she couldn't help herself. "And what are you afraid of?"

"Hmm, that's tougher. Not much. People selling stories about me to the rags, like about how my handbag designs are trash and I'm nothing but a spoiled rich girl spending Daddy's money." Tamsin's eyes started to well up, but she seemed to think better of smudging her eyeliner and got ahold of herself. "And anything at all happening to Lady Barksalot. Or any puppy for that matter."

She looked lovingly over at the dog, who was, as her name would suggest, barking loudly at her latest enemy, the lamp.

The answer to getting Tamsin excited about giving was clear, even though it pained Lucia to suggest it. It wasn't that she didn't love animals. She too melted every time she passed a French bulldog on the street, like any normal, red-blooded human. But animal charities didn't need Tamsin's money— some of them were enormous organizations bringing in hundreds of millions a year. For *cats*. That's a lot of yarn. Lucia thought about all the people who could benefit from just a fraction of that money, about how many families ArteAustin could have supported in getting their immigration cases heard or by finding them jobs or homes.

But this was about getting Tamsin to care about something— anything—enough that she wanted to take a first step. Lucia and Melissa agreed that philanthropy was like a gateway drug. Once people gave a little, they became addicted to that feeling of helping.

It's a journey, Lucia thought. Just get her on the journey.

"There are some amazing nonprofits helping dogs and cats right here in London. Why don't we visit some together? You can learn more about their work, and maybe you'll find something that excites you?"

Tamsin considered. Even Lady Barksalot stared at Lucia, who didn't dare look at Celeste, whose eyes were now burning a hole into the back of her skull.

"Yeah, alright," she said slowly. "Why not? Plus that would make great content for my fans. OK, I'm in. My assistant will email you to set it up."

Tamsin stood up and scooped the dog back into her Birkin bag. Then, out of the blue, she enveloped Lucia in a hug. "We're going to have fun, you and me, I can tell."

She offered air-kisses to Celeste again, and like a puff of smoke from a Diptyque candle, Tamsin was gone.

In the town car on the way back to the office, Celeste said nothing. The silence was so tense that Lucia felt a trickle of sweat run down her spine. Why on earth did she care so much about pleasing this tiny French torturer?

But three hours later, as she was eating a ham sandwich "al desko" (Lucia rarely managed to leave her desk for lunch), her inbox pinged with an email from Celeste, forwarded from Tamsin's assistant. The note was brief, confirming Tamsin's RSVP for a cocktail reception the bank was hosting the following week.

Later, Melissa would tell her that this was a coup. Tamsin had never attended an after-hours event at the bank. Not one. Brendan would be thrilled, and Celeste could take full credit.

A victory of this magnitude was met with a level of enthusiasm commensurate with what Celeste was able to give. Her forwarding note contained only one word: *good*.

Chapter 10
Henry Perry

Lucia hated being late. Even when it wasn't her fault, it felt like a personal failing. Horns blared all around her. The crush of cars, their drivers clearly frustrated by the standstill traffic on Kingsway, only added to her mounting anxiety. She knew Sooz would already be waiting at the Savoy, drumming her neon-painted nails on the white tablecloth, wondering why she had agreed to come in the first place.

They hadn't seen each other for weeks—Lucia's fault. Ever since landing the Great White Whale, a.k.a. Ms. Tamsin St. James, she'd been busier than ever at work. On the upside, Celeste, at long last, had begrudgingly accepted Lucia's value went beyond that of being the office punching bag. The downside, now that she was no longer considered a giant waste of space, was that her coworkers were pulling her into things left, right, and center.

This date with Sooz was blocked off in her calendar with the label: "LUCIA NOT AVAILABLE THAT MEANS YOU TRISTAN." She had done everything possible to leave the office on time, but just as she was headed out the door, Tristan yanked her, sleeve first, into a conference room. There sat a man all in tweeds, apparently a third cousin of a board member, who wanted a consult on how to set up a foundation. For "something to do with needy people," he'd explained, his nose literally in the air.

At last, just as she was about to grab a taxi, Tristan had called after her again.

"Luce, I have a run-of-the-mill medical appointment today." Lucia knew this was code for Botox. "Can you be back by three to take a meeting with Henry Perry?"

She wasn't in any position to say no. Even after an encouraging start with Tamsin, Lucia still hadn't been allowed to spend time with clients on her own; a one-on-one with a client was exactly what she had been waiting for. She agreed, knowing this would squeeze her teatime to a scant hour, fifteen minutes of which had already been wasted listening to the symphony of central London gridlock that surrounded her.

"You know what, just pull over here, I'll run the rest of the way."

"Are you sure, love?" the cab driver asked, looking at her feet clad in patent leather heels. "Those don't look much like running shoes."

"I'll be fine, but thanks." She tapped her phone on the payment terminal, hopped out of the cab, and set off down the street at a sprint, downgrading almost immediately to a light jog (her heels were definitely not running shoes). Just as quickly, traffic started moving again; her taxi driver honked at her as he sped by. Typical, she thought, throwing her hands in the air. Getting back to the office by 3:00 p.m. when she was now twenty minutes late was going to be impossible, but she had no choice. Surely, Sooz would understand.

Lucia blotted her forehead with a tissue as she rushed into the dining room and spotted Sooz alone at a table, her impeccably made-up face screwed up in annoyance.

"Hi, darling," she said, offering an air-kiss. Sooz was dressed in tight faux-leather leggings and an oversize sweater that had the words "Posh Twats" embroidered across the front. "Nice jumper."

"I thought I'd try to blend in with this crowd. All posh twats and . . . sorry . . . American tourists."

There was a forced lightness in her voice, as if she wanted Lucia to think she was joking even though she wasn't. The tea had been Lucia's idea, a way to make up for the mounting number of unanswered texts and canceled playdates since she had started her job. "My treat," she had promised when she'd phoned Sooz with the invitation. Even though she knew the Savoy was not Sooz's scene, it was the nicest place closish to Lucia's office (although, she thought, her heartbeat still elevated after her attempt to break the world record for the 400-meter dash, not close enough).

"It'll be fun. Just you, me, a bunch of tiny sandwiches, and a whole lot of gossip about romance novels." Sooz had agreed.

But now that they were together, Lucia wondered if it hadn't been a miscalculation from the start. Sooz seemed on edge, and Lucia wasn't sure why: Was it the vibe at the Savoy, the fact that she was late, or their relationship in general? Maybe it was all three.

"Let's order, shall we," Lucia said, attempting to make eye contact with their waiter. He was two tables over, pouring tea from a silver pot with such flourish and precision that it would have been lovely to watch if Lucia hadn't been on the clock.

Finally, the waiter arrived, toting a tea menu thicker than the Bible. Lucia sweetly asked if he would please bring out all three of the courses—savories, scones, and sweets—at once. He recoiled in horror but agreed.

"Have you made your tea selection?" he asked Lucia.

"I'll just have . . . Which tea tastes the most like coffee?" He shot her a look of pure disgust. For a second, she thought he might ask her to leave the premises, but he mumbled something about Assam and then looked over to Sooz.

"Just water for me, thanks," she said. "Unless you have any fair-trade-certified teas?"

His face contorted into an exaggerated grimace, and Lucia debated telling him to stop or it would freeze that way. But there was no time for motherly admonitions.

"I thought not," Sooz frowned. "Tap please, not bottled," she added, closing her menu and handing it back to the waiter, who couldn't get away from them quickly enough.

"So," Lucia started. "Can't believe what a nice day it is, given the rain all week."

"We've needed it. It's been so unusually dry," Sooz said, not making eye contact.

Lucia tried again with another uncontroversial topic. "How's Atticus? I know he gets to see Marley with Gretel, but I miss him."

Sooz took out her phone to show Lucia some pictures of the pair going down the slide together at the playground. This reminded Lucia of an advert for Tilly Willington's latest book, which she hadn't yet found time to read, about an Olympic rhythmic gymnast who falls into a BDSM relationship with her biggest rival (*Double Stag*). Sooz had just finished it and began to describe the story in all its gratuitous detail. "It gives a whole new meaning to the term *apparatus exchange*," Sooz declared with dramatic flourish. The two older gentlemen in suits at the next table nearly choked on their macarons.

The safe subjects—weather, kids, X-rated novels—made Lucia feel like they were back on the playground bench together. She had missed the comfortable ease between them and was glad it still existed, so long as they avoided the topic of Lucia's job at Eastern Currents.

But as Big Ben chimed in fifteen-minute increments, Lucia started to grow anxious, which did not go unnoticed. "Listen, you go. I'll pay the bill," Sooz offered, after Lucia checked the time on her phone for the third time in thirty seconds.

"No way, my treat, I promised," Lucia replied half-heartedly, but she had already started to grab her purse. If she left now and there was no traffic, she'd just make it back in time for her meeting.

"Go. Wouldn't want to keep those spoiled hypocrite clients of yours waiting," Sooz insisted.

Lucia stopped. She knew Sooz wanted her to agree, to laugh and tell her how awful her rich clients were. But she didn't want to lie. On the surface, some of her clients seemed like hypocrites—they made money in unsavory ways only to give it away (well, some of it) to great causes—but at least they were trying to do some good. On balance, Lucia felt it was better to do something than nothing at all, and insulting her clients, even just to appease her friend, seemed weirdly disloyal.

Lucia didn't want to cause a fight, nor did she have time for one. "OK, thanks so much, babe. This was fun. I'll get the next one," she said.

"Right, so that'll be next year at this rate." Lucia pretended not to hear as she rushed out of the Savoy and into a waiting taxi.

Lucia sighed to herself—this was not the grand reunion she had hoped for. It only reinforced the nagging feeling that had crept up on her recently: that she was not entirely succeeding at any element of her life right now. A definite C-average student at best—her skin prickled at the thought. At home, she was barely operating at 50 percent, if that. The lack of sleep was killing her. She had even fallen asleep during sex the week before.

"Am I boring you, *cariño*?" Ollie asked in the morning, a hound dog's look of dejection in his eyes. "It used to drive you mad when I whispered lines from *Mansfield Park* in your ear."

"Never, love," she promised, rushing to get ready for work. "It's not you. It's me. I promise I'll be wide awake tomorrow." But the next night she was drooling on her pillow before he even made it into bed.

It was going to be OK, she convinced herself. She just needed to stay the course. She had only been in the job for a couple of months, which was no time at all. After moving to the UK, it had taken longer than that for her to get used to which direction traffic was coming from as she crossed the street. (To be fair, she always looked both ways, frantically, like she was refereeing a high-stakes game of Ping-Pong. She hadn't been run over. Yet.)

Thanks to her so-called "spoiled hypocrite clients," her job had already given her experiences far beyond those she had ever imagined. Last week, she had dined in the Cloisters at Westminster Abbey at the invitation of a client who had provided two million pounds in scholarship funds to support the choir school. As the guests feasted by candlelight, they were serenaded by the choristers' angelic voices.

At one point, when Lucia surreptitiously bent down to retrieve her fork from under her chair, she realized she had spent the evening sitting on the grave of seventeenth-century English writer Aphra Behn. "Sorry," she whispered apologetically to the dead woman, determined not to drop anything else. "I hope you liked whipped meringue."

The traffic lightened up, a small miracle. She opened the dossier Tristan had sent while her cab sped across town, pushing her thoughts toward what was coming: her first solo client meeting. She couldn't wait, even if no one else deemed Henry Perry important enough to warrant their attention. Henry was the second son of the Duke of Eaton, and you didn't need a PhD in social climbing to know that the second son wasn't worth as much as the first ("an heir and a spare," as the saying goes). Henry was still very, very wealthy and had an eye-wateringly large trust fund that meant he'd never have to work a day in his life. But he was small potatoes compared to his parents and elder brother, the third-largest landowners in the country. (Behind the royal family. And Tamsin's dad.)

Henry was twenty-eight, unmarried, and interested in "progressive" causes—the bank's code word for radical and not to be touched. He was constantly requesting meetings, trying to get the bank to sponsor fundraising dinners or offer space to his "pet charities" (not in this case actual pet charities, but those pesky progressive causes). Perish the thought of someone who genuinely wanted to use their privilege to do some actual good. For humans.

Her cab pulled up to the Eastern Currents building with a whole six minutes to spare. Surely that was enough time to grab a coffee? Though she'd only taken a few small sips of her tea, she needed something to rinse the awful taste out of her mouth.

She rushed across the street to Amplify, the needlessly posh hipster coffee spot that she usually avoided. (Amplify refused to serve sugar or dairy on principle, and while Lucia applauded their environmental efforts and could make do with oat milk in a pinch, she refused to give up sugar. Yes, she would live longer without it, but what would the point of those joyless extra sugar-free years even be?) However, these were desperate times.

She joined the queue to order, tapping her toes on the polished cement floor and craning her neck to see what was taking so long. Were they milking actual oats back there? There were four people in front of her, and she sighed loudly in exasperation. So loudly in fact that the man in front of her, smartly put together in a well-cut suit and expensive dress shoes, turned around and faced her with raised eyebrows. She shrugged and smiled sheepishly before going back to her counting. Three people to go.

Finally, after contemplating the possibility that she might just die if she didn't get caffeine into her body soon, only she and Mr. Dress Shoes were left. He asked for a triple shot, dash of almond milk, and then turned to ask what she wanted. (Chivalry, huzzah; maybe it wasn't dead after all.)

"You seem like you're in rather a hurry," he said. "It would be my pleasure."

"Is it that obvious?" she demurred, knowing it was. "I'm sorry. I'm just *so* tired, and I have a meeting with an important client. I can't be late. You know the drill, I'm sure." She stopped, out of breath; he grinned at her. "Sorry. I always talk too much when I'm undercaffeinated. Sorry again. And yes, an oat milk cappuccino. To go . . . or, what do you say here, takeaway. Please. Thank you."

The barista started tamping down the grounds. Lucia felt moved by the random act of kindness from a stranger and horrified by how desperate she must look.

A minute to go as the milk frothed and the coffee machine hissed with steam. His drink was ready first, and he offered her a "hope your meeting goes well" as he walked with his cup over to the bar. What a gem, she thought, grabbing hers as soon as it was ready and throwing a "thanks again" over her shoulder at him as she sprinted, for the second time that day, to avoid being late.

Lucia rushed up to the tenth-floor conference room and managed to rip open three sugar packets and dispose of the evidence just before the door opened. She almost spilled her hard-won drink in surprise when in walked fancy dress shoes from the coffee shop—none other than Henry Perry himself.

"You!" she said. "My fairy godfather!"

He laughed, his smile lighting up his whole face. "Nonsense, it was nothing."

"Are you kidding? It was everything. If you ever need a kidney somewhere down the line, I'm your girl."

Henry sat down, and Lucia followed suit. "I can see now why you were in such a hurry," he said. "After all I am a very important client."

Now caffeinated and in better lighting, she assessed him. He seemed the epitome of the upper crust, in her mind at least: pale skin, blue eyes, and light hair slightly balding at the temples. A bit stiff looking, until he smiled—then his eyes crinkled up at the corners in the kindest way. And, she noticed, he had a cleft in his chin. All the best ones did.

Henry shook his head and her hand at the same time, saying, "I'm joking, of course. I'm sure we both know you drew the short straw today."

"I beg your pardon?" she asked. Celeste had, mortifyingly, made her practice using this expression as her default, "Excuse me?" having been deemed too common a phrase.

"You've gotten stuck with this meeting. Come now, you must be new here if you consider me an important client." He shrugged his shoulders. "I don't have the cachet of my elder brother."

She considered lying but decided against it. She trusted his kind eyes. "Sort of. I mean, personally I feel lucky to be here. But no one fought me over taking this meeting."

"Hmm—honesty from someone at Eastern Currents. I had always assumed they beat that out of you at your orientation. Everyone is always so obsequious to my face. But I can see they have hired well with you. So, who are you?"

Lucia was taken aback—few clients had asked her any questions about herself. She'd be shocked if any of them knew her last name. Or her first name, for that matter. Most of them called her Lucy.

She introduced herself like she was writing one of the dossiers she had become intimately familiar with. "Lucia Gutierrez-Barrow, Venezuelan American, from Texas, British husband. My background is in fundraising, and I worked at a nonprofit in Austin for many years before moving here. I have a one-year-old daughter who is teething and therefore up all night, requiring me to drink at least three or four coffees a day. And, if honesty is your bag, I'll admit that I'd be happy getting them from Starbucks every morning, but it has been deemed terribly uncool by everyone I've met here."

"I'm very pleased to make your acquaintance, Lucia. I suspect you already know a fair bit about me. Second son, et cetera, et cetera. I have a reputation for being a bit of a black sheep in my family. Well, maybe more like a mottled gray. I'm in the inner circle, but they'd all rather I kept my mouth shut. Personally, I enjoy the bitterness of a posh macchiato, but I see your point."

There was a hum of satisfaction in the air. They were clearly enjoying each other's company. Henry waited until Lucia sat down before taking his own seat. It was only afterward that she wondered if she should have curtsied now that she (sort of) knew how to do it.

"So, let's get right down to it then—we're here to talk about your giving," Lucia said, opening her notebook to a blank page. "You have supported an impressive list of causes. What do you want to do next?"

"Indeed," Henry said, settling back into his chair. "My family has had a foundation for eons. Nothing surprising, very traditional. We give about one hundred million pounds a year, give or take a bit depending on the markets. The usual causes—donations to my old school, which hardly needs the money. Art exhibitions. Upkeep of Kew Gardens. Charities where the royals are patrons. Always the same things. It's a bit of a snooze, if I'm being honest."

She had read this in the file. The Perrys were some of the UK's most generous philanthropists, in terms of amount at least. You couldn't walk into a major museum in the country without seeing their name on a plaque over a wing.

"What Daddy and Mummy contribute is extraordinary, of course. It does a great deal of good. But I feel like . . . Well, I feel we should be doing better." Henry got up and walked to the window, folding his hands behind his back as he looked out over the city. "We should be doing *better*. We have an excessive amount of wealth, even though no one in my family has been required to work for generations. We made it off the backs of others."

Again, Henry had surprised her: His statement was categorically true—much inherited wealth in the UK came from somewhere unethical (colonial rule, the slave trade, unfair land-ownership laws, pick a card)—but she had yet to hear anyone acknowledge that fact, even in veiled terms.

"My family owes much to this country—everything, really—even if they don't want to admit it. And I want to have an impact, do something that matters, go beyond the safe causes that don't anger anyone. I have been trying, working more closely with charities, particularly ones that support asylum seekers. For obvious reasons."

Lucia wasn't sure what obvious reasons he meant, but he was speaking her language.

"After years of pleading, I've been given two million pounds a year in discretionary funding. I can donate it wherever I want, as long as it's done anonymously. Heaven forbid the Perry name be associated with helping the people who need it the most." He sneered. "I have ideas, probably too many. I have shared them with Tristan, of course, but he has advised me to wait until Daddy passes on and my inheritance properly comes in, and not to rock the boat until then."

Lucia nodded; that sounded just like Tristan. "Tristan is pragmatic. But he and I, we have . . ." Lucia thought about her next words. "Let's just say, different views on how philanthropy should work. Not miles apart, of course, and I see his reasoning." She didn't know their relationship and, more than that, didn't want to throw Tristan under the bus, no matter how much of an ass he had been to her.

But something about Henry's open and guileless expression made her feel like she could be honest with him. "My last job was as fundraiser for a nonprofit that helped immigrants from Central and South America in the US. Their needs were urgent and immediate—food, work, housing, childcare—and every penny I brought in was put to good use almost as soon as it came through the door. I didn't have the luxury of waiting around for—forgive me—some old rich guy to croak." At this she glanced at him, and his eyes danced. His amusement was enough to encourage her to continue. "I needed to find ways to raise as much as I could as quickly as I could. Lives literally depended on it. And trust me, we could have done a whole lot with two million pounds a year."

"Well then, Lucia," Henry replied, grinning widely now, "what do you suggest we do?"

Lucia's mouth could barely keep up with the pace of her thoughts, which happened when she was excited. "What if we start with some research—if it's OK with Tristan of course? Visit some charities, meet some leaders and some new arrivals themselves. Let them tell us what they need. And then figure out the best way for you to help.

"And," she added as an afterthought, "your family is welcome to join us, if you think they'd be interested."

Henry laughed, and she frowned, worried she had gone too far. "No, I'm not laughing at you, Lucia. It's brilliant. I'm just trying to imagine Mummy taking tea with anyone who isn't listed in Debrett's."

"It's a journey," Lucia said. "You're further along than most, but your parents need to start somewhere. For now, we can keep this *entre nous*, if you'd like. Let's start by figuring out how to make the most of your money—and then, we'll determine how to better direct theirs."

"Why, Mrs. Barrow," he replied, his gaze full of mischief. "Are you recommending all-out treason during our first meeting?"

"Not treason. More like some harmless scheming in pursuit of the greater good. Less Benedict Arnold, more Mrs. Bennet from *Pride and Prejudice*. Plus, you do have a bit of Mr. Darcy about you."

Henry gave her a questioning look. "Firth or Macfadyen?"

"Firth, obvs," she replied.

"Oh thank heavens."

They sat back down, eager to start brainstorming. It wasn't until after there was a gentle knock on the door and an assistant poked in to politely kick them out of the meeting room that they noticed the hour had long since flown by. She and Henry parted ways in the elevator—Lucia getting off on the eighth floor—with a promise to start setting dates to visit some prospective grantees.

Lucia was flying. Finally, *finally*, something that lit her up inside. She hadn't felt this way in forever, at least not since leaving Texas. The passion, the fire, the knowledge that she was working toward something bigger than herself, and with a partner who seemed to get it and had the assets behind him to see things through.

"Well don't you look like the mouse that got the cheese? Isn't that accurate? All you Americans are so enthralled by that Mickey Mouse?" Tristan's droll voice greeted her. He was back behind his desk, and although his eyes were laughing, his forehead was frozen in place.

"Hilarious," she said. "But I should be thanking you. Henry was awesome. I really liked him, and we have a plan. That is, if you'll let me spend some time with him."

"That's why I scheduled my procedure . . . er, appointment . . . for this afternoon, to give you two a chance to connect. I thought you might hit it off. Henry's already texted me to tell me you were a delight. And trust me, he doesn't say that about everyone."

"You guys are text friends?"

"Indeed we are," he said.

"Well isn't it just a small world after all?"

Tristan rolled his eyes, but he was not mad. In fact, Lucia thought she spied . . . Could it be? A smile?

"Look, it's time I stopped hazing you. You really saved my arse with that Tamsin thing, and truthfully, I couldn't be happier about giving Henry over to you. I love him as a mate, but around here he's damaged goods. Celeste only cares about the biggest fish, and Henry's parents, whom he loves to pester with his good deeds, are the biggest of the big. The only one bigger is the White Whale, Ms. St. James herself. It's all about succession at the end of the day. In the families and, of course, here at the bank."

"What do you mean, succession?" Lucia asked.

Tristan moved closer to Lucia and dropped his voice. "First of all, we agree—nothing between us leaves us. If you ever say I told you anything, I will deny it, and also, I will crush you."

She believed him. "Cone of silence, agreed."

"Brendan is a waste of space. He joined the bank during medieval times, when being white and having a penis were all you needed to get promoted."

Lucia had thought as much but had never dared to say so. If Tristan was throwing shade at the head honcho, he must trust her at least a little bit.

"Yeah, you see it already, I can tell. He once told us that the secret to his success was not to piss anyone off. That ostrich has buried his head for his entire career—so here we are, all listening to him. But not for long."

"Much more of a walrus than an ostrich, but go on."

Tristan's eyes twinkled. "Exactly. Celeste, in all this time, has been priming herself to take Brendan's job. She may be harsh, but she's had to be. She's worked under that idiot for five years, and now that he's retiring, it's going to be her time to shine. If she gets the promotion, she would be the second woman to serve on the management team in the bank's four-hundred-year history.

"She's got more balls than he does, but still she knows not to piss anyone off—at least until she's risen high enough that it doesn't matter. Anyway, that's why you must be careful around Henry. If anyone's likely to cause trouble with the Perrys, and make trouble for Celeste, it's him. He's brilliant on a night out, but he's a liability. So, darling, he's all yours."

Lucia couldn't help herself—she hugged him. He stiffened, but right before she let go, she thought she felt his muscles soften.

"Thank you, thank you, thank you! You won't regret this."

"Ugh, stop with the emotion. I may be Nigerian by birth, but I'm British by upbringing and we do not. Do. Emotion."

"What are you two chickens clucking about?" Melissa poked her head around the corner. Lucia was about to respond when Tristan said, "Oh, nothing. Lucia was just regaling me with the most boring story in the world about her infant." He threw a conspiratorial glance at Lucia. She wasn't sure why Tristan would care if Melissa knew about her meeting with Henry Perry, but she didn't want to do anything to damage their fragile truce.

"Yep, that's me," she said, standing up and smiling at him. "Tomorrow's lesson will be a how-to on using a breast pump. Spoiler alert: Your nipple really can double in size."

Tristan's face twisted in horror (even without the ability to raise his eyebrows).

She walked back to her own desk with a spring in her step. She had a new client, a great one. She had an ally. If she could just figure out how to win over Celeste, stay awake during sex with her husband, fix her friendship with Sooz, and get Marley to stop waking up every two hours, she'd be golden.

Chapter 11
The Pipeline and the Aubergine

The Zone.

Lucia was so close. It was in her grasp.

She couldn't see it, but she could imagine it, like the edge of an infinity pool blending into the horizon. In fact, she'd been in a rooftop infinity pool just last week, taking a meeting. Rona had insisted they swim while they chatted, and Lucia, unprepared, had needed to borrow one of her bathing suits. Unfortunately, it was two sizes too small. She thought she had gotten away with it until she realized the pool was glass bottomed and sat above Rona's living room, which made it 95 percent certain that her husband, Francis, and his business associates, there for a non-pool meeting, had seen 100 percent of Lucia's bare ass.

This was different. The Zone was elusive, rare, like a once-in-a-century eclipse. It happened when everything was functioning smoothly, at home and in the office, and she was firing on all synapses. Last night, she felt the outer rim of it. Celeste uncharacteristically left the office early, giving Lucia the chance to zip across town to Notting Hill and spend a rare, precious prebedtime fifteen minutes with Marley. She sang the *pio pio* song (almost on key), grateful for the chance to inhale her baby's lavender-soaked essence before she drifted off to sleep.

Ollie arrived home, and his jaw dropped to the floor when Lucia greeted him with a martini at the door and dinner on the stove—homemade arepas and a chilled bottle of white wine.

"What's all this?" he said delightedly, undoing his tie. "Wait? Is it Tuesday? Oh hallelujah."

Tuesday night was scheduled-sex night. People with no children might find this sad, but with a baby at home, finding time for sex on a regular basis was like getting a bikini wax: hard to fit into the schedule, but you always end up glad you did it, and with an experienced technician, you can leave satisfied in less than fifteen minutes.

"It *is* Tuesday, *amor*," she said, handing him the martini. "But first, dinner. The arepas have to be eaten hot."

"In the interest of propriety, I'll spare you the crude pun that just popped into my head." He smiled devilishly at her. "Let me change, and we'll have dinner together."

They ticked off every box on their Tuesday to-do list, leaving Lucia with a satisfied glow. Then, after Ollie fell asleep, she snuck out of bed to work for another few hours. Tristan was also online, messaging her back in real time, which made her feel less lonely.

"Shouldn't you be in bed with your baby, Mildred, or whatever she's called?" he wrote.

"Dare I ask how many people are in your bed tonight?" she replied.

He sent back a devil emoji, and they both continued plugging away.

Lucia passed out around 2:00 a.m. The Zone felt more achievable in the evenings (as long as she wasn't including hours slept as part of her calculus). But the mornings, especially the following one, when she hit snooze twice, weren't as Zone adjacent as she would have liked.

"Hey, thanks for last night," she said, smacking Ollie's bottom as he made them coffee.

"My pleasure, Mrs. Barrow," he replied, handing her a cappuccino, which she gratefully received. Today would be a four-coffee day, she decided, taking her mug with her to get dressed.

"Listen, love, Gaz is hosting a pub quiz tonight, and the whole gang is going to be there. It starts at half six, and I'm sure you won't be home by then," he yelled from the kitchen. "But maybe you could join us for the last few rounds? We're in desperate need of your popular-culture knowledge."

"You know I'd love to," she replied, which wasn't true—the last one was about as fun as those dreams where you show up to an exam only to realize you haven't studied and don't know any of the answers. She was asked the color of the football used in the 1966 World Cup, and when she said brown (weren't all footballs brown?), she was basically laughed out of the pub because (1) it was a soccer ball, and (2) it was orange.

Thankfully this time she had an iron-clad excuse not to attend. "The thing is I have that event tonight for Tamsin. At the animal shelter? Cupcakes for Pups?" This was not her idea of a good time, either, but at least it got her out of a night with Belly and the crew.

He walked into the bathroom to face her. "You're at another event? That's the fifth one in ten days."

"But who's counting?" she retorted.

"Me," he parried back. "Pardon me for actually wanting to spend an evening with my wife."

"Right," she muttered. "Your wife and six of your closest, drunkest friends who make me feel stupid for not knowing the year Guy Fawkes didn't bomb Parliament or whatever."

"What was that?" Ollie moved in closer.

Lucia thought about airing her grievances with his friends, telling her husband how left out of their little private club she felt, reminding him of how many client events he had attended recently himself.

"Let's not fight, OK? I have a long day ahead, and so do you. You need to study up on Cockney slang and the number of members of the Welsh assembly, or whatever else you might get grilled on tonight. Plus"—she wrapped her arms around his waist—"I have it on good authority that I'll be home early tomorrow night again, which means we can schedule a bonus session."

Ollie looked at her, deciding whether he wanted to fight or concede. But the promise of a second night of lovemaking in one week seemed too much for him to pass up. "Fine. I'll admit, things have been busy. And Christmas is right around the corner—we're going to have a lovely time away at Mummy's with the family."

Lucia hid her grimace. Christmas at Moira's. Joy to the world.

"We'll talk about this later. Maybe Thursday." He smiled. "Anyway, we've got a well-rounded team. Belly's knowledge of American popular culture rivals even your own. Did you know she once won us a bonus round by naming every Kardashian child in order of age?"

A little voice in the back of her head wondered at how quickly he'd gotten over her absence. Was she so easily replaced? While she was glad not to be arguing, couldn't Ollie have fought a little bit harder for her to join? Maybe he was relieved she wasn't coming, so he could have alone time with his friends without having to explain things to Lucia or smooth over her gaffes and errors. Or alone time with one friend in particular, she wondered.

She told the little voice to pipe down. She didn't want to go there, especially not now, not with so much to do. "Oh, we won't have much time to talk on Thursday," she replied, kissing him, relieved that this now oft-repeated argument between them had passed.

There it was again. The Zone, ahead in the distance. She could almost taste it.

* * *

The morning had been hectic, full of meetings and calls. Tamsin phoned just after 12:00 p.m. from her foundation's new offices, on the forty-second floor of a giant skyscraper that, due to its unfortunate shape, had been nicknamed the Aubergine—the British word for eggplant. Lucia had to admit that it did look like the naughtiest emoji blown up to one kajillion times its normal size.

"So what do you think? The St. James Foundation for the Rehabilitation of Dogs and Cats or PFP, Prosthetics for Pets?" Tamsin repeated.

"Both great. Which do you prefer?" Lucia said hurriedly, as she desperately tried to finish off a dossier for Celeste before lunch.

Without knowing the first thing about prosthetics, Tamsin had decided to invest all her foundation's funds into making new limbs for animals and had rented a three-thousand-square-foot office space, although she had zero staff to work there.

She now planned to carpet the luxurious balcony of said office, with its stunning view of the entire city of London, in Astroturf, so pets could use it to relieve themselves.

"I think we need my name on it. Our name. It's Daddy's money after all. Oh, I hope he likes it."

In moments like these, Lucia sensed Tamsin's vulnerability. It was clear that her ultimate motivation was her father's approval. Despite all her wild ideas, Lucia couldn't help but feel protective of her.

"He will, I'm sure of it," she replied confidently. She looked up to see Melissa standing next to her desk, coat already on and purse in hand. "I have to run now. I'm in meetings all afternoon, but we'll catch up tomorrow. OK . . . Yes, the ball pit is a great idea . . . Uh-huh. I really have to go. Bye, Tamsin. Bye bye bye." She hung up the phone.

"Lunch?" she said to her friend.

"Absolutely. I'm famished. Let's go to Earl's," Melissa said, naming her preferred local deli. It was too cold to go far, but Melissa insisted they travel at least a five-minute walk from the office. "The air is too stagnant around here," she told Lucia the first time they went out to lunch together. "You don't lose the smell of banker for at least four blocks."

They joined the queue as they arrived, ordered at the counter, and then sat down with their sandwiches at the vacant table in the corner. Lucia always looked around for any familiar faces before they started gossiping about work.

"So how goes the doggy-prostate charity?" Melissa asked between bites of sweet corn and tuna on a bap. Lucia loved tuna but would be too concerned about smelly breath to order it on a workday. Melissa never seemed to care. She loved that about her.

"Ha! Prosthetics, not prostates. Although, given that she's put her office in the Aubergine, that might have been more appropriate. Not that it matters what she chooses," she said, digging into her turkey-and-avocado wrap. "Either cause would have made an equivalent impact. By which I mean, none."

Melissa nodded. "It is absolutely mad. But at least it's something. And I hear she's running the cash through the bank's accounts, so that's good for AUM. All those pampered pooches will make your bonus a bit fatter this year," she said wryly.

"I know," Lucia sighed. "It's a journey, she has to start somewhere, blah blah blah. I do agree with you. But even though it's a substantial amount of money for charity, it's a vanity project at the end of the day. I wish we could secretly redirect the payments somewhere else. Anywhere else."

"Hmm, like your supersecret special little project with the yummy Henry Perry?" she asked with a twinkle in her eye.

Lucia and Henry had agreed to keep the details of their research hush-hush while they worked out a concrete plan, lest his parents get wind, but Lucia needed someone to brainstorm with, and there was no one better for that than Melissa. She was the only one at the bank who had actually worked inside a UK charity, and she understood the landscape better than anyone.

"Now now, he's much too young for either of us. And anyway, it's not like that. My interest in Henry is strictly professional." Lucia smiled. "But in a professional sense, I'm ardently in love with him. I'm meeting him later today at a refugee center in North London that he might want to fund."

"I'm happy for you, pet. Just make sure Celeste doesn't catch wind of your little field trips."

"Never," Lucia said, crossing herself for good luck. "She'd lose it if she thought I was planning anything to upset her precious Perrys. You won't tell her, will you?"

Melissa snorted. "As if I'd give the Dragon any ammunition to use against you."

Just then, both their phones pinged, loudly and repeatedly. Lucia pulled hers out of her coat pocket. "A message from Tristan," she said. "It says, 'Leave whatever giant cookie you're eyeing and get back here, stat.'"

"I've got an email from Thomas," Melissa said. She was quiet, her eyes darting back and forth while she read the email. "It's to everyone. It just says, 'Urgent huddle, five minutes.' We'd better go now."

Lucia had no idea what was so urgent that she couldn't finish her sandwich, but knowing Celeste, she had waited until she saw them leave for lunch only to summon them back—just to prove she could. Lucia took her turkey to go (yet another lunch al desko, after all). She contemplated trying to eat it on the brisk walk back to the office, but she knew she would get avocado on her yellow coat, which was pretty much the only splash of color left in her work wardrobe. She usually hid the coat under her desk during the day to avoid Celeste making any comments about how much she looked like a banana.

By the time they made it back, most of the team were assembled around Celeste and Brendan, who were standing in the middle of the floor. The fake smile plastered on Celeste's face struck Lucia as terrifying. The only thing scarier might have been a real smile, but Lucia had never seen her boss crack one of those and didn't suppose she ever would.

"Thank you all for gathering on such short notice," Brendan said, puffing up his chest, looking more like a walrus than ever. "We've called you together today for an important announcement that cannot wait. Our team has been working on a huge project that we were hoping to share with you at the appropriate moment, in due course, but unfortunately the papers are planning on breaking the story this afternoon. It's good news but will require some . . . What's the word, Celeste?"

"Careful and consistent messaging," she said firmly. Brendan looked at her pleadingly, and she rolled her eyes, a movement so tiny it was imperceptible—except to those who were subject to her annoyance on a daily basis. "Shall I go on?" she asked Brendan, who nodded, his relief palpable.

Celeste stepped in front of him, commanding the attention of the entire floor. "You all recall our decision to support Fredrick Sanderson in keeping the funds of his late father away from his stepmother, Sunita."

Of course they remembered, Lucia especially. How could she forget Celeste's decision *not* to help Sunita create a fund for climate change when the conflict came up during the team meeting on Lucia's very first day on the job? Lord Sanderson died just a few weeks after that, resulting in a raging battle over his will that Fredrick, the new lord, had recently won.

"Lord Fredrick was very grateful to us for all our support and, as a thank-you, decided to offer us an opportunity to take on an . . . exciting . . . joint project." If Lucia didn't know any better, she would have thought she saw Celeste's eye twitch— but she must have been mistaken. The woman never lost her composure, plus her regular cosmetic enhancements didn't allow for unintentional facial movements.

"A new foundation?" Melissa exclaimed, and everyone started murmuring in excitement. Fredrick had now inherited a huge fortune. The amount he would have at his disposal to donate would be game-changing.

"Not quite," Celeste said. "Something more lucrative." She paused, and again Lucia thought she saw Celeste flinch but chalked it up to her imagination. "Fredrick has offered us the chance to finance the building of the Taraknor Project."

The silence was deafening. Lucia looked over at Tristan, whose face was the picture of genuine confusion. They all must have misheard. She glanced at Celeste, but her boss was surveying the group, her face unreadable.

At the risk of being sent to the stocks for impertinence, she piped up. "Celeste," Lucia said, all eyes in the room turning toward her. "Could you repeat that, please?"

Celeste sucked in a breath and, looking Lucia right in the eye, enunciated every syllable. "The Taraknor Project. I'm sure it is familiar to you, if you read anything that is not *Parents* magazine. It has been in the news for many months now."

Like a spell had broken, the room erupted in noise, but this was no longer the sound of excitement. Even Tristan's face, normally composed in every situation, was the picture of shock. Muffled cries of "What?" and "Are you kidding?" could be heard among the assembled staff, but no one wanted to offer an opinion loud enough for Celeste to pick them out of the crowd.

Except Melissa.

"You cannot possibly be serious. Is this some kind of sick joke?" Lucia heard the voice next to her exclaim, punctuated by the jangling of her bottle-top necklace. "Taraknor is a crude oil pipeline. It will cut across the Arctic Circle, turning the clock back on the fight against climate change. This is the opposite of good news. It's apocalyptic news," she finished firmly, crossing her arms.

Brendan, unused to anyone ever disagreeing with him, looked to Celeste like a deer caught in the headlights. "Well, yes, um, right. Celeste, I'll let you respond to that first," he said. Chicken, Lucia thought.

Celeste was a woman of small stature, but she seemed to grow half a foot as she faced Melissa. "We have given our opinion to the management team about the impacts of this project, but they have made the final decision. It is out of our hands. We needed to tell you before the news went public to avoid any staff speaking out against it."

But Melissa couldn't stop herself. "Let's set aside the catastrophic impact on our planet for just a moment. How could this possibly make good business sense? There will be protesters outside our doors day and night. Our nonprofit partners, especially the environmental ones, won't talk to us, they'll decline our clients' donations . . ."

"Stop," Celeste said firmly, holding up a hand mere inches from Melissa's reddening face. "That will not happen. Yes, there will be a bit of disruption at first. But people, even charities, have short attention spans, especially when there is money on the table. Besides, this project will make the bank a lot of revenue that we will use to finance other things we are excited about."

Melissa's chest visibly rose and fell as she glared at Celeste, who met her gaze with equal defiance. Everyone else seemed to hold their breath, waiting to see who would back down first. It felt like an eternity, before Melissa took a step back, her shoulders sagging. Celeste had emerged victorious from this battle, and she knew it.

"No one speaks out of turn, no one responds to the press about this," she said, releasing Melissa from her deadly stare and glancing around at everyone assembled. "It is imperative we respond with one voice. The penalty for defiance will be severe. No one speaks out of turn," she repeated, finishing her speech with her eyes locked on Melissa's again.

Melissa bowed her head, nodding silently.

"Well then, I'm glad that's sorted. Let's get on with our day," Brendan chirped. Everyone scattered back to their own desks as if nothing had happened—but their hushed tones suggested otherwise.

Lucia was stricken—she had no idea how to even begin processing what had just occurred. She was proud of Melissa for speaking up, but also mortified for her. She wanted to say something supportive, but her phone was beeping aggressively with a reminder. If she was going to make it to her meeting with Henry in far North London, then she had to leave now.

"You OK?" She put her hand on Melissa's shoulder. "I have to run, but let's put our heads together later. We'll figure something out. There must be a way to stop this, or mitigate it at least."

Melissa smiled ruefully, a forced gesture that didn't reach her eyes. "Yeah, yeah, alright."

"You're my Yoda," Lucia replied with as much enthusiasm as she could muster. "Remember, in this fight, together we are."

"Go on now, you'll be late," Melissa said, shooing Lucia out the door.

Chapter 12
Operation Bridget Jones

The air was cold and brisk as Lucia walked the few blocks from her office to Liverpool Street Station, the sunshine and festive Christmas decorations at odds with her downbeat mood.

She couldn't stop thinking about what had just gone down at the office. Sure, a lot of decisions she had made or witnessed since starting this job toed a fine line between doing what was right and doing what was profitable. But each time an action seemed to teeter over to the side of questionable morality, the trade-off had been justified by a clear, long-term benefit: Make a small compromise now in order to make a bigger impact later. *Later* had become a constant refrain, and one she had come to truly believe.

But it was difficult to see any rationale for the bank investing in the Taraknor pipeline. Unless that rationale was pure, selfish greed. It felt backward, retrograde, drastically misaligned with the values she so proudly purported to hold herself to. It would make a ton of money, but at what cost? She could feel a headache forming at her temples.

As she descended into the station and boarded the Tube, some of her negativity started to dissipate in the face of an unusually merry aura. The holiday spirit was pervasive in London, even among the most hard-hearted commuters. Everyone seemed to have a bit more pep in their step. A family of American tourists boarded at the next stop and asked a man dressed as Santa if he knew the way to "Lie-chester Square." As he patiently directed them, Lucia exchanged glances with a woman seated across from her, who rolled her eyes in a knowing gesture. Lucia smiled, feeling more like a Londoner every day.

By the time she emerged at ground level, she had put the pipeline problem squarely away to be dealt with later and felt nearly merry at the thought of what she and Henry were about to do. This, their visit to the North London Center for Migrants and Refugees, was the beginning of what she hoped would be something big, exciting, and not at all morally questionable: They were about to do some good.

She had arranged to meet Henry outside of the center, but when she arrived, bang on time, he was nowhere to be seen. She had been researching for weeks, mapping the refugee and migrant centers across London, trying to find organizations that met their criteria. The organizations had to be the right size (big enough to deploy Henry's money, but small enough that the amount he was offering would make a difference), and well established and respected with a solid track record (or Henry's parents would nix the idea without a second glance). They also needed to boast big ambitions to advance the fight for human rights. She'd narrowed her list down to eight and pored over each of the short-listed nonprofits' annual reports and tax returns, seeing the sun rise more than once until she found the organization that ticked every box. The North London Center for Migrants and Refugees seemed just right, the Goldilocks of charities.

This area of North London was unfamiliar to Lucia. She waited in front of the four-story brick building that housed the center. Its sloping roof had seen better days. Still, the place looked inviting. The door had recently been painted in a shade of bright blue and was decorated with a wreath tied with a big red bow. There was also a taped-up sign, written in English and ten other languages, including Spanish, that read, "All Are Welcome Here."

Lucia was hit with a wave of nostalgia. She'd spent half her childhood inside places like this, sanctuaries set up to support strangers in a strange land. As the first of her family to be born in the US, she had a comfort and facility with American culture and the English language that her grandparents never attained. As soon as she was old enough to read and write, she accompanied her *abuelos* to the many migrant centers that acted as hubs for the Venezuelan community.

She remembered the first time she went with them so vividly. She was only eleven but was ready to do whatever she could to help these people who looked and sounded just like her but whose lives had taken vastly different paths. She remembered how her *abuelo* beamed at her as she sat patiently with a Honduran couple and their baby, translating the asylum application forms into Spanish for them. She felt useful and very grown-up, grounded in her sense of purpose. It was a feeling she had spent her entire professional life trying to recapture.

Lucia's phone buzzed with a text from Henry: I'm inside already, it read. She turned the knob and went in.

The reception area was lined with sofas and comfy pillows, as well as rows of extra folding chairs. It was empty, but she could smell the remnants of the lunch that had been recently served—cumin and coriander that made her wistful for the *hallacas* and *caraotas* at the places she'd volunteered as a child.

Behind a door off the main hallway she heard shrieks—the happy kind—and went in to find a dozen children, ranging from Marley's age to four or five, climbing all over some poor soul sitting in the middle of a rainbow carpet. Their faces transformed into a mix of terror and glee as the center of their mountain roared like a lion. Several of them ran away, leaving only the lump in the middle. The lump looked a lot like Henry.

"Oh hello, Lucia, I see you've found me." He was red-faced, and his hair was askew, but his smile was bigger than she had ever seen it. "I was waiting outside when Amina told me to stop loitering and come in." He freed one arm from a toddler and pointed at a woman in the corner, doubled over in laughter. Amina, the executive director of the center, was short and slim, wearing black jeans, a long-sleeved brown shirt, and a black hijab wrapped loosely around her hair. She waved.

Lucia walked over and stuck out her hand. "It's so nice to finally meet you in person," she said. "I'm the one who has been pestering you with emails."

"Nonsense, we are always happy to hear from new friends here, especially when they have an Eastern Currents email address." She clapped three times loudly, and the children gave her their full attention. "I need to borrow your monster for a moment," she said. A collective *aw* went up around the room. "It's time for snack now, anyway." Henry was forgotten as two adults walked in with trays of fruit, digestive biscuits, and juice boxes.

Amina walked them out of the nursery and down a long hallway. "The nursery is open Monday through Friday, and we try to accommodate as many children as we can. Often the parents don't get much notice for an appointment with a lawyer or a job interview. There are rules about how many adults must be present per child, so I got my qualification, and I jump in to assist them whenever needed. Luckily today is a quiet day," she said.

Henry's eyes widened. "If that was quiet, I shudder to think what a loud day is like."

Amina laughed. "You have no idea."

She walked them to a small office in the back. Six desks were packed into the room like sardines. A pot of cheerful, red poinsettias was perched on a small folding table by the window.

"Our team is never in here all at the same time," she said. "It's hard to fit. Our two advocacy officers are at the House of Commons today, speaking to the All-Party Parliamentary Group on Refugee Rights, and the rest are busy around the building. I'll introduce you if we have time."

They sat down at the table just as the receptionist entered with a steaming pot of tea, three mugs, and a plate of spiral pastries coated with green dust. Never one to resist a fried treat, Lucia reached for one. A syrupy blend of honey and pistachio filled her mouth, and she involuntarily moaned. "Oh my god," she said through sticky teeth. "What is this?"

"It's called *mshabak*," Amina said. "It's sort of like the American . . . How would you call it?"

"Funnel cake," Lucia responded, still enjoying the taste. "We had it at the state fair every year growing up. But this is sweeter somehow. I am obsessed."

"Yes, they are addictive," she said, taking one for herself. "They are Syrian. That's where I'm from. I ate them for special occasions as a child. Now, we bring them in for our guests. Yet another reason why I am so glad you are here."

Lucia brought herself back to earth. "Right, so as I mentioned in my *many* emails, we just want to learn a bit more about the organization and what you do, as well as what you could do, with the right funding." She looked at Henry for agreement, and he nodded.

Lucia had already learned quite a bit from her research. She knew the UK's seventy thousand annual asylum seekers endured long waits as their applications made their way through the system. While they were being processed, they couldn't work and were supported by the government with a daily stipend that was less, she thought shamefully, than she spent on coffee.

"Our focus here is on providing holistic support to anyone who passes through our doors. Anything they need, we will try to get it for them. Everyone from those who have literally just arrived to those who have received a positive decision. You may not expect it, but when a claim is approved, the paltry support they receive stops completely after twenty-eight days. Twenty-eight days to find a job is not a lot of time. But here you can get English lessons, childcare, advice on drafting your résumé and interviewing skills, pro bono legal support. For a while we had an in-house therapist, but she left, and we haven't had the budget to replace her. I investigated training myself to replace her, but it was too expensive."

"Executive director, nursery teacher, in-house therapist?" Lucia questioned. "You can't do it all yourself. Trust me. I used to work at a nonprofit, I tried." And she had. Lucia had nearly killed herself helping with individual cases at ArteAustin on top of her fundraising load until her boss had made her stop.

"I know." Amina sighed. "My job is supposed to be outward facing, leadership, fundraising, all of that. But I find it hard not to get attached."

"I hear that," Lucia agreed.

Amina explained that recent government cuts meant their funding had dwindled while the need for their services only grew. They needed to fill the gap, or else thousands would fall through the cracks.

Lucia took diligent notes while sneaking the occasional glance at Henry. His focus remained on Amina as she told a story about a pair of twins, only thirteen, who arrived last week after a harrowing journey by sea. Amina had helped them find their cousin who lived just outside of London. Their parents, who they hoped were still in a refugee camp in Calais, were uncontactable. Henry's eyes glistened as she spoke.

"Well. It's extraordinary what you're doing here," Lucia affirmed. "This place has such a positive and welcoming vibe." Sometimes this threw donors for a loop—they expected places like the center to be depressing, but often they were the most joyful examples of the resilience of the human spirit.

"Yes, quite," Henry said quietly. "Extraordinary."

"It is such a wonderful place," Amina agreed. "I was a client, you know. I wouldn't be here if it wasn't for the center. If only we could guarantee its survival forever. The owners of the building are selling. We have been trying to pull together a fund, but the cost is substantial. It needs a whole new roof, rewiring of the electrical system—the upkeep would be astronomical. So in a few months we will be looking for a new site. It would be great to find somewhere bigger. We are bursting at the seams even now."

Lucia wondered if Henry was thinking what she was: that it was a shame they only had two million pounds to give. That amount could probably pay for a good chunk of the building cost, but the repairs and upkeep would be more. Of course, a large sum from his parents' foundation, even as a one-off gift, could maintain the building forever, like an endowment. They could build bedrooms on the upper floors, expand the child-care facilities. Hire more lawyers, run more campaigns to advocate for changes to the asylum system. It could be huge, if only they could access that larger pot of family money.

Henry's face was unreadable. Lucia thanked Amina and told her she'd be in touch, and Henry did the same, shaking hands. He managed a haphazard wave to the nursery staff on the way out, but the children were quietly listening to a story, his tenure as the evil monster already a distant memory.

They walked in silence down the street toward the Tube station. Lucia had experienced this before, the blank out, she called it. In Tamsin's case it was often because she was bored, but she didn't think that was what was happening here. Sometimes being faced with the reality of privilege, how lucky or unlucky one could be by the sheer circumstance of their birth, was sobering. It was easy to forget when inside one's own bubble, but site visits often drove it home for people.

"Penny for your thoughts?" Lucia said after a few minutes. "Or is it a pence?"

"Either works," Henry said, coming out of his fog. "Sorry. I was just thinking."

"About what?"

Henry was quiet for a moment before speaking. "My father's family, they are among the oldest of old money. As in 'close personal friends of Henry VIII who retained their heads' old money."

"I know," Lucia said. "You're basically royal."

"Indeed," Henry said with a wry smile. "On my father's side. But my mother's mother, she was actually born in Germany. Have you heard of the Kindertransport?"

Lucia shook her head.

"Just before the outbreak of the Second World War, Jewish children from places like Berlin, Prague, and Vienna boarded trains and boats alone to be evacuated to Britain, where they were resettled. My grandmother was one of them. She was brought up here, sent to good schools, met my grandfather, and became a full British citizen. Before she died, she told me stories about her childhood in Germany—she had so few fragments of memory to latch on to. My mother, on the other hand, never speaks of it. You would never know her own mother's maiden name was Schulz."

"Funny that," Lucia said. "Both of our grandparents were immigrants."

Henry smiled. "That must be why you and I get on so well. When we were in there, I was thinking about my grandmother, how she was taken in—how different her life would have been if she hadn't had people like Amina looking out for her and caring for her. How terrified and lonely she would have been in a new country. How fortunate she was. How fortunate I am." He looked at Lucia and placed his hands on her shoulders. "We have to do something."

"I'm glad you said that," Lucia responded. "Within your existing two-million-pound budget, we could begin by offering a six-figure unrestricted tester donation, maybe two hundred and fifty thousand pounds. Something that will allow them to find their feet in a new location. Once they settle in, we can set up a multiyear operating grant, maybe help them expand their reach . . ."

"No," Henry said. "Not just my money. And don't act like you didn't think about it, too."

She grinned wolfishly. "Yes, of course, we could use your money to buy the building, but if we really wanted to expand, we could . . ."

". . . get my parents to create an endowment, hundreds of millions, so the center can run in perpetuity, maybe expand across the country," Henry finished.

Lucia clapped her hands together and squealed. Henry looked mortified at her public display of emotion but smiled, anyway. "Yes! Yes yes yes," she said. "This is how we will get your parents on board with making bigger, bolder gifts. We can course correct the *Titanic*. Should we call our mission that? *Titanic*?"

"Absolutely not," Henry said. "I am all for code names, of course, but *Titanic* is too American and entirely too morbid."

"Hmm," Lucia thought. She only needed to cycle through a few other options before landing on the right one. "I know! Operation Bridget Jones. Featuring the OG Mr. Darcy himself, Colin Firth, and just like Bridget, our plan is crazy, lovable, but deserving of a happy ending."

"Done," he said. "Let Operation Bridget Jones commence. Let's authorize two hundred and fifty thousand pounds right now as you suggest but start quietly inquiring about the building purchase at the same time. I'll think about the best way to convince Mummy and Daddy this isn't about politics. It's about humanity."

"Up top," Lucia said, ebullient, raising her hand in the air, fingers splayed and ready to receive a high five.

Henry looked around to make sure no one was watching, then begrudgingly met her outstretched hand with his own. She headed back to the Tube as Henry hailed a passing cab.

Back at her desk, Lucia was on cloud nine, a miracle after how the day had begun. Her mind flashed back to the pipeline bombshell from earlier—she still couldn't believe the bank had agreed to it, and Celeste had let it happen—but she tried to stay focused on the positive. She couldn't wait to text Sooz about how amazing this project was. That night, she'd tell Ollie that it was worth it, all of it, because she was going to make a generational impact.

But first, there was a blinking red light on her phone that had to be attended to. She listened to her voicemail and then dialed the number that had been left. "Hi, is this Sandro? This is Lucia Gutierrez-Barrow from Eastern Currents, returning your call . . . Uh-huh. So, allow me to just confirm, you're Tamsin's dog groomer, and she told you that you could be a trustee of the new foundation? . . . OK, let me just start by taking down some details."

Chapter 13
Christmas, Actually

The laws of air mattress physics dictated that if one person moved, the other would be launched into oblivion. Holding her breath, Lucia carefully turned to face the window. Ollie stirred slightly under the covers but quickly settled back into a deep sleep.

This Christmas, with her in-laws, she had decided to take even the most minute victories as wins. The lead-up to the holiday had been exhausting, full of Christmas parties, Christmas drinks, Christmas dos, and Christmas dinners. She had been out every night and barely seen Ollie (which hadn't gone unnoticed).

Christmas was, in her mind, officially over, although they were still waking up in Moira's attic, the place where the least important guests were banished. Or at least that's what it felt like.

Marley was in Ollie's old room—the only change since his childhood were the guardrails added to the tiny single bed to keep her from rolling out. Otherwise, the room was a time capsule of posters of football players (the soccer ones), tennis trophies, academic-achievement certificates pinned up neatly on a flaking corkboard, well-thumbed comic books, and on the ceiling, a picture of three bikini-clad members of a British pop trio that even Lucia, culture vulture that she was, had never heard of. She was grateful that Marley was a stomach sleeper.

Moira had her own bedroom, of course, all dainty florals and chintz (Lucia could only assume, as she had never been invited in there), and Ollie's little sister, Isabel (the Princess to Ollie's Peanut), maintained her large room with a king-size bed. Lucia didn't begrudge her sister-in-law for wanting the most comfortable room, neither did she lay into her kind-hearted husband who doted on his sibling for not asking if they could have it, but none of those magnanimous feelings changed the fact that her back ached like she was 102 years old. She was counting down the hours, minutes, and seconds until she could return home to her normal, noninflatable bed.

Soon, but not yet. Christmas Day had passed, but there was one more holiday to celebrate: Boxing Day. What even was Boxing Day? No one had sufficiently answered that question for her, though she'd asked numerous times.

"Who cares, it's another holiday." Isabel shrugged. "Who wouldn't want an extra day of Christmas?"

Lucia started to raise her hand and then, remembering that she was supposed to be on her best behavior, pretended to use it to smooth down her hair instead.

Google said it had something to do with the day the well-to-dos boxed up their Christmas leftovers and gave their servants the afternoon off. She could not for the life of her imagine how a Tupperware full of congealed turkey and (ugh) brussels sprouts was anyone's idea of a gift, but she added it to the list of things she would never understand about her adopted homeland, along with cricket, tea, and why a word spelled Cholmondeley was pronounced "Chumlee."

The root of the holiday mattered less than the fact that Boxing Day meant adding yet another cheer-filled twenty-four hours of family fun to her already interminable-seeming exile to the countryside.

There was a meal to be eaten, and after much negotiation, Moira had agreed to let Lucia cook. She was going to make a crowd-pleaser: *arroz con pollo*. The classic, pan–Latin American chicken-and-rice dish was simple, flavorful, and not too spicy. And it reminded Lucia of a different time, when her grandparents hosted big *Noche Buena* dinners on Christmas Eve. After a day of cooking and serving food at the migrant centers where they volunteered, they would sit down to a large, jovial meal with all their church and neighborhood friends, people Lucia called her aunts, uncles, and cousins— their lack of shared DNA was irrelevant. The next day, exhausted, her *abuela* would whip up her famous *arroz con pollo*, a simple one-pot dish that the three of them ate together in front of the TV.

Those days were wonderful. After her grandparents passed away, Lucia spent Christmases alone with a bottle (or three) of wine and a steady diet of rom-coms and takeout. That was until Ollie came along. His family had their own traditions, and he loved them so much that she did her best to go with the flow. But having Marley had changed things. Now that her daughter was old enough to eat solid food, Lucia ached to share one little piece of herself at that table.

She heard Marley's chatter downstairs, and since there was no way she was going to be able to fall back to sleep, she held her breath once more and rolled off the mattress with precision, turning back to make sure she hadn't disturbed Ollie before tiptoeing across the creaky floorboards and closing the door behind her.

She scooped up her daughter from Ollie's room, along with Marley's new appendage, a giant stuffed bunny that had been waiting for her under the tree yesterday, and brought both baby and bunny down to the kitchen. Moira's house was beautiful, she thought to herself as she looked out the window onto their pretty garden and beyond to the village green, covered in glistening frost. The tiny hamlet of Kington-on-the-hill was something straight out of *The Holiday*.

Despite the cold, the kitchen was toasty and comfortable, thanks to the AGA that warmed the entire room, including the flagstone floors. Lucia set Marley in her high chair and peered around to make sure no one was coming. Then she reached up in the cabinet over the fridge where she had hidden her espresso maker, portable foam-frothing wand, and bag of freshly ground beans so she could start her day properly.

She had just placed the *cafetera* on the stovetop when she heard a rustle behind her. "It's not what you think," she said, whipping around guiltily. "Phew, it's just you."

Ollie went to Marley first and tousled her hair, before giving Lucia a light kiss. She loved that he didn't care if she had bed head (she did) or morning breath (she *definitely* did). Those things didn't seem to register with him. "I can't believe you brought that," he said with a wry smile. "You better not let Mummy see it."

Lucia pulled her mug to her chest and gasped. "Never. I'd like to keep my head, thank you very much." She eyed the giant jar on the kitchen counter filled with instant coffee that Moira had probably purchased in 1981 and insisted was "just as good as what any spendthrift might get for three pounds twenty at a coffee shop."

The first time she'd stayed at her mother-in-law's, Lucia learned the hard way that she couldn't survive on expired Nescafé without experiencing major cappuccino withdrawal. Likewise, she discovered that Moira would take extreme offense if Lucia dared to express a preference for anything other than the ancient coffee crystals in the jar. Instead, she chose to hide her dirty habit from everyone.

"Is there enough for me?" he asked sheepishly. She expertly frothed the milk and prepared two steaming mugs. They brought their coffees, Marley, and the bunny into the living room, where the tree was still lit. Yesterday's opened presents were piled underneath, waiting to be enjoyed (or, in a few cases, regifted). Ollie went to light a fire in the hearth as Lucia sank into the soft couch with Marley snuggled on her lap.

"This is nice," she said. "Just the three of us. Four if you count Bunny."

"Indeed," he said, blowing gently into the embers so the flames would catch. "I can't even remember the last time the three of us were together and all awake."

"Is that a jab at me?" she said, crinkling her nose in his direction. "Because last time I checked, you were out at your fair share of Christmas parties, too."

Ollie stood and looked over at Lucia—he started to say something, then stopped himself. "Sorry. You're right. I'm just tired. It's been a busy time for us both. I miss you, *cariño*. I feel like I never see you anymore."

Lucia heard sweetness in his words but also blame. Yes, she had been out—a lot—but so had Ollie. Plus, most of it was for work—she was out with clients, not friends. Meanwhile half of his Christmas events seemed to be with his mates, Gaz and Pip and, ugh, the dreaded Belly and her lack thereof. She'd hoped to escape them this week, but no such luck. They had all grown up in the same village and were back home in their childhood bedrooms, too. Lucia felt a fresh pang of jealousy over their decades of shared history, a history that didn't include her.

But it was still Christmas (or Boxing Day), and he had the home-court advantage. Moira's house was not neutral territory on which to launch a battle.

"I'm sorry, too, love, it's just been crazy. Things will be quieter in January." She didn't know that but hoped it was true. She would will it to be so.

"And hey," she said as she pulled him in toward her. "It's Christmas. Look at how happy our baby is."

They both focused on Marley, who had wriggled out of Lucia's arms to seek out the other gifts she hadn't played with yet, and the moment of tension passed.

They sat quietly, the oversize bunny between them, until they heard noises coming from the bedroom upstairs. "That'll be Mummy," Ollie said. "Better drink fast."

Lucia downed her coffee—it scalded her throat, but that was better than getting yelled at—and readied herself to face yet another day of the most wonderful time of the year with her mother-in-law.

Morning pleasantries exchanged, Lucia excused herself to get dressed, lingering as long as she could without a search party being sent upstairs to find her. Finally, when she had brushed every strand of her freshly straightened hair at least forty-five times, she went back down into the fray. Breakfast was over, and the dishes were done. She might as well get a head start on the arroz con pollo, she thought, which was always better the longer it simmered.

She lost herself in the comfortable rhythm of chopping, peeling, and stirring when she heard the door to the garden creak open and a voice that was her own personal equivalent to nails on a chalkboard.

"Whatever is that smell? It's quite potent."

"Oh come on. Her? Now?" Lucia muttered under her breath as she took a swig from the bottle of white wine next to her. She only needed a cup for the arroz con pollo, but no one else needed to know that.

"Belly," she said as her alleged friend/actual nemesis swanned into the kitchen decked out in head-to-toe Lululemon. Somehow Belly managed to look sun-kissed, like it was August in Spain and not UV-free December in Britain. Lucia, wearing a frilly lavender apron that was spattered in the red-and-yellow sauce that was bubbling in the pot, tried her best to greet her graciously. "That 'potent smell' is arroz con pollo, a Latin American delicacy," she said standing up straighter. "And our lunch."

"Part of it at least," said Ollie's sister, Isabel, breezing into the kitchen in an equally glam ensemble. "Keep up the good work, Lucia," she said as she crossed the room to greet Belly with air-kisses. The two of them, Belly and Bellz, were (of course) best friends from school. "Ready?"

"Off to restorative yogalates?" Lucia said, wishing she could take just one more swig of wine without them noticing.

"Lulu, you cad," Belly laughed. "You know we're training for the tri next month. No breaks for us!" She gave Lucia a poisonous smile. "Thank you so much for your donation, by the by. You were both too, too generous. I love seeing Ollie's name at the top of my fundraising site. Yours, too, naturally.

You must be making quite a bit of dosh yourself these days given how hard he says you're working."

"Is that Belly?" Ollie called out as he entered the kitchen. "Ah, I thought I heard your dulcet tones. Off for a run then? Don't get lost in the forest."

"Oh you are naughty," Belly said. "Remember that time we spent all night out there?" She grinned up at him in a way that activated nausea in Lucia that was completely unrelated to the vast quantity of pinot grigio sloshing around in her stomach.

"I have a vague recollection," he said, looking down at a fascinating spot on the floor. Lucia couldn't be sure in the dim kitchen light, but was he blushing? Before Lucia could react, he backed out of the room.

There was an awkward pause. Lucia wondered if this would be an appropriate moment to take a swing at Belly, maybe knocking out a tooth or two. ("Mind the shot," she'd warn as she recoiled her arm and launched her fist toward Belly's face.) But just then, Isabel grabbed Belly's sleeve and pulled her out the door.

"Let's go, I have so much to tell you. Bye, Lucia," her sister-in-law said as she and Belly jogged away at a brisk clip. Lucia watched them pass through the garden and head through the gate into the meadow, their high ponytails bouncing with each step. "A triathlon," she huffed to herself. The only triathlon Lucia could imagine training for right now was one that involved sleeping, drinking, and working. Maybe she'd email Belly and ask her to sponsor her for that.

Lucia unlocked her phone to check her email, a reflex in moments of stress. She was like one of Pavlov's dogs, she realized, except instead of salivating at a bell, she threw herself into work whenever something, or someone, at home pissed her off. Tristan had sent her a note:

Thought you might need this to survive the interminable yuletide season. You'll have noticed that by Boxing Day, the Brits are all quite feral. Bisous from Barbados xx

There was a link to an article with the headline "What the Brits Say vs. What they Mean." Ha! She scrolled down to the first one: "what a bold sentiment" meant "you are totally insane." She wished she had seen this before she started working at the bank—her ideas had been called bold at least half a dozen times.

She read most of the article, committing the phrases to memory, until the pot bubbled up again, demanding her attention. She put down her phone and turned the fussy AGA down to a simmer. A peppery saffron smell filled the kitchen, and she was, for a fleeting moment, transported to her childhood. Even though she had halved the spice quantities in an attempt to meet Ollie's family's palates where they were, the scent was familiar and warm.

Lucia ran upstairs to finish packing. She had insisted, as sweetly as possible, that they leave after lunch, making up an excuse about needing to get home to do some laundry before the workweek started.

"Mummy can do that for us" was Ollie's response, but when she replied that her mother-in-law would only wash her underwear over her dead body, he conceded.

She left the bags in their attic room so as not to seem too eager and went back downstairs to check on the arroz. Almost done. Moira was in the kitchen reheating leftovers from yesterday's Christmas lunch.

"Moira, you don't have to do that," Lucia offered. "I've made enough arroz to feed us and probably the whole village. And their visiting relatives."

"Oh, it's no trouble. I just thought we might give people options, in case anyone wants something a bit more *traditional*."

Lucia frowned. "This dish is traditional to me, you know."

"Yes, yes, dear, of course it is . . ." Moira trailed off, turning her back to Lucia as she reached up to retrieve a stack of plates from the cabinet and set them down next to the utensils that were ready to be parceled out to their places.

Lucia stifled a sigh, and then hollered to her husband in the living room. "Ollie, can you come set the table, please?"

"Don't worry, Peanut," Moira shouted in response from the kitchen. "You rest up. I'll do it. I'm nearly done here." She walked out of the kitchen and started making up each place setting. "He works so hard during the week, don't you think, Lucia? We ought to let him have a little break while we ladies take care of things."

Two more swigs of wine later, everything was ready to eat (also, the bottle was empty). Lucia felt a mix of pride and nerves as she scooped out the arroz con pollo onto their plates. She loved how the bright yellow of the rice, red of the peppers, and green of the peas popped on the backdrop of Moira's vintage blue-and-white Royal Doulton china. This meal in this setting was like her and Ollie, she thought wistfully. They shouldn't go together, but they did. A tear came to her eye. She realized she was a little bit drunk.

Lucia sat down, and after Moira led them in saying grace, she dug in. She sighed to herself, savoring the flavor of the first bite. A bit bland, but it was the same taste she remembered from her childhood. She was proud of how well the meal had turned out. She closed her eyes, just for a moment, in silent prayer to her grandparents, and then opened them to survey the response around the table.

First, she looked at Marley, who took a big bite and did not spit it out (the equivalent of bestowing Lucia with a Michelin star). Then over to Ollie. "Darling, it's spectacular," Ollie said, his mouth partially full. "Why haven't you made this for me before? I love the combination of flavors. Don't you think, Mummy?"

"Mmm," Moira said, making a big show of taking a small bite. "It's quite good, Lucia, thank you."

"Yes," Isabel replied. "Quite good. I'm just going to refill this water jug for us. Spicy."

Lucia felt her stomach sink. The third entry in the article from Tristan covered use of the term *quite good*. To Brits, she recalled clearly, it meant "hugely disappointing."

She hadn't thought, not once, when she and Ollie were dating that she would stick out like a sore thumb in his universe. Her fantasies, rooted firmly in British rom-coms, always featured her picking up a Victoria sponge at an adorable little bakery as she crossed Hyde Park to meet her best friend, Elizabeth Poshington, at her quirky but altogether charming city-center flat. Lucia's difference would be her superpower; they'd all adore her Latina spice, her American accent, her brightly colored clothes and bubbly personality and the fact that she was not the same as the rest of them. Never did she imagine a world like the one she was in—a place where no matter how hard she seemed to try, she would never be accepted for who she was.

Lucia was quiet as she finished eating. Ollie had seconds, but she had lost her appetite. Marley's big yawns provided the perfect excuse to make a speedy exit before her nap time.

"Thank you, Moira," she said, offering her mother-in-law a limp hug. "I had quite a good time."

On the way home, Lucia fell silent, lost in her own thoughts, but her feelings of doom seemed to lessen the farther they traveled from the boundary of the village.

It wasn't until they were on the highway that she noticed Ollie was strangely pensive, as well. He looked straight ahead, not glancing over at her once, not even when "All I Want for Christmas Is You" came on the radio, a song that usually provoked an automatic reaction; neither of them could resist belting it out at the top of their lungs. But this time, as Mariah crooned and Lucia started to sing along (off-key), his lips stayed firmly pressed in a line, his eyes focused on the road. She didn't dare to venture a guess as to why.

Chapter 14
Bartholomew's

It was a relatively quiet February afternoon on the eighth floor. January had passed in a melancholy blur. Everyone around Lucia had embraced dry January where they didn't drink alcohol for the month. This boggled her mind. If there was ever a time anyone needed a cocktail, it was in January, the dreariest, coldest, most miserable month of the year.

Somehow they had made it through, and now February, with its short gray days, was nearly over. The parents of the older children, beholden to the school calendar, had settled back into their usual work routines after the half-term break, their memories of snow-dusted ski slopes, hot tubs, and mulled wine long forgotten. Why, Lucia wondered, would you ever spend money to leave one cold place to go on vacation in another, even colder one?

Brendan was still away, having decamped to his holiday home in Marbella with his wife (about whom Lucia was eternally curious—was she entirely lacking in good judgment? Or did she lose a bet?). Celeste had been only moderately pissy in his absence. So far it was a regular, run-of-the-mill, not-at-all-special Thursday. Until all hell broke loose.

Lucia was taking a breather from the never-ending stack of dossiers to read a few thank-you letters that had arrived from Rona's grantees in Pakistan. Melissa was right—this was a highlight of the job. She was halfway through a note on a supersized greeting card signed by the Pakistani girls' cross-country team Rona had funded for a championship race in Malaysia, when she heard the distinct crunch of four-inch heels on carpet. She half expected the glass of water beside her to start rippling. Celeste was on the warpath.

Lucia froze, bracing for impact, but Celeste marched past her desk, instead stopping in front of Melissa's. Though immediately sorry for her friend, Lucia couldn't help but feel a little bit relieved.

Melissa, who had not been skiing the week prior, was shutting down her laptop and getting ready to head out. She didn't flinch as Celeste towered over her and, in full earshot of everyone in the office, began to rail.

"How dare you go behind my back for this nonsense? And where do you think you are going?"

"Celeste," Melissa said calmly without even a hint of fear in her voice (as it was, Lucia was afraid enough for them both). "I didn't go behind your back. I told you I was starting an internal petition to get the bank to divest from the Taraknor pipeline project and all future fossil fuel investments. I also told you," she said as she zipped up her purse, "that my daughter has a piano recital today and I would be leaving early."

Celeste released a torrent of French expletives. "Do you not understand our position here? I could not have been clearer about one voice. That meant internally, as well. We are trying to raise our profile in the bank for our impact, not your silly attempts to stop one project. It's not about a single project; it's about all of it."

No one was even pretending to work. They stared at Melissa and Celeste like they were watching a scene from a soap opera and one of them was about to slap the other at any moment. Lucia realized she had been holding her breath and tried to exhale quietly so as not to draw attention to herself.

Melissa lowered her voice, but Lucia could still hear her. "Please, Celeste. Let's discuss this rationally, like adults, but later and not in front of everyone." She gestured at her coworkers, who, on cue, looked down at their screens, embarrassed to have been caught openly gawking. "OK?"

Celeste was breathing heavily, only then seeming to notice that she had become the office spectacle. "I expect you in my office first thing tomorrow morning." She turned on her heel and headed back to her desk.

"Yes, of course, Celeste," Melissa said loudly, a way to make Celeste feel like she had won. Lucia was in awe of her bravery. She had seen the petition and made an excuse not to sign it, worried that it would piss off Celeste and put her work with Henry at risk. She tried to make eye contact with Melissa, to offer a look of solidarity, but Melissa cast her glance downward as she made her way out.

Tristan sidled over to her desk. "I don't know about you, but I really need a drink tonight."

Lucia's muscles unclenched. "Jeez, me, too," she replied. "But just one. I want to be home in time to eat dinner with Ollie."

Tristan had finally stopped "hazing" her, as he'd called it, and they had formed a friendship based on hating Celeste and a shared passion for snark.

Lucia was still getting accustomed to this nicer version of Tristan, so when their cab pulled over onto a quiet side street in Mayfair, she immediately rifled around in her purse to pay the fare. "I've got money somewhere," she said.

"No worries, Luce," he said, tapping his phone to the cab's credit card reader. "It's on the bank. Haven't you learned? Never, ever pay for anything, especially your own cab fare."

"Even a social outing?" Lucia laughed. "I guess any outing with you is technically work. I have to admit, not paying for anything myself has been easier to get used to than I expected."

They disembarked onto the sidewalk, Tristan leading Lucia by the arm while using his free hand to send a text. The pair wandered away from the lights of Old Bond Street, where the highest-end designers jockeyed for space and eyeballs, each putting on a more eye-catching display than the next. She didn't know whom their wares, wild and extravagant, were for. With the exception of Tamsin, her clients wouldn't be caught dead in garish dresses with thigh-high slits or dripping in diamonds (or, in the case of the outfit Tamsin wore to the inaugural board meeting of her new foundation, both). Their tastes skewed boring: muted tones, classic cuts, and understated accessories, all ridiculously expensive, of course, even if they didn't look it. Although there was something to this—Lucia had recently found herself judging people for showy sartorial choices she would have once found glamorous.

During the day, Mayfair bustled with office workers, tourists, and ladies who lunched, but after 5:00 p.m., it was dead. Tristan guided them onto a side street lined with one-room art galleries. They too were shut for the night, their doors locked tight. Lucia caught a glimpse of a Picasso pencil drawing and a small Basquiat canvas in a window, just waiting for a buyer with six figures to drop on a random weekday afternoon.

No one frequented this part of Mayfair for the nightlife, but Tristan said he was taking her somewhere she had never been and "wouldn't ever get into, anyway." Her curiosity was piqued. Friday would be busy, but she had vowed not to work this weekend. Just one drink and a quick bitch session about Celeste and she'd be home and in bed before you could say, "Gin martini, hold the olives." She really needed to blow off some steam.

The Melissa debacle had capped off a few weeks that had been a mixed bag, to put it mildly. She was grateful for the amazing opportunities she had to do good work that made a real impact. She and Henry had paid another visit to Amina's North London center to meet the two new trauma therapists hired with his funding. The first grant to the center from Henry's discretionary fund had gone surprisingly smoothly with no pushback at all from the trustees (it didn't hurt that the donation was timed to just before the end of the foundation's fiscal year, always helpful for tax purposes).

Rona, too, was doubling down on her funding commitments to girls across South Asia. Lucia had had the pleasure of calling Seema, the director of the girls' school in Pakistan, to confirm their bank details for the additional donation Rona was making to them; those moments were precious highlights.

They were worth the little trade-offs and compromises she made along the way. Tamsin was . . . Well, she was Tamsin. Lucia sent over documents detailing her legal responsibilities as a charity trustee; in return she received TikToks of elaborate dog birthday parties. At least, she had gotten Tamsin to agree to set up a scholarship fund for trainee veterinarians on the grounds that it would allow for more operations on dogs. Any money Lucia could direct toward helping humans was progress.

Progress or not, her workload felt like it had doubled, especially now that Celeste seemed to be leaning on her more, asking Lucia to take on clients that probably should have been Melissa's. Lucia couldn't wait until GIFGAL, just six short weeks away. She wasn't going, of course, but Celeste was. One whole week without Celeste seemed almost too good to be true. Lucia was planning to arrive late, leave early, and you know, spend some actual quality time with her family every day her boss was out of the office.

In the meantime, cocktails were sure to help with the guilt.

Tristan stopped in front of a black iron gate. "Hold on, Yank," he said pulling Lucia back by her elbow—lost in thought, she had continued walking. "We're here."

"We're where, exactly?" Lucia replied, backtracking to where Tristan was standing in front of a tall, redbrick neo-classical building that looked like it had once been someone's luxurious private home. There was no signage, nothing bearing a name, just a solitary iron lamp with a flickering flame. "I thought we were going for a drink. Are you going to murder me?"

"If I was going to murder you, I wouldn't choose somewhere as cliché as a dark alley. And you'd never see it coming." His mouth slyly turned up at the corners, and she was only the tiniest bit terrified.

Tristan opened the gate and led the way to an oversize plain wooden door. So plain in fact it was almost as if it was designed to be intentionally unremarkable. He pulled down on a braided cord. Lucia heard no bell, but the door was suddenly opened by a sleek-looking woman dressed all in black. "Welcome back, Mr. Adebayo," she purred, receiving his coat with her out-stretched arms. "I see you've brought a guest."

Lucia stood dumbfounded, rubbernecking as if she had entered Narnia. The lobby was dark-wood paneled, with a roaring fire and, over the mantle, a large portrait of a refined-looking British gentleman in a three-piece suit. A central atrium rose at least five floors, each reached by a long twisting staircase, and somewhere inside, she could hear the sound of a cocktail shaker shaking what was sure to be a martini.

She was still frozen in awe when she noticed the hostess's outstretched hands. Was she expecting an entry fee? What did one offer for admission into a place like this? Gold bars? State secrets? A blood oath?

Or, she realized, coming back to her senses, the hostess was simply gesturing for her coat. Lucia shuffled out of it and passed it over. "I thought you were asking for my ID," she joked. "You know, to card me?"

Tristan groaned in response.

They were led down a long hallway lit on either side by softly glowing glass orbs. Off the corridor, she caught glimpses of lush sitting rooms, each full of people laughing and clink-ing glasses. She thought she smelled cigar smoke.

"Tristan," she whispered loudly. "Are people smoking in here? I thought you weren't allowed to smoke inside anymore."

"She's never been here before," Tristan told the hostess. "Obviously." He looked back at her, snorting. "Relax. You look tighter than Celeste's forehead. Welcome to Bartholo-mew's, where you can do pretty much anything you want."

"What is this place?" she asked out loud this time.

"London's oldest and most exclusive members' club," the hostess responded as they turned a corner and headed up a set of stairs. "We have been operating consistently since the 1650s."

"It's impossible to get in," Tristan added. "In fact, you wouldn't be here if it wasn't for me. Remember that."

They were ushered into a large room with a massive bar in the center. It hummed with energy but still felt intimate. She followed Tristan through a maze of leather armchairs and plush velvet sofas. "Oh bless, look at you," Tristan said facetiously. "Come now, let's get you a drink before you strain your neck."

"OK. But just one." She sank down into one of the buttery leather armchairs next to the fireplace, inhaling the mix of peat and cedar that permeated the air. Instead of being stiff and formal, the room was comfortable and worn in, confounding expectations—kind of like Tristan himself. "And then I've got to get home."

"Yes, of course, how is baby Maleficent?"

"Very funny. We both know there's only one Disney villain in our life. Although damn her, she does look good in purple and black. I seriously could not believe how she raged on Melissa in front of everyone today."

"You couldn't?" Tristan was skeptical as the waitress arrived with their martinis. "It has been quite the week with the Dragon, but you should know by now her favorite form of humiliation is public," he replied. "However, I agree that she has been on the warpath of late. We all saw her little outburst at your desk on Tuesday." She had nearly forgotten (or willfully blocked out) the other Celeste debacle of the week. Lucia had been on the phone with a client's grantee from Mexico, chatting excitedly in Spanish, when Celeste marched over, grabbed the phone out of her hand, and rudely hung up the receiver. "Shut up your ridiculous nonsense," she had yelled at Lucia in front of the entire office.

Lucia reddened at the memory.

"Aw, Luce, don't let it bother you too much. Brush it off and get your work done. You can't take her too seriously. You need to be more like me," he said, catching a glimpse of his reflection in the mirror on the wall and smiling at himself. "Celeste is just a means to an end."

She took a sip of the martini, so perfectly chilled that she wondered if they tested the temperature at the bar before bringing it to the table. God this place was nice. "And what end is that? World domination?"

"In a manner of speaking," he replied. She laughed, but Tristan went on. "I'm not joking. You know I'm biding my time here in London, in philanthropy. It was the only client-facing job I could get, and my father has insisted I get 'proper banking experience' before I come home."

"What?" she said, clutching a set of invisible pearls to her chest in mock horror. "You mean to tell me that philanthropy isn't your deepest, most soul-affirming passion? I never would have guessed."

"Christ no," he exclaimed. "I mean, it's lovely doing good. But dribbles of generosity here and there, that's not going to solve anything. No, my sweet little dolt, I'm just learning, watching, waiting to pounce." Tristan signaled for another round. "And, by pounce, I mean lead Nigeria into the solar revolution."

She snorted. "Oh yeah? You and whose bank account?"

"Um, mine. I'm the heir apparent to Addixo Oil. You didn't know that?" He laughed. "Maybe you should do a dossier on me."

Lucia nearly choked on her drink. Addixo was one of Africa's biggest oil companies. She knew Tristan had money, but she had assumed he was rich . . . not, like, rich rich. She told him as much.

"Correct, darling, I'm one of us," he said.

"One of them, you mean," Lucia said, taking another sip, noting a hint of elderflower. Delicious. She'd have just one more after this, and then she'd go home.

"Come on," he said. "It's privilege, and you've got it. You scream it from your bag to your shoes to your holier-than-thou attitude." He placed his hands in a prayer position.

"Please," she said. "My grandparents were working-class, friend. I went to public school—and not like a British public school, the free, state-funded kind. I attended college on a full scholarship."

"Poor thing, I'm sure you had a tragically humble little-match-girl upbringing with barely enough money to go to the mall on the weekends. Doesn't matter now," he said. "You have a full-time nanny and a husband who has the money and sense to buy you this season's Balenciaga," he said, pointing to her bag.

"Christmas present," she gulped, pushing the purse under her chair.

"I'm just saying, we're different but not that different. You're hobnobbing with the point-one percent, but you are the one percent. Just own it."

He wasn't wrong. She was of course aware of the fact that her marriage to Ollie had put her in a different social class, but she hadn't stopped to think about how different she might have become because of the move, and now the job. Was she a rich person?

Nope, absolutely not, she thought. She was still the same. Just a bit buzzed. She needed to get home, not drunk, just as she had planned. "I should go, it's a school night. Let me get this round," Lucia said, catching their waitress's eye and making the universal sign for "bring me the check."

"Put that plastic away," he hissed. "What did I tell you in the cab?"

"I was listening. It's my corporate card."

"Money does not change hands here. Everyone operates on the honor system, and anyway, Eastern Currents has an account. This is a business dinner after all. Well, a liquid dinner. Order me another will you? I need to go powder my nose."

Tristan was quickly swallowed by the crowd, leaving Lucia on her own.

She pulled out her phone and shot Ollie a quick text:

Hi babe. Getting the bill and then coming home. I think I've finally convinced Tristan to be my friend.

The response came back quickly:

Don't rush, love. Belly and Caz popped by, and we're going for a quick dinner. Marley's with Mummy, so all is well. Well done on Tristan, I knew he'd come around. Miss you. xx

She felt a rush of emotions: Guilt at the thought of Moira snuggling Marley, drying her soft skin after the bath, putting her down. Fury with a dash of jealousy at the thought of Belly, again. Maybe one day she'd write a book called *Belly, Again*. It would be a horror novel.

Why was he spending so much time with her, anyway? She knew they were friends, old friends, but why didn't Belly's husband ever show up to these impromptu *tête-à-têtes*? And why was she thinking in French, she admonished herself. She had been spending too much time with Celeste.

She slumped back into her chair, deciding what to text in response. She could rush home to head off Ollie, but a feeling of doubt gave her pause. Maybe he didn't want her to come home. Maybe he'd prefer to spend the evening with Belly. It would be lovely, they could reminisce and gossip about their friends, and he could pretend he was still in his old life, the one he'd had before he was saddled with her.

When they were in Texas—which seemed like a lifetime ago—she was sure they were two halves of a whole. But maybe, like timber in a cold climate, their pieces had warped and changed shape. Maybe they didn't fit together so well, after all.

It was a maudlin thought. She knew herself well enough to realize that rushing home now would only result in an argument where her temper might snap and her jealousy would get the best of her.

She couldn't let that happen. They had never had a big fight. Ever. Secretly, she worried about whether their relationship, built on love-at-first-sight-type romance and not a lot of getting-to-know-each-other time, could survive it.

Instead of rushing home, there was another option, the option where she had another martini, or maybe two, and forgot all about stupid Belly.

Thanks, babe, she texted back. **Miss you, too.** She added a kissy-face emoji at the end for good measure and put her phone back in her bag just as Tristan returned to the table.

"Let me guess," he said. "A good night text to little Molly?"

"Shows how much you know," she lied, wanting to put all thoughts of her home life behind her. The gin made her feel warm inside. "I was just checking my work email. It was Mrs. Kalaya, writing to make sure all the children at the orphanage will be wearing her company's branded caps in the photo we take." She gave an exaggerated shrug. This cringe-worthy request had in fact come through just before she'd left, but Tristan didn't need to know that.

Tristan sighed theatrically. "Luce, you bleeding heart. You're doing it all wrong, you know."

"Blah blah, keep your head down, don't get attached," she mimicked his voice. "That's never been an easy one for me." Lucia thought about Amina and the center. She was willing to put up with all manner of Celeste-ian outbursts if it meant getting what she wanted for her grantees. She crossed her legs and leaned toward him conspiratorially. "So what am I doing wrong? Caring too much? Enlighten me, oh wise one."

"You are working so bloody hard to row against the current when all you need to do is let it sweep you up. Take me, for example. My family are Nigeria's third-biggest charitable givers. Yes, we've done some good, but it's a drop in the proverbial bucket. Real change, sustainable change, will come when we can switch the entire company to solar. I wasn't kidding about the revolution. I'm going to do it."

"And I'm proud of you for that." She raised a glass to toast him. Another two martinis had materialized on the table while she wasn't looking. "What does that have to do with me?"

"The way I'm going to get there is to work *within* the system. I need to prove to my father I can handle a corporate job, not shake things up too much until I'm in charge. Then I won't just have the money, I'll have the power. The influence. The networks. That's how I'm going to make the real change. Trust me, I've been here long enough to know that without power, you're nothing. Even if you have money. You need to be palatable, accepted. Then you can usher in your own agenda. I learned it from the best."

"Who? Your dad?"

"No, *le grande dame* herself. Celeste, that evil witch." Tristan looked like a cat who had caught a canary, alight with the glow of good gossip. "You know, I knew her from before. Or knew of her. She used to be an activist. She was arrested, at least twice, for sabotaging Addixo's drilling operations."

"Celeste? Our Celeste?" Lucia tried to imagine her boss burning her custom Agent Provocateur bras and failed.

"The very same. When I was hired, my dad sent me a photo he had of her protesting his oil company. He told me to watch out for the 'radical influences' at Eastern Currents." Lucia snorted. "Once I'd earned her trust, she told me the whole story—how after her last arrest she left the country and went home to Paris to lick her wounds, how frustrated she was that she put her body and reputation on the line and no one cared and nothing changed. She went and got an MBA at the Sorbonne and started working at Eastern Currents. She realized that she could beat them at their own game."

Lucia scoffed at the assertion. "Maybe she's playing their game a bit too well. That must have been what she was doing today when she reamed out Melissa in front of everyone, not to mention letting the bank invest in the Taraknor pipeline in the first place." Her voice was soft, but the comment was sharp in a way that surprised even her.

"Touché," Tristan replied, cocking his head to one side as if noticing an edge to Lucia he hadn't seen before. "But you're still missing the point. She'll be in charge soon, and then she can make everything happen."

Lucia was tempted by this fantasy. In fact, it sounded downright logical. Work hard, amass power and influence over those with the most money, then do good at a level you couldn't from outside. Maybe Celeste wasn't crazy; maybe she was brilliant.

"This could be the gin talking, but you might be making sense."

"Did someone say gin? Sorry, loves, we're moving on. Flaming tequilas all around please," a voice above her interjected.

She looked up to see Henry Perry standing over them with a tray of shot glasses and a blowtorch.

Henry placed the tray down and greeted Tristan first, whispering something in his ear that made him laugh. He put his hand on his back and rubbed it slowly up and down, seductively. Was it possible they were flirting?

"Oh drat, I forgot the lime. I'll be right back," Henry said and beelined to the bar.

"Hey, let me ask you something about Henry," she said.

"Will he allow you to skip these shots? Absolutely not." She hadn't taken a shot since college, but she was so far gone already, what was one more? "One, you're practically Mexican." She shot a dirty look at him. "And two, you can't say no. The client is always right."

"Is Henry gay?"

He looked at her like she was an idiot. "Are you having a laugh? It's the worst-kept secret in town."

"Does his family know? I know they are . . ." She grasped for the right words, vocabulary eluding her. "Traditional," she settled on, cringing at the memory of the last time she heard that word: a barb straight from her mother-in-law's pursed lips.

"He's told them. Many times. But they continue to ignore him. Everyone else knows, though. Henry is out and proud. As out and proud as a very reserved Englishman can be. Speak of the devil." Henry was back with limes, salt, and a wicked grin. "Henry, darling, Lucia and I were just discussing your homosexual proclivities."

"Ah yes. They've tried to beat them out of me, but they continue to return, I'm afraid." Henry smiled, and Lucia leaned in for the double air-kiss.

"I suppose that explains why you didn't try to ravish me when we first met," she said. Oh god, she really was drunk. "I usually have that effect on men."

"Sadly, you're not my type. But in every other way, my dear, you are truly delightful." If the lights were brighter, they might have seen Lucia blush. "It's why I do what I do, didn't you know? I have to be the family agitator. Even though it may not seem like it, I know keenly what it feels like to be an outsider."

The rest of the night was a blurry haze of smoke, gin, and tequila and more gin and eventually some absinthe. Whatever happened, it was enough to make her forget all about Celeste, and Belly, and how awful her hangover would be in the morning. At some point there was dancing. On a table.

Before she knew it, she was in the back seat of someone's town car and at her front door. She shushed them all (loudly) as she tiptoed inside. She might have been wasted, but not wasted enough to court a Marley wake up.

Lucia peeked in on her baby first—sound asleep and breathing softly—and then turned toward her bedroom door with trepidation. What if Ollie wasn't inside? Her heart started to beat faster as she put her hand on the knob, turning it quietly. When she saw the large, snoring mound, she let out a huge sigh of relief.

Ollie was there—of course he was there. Where he had been before, what he had been up to, and with whom was another matter—but it was one that, in her inebriated state, she wasn't going to uncover tonight.

He stirred only slightly as she curled her body up into his. It fit there so naturally, like they were both designed for this exact purpose. Asleep or awake, she wasn't sure, but he threw an arm over her and pulled her into him.

Tomorrow—or today, just a few hours from now—she'd be back at her desk. But for the moment, she burrowed deeper into the curve of Ollie's chest and tried to stop the room from spinning as she drifted off to sleep.

Chapter 15
Bloodshot

"Ma, Ma, Ma, *Mama*."

Lucia opened one eye; the other was crusted with sleep and refused to budge. She could just make out a smiling, beatific face, dark curls backlit by sun streaming in behind her. But this was no angel. It was Marley, straddled across her body, perched directly on top of her bladder.

"Good morning, Mama, good morning," Marley chirped, a tiny, energetic alarm clock. She bounced as she spoke, as if Lucia were a trampoline. If she pressed down on her stomach even one more time, Lucia was sure she was going to wet herself.

"*Buenos días, amorcita.*" She lifted Marley off her stomach and placed her on the bed. With Marley cradled in the crook of her arm, Lucia began to sit up, trying with all her might not to give in to the overwhelming urge to vomit. She did not know the time of day or day of the week and struggled to remember what the hell she had done last night. Hangovers in one's late thirties were not for the fainthearted.

She peeked under the covers: T-shirt, no underwear, one shoe, and a nasty bruise on her thigh. Lucia turned to face Marley, who reached for her cheek and pulled off something furry and caterpillar-like. One set of false eyelashes. Where was the other set? Also, whose false eyelashes were these? Not hers; she hadn't been wearing any.

"Let's go find Daddy, shall we?" Lucia got up, pulled on a pair of Ollie's sweats, and shuffled into the bathroom first, Marley toddling after her agreeably. She avoided looking in the mirror, not sure how much of a disaster she would find there, and then padded into the kitchen.

"Coffee?" Ollie asked, handing her a "World's Best Mum" mug. The irony. It was unclear if she could drink anything without heaving but was grateful for the gesture.

"Thanks. So, do you know what time . . ."

"You got home?" Ollie finished, leaning back on the counter. "Not sure. I got in just after midnight, and you were nowhere to be found. My phone however was fairly full."

Ollie handed his phone to Lucia.

[11:18 p.m.] Lucia: Hey boo. Still out. What about you? Is Belly there? Whatever. Love you xxxxxxxxx

[11:20 p.m.] Ollie: Still out, Belly sends a big kiss back.

[11:21 p.m.] Lucia: Blech.

[11:21 p.m.] Lucia: Sorry that was for Tristan, he said something gross.

[1:07 a.m.] Ollie: Home now and going to bed. Left you a glass of water next to your nightstand. Drink it.

Lucia had not.

[1:49 a.m.] Lucia: LOLLLLLLL Henry just told me a hilar jokke re queen victria and a priest, remind me when home, coming there soon ok byeeeeee

That was the last text message, but there was a voice memo. She pressed Play. It was a muffled conversation, and Lucia could tell she was yelling in Spanish.

She put her head down on the table in embarrassment, her curls cascading around her. The marble of the kitchen counter felt surprisingly cool and quite nice. "I'm never drinking again."

Ollie laughed. "I've heard that one before. Remember Paris?"

"Low blow," she said. "That was different."

Paris had been their first trip after Marley was born. The combination of not having consumed alcohol for months and being child-free for the night meant that she was feeling buzzed *before* they even sat down to dinner. And then, the wine came. Instead of spending the next day wandering along the Seine, taking in the sights of Notre-Dame and the Louvre, Lucia laid in bed while Ollie played nursemaid. He popped out quickly to buy her a ham-and-cheese croissant and a café au lait, and then they spent the rest of the day curled up together, binge-watching *Friends*. It was perfect.

"That was different," he sighed, looking wistful. "*Amor*, in all seriousness, though. I don't mind you cutting loose on a weeknight. But at the risk of sounding like a broken record, I feel like I barely see you anymore. We haven't been out together, just the two of us, in ages. I suspect Patricos has forgotten our regular orders."

"Um, maybe you forgot you were out last night, too?" The residue of her jealousy coated her memories of the previous evening's escapades. "Wait. Did you say weeknight?" She looked at the clock on the oven. It read 10:14 a.m. "What day is it?"

"Friday, of course. I'm working from home. But I really think we need to talk about balancing work and home life, and you know . . ."

"No! No no no no," Lucia exclaimed. "I am so late."

She sped around the kitchen counter, as fast as she could in her delicate state, and kissed Ollie on the cheek. "I'm sorry, love. I know it's been a lot. I hear you, I really do. Let's talk about it later, tonight. I have to run."

Ollie's eyes followed her as she went back into the bedroom, but she didn't turn around to scrutinize what they were saying to her.

Lucia hoisted herself into the shower. The idea of putting on a bra seemed too onerous, but somehow, miraculously, she managed to assemble a presentable enough outfit and transport her tender body to the office. On her way out of the Tube, she stopped at Starbucks. Now was no time for keeping up appearances. She needed sugar, and she needed it badly. One caramel Frappuccino and half a vanilla bean scone later, she donned her largest sunglasses and snuck into the office. Or attempted to.

"You are late," Celeste yelled from her office across the floor. Everyone looked up to watch Lucia's walk of shame.

"I was . . . out with a client last night," she said, throwing a glance at Tristan. He looked fresh and sunny and was drinking a green juice and smiling at her. How was it possible that he didn't feel as awful as she did? More practice maybe, she thought. And the superior alcohol-processing power of a younger liver.

"That is not an excuse. Don't get settled in. We go to the Perrys today *tout suite.*"

That tequila must have been one hundred proof. How else could she have forgotten about the Perry Foundation board meeting? Celeste always attended, since the elder Perrys were her clients, but Lucia had been invited to come along this time at Henry's request. They weren't ready to pitch Operation Bridget Jones yet—although the proposal they were working on was a thing of beauty—but Lucia thought meeting his parents and seeing how the foundation operated would be a great opportunity to gather intel and observe them in their natural habitat. Henry had agreed.

Also, Lucia couldn't help her curiosity about Henry's family. He spoke of them in veiled references and riddles when they came up at all, which, despite how much time they spent plotting and scheming and yes, drinking together, was relatively infrequent. She never sensed a lot of love in that relationship. Loyalty or duty, sure, but not affection.

She and Celeste got into the town car, and for once, Lucia was grateful for Celeste's habit of completely ignoring her whenever they were alone together. That way she could focus on her primary objective: trying not to throw up on Celeste's camel-colored cashmere coat.

Lucia must have dozed off because she woke up to a small puddle of drool on her own shoulder and peered out the window to see a security guard waving them through a set of tall wrought-iron gates.

"Blimey," the driver exclaimed as they drove down the gravel path bordered by manicured hedges on either side. She couldn't help but agree. When the drive opened up to a view of a mansion that put the Downton Abbey estate to shame, she and the driver both gasped in unison. Celeste rolled her eyes.

Lucia had been to the Perrys' London town house a few times before to drop off papers for Henry. It was impressive in the sense that having a whole house in the center of a big expensive city was impressive. The town house itself was lovely, but among her clients a city pied-à-terre in the shadow of Buckingham Palace was almost a prerequisite.

Their country estate, however, was something else entirely. Set against the backdrop of the stunning rolling hills of Hertfordshire, the palatial main house—with its sixteen sets of double windows across the front—was built of stone, weathered to perfection by history and time. Vines of ivy climbed the facade, making the towering palace look oddly quaint. Lucia thought she could make out a barn in the distance, bigger than her entire childhood home. What a shame she was married. And that Henry would not be interested in her even if she wasn't. This was the Pemberley of her wildest dreams.

In the distance, she saw a dog chasing a flock of sheep with unbridled joy. She had a fleeting thought that maybe stupid Belly had been right: You really did need a country house for your dog.

"Stop here," Celeste said to the driver, who reactively slammed on the brakes in the middle of the drive.

"Lucia," she said. It was probably the first time Celeste had said her name correctly without making it sound like a curse word. "Listen to me, this is important. I realize that you and Henry are working on his little personal projects," she said.

Did Celeste know about Operation Bridget Jones? Was she going to shut it down? As if this day could get worse, Lucia thought she was going to hurl, but she forced herself to look Celeste right in the eye.

"Well, let me just explain," Lucia sputtered, ready to say anything that popped into her mind to keep the project alive.

But Celeste held up a hand. "*Non*. This is not a problem. He has his small funds; he can do what he wants. It is good. I want you to keep Henry happy. He is not as important as the older brother but important still."

Lucia was relieved—she clearly had no idea what they were planning to pitch to the elder Perrys. Plus, Celeste's use of the word *good* sent a thrill down her spine. It didn't matter how awful she was, she desperately needed Celeste's approval. A therapist could have a field day with her mommy issues.

"But you must listen, the Perrys, they are not the same as Henry. Or as you and me." The same? The only similarity Lucia could imagine between her and Celeste was that they were both humans. Although, the jury was still out on Celeste, who had continued talking. "They are very old-fashioned, they like tradition and formality. They have a lot of money, and one day much of it will be Henry's. They are *vraiment importants*. For the bank, yes, but also for me. I have some significant things coming in the future. When I am in charge, maybe we will do things a bit different than Brendan."

This was the first time Celeste had ever referred to herself and Lucia as a *we*. Obviously, Lucia knew Celeste would take over, but she'd never considered what that might mean for her: a possible promotion? She hadn't dared dream but nodded vigorously now. "Absolutely," Lucia said, hangover momentarily forgotten, people-pleasing senses on high alert. "What do you need from me?"

"Today you must not, how do you say, rock the boat. You must not do your American thing where you say what you think. I hate it always, but especially here."

She resisted the temptation to roll her eyes in Celeste's face. "And you must keep Henry under control. Sometimes in these meetings he becomes upset, like a child. But it will not help him. Or you." She motioned to the driver to continue. "Or me."

Georgia, the family's assistant, gave them a cheery wave from the front of the house. Just before opening the door, Celeste put her hand on top of Lucia's and patted it. "Stay quiet, do not make them angry. In this way we will get what we want."

"Got it," Lucia replied, close to tears. Had she temporarily tamed the Dragon? She couldn't wait to tell Melissa.

They got out of the car, greeted Georgia, and followed her into the house. Lucia was trying so hard to keep her cool, but she could not resist a small "Wow."

"Oh yes, it's really quite special," Georgia assented. "It's on the site of an abbey from the 1100s, but the current structure was built sometime around the mid-1800s. The barn dates back to the 1600s, we think."

Thanks to Tristan's many lectures, Lucia had begun to differentiate between an old-money family home and a new-money family home. This was the *oldest* of old money. She'd visited Tamsin's mother's country pile just a few weeks before. That sprawling mansion had been purchased from a famous rugby star and his wife; although they did some redecoration, they had decided to keep the bathroom with the solid-gold toilet and taps as well as his-and-hers matching thrones in the formal living room. "Aren't they fabulous?" she'd said on the tour, without a hint of irony.

The Perry estate was the opposite: classic, full of heirlooms, and Lucia thought, a bit stuffy (although that could have been the hangover talking). Georgia led them into a large formal dining room, at the center of which sat a huge wooden table that could easily seat thirty people. The walls were covered in portraits of old men and women who must have been Perrys throughout history; they all shared the same excellent cleft chin.

Celeste made the rounds, saying hello to everyone, but Lucia felt a wave of nausea roiling and stayed near the door, leaning on the frame for support. This was worse than morning sickness.

Almost.

Henry, wearing jeans and a sweater with the collar of a button-down peeking out, caught her eye and walked over. He looked as refined as ever, completely unaffected by the alcohol.

"I'm sorry, but how are you this put together? Is the ability to get rip-roaring drunk and not show it something you all are born with here, or is it carefully honed and developed over time?" she asked, but as he came closer, she noticed his blood-shot eyes. "Thank goodness. I was beginning to think everyone else was drinking water last night and I was the only one down-ing tequila." She shuddered at the memory.

"No indeed, my morning was rough. But not as rough as yours, I suspect." He laughed, and she flashed back to a mental image of Henry walking over with a tray of flaming shots. "Only one of us danced on a table last night. I'll give you a hint—it wasn't me."

"Alright, Judgy McJudgerson," she said. "I'm here, aren't I?"

"How dare you, you peasant. It's Lord McJudgerson, if you please."

"Hold up," said Lucia. "Are you really a lord? Was I sup-posed to be calling you Lord Perry this whole time? I'm so sorry. Your majesty."

"Don't you dare ever call me anything but Henry. OK, let me give you a rundown on the assorted here before we start." Henry leaned in closer to Lucia's ear so no one else could hear. "Right, so Mr. Beans One, Two, and Three are the accountant, lawyer, and wealth manager, respectively." He was referring to a group of three men, all in black suits, with graying hair on the other side of the room. "Don't bother to learn their names. All they will do is agree with everything my parents say. And charge by the hour for the privilege."

"Got it, Messieurs Bean. And I'm guessing that put-together woman is your mother?"

"Yes, the lovely duchess. Mummy will be kind to your face but cruel behind your back. She is ruthless. Talk to her about horses and roses, and steer clear of any of your fanciful ideas about philanthropy being anything but a gift of kindness to the less fortunate. Always call her Your Grace."

"So what does that make you?"

"Well a lord, of course, but I never use my title in public."

"Indeed, milord." Lucia curtsied at him.

"Oh, do shut up." He laughed.

"And your brother? Is he a lord, too?"

She looked over to see a taller, stockier version of Henry, who appeared to be brimming with something like confidence . . . or was it arrogance? He cast his blue eyes—the same shade as Henry's—down at a cup Georgia had placed in front of him and sneered, sending it back. Arrogance.

"Billy? No, he's William, Earl of Cheshire. Eldest son gets to use Daddy's subsidiary titles."

"Christ, I should have had more coffee."

"I'll get you a cappuccino. With sugar." He gestured to Georgia to come their way. "No Starbucks in the vicinity, unfortunately."

"I love you for even suggesting it." He gave her order to Georgia. "Two sugars please," Lucia added. Georgia's eyes widened. "Certainly. I'm not sure we have any sugar in the kitchen, but I think there are sugar cubes in the barn. We feed them to the horses."

Lucia would have been mortified if she wasn't in such a needy state. She probably would have eaten hay if it had been covered in chocolate or bacon grease.

"Thanks, Georgia. Much appreciated."

There was only one unidentified person left, and even without the process of elimination, she would have recognized the duke anywhere.

"Yes," Henry said, following her eyes. "Daddy dearest."

Henry's father looked as if he had stepped right out of one of the paintings on the wall. He and Henry looked remarkably alike, but the duke's eyes, that same Perry blue, lacked the sparkle of Henry's. He had a hawkish nose, the family chin, and a cold, stern expression.

The duke moved toward the head of the table, and everyone else scurried to their seats. "Listen, Celeste said something weird to me in the car. She told me to make sure we don't rock the boat in this meeting. I don't think she knows what we're planning with Operation Bridget Jones, but still, I'm on high alert."

"Hmm," he murmured back. "Did you tell her where else she could shove that stick that's always up her backside? We're making change, dammit." His voice took on a louder tone.

"Shh," she said. "I hate to say it, but I think she's right. We've come too far; I don't want to jeopardize anything. It's too important. Let's just follow her advice, OK?"

Henry scowled. "I'm surprised to see you agreeing with Celeste on anything. However, I trust you. I'll try my best, but no guarantees. Mummy and Daddy hate when we argue in front of company." The look in his eyes made it clear that he didn't dislike it nearly as much as they did.

The duke's family flanked him in order of importance—his wife and William took the chairs on either side of him. Henry sat down one seat away from his brother, followed by Bean, Bean, and Bean. Farther down the line, Georgia, who had returned with Lucia's coffee (which smelled vaguely of manure but she was so desperate she didn't care), took her place to record the minutes. Celeste filled the following seat, while Lucia sat down in the spot farthest from the duke.

"Georgia, please note that the board meeting has officially commenced. It is thirteen hundred hours on Friday the twenty-sixth of February," the duke said in a booming voice.

"Yes, Georgia, make sure you spell that B-O-R-E-D," Henry piped up. His father glared at him. So much for hanging back, Lucia thought. Henry was indeed in a petulant mood. He winked at Lucia.

"Strike that please, Georgia. To continue—have we all reviewed the minutes from the last meeting? Can these be approved?"

"Approved," the duchess said.

"Seconded," all three Beans said at the same time, desperate to get their names in the minutes.

"One moment please," Henry said. Everyone turned to face him. "Last meeting, I proposed cutting our annual donation to Suffolk in half and giving the balance to the local state schools. Particularly those that are housing the largest influx of migrants. That has not made it into the minutes."

Suffolk, the public (i.e., private) school attended by generations of Perrys, including Henry, already had an endowment of £250 million, Lucia knew.

William bleated, exasperated. "This again?" he said. "I thought we voted you down already."

"Why yes, brother, you did," Henry said. "But it didn't make the minutes. I'd like it noted for the record."

"Dear, we discussed this," his mother said in the same soothing voice Lucia used to address Marley whenever she threw a tantrum over something like the sky being blue rather than her favorite shade of pink. "Suffolk is looking to build a new observatory. They need the funding. Don't you think children should have everything they need?"

"I do," he said, his voice rising in anger. "Like basic computers. Art supplies. A hot breakfast, for heaven's sake. Which the children in the state schools are missing."

"Henry, darling," his mother started again. "Why don't you use your discretionary fund to support this? Just ensure it's done anonymously."

"Anonymously, of course. I'd never dream of dragging our family name through the mud by associating with refugees and migrants, even though we all know we wouldn't even be here if not for the generosity of others, people who didn't care about being too political."

"Henry," his father barked. "Do not speak to your mother that way. This has already been decided. Georgia, the minutes are approved."

Henry leaned forward as if he was going to continue. Lucia glanced at Celeste, whose eyes were darting back and forth between the younger son and his father. She had to say something.

"Henry," Lucia said, mimicking his mother's soothing tone. "Your mother is right." She smiled generously at the older woman. "I'm happy to help you craft a grant from your funding to the local school. We wouldn't want to *jeopardize*"—she emphasized the word—"our time in this meeting by continuing along this vein of discussion."

Henry slumped back into his chair and stopped talking. His mother looked relieved, smiling gratefully at Lucia. His father ignored the entire outburst.

"Moving on. The parking facilities in front of the monument to Lord Nelson we funded in Hampshire are atrocious. Can we have a report on . . ."

She caught Henry's eyes and mouthed the word *sorry* at him, and then tapped her wrist. Patience and time, that's what they needed. He smiled back, but she could tell he was deflated. Lucia had spent her whole childhood wishing she had parents to fight with, but now she thought maybe she had been better off with her docile *abuelos* for company.

Henry didn't say anything else for the remainder of the meeting, during which no one spoke except to agree with whatever the duke was proposing. They finished at 2:00 p.m. on the dot. Celeste and Lucia said goodbye and got back into a waiting town car that would ferry them back to the office.

Celeste was quiet for the first part of the journey, but once they were clear of the Perry estate and back among the quaint thatched houses of the village, she spoke. "Lucia," she said. (Lucia perked up at the sound of her actual name being used twice in one day!) "Well done. You did a good job of controlling Henry's more outrageous tendencies. I knew I could trust you to do the right thing."

It was a victory of sorts. Lucia knew she should be glad Celeste was paying her attention, and not the toxic kind she has become accustomed to. Still, she couldn't help but feel like she had somehow sold Henry out.

"I need people I can trust around me. Not everyone on my team is trustworthy anymore." She eyed the driver and raised the partition between him and them. "For example, Melissa. This new campaign she is doing about divestment, *c'est ridicule*. Ridiculous. The bank will not quit the Taraknor pipeline. The only way to mitigate the worst of the damage is to stay close to the project, not go against it. Melissa doesn't seem to understand anymore what we are doing here and how to get things done."

Lucia opened her mouth to protest, but Celeste continued her rant.

"And what's worse, she has missed so many days lately. You are always in the office, and you also have a child, yet Melissa cannot seem to handle her responsibilities. It is true we need a proper charity person on the team, to show we are serious about our commitment to impact, nonprofits, whatever. But now we have you . . ." She looked away from Lucia and out the window.

"GIFGAL is coming, and it is too important to risk on someone I don't know if I can trust. What if her child gets a loose tooth? Will she fly home immediately? It is too important. Even Nigel will be there. We cannot have any mistakes."

Nigel Petersham, the CEO of the bank, was a key player. It would be important for Celeste to get him on her side if she wanted to replace Brendan once he retired.

Now she turned back and looked at Lucia with her clear, cold, wrinkle-free eyes. "I am asking you: Do you think Melissa is right for GIFGAL? For our team?"

The words were right there on the tip of Lucia's tongue: "Melissa is too good for GIFGAL, for the bank, and especially for you. She is the only person who won't compromise herself to get what she wants. She lives her values. That's more than I can say for anyone else here, and I wish I was more like her."

But nothing came out.

"Well?" Celeste said. "Do not sit like a gaping fish."

Lucia remembered the email she had gotten yesterday from Amina, with the floor plans for the North London center's new building. Henry's ambitions were increasing with every conversation they had, and Lucia couldn't help but get caught up in the excitement. If they pulled off Operation Bridget Jones and secured a nine-figure endowment from his parents, everything would change. They could afford the building, maintenance for years to come, and the expansion of their programs.

Yesterday, Amina had proposed the idea of the Perry Enterprise Center, which would help their clients set up and launch their own businesses. They'd offer seed funding in addition to business training, giving them a leg up at the start. She calculated that in two years alone, they could help seed five thousand businesses. That was five thousand immigrant families who would not only be able to pay their bills, but also take pride in starting something of their own, after losing everything. "We could be helping them thrive, instead of just survive," Amina had said.

What would her *abuelo* have done with that sort of support when he'd arrived in the US from Venezuela? Maybe he would have been able to pick up his engineering career where he'd left off, maybe invent something or start a business? Maybe instead of working as a janitor making minimum wage, he'd have had the time and space to come up with the next big thing in renewable tech. It was easy to dream about starting a solar revolution when you had Tristan's cash and connections. But without a safety net, a champion, or the basic language skills to succeed, it was much harder to convert those dreams into any sort of reality.

Celeste didn't want Lucia's opinion. She wanted her agreement. Lucia couldn't give that to her, but she also did not want to piss her off. If she made an enemy of her now, everything, all the sacrifices, all the nights away from her family, all the goddamn dog prosthetics, would have been for nothing.

"I think Melissa has a lot of great qualities," Lucia began tentatively. "She's dedicated to the work and to the impact. But ultimately you're the boss," she hedged. "It's your call."

Celeste looked like she was about to say more, but they were saved by the bell—her phone rang, and the subject was forgotten.

Chapter 16
Relics of the Raj

The treacly pace of winter was giving way to a speedier and snappier spring. Lucia was ready to shed some of her winter layers—the clothing as well as the emotional sluggishness of the freezing months. Several weeks had passed since the meeting at the Perry estate, and she was beginning to embrace the fact that she was feeling in the swing of things.

She rushed home after work to change into something that qualified as cocktail attire. The evening's event would be a who's who of the London scene, but she opted for a simple black dress—boring, she knew, but every time she wore a bright color, even on the weekends, she heard Celeste's voice in her head saying she looked like an overripe pomegranate or a wheel of Parmesan cheese.

In a nod to tonight's theme, however, she had accessorized with oversize pink, yellow, and orange hoop earrings that reminded her of one of Malini Shambala's classic works. Celeste would have said they looked like doughnuts—if she had ever even seen a doughnut—but Lucia loved them.

She debated bringing a coat but decided against it. Although technically spring, the weather in London was so fickle that one had to be prepared for anything. A hailstorm had blown through earlier that afternoon, but tonight, the temperature was an unexpectedly mild sixty-eight degrees.

Lucia's outfit didn't matter nearly as much as her date. She was genuinely excited about the prospect of a girls' night out with Sooz. They hadn't seen each other in person since their tea at the Savoy, but there had been a few texts, funny and friendly with no animosity, and a handwritten thank-you card for the Christmas gift Lucia had sent, a signed first edition of Tilly Willington's latest novel. Things had been looking up; tonight was just what they needed to resolidify their friendship.

She took a long look at herself in the full-length mirror. She looked different. With the exception of her earrings, everything she had on was designer; even her plain black dress was picked out on one of her now-regular visits to Crease, self-funded this time. Her hair was straight, thanks to regular blowouts (once a special-occasion-only treat, she had found she was more palatable to people at work when her curls weren't flying all over the place). She supposed that, even if she felt like she didn't always belong in environments like the one she was headed off to tonight, she at least looked the part.

"Your taxi is here, Lucia," Moira called from the living room. Ollie was working late again, so dear old Mummy was babysitting Marley. Lucia scooped Marley up in her arms, pressing her nose into her cheek.

"Pretty Mommy! Kiss?" Marley asked.

"I have lipstick on, darling." Marley looked crestfallen. "OK, OK, you win. Just one or you're going to look like you've been attacked by the kiss monster." She gave Marley a light peck, leaving only a trace of pink. "One now, and next week Mommy will be home lots and we'll have kisses every day."

GIFGAL couldn't come soon enough. She planned to work from home all week so she and Marley could hit up all their old haunts, even Singy Songy. Plus she was going to cook for Ollie every night. She couldn't wait. It was her week to make amends for how absent she had been the past few weeks. Months?

"You do look nice," Moira said, taking Marley from her. "Especially those earrings. Very . . . exotic."

Lucia almost quipped back, *Yes, and you look so interesting tonight yourself,* which a Brit would clearly understand to mean, *I wouldn't be caught dead in what you're wearing*—but, given how much Moira had babysat for them lately, she refrained. She muttered a quick thanks and headed out the door quickly to avoid any further opportunities for Moira to offer up microaggressions in the guise of compliments.

She hopped into her taxi and scrolled through her emails as quickly as she could; the ride to the Victoria and Albert Museum was a short one. It was a place Lucia had long wanted to visit but hadn't found the time—its neighbors in South Kensington, the Science Museum and Natural History Museum, were much more child friendly. She shuddered at the thought of the damage a pair of sticky toddler hands could do to a priceless sixteenth-century Islamic rug or a betel nut container shaped like a chicken from 1700s Myanmar.

There was a note from Henry in her inbox, with some questions about their revised pitch for Operation Bridget Jones. Once the plans for the North London center had been set, he wondered why, with a bigger budget, they couldn't replicate them all over the country. Operation Bridget Jones was going national. His email confirmed that she should start looking for nonprofits to partner with in Bristol, Birmingham, Glasgow, and Manchester to begin.

There were a few other emails that could wait until tomorrow. She skimmed one from the head of building operations at the bank, a reminder that the priceless Damien Hirst shark-in-formaldehyde sculpture on the sixth floor was not, in fact, a coffee table and therefore shouldn't be the place where dirty mugs were discarded. There was also an email about contributing to Brendan's birthday gift. "It's a BIG birthday," his assistant wrote. "Make your contributions accordingly." It did not seem like a request.

Lucia had already contributed, and happily. This "big birthday" meant his retirement was imminent, and not a moment too soon. She was rarely forced to interact with him, but last week she was summoned to his office to brief him on the work her clients were doing on empowering women, a topic that only seemed to matter when International Women's Day was around the corner.

His office wasn't small but felt claustrophobic, probably because every inch of wall space was covered in red—the color of his favorite soccer team. She had prepared a thorough briefing document for him, staying late for three consecutive nights to finish it, which he, of course, had not bothered to read. When she started to summarize the facts about how little global funding went to women and girls, he interrupted her. "Lucy, I'm going to stop you right there," he said, holding out his hand like a red card on the football pitch. "I don't really need you to tell me about women. I have three daughters, a wife, and even the dog in my house is a bitch." He laughed loudly at his own joke. Lucia managed a wan smile before continuing.

Celeste may have been rude, but Brendan was downright incompetent. She was hopeful that things would improve when Celeste was promoted. Maybe she'd get promoted, too, get a bigger portfolio, relax more, work less, and do more good. Short-term pain for long-term gain.

She pulled up just as her phone buzzed with a text from Sooz saying that she was running a few minutes late. That was fine; there was a long line of cars waiting to deposit their VIP guests ahead of her. She watched out the window as each arrival walked down the magenta carpet and took their place in front of the step-and-repeat wall to face the flashing bulbs and indecipherable shrieks of the gathered paparazzi. There was Britain's most recognizable Olympian, a hot diver, posing with four floppy-haired boy band singers, young enough to be Lucia's sons. Fans squealed at a pitch not made for human ears. She snapped a blurry photo through the window to send to Tristan, who would die of jealousy.

Finally it was her turn. Lucia disembarked from the car and sashayed down the carpet on her own. No one wanted to take her picture, but she did stop once to do a double take at the giant stuffed tiger, three times the size of an actual tiger, that greeted her at the door. She allowed herself one "Wow," then pulled out her invitation for the guard before being ushered past the velvet ropes.

Tonight's opening was the talk of the town—*Relics of the Raj* was a dazzling showcase of clothing re-created from nineteenth-century drawings. The designs themselves had been unearthed from beneath a stack of East India Company tea and sugar invoices during a recent inventory of the museum's archives. A very savvy curator, knowing how popular fashion exhibitions were, decided the never-before-seen Indian looks would be guaranteed to generate buzz.

The entire atrium underneath the V&A's iconic soaring dome had been made over to resemble a palace during the time of the Raj. The enormous marble columns were strung with delicate fairy lights, giving the room an ethereal glow. Live mannequins paraded around, modeling the exhibition designs—they stopped every few moments, posing in perfect stillness so guests could appreciate them up close.

Lucia looked up at the famous Chihuly chandelier, dressed up for the occasion with strings of purple-and-white orchids that hung down from the ceiling. In the center of the room, a pond had been constructed to approximate a palace court-yard. It had been filled with real water and pink lotus flowers, then covered in plexiglass, delighting anyone who walked across. Two traditional Indian musicians played the sitar and tabla, as a singer, dressed in a resplendent gold sari, crooned softly over the thrum of people. More than half the crowd wore culturally Indian attire in every possible color, and Lucia immediately cursed her inner Celeste for forcing her into a black dress. If there was ever an opportunity to be mistaken for a pomegranate, this would have been it.

She scanned the room for Sooz. Instead, she caught another set of eyes and frowned. Belly and Caz were across the atrium, waving her over. Ugh. She plastered a smile on her face and made her way over to them.

"How lovely to run into you," Belly said, proffering her cheek for air-kisses as Caz did the same. "Ollie says you're so busy at work these days it's hard to pin you down."

Lucia ignored the jab, craning her neck in search of Sooz. "Tonight is work for me. One of my clients is funding the exhibition. Do you know Rosemary Chatto?" Rosemary was nice but a bit of a headache. She was trying to set up her own nonprofit focused on biodiversity. Rather than starting a new nonprofit, Lucia had tried to convince her that there was almost always a better, more effective option in an existing organization that had already been doing the same type of work for years. But the client was always right, so for about a month now, she had been helping Rosemary to establish the

Rosemary Chatto Foundation for All Living Things—it would, at least, be run through Eastern Currents, which boosted AUM and made Lucia look good.

"Of course, silly, we went to school with Rosie's older brother. And anyway, I'm on the board here, so I never miss an opening."

"Right. Well, you both look lovely." Belly and Caz had leaned heavily into the theme, draped in jewel-toned saris with layers of gold jewelry. Even though she was sure her closet was now full of the same labels as these women, she had once again miscalculated what was required to fit in. Maybe she would never figure it out. "That necklace is stupendous."

"Isn't it just? It belonged to Colz's grandmother. Did you know she lived in India during the Raj? Those were the days."

Before Lucia could respond, a waitress appeared with a tray of canapés. "Vegetarian samosas with mango chutney?" she asked with a smile.

Belly waved her hand carelessly, shooing the waitress away, which infuriated Lucia perhaps more than anything else. "I'll have one," she said, making eye contact and smiling. "They look delicious, thanks," she said.

She shoved the entire samosa into her mouth. It was too large, but dainty bites would have very likely resulted in half of the samosa's innards ending up on her bosom; plus, she could channel her rage at Ollie's friends into vigorous chewing.

"Are you on your own tonight?" Caz asked.

"I'm sure you must be," Belly interjected. "Ollie is stuck at work."

Lucia swallowed in a huge gulp and arched an eyebrow. How did this woman seem to know more about her husband than she did? "I'm meeting a friend." She willed Sooz into existence. Luckily, just then, the crowd parted, and her wish came true.

Sooz, glamorous and gorgeous as ever, made her way over to Lucia and the group. Her face was perfectly made up, and she wore a bright-yellow dress that would have looked like a radioactive potato sack on Lucia but looked nothing short of avant-garde on Sooz's svelte frame.

"My love," Lucia said, offering a cheek for Sooz to kiss. "You have no idea how happy I am to see you. Belly, Caz, please meet my guide to all things British, Susanna."

"Just Sooz. Pleased to meet you both," she said, holding her hand out. Her nails today were neon blue, setting off the yellow of her dress in spectacular fashion.

"What fabulous nails," Caz said, grabbing her hand. "You *must* tell me who your manicurist is."

"I usually see Carina at Elephant and Castle Nails, just opposite the station."

Belly laughed. "My word. Do you know, I've lived in London my whole life and never actually been to Elephant and Castle. Do you need a passport to go south of the river?"

Caz cackled like this was the funniest joke she had ever heard, but Sooz gritted her teeth, and Lucia knew she needed to pull her away before she made it crystal clear to Belly just where she could shove her passport.

"Ladies, it's been nice to see you, but I must get Sooz a drink. See you soon," Lucia said, making a speedy exit.

"Yes, we're all meant to be out to dinner together next week. Check with your husband!" Belly yelled in parting. Lucia seethed.

Sooz grabbed a rhubarb gin and tonic from the bar. "As if Elephant and Castle is another country. It probably is from whatever crumbling estate she lives in with her seven children, all named George, and fourteen nannies."

"Easy now, let's let the drinks settle first." Lucia took a margarita and offered it to Sooz in a toast. "Not that you need yet another reason to despise her, but that's Belly, the one I've been telling you about. I, of course, hate her, but I'm supposed to act like I don't. How did I do?"

"*The* Belly? Ollie's ex? In that case, cheers. You handled that better than I would have. Why do you think I keep my nails so long? It's to stab out the eyeballs of my enemies." She took a sip. "My friends' enemies naturally being my enemies, as well."

"I appreciate the loyalty," Lucia responded. "So what do you make of this whole spectacle?" She gestured around the room, and they watched as a guest hung his coat over one of the live mannequin's outstretched arms, only to let out a shriek when she dropped it and continued walking. "Pretty wild, huh?"

Sooz gave a shudder. "I know this is work for you, but something about this whole thing is just giving me the creeps." She sipped her drink and glanced around. "Anyway . . . You know what else was wild? You put on a British accent when you were speaking to Belly just now. Very Madonna in her Guy Ritchie era of you."

Lucia laughed nervously. Was she putting on a faux accent? How embarrassing. Why hadn't anyone told her?

"Good thing you're here then to keep me from making a fool out of myself. Now update me, how's Atticus? I miss that squishy face."

They walked farther into the museum, and Lucia let her friend's vivacious energy and dynamism cascade over her like a wave. Sooz regaled Lucia with the tale of the latest mummy-and-baby art class she had been taking, demonstrating how Atticus tried to eat the fruit bowl they were supposed to be painting, then she summarized the research she'd been doing for an article on the best mica-free foundations for darker skin tones. Lucia was in awe of Sooz's ability to seamlessly blend her work and life. Balance wasn't an effort for her, it just appeared to come as naturally as breathing. Sooz gave everything 100 percent and still had room for more. How? How did she manage to fit those two distinct piles—work and motherhood—neatly into one bag? (And knowing Sooz, it was a really cute, vintage designer bag at that.)

As they made the rounds, Rosemary Chatto caught Lucia's eye and waved at her from across the room. She mimed a phone, and Lucia took her own out to check her messages. There was a text from Rosemary:

I've got some updates, come find me in ten. PS love your friend's dress! Where's it from?

She showed Sooz the message. "You're making quite the splash," she said. "Rosemary's sponsoring tonight. Maybe she'll offer you a job as a model at the next one."

Sooz made a face and stuck out her tongue. "No thank you, babe. Anyway, she couldn't afford me."

"Rosemary Chatto?" Lucia scoffed. "Uh yeah, she probably could."

Sooz stopped. "Rosemary Chatto?" she repeated.

"Have you heard of her?"

"Isn't she the daughter of Charmless Chatto?"

Lucia had completely forgotten—or maybe willfully ignored—who Rosemary's father was and where their money had come from. Her mind flashed back to the first protest she and Sooz had attended, the realization dawning on her in horror.

Lucia took a bigger gulp, finishing her drink. "Yes. Lord Charles is her father."

If they had been in a movie, Sooz would have done a spit take. "I can't believe you."

Lucia was taken aback by the hostility in Sooz's voice. "She's not that bad. Clueless about some things, but her heart is in the right place."

"Are you flipping kidding me? How do you even stand to work with her? Her money is the definition of dirty money, made off the backs of the workers she pays pennies to."

"I don't disagree with you, not exactly," Lucia said, putting a hand on Sooz's shoulder, a conciliatory gesture. "Personally, I would never shop at Plus Ça." Anymore. It wasn't entirely a lie since she knew if she dared to wear anything from a high-street brand to work, Tristan would tease her mercilessly. "But the family, particularly Rosemary, are doing a lot of good with their donations. I'm advising on their philanthropy, and it's impressive, in the tens of millions."

"Please tell me you don't genuinely believe the total rubbish coming out of your mouth."

Lucia meekly removed her hand from Sooz's shoulder. "It's not rubbish. Just last week, I got them to agree to take a meeting with a child labor nonprofit. And they are doing a trial donation to a cool new social enterprise designing a way to reuse fabric offcuts instead of throwing them away."

"To make more clothes to go into more landfills?"

"Sooz, come on. You need to take a more long-term view. Sometimes you have to give a little to get a lot."

"At what cost?" Sooz responded, loud enough now that people were staring. "Look at you, standing here in this British-colonial wet dream of magical India. Kissing the arses of rich people who are exploiting everyone and everything just because they can. Because people like you make them feel good about themselves in the process."

Lucia met her gaze with a steely glare. "My mistake. I didn't realize that finding the perfect red lip color for fall was going to change the world."

They were silent for a moment, fuming as they locked eyes. "I'm sorry if you don't understand the bigger purpose of what I'm trying to do here," Lucia said quietly. "Or anything about making change at all. Maybe it's easy to judge when you attend the occasional protest followed by a coffee, cake, and a manicure, but I'm in the business of making an impact."

Sooz recoiled and backed away. "You're making an impact alright. I'm just not sure it's the one you think."

A group of performers in traditional kathak costumes were putting on an acrobatic display in the center of the room, drawing everyone's attention away from their face-off. A small mercy.

All at once, Sooz's posture softened, and her shoulders sagged. "Maybe I shouldn't have come tonight," she said. "Atticus has been sick, so I've been up nights, and I think I'm coming down with whatever he has. Let's get together another time, OK? Maybe somewhere . . . else." She turned on her heels and beelined for the exit.

Lucia stood for a moment, frozen in place like the mannequins around her, as she watched Sooz walk away. She considered going after Sooz—of course she should; Sooz could be self-righteous, but she was also Lucia's best friend. But just as she started to give chase, she felt a tug on her arm.

Rosemary.

"Darling, Lucy, where have you been? I told you I needed you. I've just met the most wonderful candidate for the head of my foundation. He doesn't have any work experience, but his father is on a board with my father. He's very handsome—the other stuff we can teach, don't you think? Come, give me your honest opinion."

Lucia glimpsed a flash of neon heading out the door. She'd never catch Sooz now. She'd message her tomorrow and sort things out.

"Yes, of course," she said, linking arms with Rosemary and proceeding back into the Raj.

It was three hours and two margaritas later when Lucia turned her key in the door and crept quietly into the apartment. She almost dropped them when she saw Ollie on the armchair with a book.

"Sheesh, you scared me," she said.

"Is that any way to greet the man who waited up for his"—he inhaled deeply—"sloshed wife?"

"I didn't have that much to drink," she said, trying not to fall over as she kicked off her shoes.

"Perhaps the smell of mezcal is coming from Marley's room, then. We really should sort that."

Lucia sat next to him and rubbed her feet. She was exhausted. "Babe, look, I love you, but I am not in the mood for a lecture tonight. I'm going to bed."

Ollie got up off the chair and put his arms around her. "You're right, I'm sorry. I just wanted to see you. Belly texted to say you looked radiant tonight." He kissed her on the neck. "She was right."

Just the mention of her name set a fire burning in Lucia's veins. "Thank you, darling. Now, I want to shower this whole awful day away. Care to join me?" Suck it, Belly, she thought.

"Are you trying to deflect a serious conversation with the prospect of sex?" he asked. "It's not even Tuesday."

"Maybe. Are you agreeing?"

Ollie sighed. "I suppose I am. But we're going to need to talk about this eventually. This isn't sustainable. We can't go on like this."

"You're right. This week, I promise. Celeste is heading out tomorrow for GIFGAL. How about dinner? I'll come home early, get some good QT with Marley, and we'll go to Patricos? You know that nothing is more of an aphrodisiac to me than the smell of garlic."

After the shower and the satisfying session that followed, Lucia waited until Ollie fell asleep to check her phone one last time before bed, hoping Sooz had texted some kind of apology. Nothing. There were, however, three new work emails that hadn't been there before. She knew she should ignore them until morning, but she never could resist getting rid of that shiny red circle and achieving inbox zero.

The first email was from Celeste. Lucia was in cc, along with Tristan and a bunch of names she didn't recognize. She could hear Celeste's haughty tone as she read:

Please change all tickets and travel for GIFGAL to Lucea Barrow (svp confirm the spelling). Melissa Cook is no longer attending.

Below that was a conference confirmation email and a bunch of logistics.

Oh shit. Lucia felt her stomach drop. Melissa had been so excited about this trip. She had arranged childcare—no small feat as a single parent—and had been saving up her vacation days for some personal downtime after the conference. She deserved this trip. Celeste had just snatched it away and given it to her instead.

She moved on to the second email. It was from the bank's travel agent with her plane tickets. Business class. Her flight to Miami left at 9:00 a.m. tomorrow. She looked at the time. Not tomorrow, today. She had to pack right now. What would she tell Ollie? And Marley?

There was no time to worry about any of that now. She'd go, just as she was expected to. It would only be a few days. Ollie would understand, he would have to, and she'd make it up to Marley when she returned. And Sooz. And Melissa. Oh god, she thought to herself in a panic, what about Melissa? She could fix everything . . . right after she got back.

The third email was from Tristan. It had a photo of Regina George in her iconic *Mean Girls* pink cardigan accompanied by the one-line caption:

Get in, loser, we're going to GIFGAL.

Chapter 17
Welcome to GIFGAL

"Cocotail?"

Lucia turned around to see a perky young woman, holding a tray of cut-crystal glasses filled with ice and white liquid, garnished with slices of pineapple and pink umbrellas cheerfully poking out of the top.

"It's our signature cocktail, the cocotail," she continued. Her accent was Australian and her hair so blonde it was almost white. Lucia was envious. One summer, she had tried Sun In in a misguided attempt at a similar hue, convinced that blondes really did have more fun. It turned her hair more of a burnt orange and people called her Sideshow Bob until it grew out.

This woman's hair, in contrast, looked naturally streaked by the sun. Her burnished tan appeared natural, as well. Lucia looked around at the other waiters, bellboys, concierges, and receptionists—even the guy handing out badges looked like he had stepped out of a 1994 Pacific Sunwear catalog.

"Our cocotail is made of coconuts foraged from our own trees, a splash of fair-trade lime juice, and rum, produced by a phenomenal social enterprise funded by the Sunbliss Foundation based in Guatemala." She pronounced it "Wuatemala," which would normally make Lucia cringe but not today. How could she be bothered when she was surrounded by beautiful people on an island in the middle of the turquoise-blue ocean?

"Oh, and the umbrellas are crafted by a group of Indigenous artisans, as well," the server finished, proudly handing Lucia the cold glass. "Welcome to GIFGAL." Lucia thanked her and took a sip, hoping the alcohol or at least the sugar might sharpen her focus. She was dazed and groggy. After a tearful goodbye with Marley and a cold send-off from Ollie back in London, she'd barely slept on the eleven-hour flight.

GIFGAL was the brainchild of Australia's wealthiest man and most generous philanthropist (according to his PR team), Sir Rupert Baldonshiel. Sir Rupert was also the owner of the exclusive Sunbliss Island, where GIFGAL took place every year. The event was invitation only. Being able to say you'd spent time on Sunbliss was like carrying an Amex Black Card, or maybe whatever secret level was higher: It told people you were someone worth knowing.

Sir Rupert made his money by growing his company from a single wind farm into one of the biggest renewable-energy businesses in the world. He gave off the air of a self-made man, so it was best if no one mentioned that his family's inherited wealth—used as the seed capital to start his business—was the result of decades of mining by the ancestral Baldonshiels, which had also resulted in displacing Aboriginal peoples and stripping the land. Sooz would have had a field day choosing exactly which expletives to use to describe the roots of his family tree.

Nowadays, Sir Rupert was up there with Bono and the Dalai Lama on anyone's official list of bona fide generous people. He'd started GIFGAL ten years ago, with the lofty aim of creating a World Economic Forum for philanthropy. Instead of focusing on how to grow the global economy, GIFGAL would grow generosity and goodwill. Rather than slipping and sliding down ice-covered Swiss streets in the darkest depths of January in ill-fitting suits, attendees would jet off to the Caribbean, in custom-branded sarongs designed by at-risk schoolchildren in Tibet. It was Davos, with a soul, in flip-flops.

GIFGAL had indeed become the place to be if you cared about social impact—or if you made your living from people who cared about social impact. Wealthy friends and wannabe friends of the Baldonshiels thought nothing of paying the thirty-thousand-dollar entry fee for three days and three nights of inspiration and entertainment (all in the name of a good cause), and companies like Eastern Currents jumped at the opportunity to become corporate sponsors, for an amount that could keep a whole lot of Wuatemalan rum makers in business for a long, long time.

Lucia checked her phone. Just before boarding the plane, she had sent Melissa a text. There was so much she wanted to say to her friend, but she wasn't sure how. She had quickly typed: Are you OK? What happened? She could tell her message had been read, but there was still no response.

Besides Lucia and Tristan, the bank's delegation included Celeste, Brendan, and the big boss, Nigel. The summit agenda was packed with a mix of plenaries and panel discussions (including the highly anticipated "The Royal Wee: Funding Water, Hygiene, and Sanitation"), activities that would not have been out of place on a summer-camp agenda (albeit a summer camp that offered kitesurfing, hot-air ballooning, and swimming with dolphins) and culminated in the big gala on the final night.

The gala was the pinnacle of the whole conference—this year's theme was a celebration of two decades of the foundation's support for HIV/AIDS—and the apex of the pinnacle was the gala's legendary pledging session, where the attendees would stand up and offer money or time or products or whatever assets they had at their disposal to good causes. It had a reputation for spontaneous generosity. Moved by the moment and the desire to one-up one another, people often committed hundreds of millions in a collective frenzy of good-will. Last year, she heard that tech darling Marcus Macintosh donated his two-hundred-foot superyacht on a whim. (He was between wives at the time, and the one he was divorcing had been very displeased.)

Lucia sipped her cocotail, which was so sweet and delicious she made a mental note to get the name of the rum for her own personal stash and thought about asking for another, but a little voice in her head reminded her to pace herself. This wasn't a vacation, no matter how soft the sand looked—it was work. She had a folder as thick as her wrist full of dossiers on people she was meant to court and flatter and cultivate for the next few days: existing bank clients who hadn't yet dipped their toes into serious giving but were philanthro-curious, big givers who were not yet clients of the bank, and of course, their usual port-folio of current clients with relationships that needed to be carefully stewarded. There hadn't been time to prepare, given it was Melissa who was supposed to be here, but at least she recognized a few of the names. Henry was attending with a gaggle of friends—no other Perrys, though—and Tamsin RSVP'd but had then gone off on a silent retreat in Indonesia for a month. Who even knew with her?

Still, everything around her screamed vacation. It even smelled like vacation—gardenias and sunscreen. The lobby was designed like a Balinese hut, with an open vista facing directly to the beach. Palm trees rustled in the distance as she was handed her key and a swag bag (which, she was proud to say, made it all the way to her room before being torn open).

Ignoring for just a moment the double-glazed French doors that led to a private balcony overlooking the ocean (every bedroom at Sunbliss offered an ocean view), the egg-shaped bathtub, and the pristine white sheets that looked like they were made of clouds, she spilled the contents of the bag onto her bed. The freebies were nicer than what she had been given for her birthday this year.

There was a candle made by Sir Rupert's wife Anna (second wife, younger than his oldest daughter by a number of years too impolite to mention) that smelled like the inside of a Fendi purse, several high-end beauty products they thoughtfully assumed one would need for the week, a designer beach wrap she recognized from the latest *Vogue*, scentless mosquito repellent, and postsunburn moisturizer; there was also a journal made by blind residents of a nursing home in Lesotho, recipients of Sunbliss Foundation funding, and an actual smartwatch with the agenda and a handy GPS-enabled delegate-finder function, so one could track down other attendees.

She shoved everything back into the bag and lay down on the bed. A wave of fatigue washed over her as her head hit the supersoft premium-down pillow—its filling probably collected from the molting of a flock of sustainable migratory geese. She really was in paradise. The beachfront horseback riding icebreaker started in just under an hour, followed by lunch prepared by a three-Michelin-star chef. Perhaps she would rest her eyes just for a second before diving into the melee.

The mathematics of it all unpleasantly flitted through her brain as her eyes drooped heavily. Maybe they should have given this money away and saved the carbon footprint. The cocotail budget alone would have funded Amina's North London center for a month.

But the distant roar of another jet landing on the island's private airstrip sounded exactly like Marley's white noise machine, and the velvety duvet seemed to mold to her body. How could something that felt this good be bad? Deals would be done here, commitments would be made, relationships solidified, and ideas conceived that might really change the world. You had to spend money to make money—or, in this case, to get others to give it away, she reasoned, as she drifted off to sleep.

* * *

Faraway shrieks of laughter filtered into the bedroom, causing Lucia to stir. Marley, she thought, and jolted awake. It was dark outside. For a moment, she didn't have the slightest idea where she was.

The smell of coconuts brought her back to the present moment. She was on Sunbliss Island. The bedside clock read 8:03 p.m., which meant she had slept through the entire first afternoon of sessions. Celeste was going to kill her.

How had this happened? She heard a vibration coming from across the room and then had a vague recollection of hurling something against the wall when it had started beeping at her (the alarm she had so diligently set). She was in big trouble.

The smartwatch had nine missed notifications from the delegate-finder feature. Eight were from Tristan, increasingly frantic:

I'm in the lobby, u coming down?

OK, I'm waiting five more minutes, if this is Latin-people time or whatever I am not having it.

I'm leaving.

OK, now I'm leaving.

You owe me a martini for having to take your place at the ice-breaker. MIA is not a good look on you.

I have been partnered with a very earnest Canadian who only wants to talk about some horrible neglected tropical disease—you owe me 7 martinis.

Are you dead?

If you're dead, I apologize for my previous comments. If you're not dead, I'm planning on killing you myself.

Then, one message from Celeste:

Is it too much to ask you to show up at this conference we have paid for you to attend? If it is too strenuous for you, maybe you would prefer to stay at the spa?

Lucia was beyond mortified.

How could this have happened? Something told her that this was punishment for not listening to her overtired body— she was running on empty. But she told that voice to pipe down because she needed to get dressed. She scrolled through the evening's agenda. Tonight's event was an international food truck festival, which sounded casual enough. She put on jeans and a button-down and pulled out a pair of Sunbliss-branded flip-flops from her closet, thoughtfully in her size and, of course, made from recycled ocean plastic, and dashed to the lobby to wave down one of the golf carts shuttling guests around the island.

Then she shot Tristan a message; she'd deal with Celeste later.

Alive but only until Celeste finds me. Don't worry about killing me, I suspect she'll handle that herself.

The cart dropped her off in a large open field usually reserved for Baldonshiel family cricket matches. The night was clear and cool, and stars twinkled in the cloudless sky. Did they hire someone to orchestrate the weather, too? She would not put it past them.

The field was bordered by food trucks, each a bright color with a flag signaling its provenance. Her heart fluttered—the festival atmosphere reminded her of the night she met Ollie in Austin (and how much had changed since then)—but the wave of nostalgia was drowned out by a rumbling in her stomach. She hadn't consumed any food since the flight this morning, unless you counted the pineapple garnish in her arrival beverage. Like a pigeon with a homing beacon, her eyes landed on a truck flying a Texas flag. The smell of freshly fried onions wafted in her direction, making her mouth water and her heart sing. There would be carnitas in her future.

Lucia joined the line and was considering whether four orders of tacos would be too many for one person when she heard a familiar voice calling her name, or a version of her name.

"Lucy, Lucy, it's you!" Tamsin, a vision in a bright-red *Baywatch*-style one-piece with a white crocheted sarong wrapped around her waist, ran up and enveloped her in a bear hug. "Oh, babe, isn't this place lush? I'm so chuffed to see you."

"As am I," Lucia responded genuinely. She had really developed a soft spot for Tamsin, an almost maternal desire to take care of her. "I didn't realize you were coming! How was the retreat?"

"Awful." Tamsin frowned. "When they said silent retreat, they *actually* meant, like, no talking. At all. And worse, no phones. I lasted twenty minutes, and then I chartered a copter to Bali instead. Heaven." She looked relaxed and tan, Lucia noted. "Anyway, come and sit with us, we're over there." Tamsin pulled Lucia's sleeve in the general direction of a picnic table attended by some very beautiful young people taking selfies.

"I'd love to! Let me just grab some tacos. I'll be right there," Lucia said. There was only one person in front of her in line.

Tamsin frowned. "No meat at the table, love!" Lucia had forgotten that Tamsin, lover of all things four legged, was a proselytizing vegetarian (although her buttery leather boots apparently "didn't count"). "Anyway, you won't need it, we have loads of food. Come on." She pulled Lucia toward her table.

Lucia reluctantly abandoned her spot. When she reached the table there was not, in fact, loads of food, but a half-eaten plate of meze. With one wistful glance back toward the carnitas and a tear in her eye, she sighed, took out a packet of sriracha from her purse, and squeezed it over the hummus.

"So how's your GIFGAL been so far?" Lucia asked, her mouth full of radish rose.

"It's been mental," she said. "The villa is gor-gee-ous. We had lunch at the house—Clara brought her chef." One of the selfie girls peered over her sunglasses at Lucia and waved. "And, let's see, mostly just hung out at the beach until we came here."

"You missed the opening plenary?" To be fair, so had she; the difference was Lucia had not dropped thirty thousand dollars only to skip the planned itinerary and lie on the beach all day. If that's all she'd wanted to do, Tamsin could have stayed in Bali and flown her friends over to meet her for less.

"Those things are so dreadfully dull," Clara said. "Being here is enough. Mum and Dad think we're learning and loving and giving or some bullshit."

So they were here out of filial obligation and for a paid vacation, Lucia noted. She recognized Clara from the latest

Home and Country magazine (each issue featured a portrait of a young single woman of marriageable age with a line about her professional and outdoor pursuits and, of course, name-dropped her wealthy parents). That meant she was a prospective philanthropist, even if she didn't know it yet. If she wasn't attending sessions, Lucia hoped she would accidentally learn something (possibly through osmosis) that would spur her to give.

Lucia couldn't worry about that now; she really needed to find some food if she was going to attempt to grovel before Celeste's Manolo-clad feet. She glanced over to see if any of the trucks were still serving. "Tamsin, listen, it was so lovely to see you, and nice to meet you all, but I really need to find my colleagues. Let's catch up tomorrow, OK? We should talk about your plan for the foundation's next board meeting. A surfing retreat in Belize is probably not tax-deductible."

Lucia stood up to go and bumped right into a petite (and yet remarkably solid) woman wearing a cream silk top and buttercup-yellow linen pants.

"*Bonsoir*, Lucia. Thank you for making the time for us in your busy schedule. Perhaps I should have expected to find you near the food, *non?*" The look on Celeste's face was even more murderous than Lucia had imagined it would be. She wondered what they would do with her body after she died. Probably put her ashes into a biodegradable canister made of recycled manure harvested from a collective in Buenos Aires (supported by a generous donation from the Sunbliss Foundation) and spread her at sea.

"Celeste, hi," Lucia drawled and sat back down again. "I've been looking all over for you."

"Ah yes, looking very hard I see."

"My apologies, I got sidetracked by our favorite client here," she said, laying an arm around Tamsin's bony shoulders and turning her so Celeste could see her face.

When Celeste noticed whom Lucia was with, the frightening scowl on her face morphed into a smile that was all sweetness and light. "Ah, but of course I did not see you there, you are so tiny! Lovely Ta-ma-sin, how are you?"

"Couldn't be better," she said. "This one, eh? She never stops working." Tamsin winked at Lucia.

Celeste eyed her shrewdly. "And where have you been working all day, Lucia? I looked everywhere and saw you nowhere."

"Well, um." Lucia swallowed loudly and started to sweat. She reached around in her brain for an excuse, but nothing materialized. "Earlier I was just . . . It was funny, really, I had just checked into my room and . . . ."

"And," Tamsin interrupted. "I called her and told her she must come to my villa and stay with me. As soon as she arrived, we got so caught up talking about my foundation plans and all the dogs and cats and rabbits that we totally lost track of time."

Lucia caught Tamsin's eye and gave her a quizzical look, but Tamsin just continued to smile her sweet innocent smile, as if she was daring Celeste to call her bluff.

"That's right." Lucia nodded firmly. "I was with Tamsin. I'm sorry I didn't respond to your messages, my battery died. Damn smartwatches."

Celeste raised an eyebrow. "Very well. You ladies have . . . fun. Lucia, I will see you first thing tomorrow." Celeste departed, with a final pointed look over her shoulder. When she was out of earshot, Lucia clasped her hands together and shook them at Tamsin in gratitude.

"Oh my gosh, you saved my ass. It was an accident. I slept through my alarm, and . . ."

Tamsin waved her hand. "Don't be silly. We're friends. That's what friends do."

Were they friends? Lucia supposed she was right—she had spent more time with Tamsin in the last few months than Sooz or any other actual friend.

"Anyway, it's settled." Tamsin clapped her hands together. "Go back to the hotel, pack your stuff, and come move into my villa. I'll send someone for your bags. This is going to be so much fun!"

As she left the field, her watch vibrated with a one-line text from Celeste: Ne merde pas. She didn't need a translate function to get the message: Don't screw up.

Chapter 18
A Clean Break

Lucia had barely slept. Jet lag was a bitch, but her alarm didn't care. It blared at 7:00 a.m., fulfilling its duty. She must have been in a state of hunger-fueled delusion when she signed up for early-morning "Trampolining with Crystal." Whatever the cause, she'd had a serious lapse in good judgment.

She shut off the alarm and lay in bed, listening to the villa come alive. Her hotel room had been spectacular, but Tamsin's villa, one of just twelve designed for the most important of the VIP guests, was something else. It had its own private infinity pool, beach, and dock. Situated on a point, the villa faced both east and west, so one could watch the sunrise and sunset from the same plush sofa with no more than a slight turn of the head.

Downstairs, she heard footsteps treading softly, hisses and bangs, people getting ready to start the day. The staff was up. Those omelets weren't going to make themselves.

She stretched her arms and legs wide. It was time to start her day, as well. She thought about her morning coffee with Marley as she reached over to pick up her phone—service on the island was patchy, hence the smartwatches, but it must have picked up a signal because there were fifteen new notifications. Not unusual—half a business day in the UK had passed already. She swiped up to view the first one, from Sooz. They hadn't spoken since the *Relics of the Raj* debacle. Was that only the day before yesterday?

So sorry about Marley, babe, let me know what I can do.

Lucia sat up, every nerve immediately on alert. She quickly scrolled through the rest of her notifications: two missed calls from Gretel and three from Ollie. The rest were texts.

Lucia's brain went into panic mode, and her hands shook as she dialed Ollie's number. As she waited for him to pick up, she scanned through his texts:

Everything is fine, but Marley fell off the climbing frame at the playground, and we think her arm might be broken. On the way to the hospital. Call when you get this. x

Of course it was the playground, that giant death trap. Why did Lucia ever let her go there? Or at least she should have been wearing a helmet, or a full bubble suit.

The call went to voicemail. Why wasn't he picking up?

Going to X-ray. She's being a total champ.

Definitely a fracture. Might need surgery. We're seeing the doctor in 20.

Lucia was wide-awake now. She threw a sweater over her pj's and walked with her phone to the beach, where she hoped she'd get better service. Lucia sat unmoving in the sand, willing Ollie to call back. Finally, the phone rang.

"Tell me what's happening," she said quickly, not bothering with a greeting. "How is she? Can you put her on FaceTime? Who is the doctor, and did they go to a reputable medical school?" Words exploded from her in a torrent.

She could hear relief tinged with panic in Ollie's voice. "She's been amazing, our little trooper. She doesn't need surgery, thank heavens, but she will need a cast. Four weeks, the doctor said, then a checkup. And they think she has a mild concussion, so that's not ideal. Still, she's in good spirits. I promised her every chocolate known to mankind when we get home."

"OK, good; that's good," she repeated, for her own benefit as much as Ollie's. "No surgery is good. Concussion is less good. And a cast? Do they even make them small enough for her tiny arm?"

His voice broke on the other end of the line, and Lucia could hear him trying to regain his composure.

"Hey, it's OK. It's OK, *amor*," she said soothingly. Like many parents, they had an unspoken agreement that only one of them was allowed to freak out at any given time; it was Ollie's turn by virtue of being there with Marley. "It could have been so much worse. She's going to be fine. Kids break bones all the time."

Ollie breathed deeply. "Of course. I know, you're right. The doctor said it was a clean break and should heal well. But it was so terrifying. Gretel said that when she fell she was unconscious for a split second."

Lucia felt her body flood with adrenaline, every mama-bear sense she had switched on. She would tear those monkey bars from the ground with her bare hands. "Can you put her on? Can I see her?"

"Sure, let me just turn on the camera."

Ollie's face filled the screen. He was in his suit. He must have rushed straight to the hospital from work. She pushed the thought of how terrible that journey must have been, not seeing Marley, not knowing. She would have been going out of her mind.

She watched as he walked down the hospital hall and into a room with cartoon characters on the walls. "Look who it is, darling, it's Mummy," she heard him say, and then Marley's precious face filled the screen. Lucia felt her eyes fill, but she refused to let them spill over. She pasted an enormous grin on her face that she hoped Marley would believe was genuine.

"Mama?" she cried, confused at first and looking around the room for Lucia before focusing on the phone.

Marley made an exaggerated pout, and Lucia laughed, choking back the tears. "How's my brave girl? I know, *mija*, you feel bad. But everything is going to be OK. You're gonna be OK. Mama loves you so much. By the time I'm back you'll practically be as good as new."

"Is Mama home?" She looked up at Ollie.

"Soon, Mama will be home very soon," she heard him say and then, after some fumbling to wrestle the phone back from Marley, "Do you need my assistant to help you find a flight out today?"

Yes! Lucia's heart exclaimed. Find me a flight out yesterday. But the words lodged in her throat.

She stared out at the ocean and the sun peeking over the horizon, like the yolk of an egg. She had no idea what to do. After yesterday's oversleeping fail, she could hardly imagine telling Celeste she had to leave without attending a single session. She would be fired, or worse.

She could hear Celeste's voice in her head. "Yes, of course, you waste our time and money to come here and then leave for a small malady. You are no better than Melissa, running off for every loose tooth. I see where your priorities really are. I thought you were one hundred percent committed to your job, *non*?"

But the word *hospital* was also playing on a loop in her mind over and over again. Her baby was in the hospital with a cast on her arm. Lucia wanted nothing more than to cuddle her daughter, to inspect every square inch of her and ensure that she really was intact.

Her mind raced through every possible outcome. If she left now, Celeste would be furious and almost certainly fire her. If she got fired, she would be risking Operation Bridget Jones and the impact she could make on the lives of hundreds of refugees. Every sacrifice she had made would have been for nothing.

If she kept her original flight, she'd be home in under seventy-two hours. It would take nearly that long to figure out a different way off the island and all the way back to London.

She couldn't leave now. Not with so much at stake. Marley would be fine—she wouldn't even remember this—and Ollie would forgive her. Eventually, she hoped.

"Thanks, *amor*, but I think it makes the most sense to keep my original flight," she said to Ollie.

His face contorted into a frown. "What do you mean?"

"There's still two days left of the conference, and tomorrow's dinner is important. I have to be there."

"You have to be with your family, that's where you have to be," he said, his tone clipped.

"Look, I'm in such a remote place it would take me over a day to get home from here. And you said so yourself, Marley is fine. You have Gretel, your mom," she said. "You can even call Sooz. She'd do anything for Marley. You know you guys are the most important people in the world to me. But I'm on thin ice with Celeste already. She would flat-out fire me if I left."

"Like that would be such a bad thing," he muttered. Quietly, Ollie stepped outside Marley's hospital room and closed the door behind him. "Honestly, all you ever talk about anymore is work. I am so ridiculously tired of hearing about Celeste. And how important your job is. Are we not important to you, too?"

226

Lucia thought her head might explode. "Are you not important?" she whisper yelled. "Ollie, of course you're important. I always put you and Marley first. I quit my job in Austin and left behind everything I had ever worked for to move across the ocean for you. Putting you first is literally all I have done since the moment we met."

She breathed heavily. It was like she had cracked a seal and now she couldn't stop the words from overflowing. "You knew what you were getting into when we met. I never promised to give up working, my work is too important—and not just to me, but to many people. I've found my purpose again. I'm finally thriving, and you want to make me feel bad? I can count on my fingers alone the number of bedtimes *you* were home for in the first year."

Ollie went silent for what seemed like a decade, his lips pressed into a thin line, his eyebrows drawn together. At last, he let out a sigh. "I don't want to fight with you," he said curtly. "She's fine. I'm fine. We'll see you when you get back. Have fun." That last sentence was tinged with sarcasm and sadness. The screen switched to black, then back to her wallpaper image of her smiling daughter, twirling in a tutu at baby ballet.

The audacity, she thought furiously. He hadn't even given her a chance to say goodbye to Marley. It was only a broken arm, a clean break, she consoled herself. Ollie had plenty of support. She was right to stay, she knew it.

Her heart rate was already elevated as she went back to her room, threw on her gym clothes and power walked over to the Mahalo Pavilion where twenty-five individual trampolines had been placed out in rows, each with a crystal of a different shade in the center. Not trampolining with Crystal, trampolining with *crystals*. The class was about to begin. She picked the nearest open spot, adorned with a purple crystal, and hopped on.

"Hold your crystal to your heart while you bounce and chat our mantra: WWRD? What would Rihanna do?" an impossibly fit woman with long silky hair screamed from the front of the room. Bouncing up and down to the beat of "Get Ready for This" from Jock Jams circa 1995. The forty-five-minute class passed in a blur of turquoise and pink.

When it was over, she felt high from the huge rush of adrenaline. Drenched in sweat and smelling of the patchouli burned during the cooldown ("Your body is fierce, and your aura is free," they'd chanted together while splayed out on the trampolines), Lucia headed back to the villa with a clearer head.

She knew she should trust her gut. Leaving now made no sense, not with everything she had to lose. But that annoying inner voice felt obliged to comment: What about what you've lost already? How much damage have you done to your relationship? How much longer can you avoid a state of the union on the state of your union?

She couldn't deal with that now. She had a job to do and a full day ahead of her. Her first session, "Taxes: Better Spent Elsewhere?" started at nine. She needed to shower, eat, and get moving.

Thirty minutes later, as she stepped into the villa, her phone pinged with a message from Ollie:

Marley discharged and we are heading home. She loves her cast. Got it in pink. We need to air this out when you get back.

There were three dots, followed by a photo of him and Marley pulling silly faces in the back of a taxi. There was a battle to be fought, but at least for today there was a détente.

Anyway, she thought to herself as she hopped into the shower to wash off the smell of patchouli, the worst thing that could have happened had happened. The rest of the trip would be disaster free from here, she was certain.

Chapter 19
Bonfire of the Vanities

That night, Lucia found herself sitting quietly in almost the exact same spot as she had been that morning. Instead of rising, the sun was now setting. She felt like she had aged a year in the last thirteen hours.

The sand on the beach was being whipped up by occasional gusts of wind. She rubbed her eyes and wondered why Sir Rupert's team hadn't thought to import windproof synthetic sand from a lab in Amsterdam; they'd thought of everything else. She let herself sink farther down—not into the sand, but into a soft beige-colored sofa that had been placed the perfect distance from a bonfire.

Once the giant egg-yolk sunset fell below the horizon, the sky began to darken quickly. It filled with stars, and Lucia cupped her ear, trying to hear the waves over the tunes from a popular Swedish house DJ who was spinning on the pool deck several yards away. Staff were circling with bottles of champagne (the brand Lucia had rejected at her own wedding on account of it being, as she'd said to Ollie, "stupid expensive"). But here, at this "friendly get-together"—the euphemistic phrase Tamsin had used when she knocked on Lucia's door and begged her to come down with a "pretty pleeeeease"—Lucia accepted a glass without question.

She felt bone-tired, physically and emotionally, and small-talked out after an intense day.

She had managed to briefly poke her head into the opening plenary before jumping into four hours of back-to-back meetings with clients and prospective clients. She'd scarfed down a cold vegan-turkey sandwich for lunch (which was as awful as it sounds) before taking a call with Rona (GIFGAL was not her scene or, as she put it, "Leave me out of anything to do with this group wank of virtue signaling"—and that was before Lucia had mentioned the vegan turkey).

She'd run into Tristan at the next session, "How to Give Your Money a Soul," but he'd left in a hurry as soon as they were instructed to "lie on the floor and close your eyes, visualizing your wealth as a chick about to hatch." Lucia stayed, grateful for the opportunity to nap during the floor-meditation exercise—she just hoped she hadn't snored too loudly.

She had been looking forward to an early night. Tomorrow was another full day of meetings, plus the gala in the evening. She needed rest, but instead, she was here on the beach. Still, she thought, taking another sip of champagne and grabbing an avocado-and-lime tart off the tray of a passing waiter, it could have been worse.

How easily she had slipped into Tamsin's world, the world of her clients, as effortlessly as shrugging off one designer coat and replacing it with another. She thought back to that embarrassing dinner with Ollie's friends. She was a novice then, a person who laughed at their frivolous approach to life, and yet here she was with a bag that cost more than two months' rent on her apartment in Austin, hanging out at a beach party on a private island with at least three part owners of Premier

League teams and 10 percent of the royal line of succession. Somehow, in the process of serving her clients, she had stopped seeing their lives as ridiculous and started to appreciate the upsides of being ridiculously wealthy.

Lucia unpocketed her phone and went back through her messages. A photo from Ollie of Marley in pj's, sent several hours ago, without a caption. She had responded, I love you both so much, with three heart emoji; Ollie hadn't written back. She missed them and still wasn't 100 percent sure that she had done the right thing by staying, but it was too late to change that now. She'd make it up to them when she was home.

She scrolled up to reread the message she had gotten earlier from Melissa, who had finally responded to her text:

Thanks, pet. I'm sure you can figure out what happened. I'm guessing you're reading this on a white sandy beach. Have a piña colada for me. Cheers xx

Lucia grimaced. It was too hard to infer tone from a text—was she sending two kisses (xx) or telling her she was going to poke her eyes out when she got back? Was she sincerely hoping Lucia was enjoying a piña colada or praying that she would choke on a tiny umbrella? Yet another thing she'd need to fix when she got home.

"Now, what could possibly be more captivating inside that tiny device than your surroundings, right here, right now?"

Henry's distinctive silhouette, backlit by the bonfire, loomed over her. Lucia smiled at him. "You're right. Anyway, it's certainly better now that you're here," she said, raising her glass to his. They clinked, and he sat down next to her.

"How was your day full of giving and loving and generally saving the world at GIFGAL?" he asked.

"Long. Exhausting. Exhilarating. And delightfully, mostly Celeste free. The champagne is helping. How was yours?"

"Odd, if I'm being truthful. I mean, in some ways it was extraordinary. I went to the panel on modern slavery. These four survivors told their stories, each more harrowing than the next. They were so brave. And then during the Q&A, Barty Crosslight, a mate of my parents, stood up and said he'd donate one million dollars to their recovery. Just like that, in the room. It's not even the gala yet. Then the survivors were crying, and the whole room was in tears."

"Wow," Lucia said. "That sounds incredible. I mean, he changed their lives right then and there."

"Absolutely," Henry replied. "It was beautiful. But once the panel was over, everyone mobbed the survivors for photos, and it all just felt—I don't know, icky. Exploitative." He took a big swig of his drink. "And no one thought to mention that the whole event was held in the Reginald Baldonshiel Solarium. Reginald, you know, was Sir Rupert's great-grandfather, most known for publishing a treatise, quite popular in its day, based on his conviction that using child labor in his mines was a gesture of goodwill; he was offering them professional opportunities."

Lucia sighed. "Welcome to the great philanthropic paradox," she told him. "We sometimes overlook hypocrisy in the name of doing good. But do we? We'll never really know."

Henry looked pensive at that, and Lucia remembered where she was and whom she was with. She and Henry had become close, but he was still a client. "Well, not you, of course," Lucia said, punching him playfully on the shoulder. "You do more than most people in your position—and soon, we'll have changed an entire country's approach to refugees. People like you are why I'm still in this crazy game. Not everyone is a hypocrite."

"Cheers to that."

They sat together as a little pack of revelers, led by Tamsin, started to gather on the other side of the fire. Curiosity got the better of them when the group erupted in laughter and someone loudly exclaimed, "You cannot be serious, your third-form teacher?" Lucia and Henry scooched around to find themselves in the middle of a rousing game of Never Have I Ever. By the looks of it (and the smell of alcohol), Tamsin was losing. Or winning, depending on her ultimate objective.

Their champagne glasses were quickly refilled (the absolute decadence of playing a drinking game with champagne was not lost on Lucia), and they jumped right in.

"Never have I ever . . . had sex with Archie!" said Bella, a fourth cousin twice removed of the queen and seventy-first in line for the throne.

They all shrieked with laughter, and Lucia watched as a floppy-haired boy across the fire turned beet red. Lucia was the only one who didn't drink. Tamsin, the other girls, and even Henry took sips from their glasses. Clearly Archie was popular.

"Never have I ever stolen Delphine's racing horse, painted it pink, and returned it to the stable before morning," said Penelope, Bella's younger sister (and therefore seventy-second in the order of succession).

"Never have I ever bought two of the same diamond necklaces: one for my wife and one for my girlfriend," said Archie, and Lucia wondered what was required to maintain such romantic stamina (and if it was available over the counter).

Lucia darted a glance toward the villa and her cozy bed inside, hoping she could sneak away unnoticed before her turn, given that she hadn't dated or had sex with any member of the royal family or even seen a racing horse up close.

Henry was next. "Never have I ever . . . gotten so drunk I threw up in a vase that was a prize for a silent auction at that National Children's Society gala and had to be escorted out."

Archie turned red again and took a sip.

"That's not fair," Archie said. "You know how I feel about those bloody charity galas. Everyone chewing off their arms to get a meeting with me. The soliciting for cash, it's never-ending. You know? When I go to galas I feel like a gazelle at a watering hole."

"God yes, the pressure of it all," Bella piped up. "I mean, isn't that why we're all here? I invited Rebecca"—Sir Rupert's third daughter—"to the spinal-injuries dinner at Whitehall last month, so then naturally when the Sunbliss invitation showed up, I had to agree."

Everyone nodded in agreement. Lucia had never considered how big a role peer pressure played in people's generosity. "So there's no part of you that has a genuine desire to give back?" she asked, emboldened by the frankness of the discussion and the potent combination of jet lag and champagne.

"Well, of course," Penelope said. "That was instilled from a very young age. On my birthday every year, my parents would take us to the children's cancer unit. I loved it. And needed it." She chewed her bottom lip. "If I spent all my time with you lot"—she gestured at the circle—"I'd lose perspective on what's real."

"Well said, Pen," Henry added. "Sometimes it's hard to connect coming here and sitting on the beach with fixing the state of the world. Daddy always says everything I do is open to scrutiny. So I better be damn careful where I choose to spend my time—whom I talk to, which events I attend. It will come back to bite me, he says, and him, too."

A quiet voice piped up. "All the time, I feel like such a sham. Even here." Tamsin started to get teary. "I'm only here because of my surname. Everyone wants to know about Daddy. How does your father feel about this? What will your father agree to?—like I'm not clever enough to have an opinion because I didn't earn the money I have."

There were murmurs of assent around the circle.

"And what's worse"—Tamsin was full-blown crying now—"is that I don't know what my father feels about anything." She barked out a bitter laugh. "We don't talk, and sure, I'll get all his money, but . . ." She trailed off.

"Here's one!" She raised her glass. "Never have I ever . . . heard *I love you* from my parents."

Lucia took a drink but was shocked to see no one else do the same. Bella and Penelope had pulled Tamsin into a group hug as she wept softly on their shoulders.

She looked over at Henry, who shrugged. Then he stood up and dusted his hands on his chinos. "There, there, chaps," he said. "No need to drown ourselves in our sorrows. That's what the champagne is for. And if that doesn't work, let's not forget what our inherited wealth can get us. The absolute best, class A hard drugs money can buy." He raised his nearly empty glass, and everyone laughed gently, grateful to have been saved from the excess of emotion. In a lighter mood, they disbanded.

"Get some rest, Lucia," Henry said with a half smile. "Big day tomorrow. We still have to save the world before we fly home."

Lucia was transported back in time to a memory she had long forgotten. She was about thirteen and having dinner with her grandparents. The night wasn't special in any particular way—they always had dinner together—except Lucia was upset. She had been invited on a school trip to Washington, DC, that her grandparents couldn't afford. Earlier that day, she'd told her teacher to give up her slot.

"*Mija*, don't worry," her *abuela* had said, cradling her in her arms at the table like she was a baby. "Your life is going to be filled with so many successes. You will go to Washington a hundred times over. We love you, *mija, no llores.*"

Her *abuelo* placed a hand on her shoulder as well and repeated it: "*Te quiero, amor.*" It was a phrase Lucia had heard so many times in her life that she had almost taken it for granted. She found it entirely unfathomable that someone like Tamsin or Henry, people with everything, had been denied such a basic need. No wonder they were always seeking gratification somewhere else.

She strolled back into the house, realizing that, if it were up to her, she wouldn't trade her own upbringing for all the Birkin bags or champagne in the world.

Finally, she could sleep. She put her pajamas on and had brushed the top half of her teeth when she heard the ding of a notification. One ding, then two, then four. She rushed to her phone, worried something else might have happened to Marley, but there were no messages. Another ding sent her rummaging for the GIFGAL smartwatch. Toothbrush still hanging out of her mouth, she retrieved it from her bag. It was a text from Tristan:

Emergency, Luce. Earthquake in Pakistan, and it's mega. Nothing can get in or out, and everyone wants to help—all our clients, everyone. Get down to the main building now. Celeste already here, and we have crisis headquarters set up in conference room B.

Lucia sighed. No rest for the wicked, or the good, either, she guessed. She threw on something presentable that Celeste couldn't insult (though, knowing her, she'd find a way) and quietly let herself out the front door.

Chapter 20
The Gala

"Oh my god, thank you, I love you, you can have anything you want from me. My next child? All the change in my purse?"

"Ew, a child? Do you love or despise me?"

Tristan handed over the coffee, still steaming in a compostable cup. They had been awake for almost thirty-six hours. Even Celeste, who, Lucia noticed for the first time since she'd known her, had bags under her eyes. (Given the circumstances, she shouldn't have been so judgmental, but the morning had been tough, and she was going to take a small dose of glee wherever she could get it, even if it was catty.)

The earthquake was the largest Pakistan had ever experienced, with vibrations felt as far away as China. Lucia had more than a passing familiarity with the geography of the area. The epicenter in northeastern Pakistan was not far from the girls' school that Rona supported. The area was mountainous, rural with poor roads. Rona had phoned at 6:00 a.m. UK time, beside herself with worry.

"I'll keep trying to reach them," Lucia calmed her. "Phone lines are down. But I promise, I'll keep trying."

"Thank you, my dear," Rona said through tears. "Those girls are the closest thing to daughters that I have. Please, just let me know as soon as you hear anything."

Lucia, Tristan, and Celeste weren't aid workers or volunteers digging survivors out of the rubble or bandaging wounds, but as the philanthropy hub of a major global bank, with a sizable number of donors who cared about what happened in South Asia, they had their own role to play.

This was when the vast global network of Eastern Currents came in handy. From their little conference room at GIFGAL, the team fielded phone calls and emails from their deep-pocketed clients who were eager to do whatever they could do to help in the aftermath of the disaster. As the death toll rose, the totals on their donation board climbed.

Lucia and her colleagues contacted every big emergency-relief nonprofit and the most trusted and effective small ones, facilitating the transfers from pounds, dollars, and yen to rupees. They gathered as much information as they could about the specific needs on the ground to share with their clients to encourage them to give more. They were like old-time phone operators, creating links and connections with speed, making sure the most money moved to the organizations best equipped to use it immediately.

The outpouring of generosity had been astounding; even Lucia was stunned by how much money they had managed to move into the hands of frontline aid organizations. This was philanthropy at its best.

It must have been the adrenaline that kept her going because physically it did not seem possible that she was still awake. Lucia now took a grateful gulp of coffee and looked at her watch. The gala would be starting soon. She couldn't believe she still had to go, after everything that had happened, but it was GIFGAL's culminating event, one that "could not be missed for something as trivial as sleep," according to Celeste.

She and the others finally left the conference room with a long list of still-to-dos, to get ready for the gala. Lucia allowed herself no more than twenty minutes to catnap, setting three different alarm clocks to ensure she didn't oversleep again, before dragging her weary body into a freezing shower to revive herself. After a battle to tame her curls into submission, she took an appreciative look in the mirror—she had followed the dress code requiring everyone to wear red and donned a floor-length crimson gown with a high halter neck. She felt strong and sexy, like she could take over the world. Or maybe fix it.

She took a selfie and sent it to Ollie with the eggplant emoji. He read it right away but didn't respond. Still angry, then, she thought anxiously.

Lucia hurried down the hallway and knocked on Tamsin's bedroom door. "Tamsin," she said quietly. "It's after seven. Are you ready to head over?"

"Luce? Is that you? Go on without me. I'm working on something, and anyway, you know me, I like to make an entrance."

Lucia sighed as she walked down the stairs and out front to hail a golf cart. What on earth could Tamsin be working on? What if she had been serious when she said she wanted to bedazzle the prosthetics of the first hundred dogs who received surgery through her foundation?

She pushed the thought out of her mind. Today, she had facilitated millions of pounds directly to the hands of non-profits supporting the recovery of the earthquake. It felt like the promise of her job at Eastern Currents fulfilled. Her purpose. And she was about to watch a lot more money than that change hands.

The closing gala would be a memorable affair. There was a cocktail hour followed by a multicourse dinner. An A-list performer, always a surprise to the guests, would take the stage (not, as Lucia once assumed, for free, but to the tune of up to three million dollars for a thirty-minute set—that was one hundred thousand dollars per minute).

But even that wasn't the ultimate highlight of the night. The peak would come during the pledging.

This portion of the evening had been described to Lucia as an auction with no prizes at the end—except the validation of one's peers (and of course basking in the warm glow of one's own generosity). Sir Rupert would take the stage to ask the attendees what they were prepared to give after several days at GIFGAL, and guests would respond with public pledges, delivered out loud.

Nigel Petersham, the bank's big boss, was attending specifically to deliver their pledge, a partnership to provide safe drinking water for twenty million people across Southeast Asia. It was Eastern Currents' biggest commitment to date, and it had been Celeste's idea.

The golf cart dropped Lucia off in front of a four-story modern building where cocktail hour was nearly finished. Bartenders flanked either side of the door with trays of red appletinis topped with perfect miniature-golden-apple garnishes. She took one and then pulled out her smartwatch to send Tristan a message:

Where are you? I'm the one in red holding an appletini LOL.

He messaged back immediately:

You are not as funny as you think you are. I'm hiding in the corner where the windows meet, come find me here.

Lucia pushed her way through the crowd and found Tristan behind an enormous potted palm.

"What's the matter, too many exes in here for your liking?" she said by way of greeting.

Tristan looked devastatingly handsome. He had gone for a deep-red crushed-velvet suit with a black shirt and no tie. If he did have an ex or two in the room, he should have been showing off.

"Ugh, I wish," he said. "I'm completely knackered from today. Doing good for the world is hell on my skin-care regimen, let me tell you. And Celeste is freaking out. I keep telling her everything will be fine, but you know how she gets. She made me go over Nigel's pledge speech four times." Tristan gave an exaggerated eye roll. "I escaped just as she was going to make me recite the entire ballroom's table plan from memory—again."

"A toast to her," Lucia said, clinking her glass with Tristan's. "May her triumph tonight allow her to spare the innocent children whose blood she would otherwise drink for breakfast tomorrow."

"Hear, hear."

A gong sounded, and the throng of guests started to move toward the ballroom. Lucia and Tristan hung back until most of the crowd had entered the room, then walked in together. Lucia was glad he was there for both moral and physical support—she nearly stumbled when she took in the whole scene.

The walls were covered in red roses, thousands of flowers, with tiny lights strung between them. Petals had been spread along the floor, a lush floral carpet, emitting a fragrant but not overpowering scent. Lucia weaved through the tables, each adorned with a burgundy tablecloth and a golden rococo centerpiece topped with tall white tapered candles. She felt as if she'd been transported from a tropical island in the Atlantic to a romantic French château in the countryside. Even in her zombielike state, she was impressed. She half expected one of the candelabras to start singing to her.

They were assigned to different tables, so she and Tristan parted ways in the middle of the ballroom. By the time Lucia found her seat, Sir Rupert's wife, Anna, was already deep in conversation with Celeste, who was treating Anna, a person she deemed important, like she had discovered the cure for cancer. Celeste had worked some evil magic on herself because she looked spectacular. She had gone for a wine-colored gown with a plunging *V* neckline that drew the eye to a diamond-encrusted ruby hanging around her neck. Her hair was slicked back, and her wrinkles had been smoothed away by some kind of superstrength moisturizer (a French brand, no doubt) that imparted an unusually dewy glow. No one would have guessed that she had been up all night figuring out the best way to hedge currency transfers and showing off her rusty but nevertheless impressive Urdu.

Brendan was already seated, attempting conversation with Mr. Lin, one of the bank's highest-profile Chinese clients. It appeared that they supported the same football team, Lucia noted with relief. Her Mandarin was nonexistent, but she had taught herself a few basic conversational phrases when she'd discovered he would be at their table. Brendan, however, was the kind of guy who assumed everyone spoke English (even after all his years at a multinational bank), and if they didn't, he thought yelling would help. Still, Mr. Lin and he seemed to be bonding.

Besides Tamsin, who had yet to arrive, the only others missing were Sir Rupert, who was making his way to the table dressed in a bright-red tuxedo, and Nigel, who walked with him. Lucia had not yet met Nigel in person, but she recognized him from his portrait on the tenth floor of her office: tall and rail thin with a head of white hair, a patrician nose, and small, rectangular spectacles. In keeping with the theme, he was wearing a red bow tie.

Sir Rupert didn't sit; he only dropped off Nigel, politely greeted everyone at the table, and tapped the side of his nose twice. "Time for the big show," he said as he turned and marched up to the stage.

A hush descended over the audience as he took the podium. "Welcome," he said, "to the Global Innovation Forum for Giving and Loving's Annual Closing Gala. This night is a culmination of everything we have been discussing, mulling, debating between bites from our food truck friends"—carnitas, we hardly knew ye, Lucia thought—"and lectures from the world's leaders in impact. Later this evening, as you know, I'm going to ask you to give, and give generously. But right now, we feast to the delightful tones of the Vodka Sodas, Harvard University's premiere a cappella group all the way from Cambridge."

The first course was placed down in front of them in unison as a group of young men with good hair, white teeth, and red cummerbunds took to the stage. Celeste leaned toward Lucia. "Where is Ta-ma-sin?" she hissed into her ear. She masked the harshness of her tone with a grin for the others, but Lucia could hear the poison in her voice. "She'd better be here, or you will be the one to blame."

Lucia swallowed and pulled out her smartwatch. On your way? she messaged Tamsin through the delegate-finder app. But her status read "Offline."

After a rousing set of boop-ba-pa-doos and some beatboxing, the Vodka Sodas took their bows, the first courses were cleared, and the mains were brought out. There was still no sign of Tamsin as Sir Rupert returned to the stage, but there was no time for Lucia to go search her out. This was the moment they had been waiting for.

Lucia couldn't wait to see if the pledging would be as ostentatious as everyone promised. Generally, her British clients didn't do public displays of wealth. The idea of one of them standing up and proclaiming a specific monetary amount seemed nearly as far-fetched as Celeste running around the room in her underwear.

"I hope you've all enjoyed your evening thus far," Sir Rupert began. "Now is the moment you've all been waiting for. But before the pledging begins, I have a special, yet sobering announcement. By now you will have all been made aware of the devastation in Pakistan. We have heard by satellite phone from a few of our partners on the ground, and I'm sorry to say, the situation is even worse than we feared."

The room was silent as he continued. "The Sunbliss Foundation has decided that, given the scope of this disaster, any gifts tonight that are not restricted for other projects will go directly to support the survivors of the earthquake and their efforts to rebuild in Pakistan. We may be faraway in distance, but we are with them in spirit, and we will not fail them."

The ballroom filled with rapturous applause. Even Celeste clapped loudly. She had been busting her ass just as hard as Lucia and Tristan all day, without complaint.

"Now, with our Pakistani friends in our hearts, who would like to begin the pledging?"

No one wanted to go first: Starting either too small or too big could be social or financial suicide. Thirty painfully long seconds of awkward silence followed, so excruciating that Lucia nearly raised her own hand, just to break the ice. Then, mercifully, Lady Tregarian of Sussex—once described by Tristan as "cheaper than a rabbit-fur coat," which is, apparently, quite cheap—stood up. "Two hundred thousand pounds, Sir Rupert," she said. Lucia was floored. Maybe there was something in the water. Or the appletinis.

"Thank you so much, my lady, for your generous gift. We are pleased as punch that you have chosen to be part of our mission this evening. Who's next?"

Once the cork was popped, the commitments started flowing like Wuatemalan rum. Many of the pledges, like the one Eastern Currents would make, had been planned months in advance. But others seemed to be given spontaneously, inspired by the call to arms.

An Indian steel billionaire offered up a tract of one hundred acres of land to build an engineering college in Tamil Nadu and announced an additional endowment to provide fifty annual scholarships for displaced Pakistani earthquake survivors to attend for free. A young German man cried as he expressed a gift of half a million to remember his father who'd died recently (although Lucia had heard through the grapevine that the man in question was relieved to have inherited earlier than anticipated, having racked up seven figures in gambling debts from Macao to Monte Carlo). A CEO from a multinational soda company vowed to transport as much bottled water to the front lines as possible.

"What an extraordinary offer," Sir Rupert said. "Although we are hearing that the damage and lack of coordination on the ground is making the delivery of supplies impossible. But as soon as this is resolved, we will do everything in our power to help you bring clean water there. Thank you for your pledge."

The next sound came from her own table. She whipped her head around to see Mr. Lin standing up. He began speaking in Mandarin, gesturing animatedly and stamping one foot. It took Sir Rupert's translators a minute to write the message down and bring a slip of paper up to the stage. Sir Rupert's eyes went wide, and he swallowed visibly before speaking.

"This is truly extraordinary. I'm not quite sure what to say. The munificent Mr. Lin has just offered up a donation of one hundred million dollars to support the rescue efforts in Pakistan. Mr. Lin, how can we even begin to express our gratitude? You are a gift to us all."

The entire room stood to applaud Mr. Lin, and Lucia felt tears sting the corners of her eyes. It was an incredible display of the human spirit. Everyone had an image of the world they wanted to see in their mind's eye, but only a privileged few had the power to realize their visions. If they could be moved, convinced to be bold, perhaps they could do incredible things. If you could disregard the glitz and pomp and exorbitant flower budget, tonight was what philanthropy was all about.

"I'm not sure we can top that, Mr. Lin. What a night this has been for Sunbliss, and for the world. Thanks to your generosity, we are surely going to make a difference in Pakistan where it's most urgently needed. Now, I'll invite you all to make a dent in our chef's signature molten-chocolate lava cake, which is made entirely of cocoa beans harvested from this extraordinary cooperative farm in . . ."

"*Wait!*"

The mandate emanated from behind the double doors at the ballroom entrance, which now swung open, forcing everyone's heads to swivel in that direction. There she was: Tamsin, alone, in a bright-white flowing ball gown, a slash of red lipstick her only nod to the dress code. She stood out in the sea of red dresses and suits, which Lucia assumed was the intention. So, this was what she meant by "make an entrance."

Tamsin glided past the tables and went directly up to the stage, smiling graciously at Sir Rupert.

"Why, Ms. St. James, what a pleasure to see you. You look ravishing, as ever."

"Thank you, Sir Rupert, not so bad yourself." She winked at him, and he blushed. "I just need a moment of everyone's time. Team, can you please get everything ready?"

A large screen came down from the ceiling, showing a flashing "No Input" message.

"Some of you may not know me, but you all know my father. Or know of him. He wouldn't be caught dead at one of these things." A few people chuckled nervously. Lucia felt abject terror surge through her veins. She had no idea what was coming. She glanced cautiously at Celeste, who appeared impassive, but Lucia clocked a small twitch in her eyebrow.

"My dad is very protective of his money—probably because he didn't have much growing up—but he raised me to be thoughtful to, you know, poor people and all of that. Or, at least, dogs. I've started my own foundation recently, it's really a lovely thing . . ."

Lucia put her head in her hands and prayed it would be over soon. Was she going to ask people to support dog prosthetics? Nigel had a confused look on his face. Brendan was fidgeting. Whatever happened, Celeste would throw the blame on Lucia.

". . . But that's not why I'm up here tonight. I never felt like it was my responsibility to take care of others." Tamsin made eye contact with Lucia and smiled. "But I recently met someone truly special who has shown me that I can do so much good in the world. If I try, I can be more than what everyone thinks I am, including my dad." Tamsin looked down with her gargantuan eyes, as if bidding the tears to flow. A single beautiful droplet graced her cheek (even her tear ducts wouldn't dare disobey her) before she looked back up at Sir Rupert.

"When I heard about the earthquake this morning, I felt sad, but I also felt something I haven't ever felt before when hearing about these crises happening all over the world. I felt powerful. I knew what to do, maybe for the first time ever. I knew I could give money—and trust me, I will. But I knew I could do even more. Boys, is the video ready?"

The "No Input" sign was replaced by a grainy feed. As the picture came into focus, they saw tall mountains rising in the background. There were misplaced piles of earth all around, next to collapsed buildings. A man in camouflage stood in the middle of the screen trying to get a microphone to work as a huge convoy of trucks paraded behind him.

"This is live right now in Shikargai, very near the epicenter of last night's earthquake. And that's Michael, Daddy's COO. Can you hear me, Michael?"

"Yes, Tamsin. Hello, GiffyGaffy folks."

"It's GIFGAL, but no bother," she said. "See, I knew Daddy's business already had supply chain logistics set up all over Pakistan. So I called him, and with a bit of effort, we managed to redirect all his vehicles and coordination technology to the survivors of the earthquake. Sorry to everyone waiting for an Amazon parcel today, this was a bit more important."

Michael continued. "I can confirm that we have a road open for aid workers and the UN to enter with supplies and large rescue equipment. I just wanted to pop on for a moment to show you we are here, on the ground, and we're going to save as many people as possible."

Lucia could not have been more shocked if Tamsin had pulled a live baby cheetah out of her brassiere. In fact, that might have been less shocking.

For months, she had been going to countless meetings at catteries and no-kill shelters, laced with conversations about all the assets Tamsin had at her disposal and how she could apply them for the greater good of humanity. She often glazed over during Lucia's monologues, checking for dirt under her nails or assessing her split ends. Lucia had just assumed her efforts had been ignored.

Yet here she was. This wisp of a girl and her giant eyelashes had almost single-handedly—with the help of a huge supply-chain-logistics company owned by her dad—saved thousands of lives.

The screen shut off, and as if broken out of a trance, the room exploded in wild and thunderous whooping and cheering, all propriety and decorum thrown to the wind. Lucia put two fingers in her mouth and whistled as Tamsin beamed, radiant atop the stage.

"Well, Ms. St. James. I don't know what to say," Sir Rupert offered.

"Say you'll help me. Thank you for inviting me, Sir Rupert. And I need to thank my favorite bankers at Eastern Currents. I couldn't have done it without you." Tamsin looked over and blew a kiss in their direction.

Lucia snuck a glance at Celeste. Any semblance of chill she had was completely gone, her jaw nearly on the floor. Besides the impact this would have—which was incredible—it was a professional coup. Their AUM would skyrocket, and Celeste would get to take the lion's share of the credit. No one would ever question Celeste after what her team had delivered tonight. Taking over Brendan's job would be a slam dunk.

The applause continued as they watched Tamsin disappear into a swarm of well-wishers. Celeste composed herself and looked Lucia square in the eye. Then she held up her glass and tipped it in her direction—a silent toast for a job well done.

Dessert was served—the cake was as good as everyone said it would be—and PTO, the hottest K-pop band in the world, took the stage to perform. Most of the guests rushed to the dance floor, but Lucia stayed in her seat, reveling in the huge accomplishments of the evening.

She reflected on all the effort—the late nights, the arguments with Ollie and Sooz, the missed bedtimes with Marley, the undercurrent of anxiety, and the way her heart skipped a beat every time she saw she had a new email from "Le Fevre, Celeste."

She wished Ollie was awake. And not mad at her. She wanted to share this moment with him so badly, not as an I told you so, but because she wanted to share every joyful moment with him. "See?" she would have said. "How can you be mad at me? Look what I've achieved! Wasn't it worth the sacrifice to help so many people? Isn't this the example we want to set for our daughter?"

She had done good. A lot of good.

"Absolutely splendid work, Mrs. Barrow. Truly. You secured the future of the St. James fortune for the bank. It's something we've been working for years to achieve." Lucia turned to see Nigel standing over her.

She stood up quickly and shook his outstretched hand. "Wow, yes, thank you so much, Mr. Petersham. It's been a pleasure. I didn't even know you knew my name," she blubbered.

"I make it a point to know the names of all our rising stars. You have a bright future here at Eastern Currents, I assure you."

"Thank you, sir, I love being a part of this team. And I couldn't have done it without Celeste's mentorship." It was the right thing to say in the moment, even if it rang hollow to her ears.

"Well done again," Nigel said, and with a curt nod of his head, he made to walk away.

Lucia checked her phone, which had come in and out of service at some point that night. There was an email from Seema to Rona, explaining that she and the girls were shaken up, but everyone had survived. The school building had collapsed, but no one was seriously injured. Then a text from Rona:

Tomorrow, we'll get the funding together to rebuild the school. Tonight, I finally sleep knowing everyone is OK.

Tomorrow. There would be work to do. So much work— to make sure the generosity that was spilling over was harnessed and directed to the right places, and to repair the rifts in her personal life.

But tonight, she reached for an appletini—she was in the mood to celebrate a job well done.

Where were Henry and Tristan? Trying to spot them in the mass of red on the dance floor was like searching for stripes in *Where's Waldo?*

The appletini had barely grazed her lips when she heard another ding—perhaps her delegate-finder app with a pin from Tristan on where to locate his shaking hips—but no, it was her phone. A message from Sooz. Lucia opened the text immediately:

Dropped dinner off at yours tonight. Homemade lasagna. Not sure your hubs knows how to make anything besides frozen chicken nuggets, so he was grateful.

She could picture the sheer relief on Ollie's face as Sooz arrived bearing a home-cooked dish. She tried not to picture her daughter attempting to feed it to herself with only one good hand.

Then a second message came through:

Look—I know you and I are going through a bit of a rough patch, but I felt like I should tell you that Belly, that evil ice queen, was at your flat already, alone with Ollie. She looked all too at home in your kitchen—open bottle of wine, two glasses, and something of a guilty expression when I walked in. If you want, I'll find her tomorrow, kidnap her, make her ride the Tube, and if that doesn't kill her, I'll force her to come get a manicure with me in Elephant and Castle. Anyway, as your friend—even if we're in a fight—I thought you deserved to know.

The appletini Lucia was holding slipped, shattering on the floor. But no one seemed to notice; the GIFGAL staff swept and mopped up the mess before she had even made it to the exit.

* * *

The after-after-party was raging on the beach. She could hear the merriment outside her window, but there was no possibility of joining them.

It was well after 3:00 a.m., and her flight off the island was in five hours. Would she reach the end of Belly's Instagram feed by then? Only time would tell. Lucia, still in her red dress, sticky with dance floor sweat that smelled unsurprisingly like apples, was unable to peel her exhausted eyes away from the screen.

First, she had gone back through Ollie's messages. Why hadn't he mentioned that Belly had come over? What was she doing there? Didn't she have her own family to take care of? And what did Sooz mean by the fact that she looked *at home*? Belly had never been to Lucia's house before.

At least not when Lucia was there.

Then she pulled up Instagram and searched until she found her—@bellyisblessed was her handle. Lucia's desire to vomit only grew the more she scrolled. The latest post was a photo of Belly and Rosemary Chatto at *Relics of the Raj*. A candid shot and yet the two of them looked like supermodels. Lucia was horrified to spot herself in the background of the photo, from the side, mid-canapé. She looked like a bear with a fish in its mouth. Her bank ID photo it was not.

She scrolled down farther. Belly in a bikini on the beach in Ibiza. Skiing (with perfect form) in Austria. On a boat, wearing an enormous fluffy hat that would look stupid on anyone else, tagging @chanelofficial with thanks for the gift. Lucia simultaneously wanted Belly to die (or maybe be horribly disfigured in a boating accident) and to be her. She couldn't stop scrolling.

A few more swipes down and her heart dropped. There was a photo of Belly on a sofa, holding a glass of wine, head thrown back in laughter. It was Lucia's sofa. And Lucia's wineglass, one of the distinctive set she had picked out herself when she'd first moved to London. So clearly, the person out of the frame must be Lucia's husband.

There was more evidence of Ollie's presence in her life the farther down she scrolled. Belly sat in front of a fireplace at a pub—someone's arm was around her shoulders. The man was cut out of the photo, but she was sure the wedding ring was the one she had slipped onto Ollie's finger with the blessing of Las Vegas's finest Elvis-impersonating minister. Another image was labeled *quick work lunch, all business*, at what she knew was the bistro around the corner from Ollie's office.

Any joy or warmth from the evening's triumph with Tamsin had seeped out of her, replaced by cascading waves of rage and jealously that washed over her in tandem and left her in despair. While she had been working her ass off, attempting (albeit not always succeeding) to do some good for the world and be a decent mother and wife, her husband had been secretly gallivanting with this woman. What else hadn't he told her?

She stayed online all night, illuminated only by her phone's screen, until the sun came up.

Chapter 21
Happy Birthday, Baby

"Sweetheart, can you get the door please? It's probably the clown . . . or the magician. Whoever it is, they need to be sent out to join the bubble man in the square so they can set up," Lucia screamed from under the hair dryer.

Hiring three separate party entertainers for a gaggle of two year olds who would remember nothing was, like every decision she'd made in relation to this party, a ridiculous one.

It had been three weeks since she'd returned from GIFGAL, three weeks of throwing herself headfirst into work all day and birthday-party planning all night, leaving little time for anything else, least of all to confront the smoldering fire of her marriage that was liable to erupt into a dumpster-sized conflagration at any moment. But, hopefully, not today.

The atmosphere between Ollie and Lucia had been so tense it was almost unbearable. She hadn't dared to confront him about Belly and the photos she saw or the text from Sooz. He hadn't said a word about her not returning when Marley broke her arm or her working too hard. Marley had become their conduit. They talked at and through her, and Lucia felt it was only a matter of time before her daughter would be trilingual in English, Spanish, and Passive-Aggressiveness.

They danced around the gigantic elephant in the room (and not the one Lucia had purchased for Marley at the airport and shared her seat with on the way home because it was too big for the overhead compartment). Lucia was angry at her husband, but she was also terrified that her suspicions were correct. The elephant—the metaphoric one—had left an enormous amount of space between her and Ollie, a gap that had started small but continued to expand the longer they ignored it. Had Belly stepped in to fill the void? Maybe all that air between them had allowed a different spark to reignite. She wasn't sure, even now, that she wanted to know.

Even worse: She felt a staggering amount of mom guilt.

It was mom guilt, that useless but insistent, gnawing emotion, that had slapped its credit card down on the counter to pay for the overpriced stuffed elephant. Mom guilt that had driven Lucia to hire nearly a basketball team's worth of party performers and to use one of Marley's drawings as the base design for invitations, which she'd handwritten until her knuckles seized up. It was the mom guilt that had pushed her shopping cart down the aisle at the Tesco Superstore and loaded it with all manner of plastic crap to fill goody bags to the brim, an activity she had worked on until three in the morning, having gotten home from work after 10:00 p.m.

What better antidote to feeling like a horrible parent than to throw an over-the-top kid's birthday party? Moms have been doing it for years. They are single-handedly responsible for the exponential growth in the custom-balloon-sign industry.

It was not lost on her that adding excessive party planning to her already punishing schedule meant she had even less time with her daughter, which was all Marley seemed to want. She had been extra clingy since Lucia had returned from GIFGAL, desperate for attention, which in turn only made Lucia feel worse. Every time she looked over and saw that cast on her daughter's fragile little arm, she felt awful, which made it even harder to leave for work in the morning. To cope, she bought personalized party napkins on Etsy.

In the end, Lucia told herself, it would all be worth it. Marley would have the best day ever. All the kids would love it; the parents would applaud her hostessing prowess and tell her what a great mom she was. And at the end of the event, they would capture that Instagram-perfect moment, the three of them leaning over Marley's two-tier mermaid-unicorn-rainbow cake about to blow out the candles. She had dreamed about that cake in her sleep. Sometimes in her nightmares, it attacked her, a giant mermaid unicorn with fangs that yelled obscenities at her in a French accent.

She refused to think about work today. Or the storm brewing with her husband. Or her mortal enemy Belly—who would, naturally, be attending the party—and whatever she had been doing in Lucia's home while she was away.

Today was about Marley, her friends, the custom-baked cake, and the Pink Paradise signature cocktail she had concocted from scratch, taking a page out of the GIFGAL playbook (the golden rule of every successful children's party: cocktails). She headed down to the square in front of their house where party preparations were in full swing. A few guests had arrived early (a habit of English people that Lucia had always found mildly annoying; being punctual at work is one thing, but being early to a party was a faux pas of the tallest order).

Children chased one another, and parents chased toddlers, all making circles around the bubble man, who was getting ready to start his demonstration. The bubbles would be followed by the magic show, and then the clown would surprise them all with balloon animals before they cut the cake and sent everyone on their way with bellies full of sugar and bags full of nonrecyclable junk that would probably end up in the garbage (she promised herself she would plant a tree to make up for that). Two hours, start to finish. Maybe after the last guest had departed and the final gift had been unwrapped, Lucia would finally feel like she had atoned for her sins (a girl could hope).

Guests lined up their Bugaboos along the gate and offered Marley carefully wrapped gifts that she was sure to ignore in favor of playing with the boxes. Lucia felt on edge and not just because Belly and her family were liable to arrive any minute; everything needed to go smoothly. She caught a flash of tangerine out of the corner of her eye—Sooz and her brood entering the square from the south gate.

Another storm brewing on another front. What was it called when two storms collided to make one giant hurricane-esque disaster? A sharknado? It was the most apt description of her personal life at the moment.

Lucia was still smarting over everything Sooz had said at the museum in spite of her text about Belly, which showed, if nothing else, loyalty, but her fury had mellowed into mild discomfort. She appreciated how Sooz had stepped up when Marley broke her arm, bringing dinner over (and acting as her spy) and even painting Marley's nails under her cast. Most of all, Lucia missed her friend, terribly. That feeling was more pressing than the need to stay angry.

Her phone buzzed in her pocket, but she ignored it—she was off the clock. It was Tristan, most likely, sharing details of whatever all-night-into-the-morning rave he was at. Well, he would just have to wait. Lucia grabbed two Pink Paradises from the table and walked over to Sooz, who was standing on her own apart from the crowd.

"Here," Lucia said handing her the cup. "It's a kid's party. You're going to need it."

"Ta," Sooz said, not making eye contact.

"Thank you so much for coming," Lucia tried again with more warmth in her voice.

Finally, Sooz looked at her and shrugged. "Atticus wouldn't miss it, would he?" she said. Her tone, in contrast, was chilly.

"Of course, Marley would never dream of a party without Atticus," Lucia went on. "But I am glad you're here, too," she added, nudging Sooz's shoulder with hers. "I've missed you."

"And whose fault is that?" Sooz lashed, then retreated. "Sorry. Look, I've missed you, too, babe. But you've been so bloody unavailable. It's hard to miss a ghost."

Making light of the situation clearly wasn't working, so she attempted another tactic: groveling. "I'm the one that's sorry," she said. "Work has been crazy, and after our disastrous night out . . ." Lucia let her voice trail off. "Well, I didn't even know if you would want to see me. But I miss you so much. You came through for Ollie and Marley when I was gone, and I just started the most over-the-top Tilly Willy yet, all about a throuple . . ."

"*Three's (Never) a Crowd?*" she asked, her interest now piqued. "Yeah, I have it on hold at the library."

"Well, let's read it together. Or do something together. Anything." She placed her hands on Sooz's shoulders. She winced but didn't shrug them off. "Sooz, you are important to me. You're my best friend."

"Too right. Your only friend," she said, but there was a small smile behind it. "Speaking of three being a crowd . . ." She gestured over at the gate. "I can't believe she had the nerve to show up here."

Lucia followed her gaze to where Belly had just arrived in a midriff-baring two-piece floral dress and, inexplicably, two nannies for her one child.

"Yeah, well, she's Ollie's *friend*," Lucia said.

"Do you want to talk about it?" Sooz asked, peering at Lucia with genuine concern.

"No," she sighed. "I mean, I do. Just not today." She shook off the unease that had settled over her. "Today is about Marley. Thank you, though." At least some of the ice between them had thawed.

Her phone buzzed again, but between sorting out the entertainers and making sure people had food and drinks while keeping one eye on Marley (the other was on Belly), Lucia was swept up in the madness.

The party was going better than she had expected. The kids adored the bubble man, were wowed by the magician, and were excitedly waiting for their balloon animals. Marley's face was joy incarnate. Lucia couldn't help but kiss her sweet little cheeks at every opportunity. Time was flying by—it was nearly time for cake and departures. Then, Marley would need a nap, and Lucia planned to soak in the tub, filled with an entire bottle of bubble bath.

The clown began wrapping up his routine, allowing each of the kids to honk his nose. The plan was that he would lead them all in a conga line to the waiting cake where they'd sing "Happy Birthday." She caught Ollie's eye and winked. He winked back. No matter what else was going on between them, today was an accomplishment. They had made this human and kept her alive for two whole years. Her heart swelled with love for this brilliant little person, who was all at once an unexpected combination of the two of them and such a unique individual. After this successful celebration of their daughter, she hoped that she and Ollie would have dinner together later. And talk. Not fight. She desperately wanted to clear the air.

Lucia pulled her phone out of the pocket of her dress to check the time and noticed a call coming in. Unknown number. She let it go to voicemail—the kids were starting to form a marching queue toward the cake table—but it rang again.

Whoever was calling was being annoyingly insistent. She picked it up to yell at them as she walked in the direction of the shimmying toddlers.

"It's Sunday," she answered. "Why are you pestering people on a Sunday?"

"This is how you answer your business phone?" the voice on the other end spat out. In a French accent.

"Celeste!" she fumbled. "Oh gosh, I'm sorry, I thought you were spam."

"Spam? What is spam?"

"Never mind," she said. She looked up to see Ollie gesturing at her. She held up two fingers and mouthed "Two seconds" at him. She had to get Celeste off the phone. "Can I phone you back later? I'm just at my daughter's birthday party, and it's nearly time for cake."

"Charming, I am sure," she said, her voice unable to hide its disdain. "Well this is something slightly more important than your silly games of peekaboo. We have had an urgent call from the palace today."

Lucia was jolted out of party mode and gave Celeste her full attention. "Of course," she said. "What do you need?"

"Apparently the prince has been caught in a, how do I say, sticky situation. There is a report airing next week that will accuse him of some very unpleasant things. Things that will be highly embarrassing for the royals."

"Oh my god, what did he do?"

"That is irrelevant," she snapped. "The issue now is how we can help him. It would be prudent for the royals, especially the prince, to be seen making a very large donation to a charity supporting women. Young women in particular."

"Right. So they want to make a big donation to a good cause to deflect attention from whatever disgusting thing he is being accused of—and probably did."

"Careful," Celeste warned. "These are our biggest clients." Her voiced dropped lower. "I do not like it any more than you, but we will do what we must. They are important, and we cannot afford any mistakes at this delicate time." It was a moment of solidarity—but it was fleeting. "I need a short list, tonight, of five organizations they can donate to. Please pick some with a photogenic executive director. That is it. Go back to your little soiree, but remember, I need it tonight." The line went dead.

Lucia was horrified but also knew she would do as Celeste asked. She put her scruples aside. Innocent until proven guilty, and she consoled herself, at least this would mean a big donation to a worthy nonprofit, no matter the motivation. Which one should she recommend?

She was shaken out of her ruminations by Belly, whom she had thus far managed to avoid. "Lovely party! Georgie had a fabulous time," she said. She looked up, dazed.

"Don't leave before cake," Lucia exclaimed.

"Oh, we had a slice—it was beautiful, if a bit dry," Belly said. "Please do give me the name of your baker next time I see you . . . so I can avoid her. Ha! Only joking. But we must run, we have another birthday party today. The diaries of these toddlers, I tell you. I need a social secretary just to manage her schedule." She spouted this in what seemed like one breath, her haughty laugh tinkling as she walked away.

Lucia looked over at the table, where the beautiful cake had been sliced into pieces and served on paper plates that were dotted over the tablecloth. Kids were licking frosting off their fingers while parents, politely using spoons, were wishing they could do the same. Marley was sitting on the floor, cake smeared all over her face and dress.

"What happened?" she said, sidling up to Ollie, who was standing over Marley.

"We couldn't wait any longer for you to handle whatever work emergency you were dealing with, yet again," he said, annoyed. "Have you ever stood between two dozen children and cake? Marley started to cry. Mummy lit the candles to turn things around. Thankfully, the party was saved."

Lucia's eyes burned. After all the planning and preparation, all the licking envelopes and blowing up balloons until her mouth and tongue felt like they belonged to someone else, the moment she had been waiting for was gone. Over. She had ruined it. No picture-perfect family moment. Lost, for what? A prince who couldn't keep it in his pants.

She suddenly felt very, very tired.

Lucia walked around the garden on autopilot, saying goodbye and picking up plates and cups and putting them into a large, black plastic garbage bag. She tipped the entertainers and thanked people for their gifts. When cleanup was complete, she picked up Marley, who was altogether filthy, and took her upstairs. She peeled off Marley's dress and her own, threw on one of Ollie's old T-shirts, and lay down under the covers with her daughter, desperate for the warmth of her daughter's little body next to hers.

Marley's sugar rush was crashing, as well, and she yawned as she burrowed her body into Lucia's. "Mommy, yummy cake," she said. Tears, ones that she had kept at bay all day, started to spill over. Marley reached her hand up to Lucia's face and patted it.

"No, no cry, Mama." She curled her body around Marley's, and the two of them, for very different reasons, fell into a deep and exhausted sleep.

* * *

Lucia woke up several hours later, unsure of the time. The flat was almost silent—she could hear rain falling softly outside but none of the telltale sounds of her daughter playing in the background. Had Marley woken up and been put back to bed already? How long had she been asleep?

Her stomach growled. She hoped Ollie had ordered something for dinner. If not, there was leftover cake. It was a leftover-cake kind of evening.

Lucia found him in the kitchen, sitting on a tall stool, flipping through the newspaper. Ollie loved a print newspaper and got one every Sunday. It was one of the many quirks she adored.

"That was some party, huh?" she said, leaning in to kiss his lips en route to the fridge. He turned his head, giving her his cheek instead. "Yikes. Frosty much?" she said.

This was going to be a fight. At the worst possible time. She had nothing left in her tank. "I know we need to have it out. But seriously, I just can't handle another argument today."

"There's no argument. Marley's asleep. I just thought we needed some time to talk before I left."

Amid all the craziness, Lucia had almost forgotten Ollie's work retreat this coming week. She couldn't think of anything worse than five days of forced bonding with corporate lawyers in a bunch of yurts in a Welsh field.

She surveyed the pickings in the fridge, which were slim. But the cake was there. It would have to do. She brought it out onto the counter, cut a slice, and took a bite. "What is this, an intervention?" she said while chewing.

Ollie was silent.

"Um, I was kidding." She swallowed, loud enough that in the quiet of the room it reverberated around her.

She and Ollie stared at each other. The church bells outside chimed for the quarter hour. She still didn't know what quarter past it was—it could have been 6:00 or 10:00 p.m. It didn't really matter because, whatever time it was, they couldn't put off this conversation any longer.

"*Amor*," she said, cocking her head to the right with a shy smile, trying a calmer tone and a seductive look—but he was steadfast, his gaze steely. "Fine. You win, OK? Let's get this over with."

Ollie chewed his bottom lip. Then he inhaled deeply and launched. The words came fast, like he couldn't wait to get them out.

"You haven't been yourself lately, and I think you know it. You're working all hours, and if you're not working, you're out. You barely see Marley, or me, for that matter. And for what? A job where they yell at you and treat you poorly and then ship you off to the Caribbean so it's all fine and dandy?" Ollie raised his voice, something he almost never did. He seemed to remember that and quieted down again.

"You're never home. You're running yourself ragged. I'm worried about you," he said, now barely above a whisper. "We're all worried about you."

At the invocation of the royal we, the fire inside her roared. "And exactly who is *we all*? Do you mean your mother?" Lucia retorted. "God forbid we do anything that worries the precious Moira. 'Oh, whatever shall I do?'" Lucia put on a high-pitched English accent. "'Heavens, my spicy Latin daughter-in-law can't make a fruitcake and is married to her job.' *Que mierda.*"

"This," Ollie said, throwing up his arms in the air. "This is exactly what I'm talking about. I know you and Mummy don't see eye to eye on a lot of things, but I thought you would maintain a modicum of decency. At least that you respected my feelings enough not to insult her to my face."

He looked genuinely hurt, taking both hands to his cheeks and rubbing them up and down, as if by massaging the muscles of his mouth, it would make it easier to say what he needed to.

"I know the past couple of years have not been easy for you. The move, the changes. I can acknowledge it has been a difficult transition," he said, more resolved than before. "And I know we didn't know each other for a lot of time before our whirlwind of a romance, but that never seemed to matter before because I *knew* you. But that person has changed. I'm aware that your work is important . . ."

"It *is* important," she snapped. "I'm trying to make things better, not just for you and our daughter. But for a lot of people's daughters." She stood up.

"Our daughter. That's rich. You didn't even come home when our daughter broke her arm."

"She was fine," Lucia said, feeling hot prickles behind her eyeballs and a tingling sensation at the bridge of her nose that signified she was going to cry. "You were there. She was fine. She is fine."

"Yes, she is fine, but that's not the point," Ollie said. "Maybe if you had offered to come back, I would have told you not to. But it was like you didn't even care about her, about me."

"Right," Lucia snorted. "You seemed pretty well taken care of in my absence."

A wave of confusion swept over his face, followed by anger. It was a difficult emotion for happy-go-lucky Ollie to show, and she could see in his languid expression what this discussion had already cost him. Lucia moved from behind the breakfast bar to the dining table. She needed to sit down, calm her agitated body and mind before she could think of how to respond properly. How to even begin?

"That is hugely unfair. How can you say I don't care? That I don't prioritize my family when that is all I have done since Marley came along? The house was clean every day, meals cooked, our daughter was educated, entertained, exercised. I dropped not a single ball, even when I felt like letting each one hit the ground and running away as fast as possible in the other direction." She was yelling now. "Do you even understand that the only reason you never run out of toilet paper is down to meticulous planning by me?

"Where were *your* priorities that first year? Huh? When I was home, lonely, googling 'does my baby hate me?' and 'how to make friends with British people,' sitting in the dark kitchen at four p.m. when the sun had already gone down."

Ollie recoiled, genuinely hurt. "I had no idea things were so bad for you. You always said everything was fine."

"Well, I guess you don't know me as well as you thought you did." Her breathing was heavy, ragged. Things she had pushed to the back of her mind, that she had told herself would be fine, would resolve themselves if she was just patient, came rushing out of her mouth, a torrent of unspoken resentments. "I gave up everything. I left Austin for you, a job I loved. I left America, the only country I've ever known. And I came here to you and all your stupid friends with their stupid nicknames."

It was right there on the tip of her tongue, the question she knew she had to ask but was afraid to know the answer to. She couldn't avoid it any longer. If he wanted to fight, she would fight.

"If you're going to tell me, now's the time. Is this about Belly?"

"What on earth are you talking about?" Ollie looked genuinely shocked, but Lucia went on.

"I see the way she looks at you. You're out with her all the time."

"I go out with all my mates."

Lucia stood up again and started pacing. "Not just out with her, in with her. She's been here, without me knowing. I had to hear it from Sooz, that she was here all cozy with you, drinking wine while Marley was in the other room with a broken arm." She knew she was about to cross a line that she couldn't come back from, but she couldn't stop herself. "Just admit it. You're having an affair, aren't you?"

Ollie stood completely still, his face impassive. "I think you must be right, Lucia. Perhaps I don't know you at all."

Lucia wiped the tears from her eyes. She was deflated. She was so tired. And she still had to put that list together for Celeste. She couldn't face any more of this. "Look, Ollie, I'm exhausted. You're angry. You're leaving for five days, and then we fly off to France." It would be the first vacation Lucia had taken in forever, planned even before she had started the job. "We can put a pin in this for now. Let's just go to bed, OK? And discuss this later."

"Later," Ollie said. "Yes, I thought you might say that." He pulled a canvas bag from behind the counter. "Seeing as I'm already packed, I'm going to sleep at Mummy's tonight. My train to Wales is quite early, anyway. I'll be back to repack for France." He hoisted the bag over his shoulder. "I think we could both use a break from each other, just until we calm down."

There was no fight left in her to disagree. "Fine," she said. "But just so I'm crystal clear, you're not denying it?"

He was quiet as he walked toward the door with his bag. "Goodbye, Lucia. I'll see you in a few days." He left without a backward glance.

Lucia went into the bedroom and threw on sweatpants and an oversize UT Austin hoodie. She thought about ordering delivery from McDonald's, but her body was crying out for sleep; her tiredness won out over her hunger. She went to check on Marley, who was in a deep sleep after the festivities of the day, blissfully unaware of the fact that her mother's life was in shambles. Then, Lucia went into her room and buried herself under the covers. She wished that she could sleep for an entire week, or maybe a month, or however long it took for the mess she had made of her life to resolve itself.

Chapter 22
Off to the Races

"I can smell the manure already." Tristan wrinkled his nose in disgust.

"Do you mean literally or figuratively? Because I am getting whiffs of both," replied Melissa archly.

It was a rare moment of camaraderie between Tristan and Melissa. Lucia, standing between them, was enjoying it. She knew it wouldn't last.

"Melissa, did you have that hat lying around in your wardrobe or did you actually need to phone Big Bird and ask to borrow it off him?"

Melissa did look a bit like the giant yellow children's character. Her rather large, feathery hat was a similar yellow to the shade of her hair, so from certain angles the whole thing just seemed to be part of her head. Lucia privately agreed that she looked ridiculous, but then again, she didn't look much better herself. Only Tristan looked elegant. In his navy morning suit with a matching vest and top hat, he appeared every inch the English gentleman. Unlike the men, ladies were required to wear hats to Ascot, and in the Royal Enclosure, the bigger the hat, the better. Lucia had borrowed one of Moira's, a wide-brimmed lilac number that made her feel like a UFO had landed on her head.

Royal Ascot, the official race of the monarchs' thorough-breds, was, like everything in British society, stratified; each tier or enclosure carried its own connotations of status and power. Anyone could buy tickets to the Windsor Enclosure ("Wouldn't be caught dead there," Tristan scoffed). The Queen Anne Enclosure had been likened by one *Town & Country* reporter to flying premium economy. And then there was the Royal Enclosure, strictly for members or their invited guests, where the three of them had been enjoying their day. Or were enjoying it, until they were harshly summoned by Thomas to meet Celeste outside the Royal Box—yet another even more exclusive level within a level. It seemed to Lucia that no matter how high a person climbed, there would always be another floor above.

It had been a pleasant morning so far, full of champagne-fueled meetings and socializing with clients—most of whom Lucia had, after nearly ten months, met several times before. Still, it was thrilling to be all dressed up at one of the season's leading social events. Even if her hat looked like it was about to take off for its home planet.

Even if her home life was falling apart.

Tonight, Ollie was coming home from his team retreat in Wales, or at least she assumed he was, unless he was planning on spending the night at Moira's so she could do all his laundry for him just the way her precious Peanut liked. Lucia genuinely didn't know. This was the longest they had ever gone without speaking to each other. She told herself it was because there was no service in his yurt. Whether or not that was the truth, she wasn't sure she wanted to know.

Lucia dealt with this crisis in her personal life the way she always did—by ignoring it and throwing herself into work all day long, a place where she was not an abject failure but rather flying very high. She had delivered Celeste the requested list of possible recipients of funds from the disgraced prince before she went to bed on Sunday and was met with a "Good work, Lucia," from Celeste the next day, publicly, in front of everyone.

She had taken advantage of being in Celeste's good graces and left by 6:00 p.m. on the dot while Ollie had been away, savoring a few precious solo evenings with Marley. Being together, just the two of them, reminded her of the best parts of her stay-at-home-mom era. So much had changed since then. After Marley fell asleep, Lucia ordered a takeaway, opened a bottle of wine, and just like the old days, watched one of her favorite romantic comedies until she nodded off. The only difference was that, this time, she cried all the way through.

Tomorrow she, Ollie, and Marley would jet off to Cannes in the South of France for a vacation that was supposed to be full of pastries, lavender, sandcastles, and sex—but instead she found herself praying that her husband, with whom she had planned this romantic/family getaway, was even going to show up.

Tomorrow she would have to face him, her marriage, and the problems that couldn't be ignored or swept under the rug. But today, she was about to meet the queen herself.

"I think my curtsy has improved, don't you?" she asked Melissa with a smile, turning to her and giving her best attempt. "I've been practicing."

"What? Oh right. Sorry, Lucia, I'm so distracted at the moment. If you'll just excuse me." She looked down at her phone, which was not ringing. "I just have to take this—call me when Celeste comes to the door."

This new awkwardness between them had been present since Lucia got back from GIFGAL, and she was sure that's what was eating at Melissa. She felt awful. It didn't help that while Celeste was heaping praise on her, she often berated Melissa for ridiculous little things in the same breath. Lucia had come to see this as one of Celeste's many power moves—divide and conquer, pit your staff against one another and watch them compete for your approval. She had tried her best not to engage, shooting sincerely apologetic glances at Melissa throughout the day. Melissa continued to ignore her, always pretending to be busy doing something else.

Speak of the devil: Celeste popped her head through the entrance to the Royal Box. Lucia felt her eyes widen involuntarily. The hat perched upon Celeste's head would have looked certifiably insane on anyone else: It was tall, maybe a foot and a half above her head, in vibrant blue, purple, and green. She also resembled a bird—a regal peacock, fanning its extraordinary plumage—and in her electric-blue slim-fitting suit, she looked chic as hell.

"Come, now, why am I waiting for you?" she snapped. Melissa ran over, and with Tristan, the three of them filed inside.

Lucia was bringing up the rear, lagging behind due to the oversize flying saucer of a headpiece that kept slipping sideways. Was it trying to make a quick escape? She readjusted the bobby pins, but as she removed one, the entire thing tumbled off her head. Lucia bent down to pick up the hat and crashed headfirst into someone's knees.

"Pardon me, ever so sorry," said a man's voice. The voice sounded strangely familiar. "Are you quite alright?"

Lucia's gaze traveled up the man's dark dress slacks and black morning coat (under which was, she couldn't help but notice, a broad, muscular chest), up to a carefully knotted tie and a gorgeous clefted chin. A chin she'd recognize anywhere. But it wasn't possible. Could it be?

She looked up at his concern-filled chocolate-brown eyes, and her breath caught. There he was: actual, real-life, bona fide Colin Firth, in the flesh. He was looking down at her.

"Madam, let me help you up." He reached a hand toward her, and she grabbed it, not sure her quaking knees could bear her weight. She managed to stand up but somehow could not control her face. Her eyes, practically popping out of their sockets, were staring at him as if she'd just gotten Botox and was temporarily unable to blink. She hoped, at least, that she wasn't drooling.

"Do you have a friend inside the Royal Box whom I could ask to come assist you?" he asked again.

That snapped her out of it. Celeste's visage did not belong in this moment, which was otherwise straight out of Lucia's dreams (although in her dreams she was charming, witty, and capable of using words more than one syllable in length).

"Um, sorry. I mean pardon. Not sorry. It's all my fault." And then because she really couldn't help it, she added, "Wow."

"Not at all," he replied with his twinkling eyes. He bent down and picked up her hat. "Here you are," he said, brushing it off and handing it back to her.

Say something, her brain commanded her mouth. Anything. "It's not even mine. Would you like to keep it?"

Inside, her brain was smacking its own forehead.

He chuckled graciously. "No, thank you. I already own a Frisbee. And you can't be caught without it here in the Royal

Enclosure or its off with your head. Now, if you'll excuse me." He sidestepped her, as her feet were frozen to the ground.

Poor Moira. She was never, ever getting back this hat now that Colin Firth had touched it. One day, when the technology was available, maybe she could use his DNA to make a perfect clone of him for her own personal use.

Lucia watched him walk away, her once dream man. This would have been the perfect meet-cute, except, she remembered with a stabbing feeling in her belly, that she already had one of those, with her own Colin Firth–esque clefted chin. Whom she missed terribly.

"I loved you in *What a Girl Wants*," she yelled after him. She thought she saw him shudder as he continued out of sight.

If she died right now, she would not even have minded. She had reached the peak of her entire life. Everything else was downhill from here. At that very moment, Celeste snapped her fingers in Lucia's face. "What is this?" she said. "You do not keep the royals waiting. And put your hat back on, you look ridiculous."

"Right, of course . . ." she stammered, reinhabiting her body and remembering where she was. "I'm coming."

Among the forty or fifty people assembled inside the Royal Box, there were several members of other royal families, a few gold medalists from the recent Olympics, an A-list actress and her husband, an exceptionally beefy action-movie star (the costar and rumored lover of the aforementioned actress), and the only British footballer she recognized standing with his posh wife. If proximity to the royals was social currency, this room was the national mint.

"Why are we here again?" Lucia whispered to Tristan.

"Probably to show off how brilliantly diverse our team is. Also I think the firm was quite grateful at how quickly we handled their scandal-cover-up donation last week."

Lucia groaned softly. She had made a lot of trade-offs since taking this job, but this one felt the worst. The donation had been made and gratefully accepted by the (highly photogenic) head of a large women's rights nonprofit. The prince's news broke a few days later, but the generosity of the family combined with their careful control of the media had dominated so much of the news cycle that it ended up being no more than a footnote. Still, the whole affair didn't sit well with Lucia. She tried to put it behind her and think of real-life Colin Firth's (slightly terrified but beyond handsome) face instead.

She grabbed a glass of champagne from the bar and made her way to the window—she couldn't have cared less about the horse race but was enjoying the people watching and hat gawking when she was corralled by Brendan.

"Lucy, come here, please. I'm delighted to introduce you to His Royal Highness."

She stood in front of the prince whose ass she had just saved and, like a pro, executed her curtsy. "Sir," she said, daintily, bending with perfect form.

"I believe I owe you a great deal of thanks Mrs. . . . Barrow, is it? I'm grateful for your quick thinking and excellent recommendation. It's always a delight—and, no doubt, a relief—to find the right charity to give one's funds to, especially on such short notice."

Internally her stomach rolled again, but she kept a polite smile plastered on her face. "Just doing my job, sir," she said.

"Nonsense," Brendan replied, patting her on the back like they were old friends. "Lucy is too modest. She's one of our rising stars here at the bank. Why, when they put me out to pasture, rather soon at that, she'll be part of our top team. Don't you agree, Celeste?"

Lucia hadn't noticed that Celeste had smoothly joined their conversation. It was like she had special radar that identified powerful people—less seek and destroy, more seek and ass-kiss. Maybe that's what was inside the giant hat?

"Of course," Celeste said, placing a bejeweled hand on Lucia's arm, as if they were dear old friends. "Out of everyone that works for me, Lucia is the best. She exceeds everyone's expectations and will go far. The others, they could learn from her." With this last barb, she looked pointedly at Melissa, who had been eavesdropping nearby. She reddened and scurried away.

"You're too kind," Lucia said. "Really. I wouldn't be able to accomplish anything without Tristan and Melissa. They've taught me so much."

"Well," the prince said, "I am in your debt. Now, if you'll excuse me, my horse is in the next race. No chance of winning, but we must show face, mustn't we?" Lucia curtsied again, and the prince excused himself.

As soon as he was gone, Celeste and Brendan both scattered without another word. Lucia picked up a second glass of champagne and went to find Melissa, who was hiding in a corner.

"Don't run away from me this time. I come bearing gifts," Lucia said, handing Melissa the glass.

"He-he," she laughed nervously. "Nowhere to run here, I'm afraid. These old bones could never keep up on that track."

They sipped silently, until Lucia decided it was time to rip off the Band-Aid.

"Listen—I seem to be on my mea culpa tour," Lucia started. "I have so many people to apologize to, and I wanted you to be the first."

"Apologize? For what?"

"For taking your spot at GIFGAL. It all happened so last minute; I didn't know I was going instead of you until the ticket had already been transferred to my name."

"I know you didn't, pet. Trust me, I know how things work around here. And I know what Celeste is like. She was mad about something stupid, and she took it out on me."

"But I should have done something."

"Like what? You couldn't have done anything but go along with it. When the Dragon makes her move to attack, you're best to go limp, curl up in the fetal position, and play dead until she eventually moves on," Melissa said without a trace of irony.

"I don't know, maybe I could have refused to go unless you were allowed to come, too. Or gone on strike." Lucia shrugged. "I just feel really bad that I went instead of you."

Melissa patted her arm good-naturedly. "Don't give it another thought. It wasn't your fault. As far as I'm concerned, GIFGAL is nothing but water under the bridge. Or under a dock, filled with superyachts." She smiled.

"Are you sure?" Lucia asked, searching Melissa's face for any sign that she was brushing her off or being disingenuous, but she seemed her usual open and honest self.

"Absolutely. Who wants to sit on a beach with a bunch of rich wankers, anyway?"

"Not me, that's for sure. Anyway, if it makes you feel better, I spent most of the time in a conference room. And I barely ate. And the cocktails were awful."

"I know you're lying about that last one," Melissa said.

"Fine, they were amazing. But the rest is true." Lucia sighed and put her arm around Melissa's shoulder. "I'm just so glad we're cool," she said. "I've felt like things have been off between us, and I didn't want that to continue. Your friendship means so much to me. I would have been fired so long ago if it wasn't for you."

"Not at all," Melissa said. "Look at you now, flying high. You'll be my boss one day soon. He-he." Lucia ignored that nervous, barking laugh, delighted to be back in Melissa's good graces.

"Honestly, Melissa, you're like the little angel that sits on my shoulder. My conscience! But wouldn't it be nice if we were both in charge one day?"

Melissa snorted.

Lucia felt lighter immediately. She hadn't realized how much it had been weighing on her until that weight was lifted. "Anyway, I'm glad this is out because I have been dying to tell you everything going on with Operation Bridget Jones. It's the only thing keeping me going these days."

Lucia explained to Melissa how far things had progressed—it wasn't just about the London center anymore. They were looking at a national program, with an advocacy strand that would work with parliament to enact policy change. "It's big, game-changing stuff," Lucia shared with pride. "First the UK, then maybe Europe, and who knows? Henry is so excited. Nervous, of course, about finally pitching this to his parents, but I think once they see his passion for it, they won't be able to say no."

"When's the big family meeting, then?" Melissa asked.

"Soon," Lucia said. "Right after I'm back from France. Henry went straight from GIFGAL to someone's yacht in the Caribbean, but he's returning next week. It has to happen before the next board meeting in mid-July. We're nearly ready."

"Well, that sounds like it's worthy of a toast," Melissa said, raising her glass again, only to find it empty. "Never mind, let's go find someone to refill these." They started moving back toward the bar. "I have to hand it to you, Lucia. When you started, I wasn't sure you'd last the week, truthfully. But you've proven yourself more than capable of getting what you want."

Lucia frowned. "I'm not sure that's a good thing."

"Nonsense. You've got Celeste's ear now. I'm sure everything will go your way." She took Lucia's empty glass from her hand and placed it on the bar next to her own. "Now, let's get our priorities straight. More bubbles, please."

Full glasses in hand, they headed out on the balcony overlooking the racetrack, where they made up limericks about people's hats while pretending to care about a bunch of horses running in a circle.

Lucia got back from Ascot late that night, Gretel having confirmed that Mr. Barrow was home before she left, and that she had washed and organized Marley's clothes for the trip. She tiptoed into the bedroom to see if Ollie would move or acknowledge her arrival, but he was sound asleep, or at least pretending to be.

She quietly collected essentials from her closet—swimsuit, sunglasses, cute wide-brimmed hat that was not Moira's and therefore did not look like a UFO, a few sundresses, the sandals it had yet to be warm enough to wear in London—and brought them out to the living room to deposit into their big suitcase.

Ollie's clothes were already stacked inside neatly, folded and pressed. She smelled a whiff of starch; eau de Moira, she thought, as she added her clothes and Marley's and zipped up the bag.

Before getting into bed, she turned on her out of office, telling her team and clients that she would be wholly unavailable for the next week. For the first time since she'd started at Eastern Currents, she wasn't worried about getting fired or pissing off Celeste. No calls, no emails. Just pure, uninterrupted family time. There would be nothing to do besides talk about whatever was on their minds.

She swallowed hard, wishing she found that thought more relaxing.

Chapter 23
Croissants and Crossroads

In Lucia's fantasy, this is how it was supposed to go: She would step off the plane onto the tarmac, one hand on her wide-brimmed hat to keep it from flying away in the light breeze. Her large sunglasses would keep the bright glare at bay as she inhaled the salty sea air and balanced her daughter, clad in head-to-toe Petit Bateau, deftly on her hip. Her handsome, cleft-chinned British husband just behind them, carrying their stylish compact leather tote down the steps. She would be one chignon away from being Audrey Hepburn.

In reality, the picture looked a lot different: The hat (smooshed during its passage through the security scanner) had a dent in it that made it sit on her head at a lopsided angle. The sky was overcast, but for that she was grateful since her sunglasses were buried deep in her purse somewhere under a biohazard bag of Marley's clothes after two mid-flight diaper explosions. Her toddler was on her hip but wearing Lucia's cardigan, fashioned as a onesie, since #diapergate meant that she had soiled her emergency backup outfit. And her handsome husband with his cleft chin was indeed behind her—but he had barely uttered a sentence to her since they'd left for the airport early that morning.

"Audrey, wherefore art thou?" Lucia murmured to herself as she lumbered across the tarmac.

After a mercifully quick wait at baggage claim and an incident-free taxi ride, they arrived at their destination, a beautifully restored château turned boutique hotel. Someone put a welcome glass of champagne into Lucia's free hand, and she thought, ruefully, how sad it would be if this was the place Ollie announced he was leaving her for Belly and, therefore, its architectural glory would be ruined for her forever.

Several hours and two naps (Marley's and hers) later, the three of them were sitting by the pool, ice creams in hand, warm sun on their faces. Lucia felt the magic of the South of France starting to work its way into her bloodstream. She peered over at Ollie and caught him peering back at her. He held her gaze for a moment, as if he wanted to say something, before turning away. A tiny, almost imperceptible chink in his armor. It gave her something she had dared not feel since Marley's party—hope.

That night, exhausted, they ordered room service and went to bed early, backs to each other, no body parts touching, not even a rogue toe. The next day at the beach, they spoke but only in reference to Marley and her needs (sleep, food, sunscreen) and the intricate process of postbeach sand removal from every crease and orifice, including a few Lucia had not known existed.

Perhaps it was the proximity to each other, the breathing in of each other's familiar scents, the distance from their usual day-to-day squabbles, the delicious wine served at every meal (that was cheaper than bottled water), the fact that the air was infused with lavender, or the hot, hot sunshine—something that reminded them both of Texas honky-tonks and falling in love. Whatever it was, the chill was melting between them.

When Ollie shyly asked Lucia if she'd join him for dinner out, just the two of them, she phoned down to the concierge to book a table and a babysitter in less time than it took him to finish his sentence.

That night, they left Marley sound asleep with the sitter and made their way to a quiet little open-air bistro by the shore. If Patricos existed in an alternate universe where everyone spoke French instead of Italian, served champagne instead of prosecco, and favored butter over garlic, this was it. The warm familiarity of the atmosphere had the desired effect of making Lucia desperately want to mend fences with her husband.

If only she knew how to begin. This was their first major fight. They had never had to make up before.

She held up the menu, sneaking glances at Ollie over the top. "I'm thinking about the mussels," she said, "but it's probably too big for one."

"Let's share then," he replied. "And for wine how about the . . ."

"Picpoul?"

"Exactly." He looked up at her and smiled, and her cheeks reddened.

They were quiet as they waited for their food, but this wasn't the hostile silence of the previous days, more pensive, as if they were treating each other with kid gloves—strangers, not spouses.

The *moules* arrived in a cloud of steam, bursting out of the pot, along with the wine and a heaping plate of *frites*. They reached for the mussels, taking turns at first and then, as the wine worked through their systems, more casually, letting their fingers graze. When there was only one mussel left, he pushed it over to her.

"You have it," he said, smiling shyly.

"No, you, I insist."

"Well, we can't very well split it can we?" She took it and thanked him.

They polished off the wine, then a second bottle along with two desserts. The restaurant was closing, but Lucia wasn't ready to go back to the hotel. She opened her mouth to speak— "Want to go for a walk down the beach?"—just as he said, "Fancy an evening stroll?" The bill paid, they turned west on the boardwalk, joining the path that circled the bay, a bright, full moon illuminating their steps.

The night was balmy, and a light breeze ruffled Lucia's hair. The ambiance was relaxed and romantic, at odds with the simmering nervousness they both felt. She put her hand by her side, and tentatively Ollie took it in his own. She looked at him, her eyes already wet, and he brought her palm to his lips.

"I'm so sorry," he said.

Oh god, here it was. All Lucia's synapses were on high alert. Her stomach twisted itself into a knot, then a second one. If he was going to tell her he had slept with that inane, hipless wench, she was going to hurl herself into the sea.

Lucia held her breath.

"I went too far, the other night," Ollie said, clasping her hand tighter. "I lashed out when I should have been asking you what was wrong. Deep down I knew something was amiss, that I should not have believed you when you said everything was fine. But I don't know, I was in denial. I didn't want anything to be wrong with us, if that makes sense."

Lucia snorted. "If that was you lashing out, I can't begin to imagine what you think of me," she said. "And?" She braced herself for whatever was coming next.

"And . . . I feel awful."

"And . . . Is that the only thing you have to be sorry about?"

He stepped back from her. "Lucia, you couldn't possibly have been serious about me having an affair with Belly. For Chrissake she's one of my oldest friends. And married to one of my best mates. I haven't thought about her like that since we were prepubescent, and even then it was fleeting. I would have had a crush on a baboon at that stage of my life if it gave me the time of day."

Lucia scrutinized his face. His eyes were wet, but his expression was completely genuine.

"She's been at our house, more than once, without me knowing."

Ollie raised an eyebrow at her. "Of course she has. So have Pip, Gaz—the whole gang. They live in the neighborhood, they pop by all the time. Honestly, you're not home often in the evenings, and I'm grateful for the company. I didn't know I needed to keep a register of our visitors or send out a missive every time someone came to our door. Do you tell me every time you see Sooz? Or every time you're out with the marvelous Henry Perry?"

"That's different, and you know it," Lucia said.

"How?" Ollie responded. "She is my platonic friend and nothing more. The level of sexual attraction I feel toward Belly is equivalent to what you feel for them. Unless there is something about your relationship with Henry—or Sooz, for that matter—that you're not telling me."

It made sense. Why had she assumed the worst? Did she lack so much faith in their marriage that she let herself get carried away by a series of not-even-very-cryptic Instagram posts? Lucia stopped for a moment to stroke the side of his cheek, feeling the rough stubble he only let grow when on vacation.

"Oh god. I feel so stupid, Ollie. I was jealous and, I guess, unsure about my place. Which is even stupider. You show me you love me all the time, but . . ." She trailed off and started to tear up.

"But what, darling?" he said, reaching into his pocket and pulling out a handkerchief.

"Of course you have a handkerchief." She blew her nose into it. "And it smells like lavender. This I what I mean," she said, waving it in the air. "I bet Belly and Pip and of course your mom, they would carry handkerchiefs in their purses. They wouldn't spill food all over themselves or mistake someone's grandfather for Winston Churchill or almost get hit by a bike twice a day because they couldn't remember which way to look. They fit here. They all fit so perfectly in your life, and let's be honest. I don't." She blew out a second time, pretty much decimating the handkerchief.

"Lucia, you couldn't be more wrong. I don't care if you know how to curtsy or recognize British historical figures. I'd prefer if you didn't get hit by a bike, but still. I love you precisely because you are just yourself, this willful, passionate, deeply caring, incredibly headstrong person who would give someone the barbecue-sauce-encrusted shirt off her back if they needed it. Those other things have never mattered to me."

She sniffled and looked up at his eyes, filled with earnest concern. "I'm so sorry."

"Far from it. I should have known what you were feeling. I just . . . I wanted our little lives to be perfect. I was worried you would regret marrying me, moving to London. It was selfish, my unwillingness to address how you truly felt."

"It's not your fault, at least not entirely. I have always been really, really good at hiding my feelings. Pushing them down into a little box when they got too big, pretending nothing was wrong."

Lucia excelled at covering up any weakness or negativity. She could handle it, by herself, always. As a kid, she'd once fractured her elbow after falling off a bike but refused to tell her grandparents she was hurt. She knew the cost of going to the doctor would be steep. For days she managed with one arm, trying not to wince when they hugged her. Almost a week passed before they confronted her after a call from the school. Her grandparents were beside themselves. Why hadn't she told them? But that was just what she did. As long as she was the only one suffering, she told herself it was fine. Lucia had been giving away pieces of herself to others for so long that it was no wonder she didn't feel whole anymore.

"No, it is my fault," Ollie said. "It's a husband's job to know his wife, respond to her needs. But I didn't do that. I watched you lose yourself, and I just want to find you again. I miss *us*. What we were like."

On this, Lucia could agree. "Me, too. Everything was so much easier before I moved here. Before we had Marley."

Ollie looked stricken, and for a moment, Lucia thought she should downplay her feelings, like she had always done. Smooth over the unpleasant, sharp edges of what she had to say.

But then she remembered: That was what had gotten her into this mess in the first place. Instead she tried radical honesty.

"Truthfully, *cariño*, I don't regret the big things—you falling literally head over heels for me, me falling figuratively head over heels for you, moving, becoming a mom. Zero regrets." Ollie's face looked relieved, and he made to speak, but Lucia raised her hand to stop him. "But it happened so fast. It's like I woke up one morning and my whole life was different. And

I was not the same, either, but I didn't know how to be this new person and also be me. That might have happened anywhere I became a wife and a mom, but to do it all in a strange country . . . I felt untethered from everything I knew, including my own identity."

"It was fast," Ollie said. "Fast but right. I probably glossed over the difficult things, hoping that maybe you would do the same. But that wasn't the solution. I wanted to keep you close, but instead I drove you into taking this mad job."

They continued strolling down the path, passing shopkeepers closing for the night, young couples strolling hand in hand, teenagers out past curfew drinking on the beach; everyone's moods were light. Lucia desperately wanted to feel that way, too. But not yet. Not until she got everything out.

"It wasn't you. I wanted the job. I was suffocating at home, doing nothing. I didn't know what my purpose was. I felt useless."

"I thought we were your purpose. Marley and me."

"You are, but also . . ." She breathed deeply, gathering her courage to say what she needed to say. She loved them with every fiber of her being, but she also knew she needed more than her family. She had a greater purpose, felt it in her bones, and it mattered to her.

"Please don't take this the wrong way, but while you and Marley complete my world, you aren't my everything. I need that other piece, too, the one that makes me feel like I'm achieving whatever I was put on this planet to do besides being a mom and a wife."

Ollie stopped walking.

"Is that something you can live with? That I need you and Marley—and something more, too?"

It was the longest four seconds of her life.

"*Querida*," he said, pulling her into him. "I can, of course I can. It's part of what I love about you, and I would never want you to give that up. You might feel a little lost, but that fire inside of you, it's right where it always was." He placed his hand over her heart. "All I want is a little piece of it. It doesn't need to be the whole thing, just . . ." He shrugged. "Just some of you."

Lucia threaded her fingers through his. "You have more than a little piece." He pulled her close to him, and she felt lighter, relieved of the burden of the truth she had been holding alone for so long. She told him, showed him who she really was, and he didn't run away. He loved her for it.

"We should probably turn around, you know," she said. "We're practically in Saint-Tropez."

"Yes, let's," he said, stopping and turning toward her. He grabbed her hips and pulled them into his, shaking his head at her. "How on earth could you think anything was going on between Belly and me?"

"I don't know. She's obnoxiously gorgeous, and so damn thin which makes me hate her even more."

"Lucia," he said, bringing his mouth to her ear and elongating her name. His breath was hot and his voice husky. "Haven't you figured out by now that she's not at all my type? I think I've made it abundantly clear to you on countless occasions exactly what—and whom—I'm attracted to."

Lucia pulled back her head—not her body, which was warming at the proximity to him—just slightly to see his face. "What were all those secret meetings then? She seemed to know everything going on in your life."

He sighed. "I wanted it to be a surprise, but I might as well tell you now to avoid any further misunderstanding. Belly has been training me on how to take on individual pro bono cases." Ollie smiled, genuine and bashful, and Lucia was immediately transported to the first time they'd met. "I thought perhaps, with the right skill set, I could assist with the immigration cases at the refugee center where you've been working. I've also been practicing my Spanish, for you obviously, but also in case there are any Latin Americans who could use my *ayudo*, too."

"It's *ayuda*," Lucia said, turning her face, her lips hovered close to his. "But A for effort." She kissed him, softly at first, then urgently. She needed more of him. How far were they from the hotel?

"I love you, Lucia." He spoke roughly, matching her desire with his own. "I love you more than I have ever been able to suitably express in any language."

"You have never been sexier to me in my life," she said. "Seriously I am so touched that you would do that. You will be amazing at it." She grinned widely. "Now, let's sprint back to the hotel. I know the French are permissive and open about their sexuality, blah blah blah, but I'm sure they wouldn't take kindly to me ripping off your clothes right here on this public beach."

He kissed her back, and together they picked up the pace. "You are the most extraordinary woman I have ever known, in every way."

"Ugh, you really are so perfect sometimes," she said. "Even more perfect than the real Colin Firth, who I met last week, incidentally."

He looked over at her with a dangerous glint in his eye. "Did you now? So I have some competition. Well then, I must rise to the challenge and make you forget all about him. Let's be quick about it. We'll relieve the sitter, and then we can make another baby."

"Hmm . . . Maybe not just now," she said, her heart rate picking up as they sped back along the promenade. "But it's a good idea to practice. You know, so when we're ready, we're really good at it."

* * *

The next morning was bright and sunny again. Lucia marveled at the reliability and regularity of the weather. She had forgotten what it was like to wake up and just know you were going to see the sun. At breakfast she had the best croissant of her life. "You know, I think I get why the French are so smug," she said to Ollie through a mouthful of pastry. "I feel like I understand Celeste a tiny fraction better. She's earned the right to be haughty. Can you please pass a *pain au chocolat*?"

After breakfast, she, Ollie, and Marley plopped themselves down on a set of blue-and-white-striped beach chairs. Marley attempted to careen herself into the water, but Ollie held her back, while Lucia unpacked the various shovels, snacks, sunscreen, and other accoutrements required for the day. Once everyone was SPF protected and Marley's water wings were blown up to a point that nearly cut off her circulation, Lucia lay back and closed her eyes, letting the sun caress her body and fill it up with some much-needed vitamin D. The tightness in her chest had loosened. For the first time in maybe forever, she felt completely and entirely content exactly where she was in life.

She sat up and pulled her sunglasses down over the bridge of her nose. "Shall we swim?" she asked Ollie.

He put his book down and turned to look at her. SPF seventy was no match for his English complexion; he was already turning a lovely shade of lobster pink. "Most certainly," he replied.

He stood and kissed the top of her head before scooping up Marley, who screamed with glee all the way to the water. They were happy together, her little family, in this beautiful moment. She dusted the sand off her thighs and ran to the sea to join them.

* * *

After a week floating on a cloud of butter and cream, Lucia was sad as they boarded the plane to head back to the UK but also refreshed. She was ready to dive back into work. She needed more balance, more boundaries. Maybe once Celeste took over Brendan's job, she could ask for a junior philanthropy advisor to report to her. Someone to deal with Tamsin's canine minutiae while Lucia took on the bigger tasks that were sure to come with the success of Operation Bridget Jones. She drafted the job description on the flight, and as they touched ground in London, Lucia switched her work email on again, for the first time in a week, to send it to herself.

She couldn't resist a quick scroll through her emails to see what awaited her. There, buried in between client updates, dossiers to complete, and event invitations, she saw an email from Henry with the subject: "Urgent—Please Send Insect Repellant." She laughed and opened it.

Dearest Lucia,

I hope your tan has not yet faded. Mine most certainly has. I didn't get a chance to congratulate you on the earthquake efforts before you left GIFGAL, particularly Tamsin's performance at the gala. How brilliant for you. Although I know how passionate you are about ensuring Britain's pets all have a minimum of four legs, you must be delighted with how widespread and impactful the disaster response has been.

Unfortunately, I don't write with good news. Mummy and Daddy got wind of our Operation Bridget Jones plan. They ambushed me with Billy last night and told me under no uncertain terms that I was not to engage in any "politically motivated philanthropy," and they would never condone any activity that could "tarnish the family's reputation." I told them to "shove their reputations up" somewhere unmentionable.

The prospect of future funding is, regrettably, gone.

Will you tell Amina for me? I can't bear it.

"Oh my god," she said out loud.

"What happened?" Ollie asked.

They've dispatched me to the north for a new project, managing the family's Scottish estate holdings. My discretionary fund as part of the family foundation is frozen for now. Still it's not all bad. I'm surrounded by wild thistle and whiskey, and I do so love the sound of bagpipes in the morning.

I'm sorry to be the bearer of bad news, and even more sorry our brilliant plan will never see the light of day.

Coffee when I'm allowed back into England? I'll be the one covered in midge bites.

x Henry

PS—Do thank *la grande dame* for me on your return to the office. You can tell her how much I appreciate her "looking after my family" and making sure they knew what we were up to before we were ready to tell them. If it's not clear, that last part should be delivered dripping in sarcasm.

"It's over" was all she could say.

She would tell Ollie everything later, when she could put the right words together. To say she was devastated was a massive understatement.

Devastated and pissed.

Celeste was going down.

Chapter 24
Fight Club

Every morning, there is a moment just before fully waking up when the subconscious is about to relinquish control but the conscious brain hasn't yet taken over. In this brief liminal space it's easy to believe dreams are real—or that reality is only a nightmare. As Lucia awoke after a fitful night of tossing and turning, she experienced a fleeting moment in which Henry's email did not exist. And then, she felt it, the anvil lodged in the pit of her stomach, as it all came flooding back.

It should have been difficult to go to work that morning, but Lucia wanted to get this over with. She sat at her desk, drinking her fourth cappuccino and rubbing her neck in hopes of dispelling the tension headache that had been throbbing away since she'd landed on UK soil the previous evening. Her eyes were glued to the elevators like she was stalking prey. It was already past 11:00 a.m., and she knew Celeste had a meeting with Brendan at noon. Normally, she would make any excuse to avoid a confrontation with Celeste, but today she was hopped up on righteous anger and caffeine.

The clock ticked on. At 11:30, unable to sit at her own desk any longer, Lucia went into Celeste's office to wait. She could count on one hand the number of times she had been in there, never willingly. Celeste preferred to do her berating on the main floor where everyone could see and hear her. On the rare occasions Lucia did have to enter the Dragon's lair, usually to get a signature or drop off a document, she tried not to linger.

She took a seat in the crisp gray linen armchair and surveyed the space. It was minimalist, cold. Classy AF, not unlike Celeste herself, Lucia thought. There was a striking new piece of contemporary art on the wall; Lucia recognized it as one of Shambala's contemporaries whom she had also studied back in college.

Anything that wasn't glass was painted a stark shade of white. She had one polished-chrome bookshelf that held very little—some books about philanthropy and finance, a few ceramic bowls, a candle that cost at least seventy-five pounds and had never been lit, and three framed photographs. Lucia stood up to get a closer look.

One was of two young adults, a man and a woman, at a graduation. Celeste's children, she assumed. They both had radiant smiles—clearly inherited from their father.

The second was of an older man with kind eyes, wearing a flatcap and sipping a small coffee at an outdoor café. The Eiffel Tower was visible in the background. Paris. He shared the same smile as the children.

It was so strange to think of Celeste as a mother and a wife. She never spoke about her family. In fact, Lucia only knew she was married because she wore a gigantic diamond. But she must have, at one time or another, faced the same conflicts Lucia was facing. She'd raised her children in Britain, away from her home country and native language. Had she also driven her career forward while attempting to be present to soothe tears and bandage skinned knees? It was easy to imagine Celeste as a monster—and sometimes she was—but she was also, like Lucia, a person who tried to pursue a passion and a family at the same time. The idea that they shared something in common was becoming unpleasant; she shuddered to think that anyone would ever compare them.

The final photo was a grainy image of a much younger Celeste. She wore casual clothes, a white button-down shirt rolled up at the sleeves, cargo pants. Cargo pants. Lucia rubbed her eyes and looked again (this picture was going to live rent-free in her head forever). Celeste's hair was pulled back in a ponytail, and she had a hand to her brow to block the sun from her eyes. There were oil rigs in the background; Lucia thought back to the conversation she'd had with Tristan about Celeste's past. It seemed incongruous, impossible really, that the woman in this photo, supposedly so devoted to change, was the same person who just killed an incredible project that would have benefited so many vulnerable people, as if flicking away a spider.

"What are you doing here?"

Lucia practically jumped out of her skin and fumbled with the photo, nearly dropping it. She set it back down with care before turning around to face Celeste.

"Celeste. Hi. I was just . . ." She trailed off, her resolve faltering. Celeste appeared her usual put-together self, but Lucia perceived slight shadows under her eyes. "I need to speak to you. About Henry Perry."

"Lucia, I have a very busy day and a meeting with Brendan in ten minutes. I do not have time to hold your head like a baby while you cry over one project that did not come to pass." She crossed over to her desk, throwing her large designer handbag aside and sitting down. "Please go."

"Go back to what? Putting braces on beagles? No way." Lucia took a seat in the armchair across from her. "This has to happen now."

She had never once stood up to Celeste. They were both surprised by it.

"You have two minutes. What is the emergency?"

"You know what. Henry told me his parents had been informed that he was developing something 'political' to support refugees, and they essentially banished him to Scotland like in some eighteenth-century novel. We had been working carefully for months to make this completely apolitical, palatable to his parents. We were going to present it to them with military precision and the utmost tact. And now that opportunity is gone."

Celeste drummed her manicured nails on the desk. "And?"

The more annoyed Celeste looked, the easier Lucia found it to access her own anger. "So you admit it. It was you."

Celeste let out an exasperated sigh. "Yes, of course. Unlike you, I am not a person who hides things." She arched an eyebrow at Lucia. "But we can discuss that another time. The Perrys are *my* clients and, I remind you, one of the bank's most important and wealthiest families. They deserve to know what their son is doing behind their backs."

"Did you even read it? Understand what we were trying to do? It wasn't just about the one refugee center in London, which, by the way, is going to be devastated when we tell them they have to pull the offer on the building they were going to buy with the Perrys' money that would be otherwise spent on, oh, I don't know, a gold-plated frame for a portrait of some dead marquess. It was about dozens of refugee and migrant centers across the UK, tens of thousands of people. Don't you care about anyone but yourself? Or anything but your AUM?"

Celeste was silent, a defiant glare in her eyes.

"After everything at GIFGAL, the earthquake, Tamsin, everything we did together. It was so incredible, the definition of impact. We have different approaches, true, but I thought we were on the same page."

"Humph," Celeste said. "We are not even in the same book."

Lucia sat back down, deflated. "At least tell me why you would ruin this."

Celeste sighed again, but it was a fraction gentler this time. Not quite sympathetic but less furious. "I was advised that Henry had been visiting some, how should I say, controversial places that might be dangerous for the reputation of the family. You have not been very discreet, Lucia. It was only a matter of time before they would find out for themselves what you were up to."

"Yes, a short matter of time before we told them with the right messaging. Amina was going to come with us to present. We had found photos of the duchess's mother on the Kindertransport. We were completely prepared."

"It is irrelevant. I could not risk the duke becoming aware, placing a call to Brendan or Nigel. You know very well what is at stake here. It is a delicate time for me, and I could not do anything to jeopardize my promotion. I did not have a choice."

"Come on, Celeste. Of course you had a choice." Lucia stood up and paced the length of the office. "Maybe it's not too late to fix this. Come with me, come see the center here in London, meet Amina. You'll see the people that we would be helping, the kids . . . the ones that migrate alone." Her voice cracked. "Just come with me and see it."

"*Non.*" Celeste waved her hand. "I do not need to see it to believe. The Perrys are too important. To the bank, yes, and to me, but also to the work we are trying to do here."

"Honestly, what work?" As Lucia raised her voice, Celeste pressed the button to fog up the windows. No witnesses. "Oh right. Our irreplaceable efforts helping disgraced royals cover up their indiscretions by using generosity as a substitute for basic human decency. You keep talking about all these big plans and amazing impact, but all I see is someone who won't take any chances. How long do you plan on waiting before you're ready to use all the power and influence you have amassed to do something—anything—good? How much damage will you do in the meantime?"

Celeste stood up and wandered over to the shelves, picking up the photo Lucia had been holding when she walked in.

"Listen to me. I will say this once and never again." Her eyes glazed over as she looked at the image, like she was looking past the photo to something else in her own mind that moved her. As if the Dragon had a heart. "I was once like you."

Lucia snorted. "What, a normal person who cares about other people?"

"Naive," she snapped. "When I was younger, I was angry, too. I believed that I would change the world all by myself. I went to protests, and then I went to jail. Have you ever spent a month in a Nigerian prison? I am sure you have not. I sacrificed my body and my soul, and for what? Nothing changed. No one listened. Nothing good came of it, for me or anyone else.

"So I went home, to Paris. I got smarter, sharper. I learned about where real change comes from—from the ones with power, with money already. Not from silly people trying to make everyone angry with their morality like a slap across the face if you are not doing it perfectly. I knew for certain that the way to make an impact, to build the future for my children, my grandchildren, was to be a person with power and money myself. That was the only way. Otherwise no one would listen to me."

"I mean, fine, you're not totally wrong. But just think about . . ." Lucia grasped for an example. "Tamsin! Look at Tamsin. Look what she did at GIFGAL, the impact that it will have. We did that by challenging her to do what was right, not just taking the easy path and giving her everything she wanted."

"You cannot be serious. Tamsin will spend millions on her stupid dog foundation because that is what she wants to do. There is your great impact. You gave her what she wanted. You made her believe her silly little project was worth something, and then when it was time for real change, you used your lever-age. *C'est vrai*, do not deny it.

"This is precisely what I am doing here. Soon I will be running the whole team, Brendan will be gone, Nigel will fol-low my advice, and then we will make some actual change. Our clients will listen to us because they trust us. And they trust us because they believe we are like them."

She hated to admit it, but Lucia could see a kernel of truth in Celeste's words. If Lucia had told Tamsin when they'd first met that she should be funding victims of natural disasters in Pakistan, she likely would have been politely escorted off the bow of her yacht. It took months of carefully chosen words and meeting after meeting aligned with Tamsin's interests. These were baby steps on the journey that eventually resulted in Tamsin trusting Lucia's expertise and guidance. It was pos-sible that Tamsin never would have gotten onto that stage at

GIFGAL and literally moved mountains for the earthquake survivors if Lucia hadn't held back her honest opinion, so many times, about her other vanity efforts.

And yet, Celeste had been working with people like the Perrys for years. What if they never changed? They might continue to send millions upon millions to superrich private schools and pave parking lots for statues of war heroes instead of directing their funds where they were really needed. It was possible to tread too carefully, Lucia thought. If she didn't help her clients—the ones like Henry who wanted to nudge the envelope—take risks with the potential for positive impact (even if it pissed some people off), then what was the point of doing this job?

Lucia felt drained. "Maybe we're already too much like them."

Celeste walked around, perched on the front of her desk, and in the most uncharacteristic way, placed a hand on Lucia's shoulder.

"We need to wait a little longer, until I am in charge. I am not happy with you for lying, but I appreciate your courage. You took a risk to make a client happy. When Brendan leaves, the team will be mine entirely. I will promote you to senior. We will hire more people, good people, and maybe I can give you the Perry portfolio so you can manage that yourself."

Is that what Lucia wanted? She had no idea. "I . . . I don't know what to think. The thing that drives me, my entire reason for getting out of bed every day has always been to leave this world a little bit better than when I came into it. To live up to the example my grandparents set for me. But I don't know if I'm doing that here. I feel like I've sacrificed so much, including seeing my family. I just have no idea if I am doing any good at all."

"You are not the only one making sacrifices, you know. My husband, Pierre, he is older now and has dementia. He needs full-time care, but I am not sitting there with him all day. I need to be here. The price is high, but I believe it is worth it, and I believe you do also."

Celeste looked at her watch. "I told you in your interview that I expected one hundred percent, and that is what I meant. You must trust me. It will be worth it for the greater good." She pressed the button to unfog the glass—from her perspective, the conversation was over.

Lucia stood up and prepared to walk out of Celeste's office and back to her desk like an automaton. She needed to process everything Celeste had said. Lucia wasn't sure she knew what was right anymore.

She put one hand on the doorknob, and a shadow passed over her face. "I just don't know how Tristan could do this to me," she muttered to herself. She thought their little inside jokes and snarky insults meant they were friends now. Wasn't that how British people treated their friends?

"*Pardón?*" Celeste asked.

"I said, I don't know how Tristan could do this to me. I mean, he warned me he would stab me in the back to get what he wanted. But I never thought he would actually do it."

Celeste clicked her tongue, and a smile crept across her face. "*Mais non*, Lucia. It was not Tristan. Although now that I am aware he knew what you were doing and did not tell me, I will have some words with him."

Lucia could see that Celeste was toying with her, but her feet remained planted. She had to know. "If it wasn't Tristan, then who was it? Who told you?"

Celeste paused dramatically, her grin widening with each passing second. Finally, she went in for the kill.

"Why, your best friend, Melissa, of course. At least one person on this team remembered that I reward loyalty above all else. Now, you may go."

With another dismissive flick of her hand, she directed Lucia out the door, leaving her to pick up the pieces of her shattered worldview all on her own.

Chapter 25
Hail Mary

Melissa's bottle-top necklace danced in the light as she sank down into the armchair of the Starbucks a few blocks away from the office. Lucia had scheduled two back-to-back conversations today, difficult ones, and she wanted to play on as close-to-home territory as she could find in London. The whiz of the steam from the milk frother and the sweet smell of caramel being swirled into macchiatos gave her the strength she needed to face her own personal Brutus. Once friend, now enemy, it seemed.

"Thank you so much for meeting me here," she started.

"Nonsense, it's just down the street. And, anyway, I feel like I haven't seen you in ages. How was France?"

"I think you and I both know we're not here to talk about France." It had been a few days since Lucia had uncovered Melissa's betrayal, and she was still in shock, made worse by the fact that Melissa had been acting completely normal. As if she hadn't thrown a bomb into Lucia's professional life.

"Alright then, Miss Serious. You're looking a bit flushed. Are you feeling well?"

Lucia was not feeling well. She was feeling the opposite of well. The Brits might say poorly, which she knew meant totally and utterly horrible.

"I'm feeling angry," she sighed. "Melissa, how could you?"

Lucia's voice held a mix of fury and pleading. Fury at feeling betrayed by her friend. And pleading because she was desperate for Melissa to tell her that it wasn't true. To respond in shock: "What are you talking about? Betray whom? Never on my honor would I do that to you!" But as she saw Melissa's cheeks redden to match her own, she knew Celeste hadn't lied.

"Oh dear," she said. "So you found out." She held up her hands in front of her, guilty. "I am sorry you got caught up in this. But you have to know it wasn't personal."

"Wasn't personal?" Lucia yelled. Another customer gave her a look, and she brought her voice back down to a normal volume. "How could you even say that? Of course it's personal. You knew what this meant to me. To Henry, to everyone. We're talking about people's lives here, their livelihoods. You took so much away from them, and from me."

Lucia thought about Amina. She hadn't had the heart to tell her yet about how their plan had fallen through, that they wouldn't be able to purchase the building or set up the endowment. She knew she had to—it was her job—but she couldn't imagine the look on her face. What could be more personal than that?

Melissa took a sip of her coffee but offered no response. Lucia glared at her, nostrils flaring, searching her face for clues about this side of Melissa's character, a side she hadn't known existed. She looked up to Melissa, had tried to be more like her—brave, willing to stand up for what she believed in, even when there was a personal cost. How could she have misjudged someone to such an extreme?

"Well, fine," Melissa said. "It was personal. Sorry. Is that what you want to hear? But I had been on the rocks with Celeste for ages. She was still mad about my pipeline-divestment campaign. She called me into her office to yell at me about my 'lack of commitment,' questioning my loyalty and my future here. I had to give her something meaningful to prove she could trust me. I only had one piece of intel juicy enough to get her off my back. I had to tell her about your project with Henry."

"Humph. You once told me your standards were higher than hers."

"I guess when it came down to it, they weren't." Melissa frowned and looked at Lucia with no contrition in her face. "Honestly, Lucia, what would you have me do? Go back to the charity sector, cap in hand? You know exactly what happens when you're on the other side of the table, asking for money instead of giving it away. Would you expect me to plead for a meeting with you, which you'd reschedule four times, only for you to tell me the bank's funds were already committed this year? Please." She laughed, but it wasn't her nervous laugh. This one was cynical and maybe even a little cruel. "I'm too old and too impatient to go around begging for scraps anymore. The system is rigged, and we both know the only way to make an impact is to play the game from the inside."

Lucia thought back to her life as a fundraiser at ArteAustin—before she held the purse strings of so many wealthy people in her hands, before their ears were attuned to her voice, primed to listen and take her advice about where to give and to whom. Back then, she was always the one holding the begging bowl, always looking for someone to give them that next big grant.

Melissa softened, her face rife with pity. "I do feel bad about hurting you, but there will be other projects. For both of us.

Celeste was so chuffed with my information, she's letting me lead a climate task force at the bank . . ."

"A task force?" Lucia scoffed. "You know that's nothing but a bullshit PR exercise."

She clicked her tongue. "Where is your sense of optimism? It's better than nothing, and everything has to start somewhere. Anyway, I hear you're getting promoted, too. You'll find a way to support all those refugees and immigrants. There will be more clients with deep pockets, and anyway, the higher you rise the more you can get away with. That's why I had to tell her. You know it, too; I know you do."

Melissa finished her coffee and stood up to leave. Lucia didn't know what to say. In her darkest times, she had viewed Melissa as proof that it was possible to do this job and do it well without losing yourself. That you could put progressive values before the bank's AUM and still succeed. But she had been foolish to believe that was possible. Melissa was just like the rest of them. Lucia was almost afraid to ask herself: Was she like them, too?

"I have to run. The Dragon needs some research on the pipeline, and 'it cannot wait,'" she said in an exaggerated French accent. Melissa got up and patted Lucia maternally. "Cheer up, pet. Remember, it's a journey, I told you that. Wait your turn, bide your time, and you'll get there soon enough. I'll see you back at the office."

With a jangle, Melissa exited the café, leaving Lucia to wonder what else she had been wrong about. Or what she *hadn't* been wrong about; that list was all too short.

Sooz's words from their shopping spree, before Lucia started the job, before everything got so complicated, rang in her ears: "Don't lose yourself," she had warned. Here Lucia was, somewhere on this journey, but without a clue as to the destination.

The little trade-offs she made to keep her clients happy had seemed worth it. Every time she held her tongue or massaged her true opinion into something her client wanted to hear, she believed she was serving her long-term goals. In her personal life it had been the same—she straightened her hair, let people call her whatever incorrect version of her name they felt comfortable with, decreased her volume, Madonna-ed up her accent. She did these things because she felt like they were crucial to making a positive impact, to fitting in with her husband's judgy friends, to being the kind of mom social media said she should be.

Who had she been before all of that? And who was she now? She had no idea.

If that wasn't the definition of being lost, she didn't know what was.

* * *

By the time her second meeting arrived, even a whipped-cream topping could not improve her mood. Henry offered her a hug and looked at her mug with disdain.

"Do you want anything?" she asked. "I'm on my third."

"Christ no. I mean, no thank you. I don't drink this . . . whatever you call it. Bilge water? It's not coffee." He grimaced.

"I can see Scotland hasn't rid you of your refined city tastes. I half expected you to arrive in a kilt."

"I thought about it, but you know you're not meant to wear anything underneath, and I think you've already had enough of a shock for one week."

"Fair enough." She drew her mouth into a line. "I'm so sorry Celeste did this to you. To us."

"It's just as well I suppose," Henry said. "It was too good to be true. Do you know, for the first time in years, I had been sleeping all night? I know that sounds ridiculous, it's not as if I have a toddler at home like you. But I was going to bed every evening feeling . . . fulfilled, I suppose. Like I had finally been doing the thing I was supposed to do." He sighed and sunk back into the chair. "And now it's all over."

Lucia's brain whirred. "Maybe we can do something else. We could fundraise for the center. I used to be a fundraiser, a great one. I can help them design a campaign to get the money they need for the building, for a start, and you can bring in all your rich friends to fund the rest." But even as she said it, she knew it would never be enough. Their ambitions had grown—they wanted a national coalition of refugee- and migrant-support nonprofits all around the country, advocating for change with one voice.

"No, it won't be enough," Henry said, echoing her thoughts. "Not compared to what my parents' funds could do. It's a shame you're not in charge of Eastern Currents. Imagine if you were in Celeste's shoes—curse her and her fabulous taste in footwear—just for a day. You could use your French wiles to convince my parents this was the most brilliant thing for their reputation ever."

Lucia laughed at the thought of it. "Ha! Can you imagine?" She put on a haughty French accent. "*Mais oui*, duke and duchess, it is *tres importante* for you to follow everything Henry says, he is your smartest and least arrogant child, and if you fund this program, you will be, how we say in France, qualified for the *Legion d'honneur*. I must go now, to my claw-sharpening appointment."

Henry smirked. "That's not bad, you know." They let the brief moment of levity wash over them. His face became serious again. "The irony of this whole thing is that if they just agreed to it, without even knowing, they would see that it wouldn't be politically charged in the least. Their friends, the ones whose opinions seem to matter so much to them, would follow their lead; they'd be the pied pipers of philanthropy, lauded as heroes."

"If only," Lucia said wistfully. "Maybe we could drug them and forge their signatures? And then quickly tell everyone so they couldn't take it back even if they wanted to."

Henry looked at Lucia oddly. A grin spread across his face, the same one that had appeared that night at Bartholomew's as he'd delivered the fourth tray of flaming tequilas. "Perhaps we can."

"What, drug your parents? No thank you. I'm not a citizen yet, and you and I both know what they do to foreigners that commit crimes in this country. Sheesh."

"No, not drug them. Something else. Follow my thinking here."

It took just one and a half more macchiatos (for Lucia, who was now 75 percent caramel) and a lukewarm bottle of water (for Henry) for a plan to come together. It was crazy. It would certainly get Lucia fired. Maybe worse. And it was by far the best idea either of them had ever had.

"So," she parroted back to him, reading from the notes she had scribbled on a napkin. "Let me make sure I have it completely correct. I will write a fake press release, from your parents, that will be sent out on the wire by the bank's PR agency."

"Correct. And I'll edit it, of course, because your language will be entirely too new-world to sound like them. It will say something like, 'The duke and duchess are sick and tired of standing by as innocent people in search of a better life for themselves and their children cross our borders only to suffer the indignities of a broken system when they arrive.'"

"Ooh, that's great," she said. "You should have my job. Actually, there will be a vacancy after this if you're looking." She joked, but she wasn't blind to the gravity of this decision— for either of them.

"I'll need to leave the continent after this. Scotland won't be far enough away from their wrath. So we say what? That the Perry Foundation is committing, at least . . . half?"

"At least," Lucia replied. "Go big or go home."

"Committing to donate at least half of its sizable endowment to support refugee and migrant charities across the UK. And we specify the first grant will be to Amina's center—to purchase the building, fund its expenses in perpetuity. Then the second is to build a national coalition for refugee and migrant advocacy. The rest to follow. Do I have it right?"

"I mean, we're making it up at this point, so is there anything else you want to add in there? Like a Christmas gift you wanted but you never got? How about a pony?"

Henry chuckled. "Darling, I have a stable full of ponies. But perhaps a new riding crop. I've plumb worn out my old one during some, shall we say, less wholesome pursuits."

She rolled her eyes. "Fine. That'll be my gift to you when this is all over, no need to ask Mummy and Daddy for that sort of thing." Lucia paused, trying to read his expression. "So we'll nail the language, their tone of voice. And then I'll release it. If we time it right, no one will have a clue what's happened until they see it in the morning papers . . ."

"After which point they won't be able to take it back without looking miserly. Or like they'd lost control of their family. Losing face is my father's worst nightmare."

"They'd be tarred and feathered if they tried to retract," Lucia added, getting more animated now. "Not literally, of course."

"I wouldn't be too sure. You've met some of our crowd. You know what they are capable of."

They fell quiet, each afraid to say what they were both thinking. Henry went first. "This is going to get you fired. You'll probably be blacklisted across the philanthropy world."

"I know," Lucia said grimly. "But honestly, I am willing to take the risk. Yes, it's against the rules and borderline unethical. But I recently saw what my future would look like if I stayed at the bank." She thought of Melissa, and a shudder ran down her spine. "A lifetime of trade-offs and compromises hoping I eventually give enough of my principles away in exchange for a seat at the top. This world, the high net worths and the ultrahigh net worths and their philanthropy—look, I don't care how many billions of dollars Tamsin gives away if all it's going to do is build hutches for needy rabbits. I want to do what I set out to do. To actually help people."

As soon as the words came out of her mouth, she could feel that they were true. No matter the consequences—this was the right call. "They're not bad people. They mean well. But meaning well and doing good aren't the same thing."

"Well said," Henry replied, standing up. "Let's do some good, shall we. And make my parents furious in the process—it's a win-win."

"Absolutely," she said. "I have a press release to write, and you better go spend some money before you're disinherited."

"Which I most certainly will be," he said matter-of-factly. "But as your very own Bridget Jones would say, 'You only get one life.' I want to make mine count."

Chapter 26
Deepfake

The next day, Lucia was a bundle of nerves at the office. Every time her inbox pinged with a new email notification, her stomach jumped into her throat. She was certain that Celeste had somehow developed ESP and was onto their plan. For a brief period in college after binge-watching *Alias*, Lucia thought maybe she wanted to be a spy; she was glad she hadn't made that choice now. She was not cut out for a life of subterfuge.

She had barely eaten anything all day and had only consumed one coffee (a telltale sign that something was amiss). Twice, she had nearly backed out. She and Henry would figure out another way to get Amina the money and save their plan, she told herself. This was too risky. But sure enough, the day passed, evening rolled around, and she was still at her desk, waiting everyone out until she was the only one left on the eighth floor.

It was nearly 10:00 p.m. Downstairs, a handful of traders were pacing back and forth in their pin-striped suits, waiting for the markets to close in the US. But up where she was, in the land of corporate affairs, it was so quiet she could hear every squeak of her seat, every tap of her keyboard and click of her mouse.

She had been over the press release so many times she had practically memorized it. Henry had tweaked the language, dreaming up a genius quote from his mum: "My own mother arrived on the Kindertransport, and I consider it my honor—more than that, my duty—to pay forward the kindness our family received." Pure tug-at-the-heartstrings perfection.

She sat with her finger over the mouse, cursor poised over the little paper-airplane icon. The press release had been ready for hours, but she was waiting for the perfect time to send it to the bank's PR team in the US—to avoid detection, it had to be after the UK business day finished but before the US team went home.

The fluorescent lights overhead, on an automatic timer, had long gone out, leaving only her desk lamp for illumination. She called Henry one more time. He answered on the first ring.

"Is it done?" he asked, not bothering to say hello.

"Almost. The email is prepped. I just wanted to make one hundred percent quadruple sure that this is what you want to do. That you've thought through the consequences."

"Oh, darling, I've thought of nothing else," he said. "I'm ready for what comes. I'm not prepared to spend my entire life living in fear—in Scotland, no less—of being who I am truly capable of being."

They were both quiet as the different paths their futures could take at this fork in the road unfurled in their minds.

"And you?" he added. "Cold feet? Have you thought about the consequences?"

"I have," she replied, and she meant it. She knew this would kill her career in philanthropy, in the UK at least. But this time she didn't question if it was worth it—she was certain that it was.

Even Ollie had agreed with her when she'd explained their plan last night.

"What do you think?"

He'd pulled her onto his lap and kissed her. "Totally and completely bonkers. But also quite possibly the bravest thing you've ever done."

"Also maybe the stupidest. I'll be unemployed. And possibly unemployable."

"Rubbish," he said, stroking her curls and delicately tucking a loose strand behind her ear. "You're brilliant, and you'll find a better home for your drive and passion. And I'll cut back on my hours a bit, to make sure you have the time and space to give it your all. I have your back, *amor*." Ollie had kissed her gently. "Always." It was all the support she needed.

"I'm ready to be who I am truly capable of being, too," she told Henry with conviction. "Or at least, to try to figure out who that is. Either way I know I'll like myself more once this is all done."

"Me, too," Henry confessed. "Go on, send it. I'll stay on the line."

"OK," she whispered down the phone to Henry. "Hold on to your butts."

"Pardon?" Henry replied.

"*Jurassic Park?*"

"Honestly, Lucia, you continually astound me with your vast knowledge of highbrow culture."

"You know what, never mind. Now I have no qualms about getting you disinherited." She brought her finger down hard on the mouse, and the email disappeared with a whoosh. "It's done."

"Right. Grand. Well, I'm off to get rip-roaring drunk and maybe buy a plane tonight before Daddy takes my credit card away tomorrow," he said and ended the call.

A sense of calm overtook Lucia. It was out there now and couldn't be taken back. She felt high. Maybe she should go out and get lit tonight, she thought. Break one rule, break them all.

She closed her laptop and traded her heels for the sneakers she kept under her desk, ready to head home. She would text Ollie, and he'd have dinner ready for her. And maybe dessert. All of a sudden, she was famished.

She packed her laptop and a few dossiers in her purse and looked around at her desk with a pang.

Depending on how early the news broke, she wasn't sure she'd be allowed to come back into the building tomorrow. The thought both relieved and disappointed her. Secretly, she hoped she'd have the opportunity to make a grand exit with a speech, à la the original Bridget Jones.

It's not you, it's me. Just kidding, Celeste, it's 100 percent you. You're the worst. You're a sellout. You'll never make any impact on the world in your high heels and your fancy bag (which I love but whatever) and your questionable morals. You like to play fast and loose with doing good, but there's too much at stake here. Some things matter more than your end-of-the-year bonus or the title on your business card.

And while I have your attention (this was for the whole office), *let me tell you something about myself. I love Starbucks, and no, my hair is not naturally stick straight, and yes, usually when I tell you the stain on my shirt was put there by my daughter, I'm lying. It was me. Lucia. LOO-SEE-YA. Not*

Luce, Lucy, Lulu, or whatever other obnoxious diminutive you can think of. Lucia Magdalena Gutierrez-Barrow. Somebody hand me a doughnut and hold the door, I'm outta here.

Then with a cardboard box full of her stuff, she'd depart, defiant, proud, and righteous.

It didn't seem likely that she'd get that moment, but it was nice to dream. Better bring all her things home tonight just in case. She was just about to reach into her drawer when the phone rang.

No one ever called her landline after hours—there was no way this was a coincidence. Steeling herself for whatever was coming, Lucia picked up the phone.

"Hello?"

"Hey, Lucia, it's Madison from Seizen PR. You're burning the midnight oil tonight, aren't you?"

The Seizen team was based in New York, which was all part of the plan. The press release contained the instruction that it was to be distributed immediately so it could make the UK morning papers. Everything would be public before anyone in London was back in the office.

"Hey, Madison! Yeah, you know what they say. Philanthropy never sleeps."

"I've never heard that one. Anyway, I just wanted to double-check a few details with you." Madison read through the press release, murmuring Lucia's carefully crafted words to herself. "Whoa. This is huge for the Perrys. They've never done anything so public. And so political. I've got to hand it to you, this is awesome."

"Yeah, it's exciting," Lucia said, her heart now beating so hard she was sure Madison could hear it across the ocean. "We've been working on them for a while. Especially Celeste. She's been tireless in her dedication to the cause."

"Excellent! OK, all looks in order here. I changed a couple of words to match our house style guidelines, but otherwise it's great. The UK team has gone home already, but I can handle it myself—I'll get this out on the wire ASAP."

"Sounds good," she replied, releasing her fists, which had involuntarily balled up as soon as the phone rang. "Just holler if you need anything else." She got ready to hang up. She needed cheese. And carbs. And a gin and tonic the size of her head.

"Oh! There's just one more thing. Is Celeste there with you?"

Lucia panicked. "Um . . . Yes, she's right here."

"Can you put her on the line? I just need her verbal approval on this before it goes. The Perrys are category-A clients, which means we need a senior lead to approve all comms."

Shit. Lucia had forgotten about this rule, brought in a couple of weeks ago when a junior PR person had sent out a release with a typo and everyone had lost their minds. It was a bad one, which resulted in that poor girl getting fired—the clients, Lord and Lady Fack, had not appreciated the spelling error.

Lucia looked around the empty room, her eyes wild. "Right. You know what, she just stepped away from her desk. To . . . use the toilet. You know how rich French food can be. Bad . . . um . . . oysters." Lucia covered her eyes with her free hand. Why was she acting so dumb?

"Well, have her call me when she's done, I guess. You get home, Lucia, go snuggle that baby of yours. Bye."

Lucia stood up and started pacing back and forth. "Oh god. Oh god oh god oh god." Her heart was beating painfully fast, and she worried she was having a heart attack. She thought of Celeste finding her in the morning, sprawled out on the floor dead. She'd prod her listless body with the toe of her high heel—or she'd get Thomas to do it so as not to soil her precious Louboutins. "What a pity," Celeste would say, stepping over her. "We will have to replace the carpet."

What had possessed her to tell Madison that Celeste was right there and would call her back? This was the definition of stupidity. She needed to buy some time. She could go home, go to sleep, and leave Madison hanging. Madison might email Celeste, but there was a chance that she wouldn't. Everyone was terrified of Celeste, after all.

Lucia's pacing slowed down. There was nothing more she could do now, she thought. She should go home and regroup, call Henry, and formulate a new plan. They would figure something out.

At the elevator bank, she looked in her purse for her ID, but it wasn't there. Lucia hurried back to retrieve it from her desk. She would have hated to leave it behind. If everything blew up in her face tomorrow, at least she'd always have that photograph—the best thing to have resulted from this job. She wondered if they made ID-card-sized frames.

Lucia reached into the drawer, feeling around for the card, when something sharp grazed her finger. She cried out and pulled her hand back—it was bleeding slightly—before checking to see what had scratched her.

Something was stuck. With a bit of wiggling she dislodged her grandmother's statue of the *Virgen de Guadalupe*. Lucia would have been devastated to have left it behind. She had so few artifacts left from that era of her life.

Her wonderful grandparents. Would they recognize the person she had become over the last few months? Or the person sitting here now, contemplating this fraudulent activity in the name of doing good for people like them? Of that, she hoped they'd be proud.

Lucia wasn't terribly superstitious, but it was hard to see the scratch on her hand as anything but a sign. She couldn't back out. If *la Virgen* thought she should go through with it, how bad could it possibly be?

She paced the floor again, racking her brain for new ideas.

"*Merde*," she said out loud to herself, mimicking Celeste's favorite expression. Then, like she had been spoken to by *la Virgen* herself, Lucia knew exactly what to do.

Calmly, she went back to her desk and put her heels back on—this was no time for flats. Then, she calmly walked into Celeste's office, which was always left unlocked for the cleaners at night. She dialed Madison's number. She took a deep breath. And she prepared to give the performance of a lifetime.

It only rang once.

"Seizen PR, seize the day, this is Madison speaking."

"*Bonsoir*, this is Celeste." No last name or company needed. Celeste wouldn't bother.

Lucia spoke as a woman possessed in the most cartoonish version of a French accent she could muster, but she was counting on the assumption that Americans thought all French people sounded like a cross between Pepé Le Pew and Lumière from *Beauty and the Beast*. Lucia could never, ever pull off a French accent that would fool a real French person, but she prayed it would be enough for this call.

"Hello, Ms. Le Fevre, thanks so much for calling me back. Lucia sent me over the press release for the Perrys, and I just wanted to make sure it had your approval. I'm sure Lucia has shown it to you already, but as you know we require your confirmation for our records," Madison said. Her voice was shaking, which spurred Lucia on.

"*Bof*, why are you people always making me do everything? Surely it should be enough that Lucy has sent it." Lucia wasn't keen to draw this out, but the real Celeste would make her annoyance known.

"I'm so sorry, Ms. Le Fevre, it is your company policy," Madison said. Lucia prayed she didn't start crying. She felt awful for putting her through this and wondered if Madison would get in trouble. She hated the thought of this innocent girl being collateral damage, even in the pursuit of so much good. There had been too many trade-offs already.

"Sorry? You are sorry. You're sorry is nothing to me," Lucia snapped, thinking quickly. "Please, do me a favor and record this call so you have my approval and I never, ever have to speak of this ever again."

"Yes, yes, just one moment." There. If Madison had it on tape, she could cover her own ass when the shit hit the fan tomorrow. Lucia was happy to take the fall but refused to bring anyone else down with her. "OK, ready."

"I, Celeste Le Fevre, tell you, Madeline"—Celeste would never remember the name of someone she deemed so far beneath her—"that I approve this press release. *Sacré bleu. Mon Dieu. Allez les Blues.* Are you happy? Now can I please get on with my evening?"

Embodying Celeste, even just for a moment, was surprisingly fun. Her veins thrummed with power, like she could crush tiny people under her sharp, perfectly manicured thumbnail. She hoped they'd play the recording for Celeste tomorrow. She would be so furious at Lucia and even more furious when she heard her hideous French accent.

"Of course, thank you so much, Ms. Le Fevre."

"Get this out immediately," Lucia barked. "I want it on the cover of every newspaper tomorrow."

"Right away. You can count on me," Madison said.

Lucia hung up the phone. Celeste never, ever said goodbye.

"*Aah*," she screamed out into the empty void of the eighth floor, knowing no one was around to hear. It was done, and what a rush. She wondered, as she now finally packed up her bag—making sure both the ID and *la Virgen* were safely stowed—how Ollie would feel about her using that voice in the bedroom. It was a little creepy, sure, but there was something about being temporarily French that made her feel vital, sexy, and ready to demand anything she wanted.

Chapter 27
The Beginning

It was an unseasonably warm September, the last bits of summer clinging on for dear life as Lucia got off the Central Line at St. Paul's, emerging in the shadow of the cathedral. She negotiated the buggy deftly, like a pro. Yes, she called it a *buggy*, and she was OK with that. She could say it, along with the words *lift*, *rubbish*, and *cutlery*, and not break out in laughter or nervous hives or both. London was her home now, and she could, when she wanted to, speak the lingo. On her own terms and, ideally, in her own accent.

The day had been busy. She and Marley had spent the morning with Sooz and Atticus running around the Barbican. She'd enticed Sooz to join her for a playdate with a promise of a hardcover of the latest Tilly Willington (entitled *Hard Cover*, about a bookseller with an insatiable lust for literature . . . and his best friend's wife) and a bag of doughnuts.

"Peace offerings," Lucia said, unbuckling a squirming Marley, who was desperate to run around with Atticus, and handing Sooz the book and snacks. "You were right."

Sooz reached into the bag, speared a doughnut with her nail like a skewer, and took a bite. "Was I now? About what?"

"Everything," Lucia said.

Lucia told her the whole story, everything she had missed since Marley's birthday, leaving nothing out. The fight with Ollie (and their makeup in the South of France); the ickiness she felt using a donation to cover up for the prince's indiscretions (to which Sooz replied, "What a dog's arsehole; see, this is why we should be a republic. There's an anti-monarchist protest next week if you want to come with."); her and Henry's grand plan to save Operation Bridget Jones; and her appalling French accent.

When she had finally shared everything, she slumped back onto the bench. "That was cathartic," Lucia said. "I feel like I'm on the twelve-step program to recovery, but instead of booze, I'm apologizing for being a world-class moron. I was so stupid to think I could change things there. Or at all."

"Lucia, Lucia, Lucia," Sooz said, shaking her head. "You're not a moron. You have a brilliant and beautiful heart. One of the biggest, kindest hearts I know. But you did exactly what I told you not to do. You lost yourself in the process." She pointed over toward the grass where Atticus and Marley were tying up another child—with pretend ropes and (they hoped) consent.

"Making change is kind of like being a mum, yeah? A lot like it. It's not about a performance for Instagram. It's about showing up, every day, even when it's hard, even when you feel like you've failed. Showing up for them, and for yourself—as yourself. Not as anyone else. The only thing you did wrong is forget that. You gave them everything, but just like with kids, you have to keep a bit back just for you. Oh shit, I think they might have actually tied up that girl. Hang on."

Sooz got up and ran over to the children. Fortunately, there was no actual rope involved in their play, only a few overactive imaginations and some tears as a result. Lucia watched as

Sooz freed the other child from imaginary captivity, tickled both Marley and Atticus, and came back to the bench.

"Anyway, you made up for it in the end. Phwoar. I am so bloody proud of you. A true champion of social good."

"Thank you. Although I'm mostly terrified of being deported."

"Never! I'll chain myself to the wing of your plane so they can't take off with you on board," Sooz said. "We should celebrate your victory against the man! What do you think, should we splash some paint on something? There must be at least one unethical item in the Barbican's collection." But Lucia demurred—she had had enough illicit activity to last a lifetime.

* * *

It had been two weeks since her Hail Mary scheme had resulted in a miraculous success. Madison was nothing if not great at her job. The press release made the cover of every major British paper the morning after Lucia's Oscar-worthy performance. And, before dawn, the BBC had reached out to Amina, booking her on *BBC Breakfast*. She gave the most genuine, heartfelt speech of gratitude, called the Perrys national treasures. She was surrounded by the children from the center. It was viewed by over seven million households nationwide.

Lucia wished she could have been a fly on the wall watching bumbling Brendan attempt to figure out what had happened. She was sure Celeste immediately knew she was behind it— she would have relished watching that exquisite moment unfold, too. But she'd decided to call in sick and see how long it took them to realize it was her. Not long, in fact, but by then there was no turning back.

Everyone was furious—but only in private. Henry had been right; any contradiction or retraction was impossible. The Perrys hated that they had been tricked, but they hated it less than everyone knowing they had been made fools of—by their own son, no less. On top of that, the response had been glowing. The gates of the Perry country estate were lined with flowers from well-wishers. *The Times*' grumpiest columnist even penned an unironic op-ed with the headline, "The Perry Family Ushers in a New Golden Age of British Generosity."

There were public commendations and congratulations from parliamentarians of every party and the royals, not to mention nonprofits working with refugees around the world. With all the fanfare, withdrawing their donation was not an option. Anyway, the Perrys thought, in the end, it was only money. They had plenty of it to follow through on their fabricated commitment and still ensure that every monument in the UK had ample parking.

Because the Perrys decided to keep quiet, the bank had no choice but to follow suit—the client was always right after all. After Lucia's betrayal was discovered there had been no yelling, no threats, not even a phone call (she was only the tiniest bit disappointed at this). Eastern Currents HR emailed her a formal termination letter, citing gross misconduct, reminding her of the contractual obligations of her NDA, and wishing her a perfunctory "good luck on your future endeavors."

* * *

They said goodbye to Sooz and Atticus with powdered sugar kisses and promises of attending a march the week after next and casually strolled to their next playdate.

"Oh look, you brought along little Monica," Tristan deadpanned with a look of true disdain. "What a treat."

Lucia pushed the buggy into the corner next to their table. "Chill, no one is expecting you to be Mary Poppins. It's her nap time." Making sure Marley was still asleep, she sat down. "Anyway, I'm unemployed now with no money to cover what would certainly be extensive therapy bills if I ever let you exchange words with her. It's great to see you, too, by the way." She leaned in for a double kiss. "Although I am a little worried about being so close to the office."

"That's why I chose this delightful spot for lunch. I'm desperate for some drama. Things are so boring without you."

This was the dish Lucia had come for: the gossip.

"You are absolutely, one hundred percent persona non grata," Tristan said to her, grinning wickedly. "It's brilliant. I still can't quite believe you pulled it off. I didn't think you had it in you."

"And how is she who shall not be named dealing with my departure?" Lucia asked through a forkful of cacio e pepe, trying desperately not to spill any of it on her sunshine-yellow top.

"*Au contraire*! You are now she who shall not be named," Tristan responded. Lucia laughed. "I'm dead serious. *No one* is allowed to utter your name in Celeste's presence. It's an unspoken rule. Once the temp who took over your job—she's reporting into Melissa, by the way, who is now very much in Celeste's good graces—asked a question about you in a team meeting, and I swear Celeste turned purple and fired her. It was hilarious. I do miss you, though."

She missed Tristan, too. And Rona—although they had plans to meet up for coffee and a tantric-yoga class (Rona assured her that she wasn't required to be naked, although it was clothing optional). She even missed Tamsin a little bit.

As for Henry, he had disappeared into a black hole since the whole thing went down. No one had seen or heard from him. Even Tristan didn't know what his reaction had been. She hoped he was OK. She knew that he had been in touch with Amina; she told her at their weekly catch-up she had an email from him confirming a few details about making payment. Lucia had been volunteering at the North London center (anonymously and behind the scenes), helping project manage the endowment setup and communication plans for the national campaign they'd be running. It wasn't going to be a smooth road ahead—their support didn't change the fact that there was still loud opposition to refugee rights—but they were on the right track.

"I wonder if this will impact Celeste's promotion," Lucia pondered aloud.

"Oh yes," Tristan replied. "It fast-tracked it. Somehow that scaly dragon came out of this entirely unscathed. She threw you under the bus, naturally. And, to Nigel, quietly blamed it on Brendan's lack of leadership. He was forced to speed up his retirement thanks to you. Celeste moved into his office and had her interior designer drawing up plans before the ink on his retirement papers was dry. The announcement of her promotion was made public this week. She won. Really she ought to be thanking you."

"Yeah right. You'd be more likely to see her march into the office in sweats and no makeup, eating a McGriddle," Lucia said.

"She told me once if I ever noticed her wearing trainers, I should escort her out behind the bank and shoot her dead on the spot."

After parting ways with Tristan, she decided to walk south, across London Bridge, with a Frappuccino in her hand, curls blowing in the breeze, and a podcast about decolonizing wealth in her ears. Around her, city workers walked with their jackets folded over their forearms, their cheeks toasted from a week-end drinking in a beer garden, making the most of the weather that everyone knew wouldn't last. Some of them were headed back to the Aubergine building where, on the forty-second floor, there was an office full of people who had finished their lunch breaks and were busy working to ensure every dog in the world had the bedazzled limbs they required.

She slurped up the final dollops of caramel and was tossing her cup into the bin when her podcast cut out, replaced by ringing in her ears. She tapped the side of the AirPods to pick up the call—it was probably Ollie phoning about dinner. "Hey, babe," she said.

"Hey, babe, yourself." The voice on the other end laughed. British yes, and familiar, but not Ollie.

"Why, hello, stranger!" she said. "Where the heck have you been hiding?"

"Oh, you know, here, there, and everywhere. Went off to Berlin to lick my wounds. The duke and duchess were not happy with me after our little stunt," Henry confirmed. "But, as you know already, our assumptions were dead-on. All the donations we committed them to are going to be honored by the foundation, so that's something."

"Something!" Lucia exclaimed, sitting down on a bench. Tower Bridge was in the distance, and farther down, she could just about make out Tamsin's superyacht. "That's everything. I'm still in shock that it all worked. You should be very proud."

"As should you. I can tell you without a doubt that I never could have done this without you."

Lucia felt a warm glow rush to her cheeks. There was plenty for them both to be proud of. Even though they were forever blacklisted.

"How's your life of poverty?" she asked.

"It could be worse," Henry drawled. "Of course, I've been told in no uncertain terms that my tenure on the foundation board is over effective immediately. My Scotland posting has been unceremoniously canceled. And I'm being cut off."

"Oh god, I'm so sorry. I was kidding, but that sounds awful," Lucia said. Marley was stirring, and she rocked the buggy back and forth. "Are you OK?"

"I've never been better," he said. She could hear that he was smiling.

"Well, thank goodness for that. Do you need a place to crash?"

"I think I'll survive," he deadpanned. "I've got six properties of my own, including two flats in the city, my Gloucestershire cottage, the farm up north, and places in New York and Paris. Not to mention my sizable trust fund, which they can't touch. I won't be needing your charity anytime soon, but you are the most wonderful friend for offering. Your generosity—it's one of the things I love most about you."

"Is it now?" she asked. "What are the others?"

"Hush now, you know you're not my type. But if you must know it's your big brain. In fact, that's why I'm calling."

A bus roared by, masking the thumping of her heart as she awaited what else he had to say.

"I've been talking about our ideas to some friends of mine. Not just doing what my parents did for the North London center to others, but really putting some proper money and influence behind the national-campaign idea. I'm talking at the highest level of government, advocating for refugees and migrants and supporting them to advocate for themselves. Here, in the EU, the US. Everywhere. It could be huge. Does this sound familiar?" The excitement in his voice was palpable as he repeated back to her the ideas they had developed together, taken almost verbatim from the Operation Bridget Jones pitch.

"Very."

"Well, turns out there are others who are as excited about it as we are. And some of them have agreed to bankroll a new foundation to do just this."

"Wow, Henry, that's amazing news!" she cried, clapping her hands together, startling Marley. "Your own foundation, you're going to be amazing at that. I'm so beyond happy for you, you're just what philanthropy needs."

"I think you mean *we're* just what philanthropy needs. I haven't been taking credit for your ideas, you know. This is our baby, and I wouldn't move forward without you. You must come with me. You'll be the executive director. You can build your own team, work closely with me to set the mission and the agenda. It's a start-up, so it will be hard work. But fulfilling work. Good work. Think of what we could accomplish together."

Marley was wide-awake now, staring intently at seagulls fighting over a discarded hot dog bun. Lucia ran her hand through her hair. A start-up environment would be intense. But Ollie had already told his firm he was going to go down to a four-day workweek so he could help out more with Marley. And Lucia knew, in her heart of hearts, that part of being a good mother, for her at least, was helping to create the world she wanted her daughter to grow up in. That was her purpose.

"Hello? Still there?" Henry said on the line.

Lucia inhaled sharply. "I need to talk to Ollie about how it would work," she said. "But I think I'm in. Oh, and I'm going to be very expensive."

"You've learned fast. I'd expect nothing less. I'll email you details. Can't wait to work together again. We're going to make a huge impact. Ciao for now, darling."

Lucia stood up, stunned, and started to push the buggy toward Borough Market. Marley craned her neck around to smile at Lucia. "Mommy happy," she said, clapping her hands. Lucia hadn't realized it, but her face was set in a joyful grin.

"Yes, *amor*. Mommy's so happy," she said, bending down to kiss her daughter on the cheek and taking Marley's empty babyccino from her. "*Vamos, mija*. Let's go do something great."

Epilogue

The doorbell rang.

"Delivery for Mrs. Barrow," a man's voice said. She buzzed him in and opened the door, surprised to see not the usual delivery-driver uniform but a man in a three-piece suit and white gloves. He was holding a small package, about the size of a laptop, wrapped in brown paper.

"But I didn't order anything," she said, puzzled. Nothing about this situation spoke of a middle-of-the-night Amazon shopping spree.

Then it dawned on her. She quickly shut the door in his face.

"Mrs. Barrow? I need a signature, please," the voice said from the other side of the door.

"No way," she said. "I know what this is. You're serving me papers, aren't you?" She had been wondering when the other shoe would finally drop. "If the bank wants to sue me, they need to speak to my husband. I mean, my lawyer. My husband is my lawyer." Could Ollie represent her? She hoped some awful rule about conflicts of interest wouldn't mean Belly had to be her legal counsel.

"No, madam, this is not a legal document," he replied. "It's a gift."

"Is this a trick? Because I don't think that's admissible in court."

"No, madam. And if you don't mind, this is not my final job of the day, and I'd quite like to get home at a reasonable hour."

Lucia opened the door a crack and peeked out. The man looked like he was telling the truth. Plus, her curiosity had already gotten the better of her. "Fine," she sighed, swinging the door wide open. "Who is it from?"

"Anonymous sender," he said, handing her a folder. "Sign here, please." She put her pen to the paper and handed it back to him. In exchange, he passed her the small package and bid her adieu. From her window, she watched him get into the back seat of a long black Bentley that sped away before her Sydney Bristow brain could click into place—she should have tried to snap a photo of the license plate just in case.

She brought the package inside, laid it on the counter, and reached for a pair of kitchen scissors to snip the twine. Carefully, she peeled the tape off each corner, unwrapping the paper and a layer of bubble wrap. Underneath was a small but stunning painting. One look told her it was a hand-finished print by Malini Shambala. The bright pinks and golds glowed in the light streaming in from her window. The print was in a delicate pewter frame that set off the colors perfectly. Classy AF.

She went back through the layers of wrapping, looking for a card or note, but nothing fell out. Not many people knew of her love for Shambala's work. In fact, the only person she had spoken to about it in the recent past was Celeste.

Lucia stared at it for a long time, a smile of realization forming on her face. A screech from Marley demanding a juice brought her out of her reverie. She delivered the sippy cup, and then brought the painting into her dressing room, where she propped it gently atop her chest of drawers. She wanted to display it somewhere she would see it every single day, a reminder that she had no regrets.

Acknowledgments

When I was eight, I wrote my first short story on a typewriter at my grandparents' law office. It was about a fictional trip to Hawaii with eight of my friends. I detailed exactly how our hair looked and what we wore, ate, and did every day. The story lacked pacing, tension, and character development, but my mother declared it "the best thing she'd ever read" (I am paraphrasing).

Then, I took a thirty-two-year hiatus from writing fiction—until March 2022. *My What If Year* had just been sent to the printer, and I was high on life and full of what-ifs, such as, *What if I wrote a novel?* With my experience limited to "Sleepover in Maui," I approached the task with the same blind faith as I had my internships. How hard could it really be?

Hard, as it turned out. The pages you've just read are the outcome of an enormous amount of help, support, and feedback from some gifted, talented, creative people, ten full drafts, unwavering faith from my incredible team, and vats upon vats of coffee.

Atop this list of book doulas is the entire Zibby Publishing squad: the brilliant Zibby Owens herself, an eternal inspiration and champion of my work; Kathleen Harris, who saw a spark in an early draft and encouraged me to make it better; Anne Messitte came in hot with her business hat on at the right moments; and Sherri Puzey gave some critical feedback just before the last push that made this story, and Lucia, shine brighter. Everyone in the Zibby-verse, the whole team, is there when I need them, for which I'm grateful every day. Thank you, as well, to my copy editor, Jordan Koluch, to my proofreaders, Madelyn Lindquist and Dassi Zeidel, and to Nicolette Seeback Ruggerio for an inspirational cover that makes my heart sing.

Coralie Hunter: Working with you has been one of the great joys of my professional life. Cory came in and told me straight off the bat that she loved my voice and that we also had a lot of work to do. I was immediately determined to impress her, *or else*. This book is a book because of Cory.

My gratitude to the many wonderful readers and writers who offered guidance, resources, YouTube videos, and constant cheerleading: Stephany Evans, Jane Delury, Andrea Dunlop, Sandra Miller, Michelle Wildgen, Sheena Cook, and Meghan Riordan Jarvis—you all motivated me when I thought maybe I'd just pack it in and see if anyone would hire me as an unpaid marine biologist instead.

To my ride-or-dies, thank you for reading this and always making me feel like it was worth the effort. Joni, Nathalie, Bec, and the whole of LAVA, love and gratitude for every ounce of feedback, support, and advice on which names didn't sound British enough (Ollie will always be Derek to me, no matter what anyone says), photos of license plates, and complete openness and transparency about the challenges of being a working mother.

To the bosses, coworkers, and clients with whom I've been privileged to be on this journey, thank you for your tireless work to champion change. I share this sector with so many people who care deeply about creating a better world. It is not always easy, it can be frustrating, but it is worth it! I'm grateful for the whole I.G. team who continues to push me to grow, as we work together to #FixTheFlow every day.

I wrote and edited the vast majority of these pages (and the many that got tossed out) at the National Library of Scotland

and the Royal Botanic Garden Edinburgh. Thank you for the frittatas, lentil soups, scones, and quiet.

To my family of Mirandas, Fernandezes and Abramses, your love and support means everything to me.

Mommy and Papi, you get the dedication on this one because I wouldn't know anything about being a good person, or trying to be one, at least, if it weren't for you.

Theo and Lola, you remind me daily about why being a mom is worth it, even in the hard times. Many feelings and even a few scenes in the book were borrowed from real life (including googling "does my baby hate me?"). I feel like maybe you like me now? Right? I hope so. I love you both to bits.

Carlos, how do I thank the person to whom I owe everything? Perhaps in *Star Trek* analogies. Writing this book was a long journey, sort of like traveling from the Delta Quadrant back to the Alpha. It involved a lot of feedback—mostly the helpful kind given by someone like Dax (Jadzia, natch), not the unhelpful kind that Quark might provide. Sometimes I felt like Odo melting into a liquid state, but whenever I wanted to quit like Tasha Yar, you kept me going. I love you more than Seska loves stirring up trouble.

Finally, a huge thanks to Kira, who I miss every day. She snored on my lap for a good portion of the writing process, and that sweet comfort might just have made this a better book.

About the Author

Alisha Fernandez Miranda is the author of the memoir *My What If Year*. With more than twenty years of experience as a philanthropic advisor, she is the chair and former CEO of I.G. Advisors, an award-winning social impact intelligence agency that consults with the world's biggest nonprofits, foundations, and corporations on their philanthropy. A Miami native, Alisha is a graduate of Harvard University and the London School of Economics and currently lives in Scotland with her husband and children.